LEVELING UP THE WORLD

L. ECLAIRE

1

aethonbooks.com

LEVELING UP THE WORLD
©2023 L. ECLAIRE

ALSO IN SERIES

YOU ARE LEVEL 1

The first thing Dallion saw after opening his eyes was the floor. The second was a blue glowing rectangle floating in the darkness.

This doesn't make sense, Dallion thought.

The last thing he remembered was returning to his dorm and stumbling into bed. There had been a wild party—wilder than he would have liked—with lots of dancing, a bit of drinking, and a few really weird games. Dallion vaguely remembered climbing on a table with a pair of plush antlers while singing some song from the nineties.

Thinking about it, maybe going out was a mistake. Dallion should have refused, or at least had a bite to eat. Since this was his first day arriving at college, it was extremely difficult to refuse. It wasn't that the party had been bad. From the fragments he could remember, Dallion was sure it had been great. The issue was that he had absolutely no memory of what happened between him falling off the table and the moment he arrived at his dorm room.

Maybe it's all a dream?

That would definitely explain a few things, mostly the flowing blue rectangle. Dallion closed his eyes, then slowly opened them again. The rectangle, now surrounded by an empty room.

"Hello?" Dallion turned around.

Rough gray stones were all about, covering walls, floor, and ceiling. There was no light source—with the exception of the blue rectangle—no furniture, no paintings, statues, or decorations of any type, not even a door. It was as if someone had dragged Dallion here and sealed off the entrance behind him.

Am I in an escape room?

Dallion stepped toward the center of the room. The moment he did, a message appeared within the rectangle.

You Are Level 1

"Level one?" Dallion asked out loud. *What's a level one?*

On cue, the window spun around, revealing additional text instructions.

You are in a small, dark room.
Smash the window to choose your destiny!

A sensible person would have taken a moment to think things through. As a visiting tech giant had once said, life was a series of carefully considered risk-reward situations. The more knowledge and information one had, the easier they would obtain great rewards for little risk. Dallion's current situation, though unusual, was no different. Using his past life experience and picking up on any clues around him, Dallion had every chance of coming to the correct conclusion. Unfortunately, Dallion wasn't a sensible person.

Without a moment's thought, he took another step forward and struck the rectangle dead center with his fist.

Crack!

The rectangle split into four equal pieces. Uncertain what was expected of him, Dallion attempted to punch the lower left piece. But before his hand could reach its target, the fragments whirled away, circling Dallion two times before forming a neat row in front of him. As he stared at them, the rectangles changed color, turning red, orange, white, and cyan. No sooner had they done so than a new blue rectangle appeared above.

Reckless!
(+2 Reaction)
Decisive reactions, though little thought.
Choose the trait that you value most so you can continue into the halls of judgment.

Despite the uncertainty of the whole situation, Dallion had to admit feeling a sense of intrigue. For some unknown reason, breaking of the blue rectangle had filled him with euphoria and a sense of achievement. At this point, the only thing he could do was follow the instruction and see where it led him.

"Do I get any hints?" he asked.

A word appeared in each of the rectangles. On closer inspection, Dallion saw that, in addition to the word, there was a number underneath.

The words were *body, mind, reaction*, and *perception*, probably the "traits" mentioned in the rectangle above. Each had a value of three, with the exception of reaction, which was at five, likely due to Dallion's reckless behavior.

Dallion was tempted to choose "mind" in the hopes it might help him figure out what was going on. However, even he knew that things couldn't be this simple. "Body" was another good choice, potentially granting him what weeks of going to the gym couldn't. Was one more point enough, though? Going by basic logic, and the thousands of hours gaming under his belt, Dallion assumed a value of three was the absolute minimum one could have. A four, even if it technically was an increase of thirty-three percent, was unlikely to provide a huge boost.

The optimal solution was to go with his most advanced trait to maximize his advantage in that area.

Gently, Dallion pressed the orange rectangle. The instant his fingers touched the hard surface, the number beneath *reaction* increased to six. Moments later, all the rectangles faded away in a cloud of pixels. A doorway suddenly appeared in the wall across, filling the room with dim yellow light.

Dallion waited eagerly, expecting something dramatic to happen. It didn't.

"Is that it?" Dallion asked, slightly deflated by the anticlimactic experience.

There was no answer.

"Hello? Anyone out there?"

Maybe I should have chosen body? he thought as he cautiously made his way outside of the room and into a torch-lit corridor. At first glance, there didn't seem to be anything special out there. The corridor was yet another example of medieval architecture. The left marked a dead end, while the right continued for several dozen steps up to what appeared to be a T-junction. The lit torches covered both walls, providing a reasonable degree of flickering light.

Having seen enough horror movies to know where this was going, Dallion tried to get a torch. However, he soon found they were all stuck in place. After several unsuccessful attempts, he admitted defeat and continued to the junction. Upon reaching it, a new blue rectangle appeared.

You are at a crossroads.
Choose the item that will serve you best.

Light flashed on either side of Dallion, attracting his attention. As he looked to the right, a small round shield appeared on the wall.

This was the first time Dallion had seen armor of this type, but, somehow, he was fully aware the object was a combat buckler. If he had to be honest, the thing resembled a metal frisbee disk more than anything else. The word "GUARD" was written above it in large green block letters.

To the left was a short metal sword pinned to the wall. It was the epitome of commonness, with the word "ATTACK" written above.

"Can I choose both?" Dallion asked.

The blue rectangle didn't answer.

That would have been way too easy. Dallion allowed himself a smile.

Attack or defense. It was the classic dilemma, and still he found himself hesitating. What if he picked the wrong item? Or worse, what if he had chosen the wrong skills? There was no indication that he'd be able to change his choice. Dallion looked at the shield, then at the sword, then at the shield again.

The sword was the obvious choice—great for attack, and possibly for marginal defense as well. The buckler, on the other hand, seemed useless for both. Or was it? The rectangle only said the item should serve him best. There was no mention of fighting.

"The hell with it!" Dallion went to the buckler and took it off the wall.

GUARD skills obtained.
You've broken through your first barrier!

A green rectangle popped up in front of his eyes. His choice had been made. Before he could turn around in an attempt to snatch the sword, everything went black. Instinct forced Dallion to recoil in an attempt to escape the darkness. To his surprise, he succeeded, thrusting his way into the light, and then into something hard and painful.

5

"Brother!" a boy's voice pierced his ears. "Brother, you made it!"

When he came back to his senses, Dallion was no longer in the dark corridor. Instead, he sat on a field next to a rather large wooden statue. A small group of people had gathered, dressed in clothes that would only be found on the historical channel or the set of a highly authentic fantasy production. Most of the people were adults the age of his parents or older, although there were a few children as well. Carefully examining everyone, Dallion could say with absolute certainty he had never seen them before in his life. Yet, at the same time, all of them seemed extremely familiar.

"I knew you'd do it, brother!" A hazel-haired boy elbowed his way through the ring of people to Dallion and hugged him like a child who'd just gotten a high-end console as a birthday gift. "I knew you'd awaken!"

"Yeah," Dallion replied, patting his "brother" on the back. "I awakened…"

What the heck just happened?!

AWAKENED

A wakening—as Dallion came to learn—was considered a pretty big deal. The village his "family" was from had less than a dozen awakened, half of which were well past their sixties. The rest were part of the village chief's family, which made sense, come to think about it. Among everything else, awakening brought with it a huge status boost, thus Dallion was enjoying a meal—the local equivalent of a feast—surrounded by a crowd of family, friends, and neighbors. The crowd was so large, it barely fit in the small house.

The food served was on the plain side, but Dallion had an inside notion it cost well more than his family could afford. Ever since he had appeared in this world, memories of his other self had slowly trickled in, making him aware of things he was supposed to know.

"I always said the boy would achieve great things," Vanessa Dull said with a nod.

She was some distant relative married to a trading merchant, who only visited during major holidays or when she had favors to ask. Dallion "remembered" she never liked him much, to the point that she had told his parents he'd be better off joining a monastery

7

of the Seven Moons. Now that Dallion had proved useful, she sang an entirely different tune.

"None of you thought he'd amount to anything, but thanks to my constant support, he has," the woman added with an attitude that implied she was owed numerous favors.

The rest of the people took little notice, anchoring their attention to Dallion.

"I'll try not to disappoint you," Dallion replied. He never liked people looking at him as he ate. Struggling to maintain a fake smile, he took a bite from what appeared to be an orange tomato and nodded. "Now that I'm awakened, what do I do?"

Intense silence filled the room. Dallion felt as if even the insects had stopped, only to gape at him.

I shouldn't have asked that question, he said to himself.

"Soul confusion," Kraisten Seene said, stroking his beard. A village elder, and Dallion's grandfather, he had seen more things than most and even spent some time in a few cities during his youth. More importantly, he was also an awakened, although his advanced age prevented him from doing anything exceptional in the last decade or so. "It sometimes happens after one awakens. No need to worry, it'll pass with time. We just have to put up with his questions until he's back to normal." He gave Dallion a pat on the back, almost making him choke in the process.

A resounding "Aaah!" filled the room as everyone let out a sigh of relief, pretending they knew what the old man was talking about.

"Now that you're awakened, you'll go to the village chief to be acknowledged," Dallion's father said. He was a massive man with an even more massive moustache. Most of his days were spent in the field, though, sometimes, he assisted with lumber gathering for the winter season. "After that, you'll be allowed to exercise your skills at home."

"And in other homes as well!" Vanessa chirped.

"Okay." Dallion went to stand when a firm hand grabbed his shoulder, slamming him down in the chair again.

"Finish your food first," Kraisten said. There was a warm smile on his face, but Dallion got the impression the offer was not up for debate. "Can't visit the chief on an empty stomach."

As if on cue, Dallion's mother rushed out of the room, only to return with another plate of food. Back in college, Dallion would have considered that a snack, but by the way the people around him swallowed at the sight of it, he suspected he was being served a delicacy.

It took half an hour for Dallion to finish everything served to him. Normally, he'd have been faster, but having to engage in polite and useless conversation every three mouthfuls prolonged the process. Once the last morsel of food was gone and even the most pointless topic was exhausted, the guests began to leave.

To no surprise, Vanessa was the first to go, explaining in great length she had very important business to deal with at home, and how difficult life was since the passing of her husband. She was followed shortly by neighbors, who actually had chores to do. Close friends and other family relations were next, leaving only Dallion's immediate family in the room. This was the point Dallion expected to be able to have a quieter and much more meaningful conversation with his parents. Amazingly, his father and younger brother also left, leaving him just with his mother and grandfather.

"You don't have to stay for this, Gertha," the old man said. "Go rest."

"He's my son," the woman stated. "I'll stay."

Dallion remembered her to be a kind but quiet woman, spending most of her time in the house. Thinking back, he remembered there was always an air of sadness surrounding her, even when she was smiling. For some reason, he had never noticed that in his "past life." Now, it was obvious there was a lot more to it.

"I know," Kraisten sighed. "Well, boy, there's no point in delaying."

Giving Dallion a stern glance, the old man cracked his knuckles, then slapped both hands on the wooden table so hard, Dallion expected it to fold in two. Instead, the piece of wooden furniture not only held its own but seemed somehow sturdier than a moment ago. A faint red glow surrounded the wooden surface, peeling away any cracks, chips, and other signs of wear until the table was as good as new.

"This…" Kraisten said as drops of sweat trickled down his forehead, "is what awakening lets you do."

The elder abruptly pulled his hands off the surface. The glow disappeared. It was extraordinary, magical, and by the looks of things, very taxing. Dallion's mother reached to support her father, but the old man raised his hand in a sign for her to stop.

"However, just because you're awakened doesn't mean you can't lose your skill." Kraisten wiped the sweat off his forehead. "Your mother also awakened but lost her gift during her acknowledgement." He clenched his fists in anger.

"It's all right, Father," the woman whispered with a sad smile. "I'm used to it."

"No, you're not," Kraisten grumbled. "And he doesn't have to get used to it either!"

"I won't," Dallion said. He still wasn't completely sure what awakening was or what he wasn't supposed to get used to, but he already knew he wasn't going to let it happen.

The old man smiled.

"The village chief will try to provoke you when you get there. Don't let him. He's an envious weasel who'd do everything to ensure that only his family has awakened." Kraisten's expression twisted with anger as he spoke. "He'll try to get under your skin and trick you into asking for a more difficult trial than you can handle." The old man paused. "He did the same to your mother."

Dallion's eyes widened with surprise. From everything he could remember, there wasn't even a hint that she had been an awakened. As far as everyone was concerned, she had been a frail woman who rarely left the house.

"Is it bad doing something more difficult?" Dallion asked.

"No." The old man shook his head. "But once you fail while using your awakened powers, you'll never be able to use them again."

A SIMPLE REQUEST

The contrast between the village chief's home and the rest of the houses was as great as day and night. Rising three and a half floors above everything else, the mansion was larger than Dallion's entire garden, made entirely of polished white granite. A path of blue tiles led through the double iron door to an inner court-yard where a few people waited.

According to Dallion's grandfather, it had been traditional for an elder or family member to accompany the awakened for support. The village chief had changed the practice twenty years ago, reducing the risk of potential challenges to his power. It also ensured the awakened couldn't rely on any advice during the trial.

"What d'you want?" a blubber of a man asked. From what Dallion could remember, he was a distant relation of the Luor family. What he lacked in skill he made up for in arrogance and laziness. No one in the Luor family liked him, so they gave him the role of pretending to be a guard.

The person beside him was no better. Tall and skinny as a twig, he had attempted awakening five times so far, each unsuccessful. Seeing Dallion, he crossed his arms.

"The chief isn't to be disturbed," the skinny man snorted.

"I was told to come here to acknowledge my awakening." *You know exactly why I'm here. You just want to humiliate me.* "Guess I'll come back later, then." Dallion turned around and slowly made his way out of the courtyard.

Three steps later, the guards reacted as Dallion knew they would. The wheels in their brains creaked to a full rotation, painting a picture of the punishment they'd get if they allowed their future victim to walk away.

"Wait!" the skinny one shouted. "The chief's waiting for you."

"You sure?" Dallion asked with a smirk. "I thought you said he was busy."

"Yeah, he is…"

Quick thinking isn't your forte, is it?

That was what happened when someone became reliant on the power of others. Everyone in the village knew the "guards" were nothing but thugs, and weak ones at that. The reason no one dared do anything about it was because harming them was the same as disputing the Luors' authority. The village chief didn't like when someone opposed him and, unlike his minions, he had the strength to cause serious harm.

"Walk this way," the fat guard grunted, leading Dallion into the house proper.

The interior was even more lavish than the exterior. While there weren't any gold or silver ornaments, the number of tapestries and marble statues was overwhelming. The floor was covered with tiles of pure jade, polished to a shine. One of these would probably be enough to keep Dallion's family fed for a month.

Back on Earth, such houses were a common occurrence in movies and online videos. And while few had the means to live in them, many had gotten a glimpse of what was inside. Dallion's past self of this world hadn't even imagined such luxury.

The group went along a wide corridor into a large hall where the entire family of the village chief had gathered around a large table.

The moment Dallion entered, all eyes turned his direction, staring as if he were a lamb walking to its slaughter.

"Dallion Seene," Aspion Luor—the village chief himself—said as he leaned forward in his seat. He was a slightly thin man of average height dressed in a series of furs and clothes of fine red cotton. Looking at him, one would think he was in his sixties, although, being an awakened, it was difficult to say for certain. Platinum blond hair, now in the process of being replaced by white, flowed way past his shoulders. Copper rings covered his fingers, an elaborate display of wealth aimed at intimidating anyone poorer than him. "I heard you managed to awaken...on your third attempt?"

A few chairs away, a youth chuckled. He was roughly the same age as Dallion, and the only male grandchild the chief had. Awakening had made him even more arrogant than the average Luor family member. Interestingly enough, Dallion hadn't been particularly bullied by him as a child, mostly because Veil Luor didn't find it particularly interesting, choosing to bully stronger victims instead.

Four of the other five grandchildren were also there, leaning back in their chairs, faces covered in a mixture of boredom and disgust. They could definitely pass as beautiful, though definitely not nice.

"Better late than never." Dallion smiled.

"Watch your tongue!" Elin, the chief's only surviving son, snapped. He was one of those who never managed to awaken despite all the support of his family.

"It's all right." Aspion grinned. "Arrogance and awakening often come hand in hand, especially among the young. People tend to forget their place. Some even believe they are invincible."

You have a terribly annoying voice, Dallion thought.

"As is the custom, you must display your powers before I can acknowledge you to the ranks of the awakened." The chief leaned back. "Any preferences?"

Nice try, old man. "A simple task," Dallion said. "I'm a simple person, after all."

"A simple task…" Aspion's grin widened. "Very well. A simple task it will be. My youngest granddaughter has been complaining that the ring I gave her for her birthday is too simple. All I ask of you is that you improve it." The man snapped his fingers.

Almost on cue, a girl took a ring off her finger and placed it on the edge of the table. Dallion felt a sudden rush of blood to his face. This world's version of him had had a crush on her ever since they were children. Often, he would use his father's knife to make clumsy wooden carvings in secret, leaving them for her to find in the hopes something would happen. Nothing ever did. She was a Luor and, as such, would have nothing to do with someone of Dallion's social standing. Although, now that he had awakened, maybe things would be different?

Gloria. Dallion remembered her name.

"Improve one ring?" he asked with a smile. "I'd have thought someone so beautiful would deserve more?"

The girl's cheeks turned pink, nearly matching the color of her blouse.

"More, you say." The village chief rubbed his hands. "Are you sure? When I asked your mother, she told me she'd improve three things of my choice, and yet she failed to improve one simple ring. Such a shame. She had so much potential, being Kraisten's daughter and all."

Why did I say that?

Anyone could see a mile away that it was a provocation. The old man wasn't even being subtle about it, and yet, for a single moment in time, Dallion felt that was the right thing to do.

His grandfather had warned him about this, and still Dallion had acted like a complete novice. Upon entering the hall, he had assumed the task would be similar to improving the table there. It was quite large and in need of repair in parts. When Aspion had asked that a ring be fixed, a voice in Dallion's head had sighed in relief, telling him he'd gotten lucky. Seeing the village chief's reaction, however, he was all but sure he had walked straight into the old man's trap.

"Well?" Aspion pressed on, his face twisted in cruel delight, gloating at his inevitable victory. "Shall I bring something else?"

Dallion went to the side of table and picked the ring up. It was just a band of metal, not even gold or silver. If he were sneaky, he could mend something else, like the table or the chair the girl was sitting on. Back in his previous life, Dallion had enough lawyers in the family to know how to exploit loopholes. Technically, he hadn't agreed to the task in any way, just made an offer. Considering the village chief's nature, there was no reason he should. However, some things were stronger than logic. Dallion had been in this world less than a few hours but, even so, refused to let this go.

Sorry, Grandpa. I have to go through with this.

"Awaken." Dallion clutched the ring in his hand.

ITEM AWAKENING

A green rectangle appeared in front of him. A split second later, everything else disappeared.

WITHIN THE RING

Dallion found himself in a large hall, though one very different to the one he had been in moments ago. All the people had vanished, along with every single piece of furniture, leaving nothing but walls and a floor of gray polished metal. The doors and windows had also magically disappeared. The only source of light was a floating blue rectangle, identical to the one he had seen before he arrived in this world.

The RING is Level 3

So, this is to be awakened?

Against all logic and reason, he knew he had entered the ring itself. More importantly, the ring wasn't just a ring; it was its very own realm. Curious, Dallion looked at his hands and arms. They were pretty much the same—slightly cleaner and without any scars or bruises—with the exception of the metal buckler attached to his left forearm.

I remember this, Dallion thought as he slid his fingers along the smooth surface. It was the same shield he had taken on the "crossroads of destiny."

Suddenly, the blue rectangle flipped.

You are in a medium metal hall.
Defeat the guardian to change the RING's destiny!

The challenge was obviously a fight, which made Dallion tense up a bit. As a child, he had gone to a dozen different martial arts classes, quitting each after a few weeks of training. Back then, he kept telling himself he could easily learn to fight if only he put his mind to it. Sadly, the years had passed, and he had yet to set his mind to it. At present, he could say he knew the basics, and he could even claim to be somewhat fit for a city kid. However, he hadn't been in a serious fight since elementary school.

"I accept," Dallion said reluctantly, tapping on the buckler with his right hand.

The rectangle remained in front of him, silent and unmoving.

"Do I get a weapon?" *I should have taken the sword,* he thought. No response.

"Do I get anything? A bottle of water? A map? Some clear instructions?"

The rectangle kept on floating, oblivious to his questions. After a while, Dallion got tired and hit it with the back of his buckler. The rectangle shattered into pixels and disappeared into the air.

Just like pop-ups.

A large arch formed at the end of the hall, leading to an adjacent room. Normally, when presented with an unknown opening, a person's initial reaction was to peek through. Dallion was no different. He suspected the guardian might be waiting for him there, but he still couldn't stop himself from moving closer.

Just a few steps, he told himself. *There can hardly be any harm in that.*

The few steps became many, then lots. Before he knew it, Dallion was at the threshold, trying to peek beyond the sides of the archway, like a cat pressing its face against a windowpane. From what he could tell, there was no enemy to be seen, or anything else for that matter. The room appeared to be an identical copy to the one Dallion was in.

Most people would have found the fact suspicious, exerting some caution before continuing. Dallion didn't, stepping through the archway without a moment's consideration.

COMBAT INITIATED

A red rectangle emerged in the air. However, that wasn't Dallion's main concern. Along with the rectangle, a seven-foot tin statue had also appeared, standing in the middle of the room.

The statue had a distinctly Greco-Roman look, depicting a woman who seemed to have spent her entire life in a bodybuilder's gym. Muscles bulged, stretching the robe she wore in fascinatingly terrifying fashion. No weapons or pieces or armor were visible on the entity, but given that she was made entirely of metal, even a slap would likely feel like a sledgehammer.

"What the heck is that?!" Dallion smashed the red rectangle away.

No sooner had he asked than a white rectangle appeared above the statue.

RING GUARDIAN
Species: COLOSSUS
Class: TIN
Health: UNKNOWN
Traits: UNKNOWN
Skills: UNKNOWN
Weakness: UNKNOWN

In theory, the rectangle was supposed to provide information, but the lack of specifics only made the guardian more menacing.

Dallion's instincts forced him to take a step back. The moment he did, his back pressed against a hard surface. The opening that had been there moments ago had vanished, leaving him no way to escape.

This was it, the trial that had caused Dallion's mother to lose her awakened powers. Judging by the size of the guardian, it looked like he might share the same fate. A fight with a colossus wasn't the first thing Dallion wanted to do after discovering what awakening powers were. Then again, since there was no way to avoid it, he might as well do it right.

Taking a step forward, he raised the shield in the air above his head to get the opponent's attention.

Acknowledging her target, the guardian bowed.

You're courteous, at least, Dallion thought.

The futility of the situation, combined with decades of watching martial art competitions on YouTube, made him do the same. After all, just because he was about to be pummeled to a pulp was no reason for him to be rude. To his surprise, the guardian smiled in response. Unlike the village chief's family, there was no maliciousness in her, just a desire to fulfill her task.

Maybe this won't be so tough after all?

Without warning, the guardian rushed forward. Her right fist pulled back, preparing for a strike.

Dallion braced himself. There was little more that he could do. Even with a sword, he would be hard-pressed to do any actual harm. The thought of bashing her on the head cartoon-style crossed his mind, only to be cast away. A much better approach would be to leap to the side, evading the blow. Which way, though?

Before Dallion could make a decision, a line of green light appeared, connecting the guardian's fist to his chest. It was a curved glowing line, more like a piece of glowing rubber tube, or a thick wire-frame projection. Not wasting a moment, Dallion leapt to his right. The line didn't budge, now linking the guardian's fist to the wall. Moments later, the two made contact. A loud *clang* resounded in the room as if someone had hit the inside of a bell.

Two new lines appeared, starting from each of the guardian's fists and ending on Dallion's chest and jaw. This time, there also were a series of green glowing footsteps on the floor, as well as semi-transparent disk representations hovering throughout the air.

GUARD SKILLS ACTIVATED
Follow the suggested markers for best efficiency.

"Is this a tutorial?" Dallion asked.

The notion was simultaneously strange and insulting. Tutorials were the one thing everyone agreed was useless and best ignored. Dallion had spent weeks of his life ranting about them online, sometimes in great detail. Right now, though, he was glad to have been proven wrong.

Following the instructions was difficult, making him feel like a marionette operated by a very drunk sailor. In both cases, there were a lot of mistakes and swearing. Even when Dallion succeeded, he did so more by chance than actual skill.

The fight turned into an exercise in evasion, in which the key was to avoid the guardian's fists, which Dallion did with perfect accuracy, following the green footprints. Keeping up felt like playing *Dance Dance Revolution*, which he had always done poorly. For every series of five successful steps, he'd miss two, and the position of the buckler was little more than an afterthought.

It took over twenty tries for Dallion to complete a full sequence right. The moment he did, time came to a sudden crawl, and a green rectangle appeared in front of him.

GUARD SEQUENCE BONUS 1 — TIME SLOW

You have successfully completed a full guard sequence. Realm time will be slowed down two times—except for you—for the next five seconds, or until you perform an aggressive action.

"Nice!" Dallion smiled at the unexpected combat advantage. There were multiple ways for him to make use of the situation. His choice was to rush up to the guardian, then slam her head with his buckler. "One for me!"

RING GUARDIAN

RING GUARDIAN
Species: COLOSSUS
Class: TIN
Health: 75%
Traits: UNKNOWN
Skills: UNKNOWN
Weakness: UNKNOWN

Twenty-five percent with one hit? It felt suspiciously easy, to the point he feared it might be a lie. There was no way his mother could lose to a four-hit enemy.

The guardian paused. As time returned to normal, she adjusted her jaw. Cold gray eyes stared at Dallion, at which point the colossus smiled.

Uh oh. Dallion felt a wave of pressure.

The experience with floating rectangles and green markers had so far given him the impression that the battle was going to be one long and arduous experience of evading enemy attacks while slowly chipping away at the guardian's health. The smile just now sent shivers down his spine. This was the point Dallion realized the opponent he faced wasn't just a brainless automaton following a predefined set of actions. There was a mind working against him, and that mind had just gotten a taste of the way Dallion fought.

The colossus took a step back, entering a low combat pose. The glowing green lines that emerged from her fist changed into cones. It was safe to assume that should any part of the cone touch Dallion's body, he risked receiving serious damage. Given the harm already done to the walls and floor, one good hit was enough to knock him out, or worse. Not only that, but, moments later, a second pair of green cones appeared, this time starting from the guardian's feet.

Hands AND feet? Dallion wanted to shout. He felt as if he had been thrown into multiplayer after completing a single step from the tutorial. In games, this would never be allowed. Apparently, life in this world didn't follow the conventions of game design.

At the same time, Dallion had to also admit he felt a bit envious. If he had known martial arts would allow him to reach a level at which point he'd be able to perform such feats, Dallion would have never skipped a single lesson.

The colossus lunged forward.

Dallion barely managed to evade her strike, when a green cone formed an arc through him.

High sweep kick, Dallion thought.

There was no time to move out of reach, so he did the only thing left, dropping down. Tendons and muscles screamed in agony, reminding Dallion how much he had been neglecting them the last few years. Despite that, he managed to push through the pain instants before the metal leg sliced the air above him. If that had made contact, it wouldn't have easily thrown Dallion across the room like a rag-doll.

Green footprints appeared on the ground, visible from the corner of his eye. Yet, instead of following them, Dallion did the unthinkable—he attacked.

Squeezing what remaining strength he had, Dallion jumped to his feet. At this point, he didn't think, acting on pure animal instinct. His left arm swung around, only slightly faster than the guardian's, managing to hit the colossus in the neck with the edge of the buckler. Sparks emerged as metal hit metal, resulting in a resounding *clang*.

CRITICAL STRIKE
Weak spot found!
Dealt damage increased by 200%

A red rectangle appeared inches from Dallion's face. It was in that moment of euphoria that he realized he was in serious trouble. His gamble had rewarded him with a critical strike, dealing significantly more damage, but it had proven to be insufficient to defeat the colossus. As a result, Dallion had rendered himself open to attack.

Four green circles as large as flying pans covered his body. Playtime was over.

Damn it! Damn it! Damn it!

There was no time for thought or elegance. Dallion jumped backward, scrambling to avoid the enemy's attacks and possibly get a guard step right. Both hands, and buckler, were placed on the back of his head in an attempt to shield him. It was a sloppy tactic, unlikely to offer any real defense. Thankfully, he didn't get to find out. The guardian's arm missed him by a hair, scratching the surface of the shield in the process.

"Wait!" Dallion shouted, still scampering forward. "Wait!"

All green markers disappeared. Dallion braced himself for a blow that would end him...but the attack never came. Glancing over his shoulder, he saw the colossus just standing there, a puzzled expression on her face.

RING GUARDIAN
Species: COLOSSUS
Class: TIN
Health: 1%
Traits: UNKNOWN
Skills: UNKNOWN
Weakness: UNKNOWN

"I-I…" Dallion turned around, breathing heavily.

One percent? he thought. All that had kept him from achieving victory had been a rounding error? Thinking about it was enough to fill Dallion with deep gamer anger. However, there was nothing for him to be angry about. It was pure luck that he had managed to pull off that attack, let alone hit the guardian's weakness. If anything, he had to be overjoyed. But still…one percent?

"I have a proposal," Dallion said.

Attempting to reason with an overpowered enemy after a sneak attack was usually a bad idea. At best, the underpowered party would lose the element of surprise. At worst, they might suffer significantly more. Strangely enough, the guardian entered a neutral stance and gestured for Dallion to continue.

"We're both at one hit health," he went on. "Whoever lands this is the winner. So, instead of dragging it out, why not finish it?"

The guardian put her hand on her chin.

"One final charge, me against you. You know my skills, and I know yours." *At least some of them.* "We both give it all we got. That way, neither of us will have any regrets." And just to be on the safe side, he bowed low, keeping his eyes aimed at the floor.

The seconds dragged like hours. After a while, Dallion could take it no longer and peeked up. The guardian stood there, arms crossed, the sincerest expression of amusement on her face. There was no way to tell whether that was a good or a bad thing. Before

Dallion could ask, the colossus gave him a wink, then started walking to the far side of the hall.

That actually worked?

"Thanks," Dallion said.

The final battle…more like a duel, the guardian's attack versus Dallion's defense skills. His enhanced reaction provided something of an advantage, although now, much was yet to be determined.

Dallion glanced at the floor. There were no guiding footsteps. Apparently, attack wasn't always the best form of defense. In order for his guard ability to help him, he had to be under attack first.

"Ready?" he shouted.

Across the room, the guardian nodded.

Here we go.

Both darted forward almost simultaneously. The guardian's speed was twice that of Dallion's, her steps shaking the entire room as she moved closer. Dallion's mind raced. It all came down to a single second, the instant before the colossus could perform her attack. If the guard skill markers kicked in on time, all would be well. If not…

One second passed. Then two. Then three. A few more and the guardian would be close enough to perform her attack. Green cones connected all of her limbs to Dallion's torso, giving every indication it was going to be a swift defeat. And all this time, there wasn't a single green marker to be seen. Maybe it was a bad idea to take this approach after all?

Suddenly, green footsteps appeared, only this time, not all of them were on the floor. Three steps away, they suddenly shot up, continuing in almost vertical fashion. For anyone familiar with physics, such an action was unachievable. People could float in the air as much as bricks. However, there was also a point at which one had to have faith.

Letting go of all fears, Dallion followed the first few steps. Upon his reaching the third, the guardian began her attack. The stat-

29

ue's left knee bent down while her right arm moved back, ready for a side hook.

Of course! It all made sense now. The marker wasn't in the air; it was at the point where the guardian's knee was, then her hip, her hand...

Similar to a mountain goat, Dallion climbed up the metal body, avoiding all attacks until there was nowhere else to go. Time froze.

Just like a statue, he thought. Somehow, despite everything, he had managed to avoid her charge and trigger the guard skill's effect. He had done what the village chief thought he couldn't. Now, there was only one thing left to do.

"Sorry," Dallion said and slammed his buckler into the guardian's head with full strength.

RING Level increased
The RING has been improved to BRONZE.
Your GUARD skills have increased to 2.

ACKNOWLEDGED

You have impressed the Ring Guardian with your behavior!
The Colossus has granted you a future boon.

D allion reached out to touch the green rectangle, but before he could reach it, he found himself back in the hall of the village chief. The sudden shift to the real world had left him slightly confused, but the disorientation quickly subsided.

The ring was still in his hand, only it was no longer made of tin. The surface had become the color of warm bronze, and that wasn't the only change. Looking at it, Dallion could swear it had become thinner, more refined, better suited for jewelry than before.

"I hope this pleases you?" Dallion placed the ring in the blonde girl's hand. As he did, the redness on her cheeks deepened. "Is there anything else you wish of me?" he turned to Aspion.

That's for you, Mom and Grandad.

A sense of euphoria ran through him as if his blood was made of it. In this state, he felt there was nothing he couldn't do. In his mind, Dallion easily saw himself take on the village chief and his entire family right there and then. However, his grandfather's warning echoed in the back of his mind. All it took was a single excuse for

Aspion to have the guards and every other awakened charge at him, and some of them were probably stronger than the ring guardian. For the moment, he had to be calm. He could always settle things once he learned what was what.

"Village chief?" Dallion asked again.

It took only a moment for the chief to regain his composure. Confusion leaked through his mask of emotion, along with a spark of pure, unadulterated hatred.

"You're Kraisten's grandson, no doubt about it." The old man offered a slow clap. "Well done. At least now my granddaughter will stop nagging me."

Judging by everyone else's expressions, they were anything but pleased. The son of the village chief purpled with anger to the point Dallion felt his head would pop.

Must be embarrassing not to have awakened, with your connections. Dallion smirked.

A few seats away, Veil—the chief's grandson—stared with a mix of anger and excitement. It was no secret he was pleased to have a new awakened, though likely because it gave him a target to fight. Remembering what Veil used to do for fun, Dallion could already see problems in his future. Even most of the granddaughters gave Dallion the stink-eye, annoyed he kept them in the room longer than they had to be.

"Did your grandfather teach you that?" The chief leaned farther forward, the tips of his fingers tapping against each other.

"I wouldn't know if he had, Village Chief," Dallion replied, "but I don't believe so."

"Either way, you did well. I officially acknowledge you as an awakened of Dherma village. Please, be sure to say hello to him and your mother." The man's face twisted back into a grin.

"Thank you, Village Chief." *I must stay calm.* "I'll do that. I'm sure they will be glad."

The final provocation failed, Aspion dismissed Dallion with a wave of his hand. The two guards, dumbstruck up to now, rushed to "escort" him out of the hall. Unlike before, neither of them dared be too close or make any offensive remarks. Once Dallion left the mansion, the massive doors slammed behind him.

Damn it, that was close! Dallion let out an internal sigh of relief. At this point, the euphoria had worn off, allowing him to realize how fortunate he had been. The guardian had been a trick, that much was obvious. Aspion had planned to seal his abilities, and it was through pure luck and persistence that hadn't happened. That, and the colossus' sense of fair play. On the other hand, if Dallion had given in to the urge to pick a fight with the village chief, things could have ended quite poorly. For one thing, the rings on the old man's hands were copper. Going by awakened logic, defeating a tin guardian leveled it up to bronze. That meant that several more levels at least would be required to transform the alloy into pure copper.

Dallion took a good look at the mansion. His past self had always stood as far away from the building as possible. Something told him he'd have to be even more careful now. That, however, was a worry for another day. Right now, the acknowledgement was over, and the awakening fight had caused Dallion to work up an appetite.

Not a soul was visible as he walked through the village. Initially, Dallion didn't think anything of it. It was common for people to be off working during harvest season. Often, they would take their children along so they could keep an eye on them. There was one major problem with that logic, though. It was nowhere near harvest season. Not only that, but the silence was so absolute, making the place feel like a ghost town.

After several minutes, Dallion began to wonder. Something definitely didn't feel right. Maybe it was worth investigating a bit before going home?

It's probably nothing, Dallion told himself. *Most likely, I'm feeling some aftereffects from the fight.*

The house Dallion's family lived in was on the village outskirts, farthest from the chief's mansion. Originally, Dallion's grandfather had had several houses, including right next to the chief's, but that had been knocked down over a decade ago. The pain of having an un-awakened daughter had made the elder move farther away. Then, once Gertha had married, it had been her decision to move out of her father's house and into that of her husband.

Similar fates had fallen a few other hopefuls, causing them to accept their new lives, or leave the village altogether. Meanwhile, the Luor family continued to grow to the point it had the greatest number of awakened, and the only one with awakened of the younger generation. Well, after today, the Seene family had one as well.

"Hello?" Dallion said as he neared the door of his house.

There was no answer. Dallion looked around. No one had said anything about going anywhere. And even if they had, at least one of the neighbors should have appeared.

Carefully, Dallion pushed the door slightly. It wasn't barred.

"Hello?" he said again, peeking inside.

All his immediate family was there, sitting at the table, somber expressions on their faces. Even Dallion's brother, who usually was so energetic and full of joy, just sat there struggling to keep tears from trickling down his cheeks.

"Did something happen?" Dallion blinked.

"It's okay, son," his father said, with the largest forced smile Dallion had seen in both of his lives. "Come, sit down. There's some food left."

"Okay?" *What happened now?*

"Here." His grandfather pushed a mug into his hands. The alcohol fumes were so strong, Dallion thought he might get alcohol poisoning just by inhaling them. "Drink up. It'll do you good."

Err, can I not? Dallion wanted to say but obediently took a sip.

The drink was definitely strong and as bitter as burned licorice.

34

Dallion made an attempt to put it away, but one look from his grandfather was enough to tell him that wasn't an option.

"Was it the ring trial?" his mother asked in a whisper.

"Mhm." Dallion nodded, wondering what to do with the drink.

"It's always the ring trial. Curse that family! I had hoped he'd have shown mercy given the state of the village, and still..." She looked away. "I'm sorry you had to go through that."

"It was tough all right, but everything worked out in the end."

Dallion's words had the effect of a lightning bolt on a cloudless day. The surrounding people froze, then stared, then looked at each other as if to confirm they hadn't misheard.

"You...you completed the trial?" Dallion's grandfather asked, hands shaking.

"Sure did. It wasn't easy, but I did it." Dallion smiled. "It was mostly luck, but—"

"You completed the trial!" The old man grabbed Dallion, lifting him from the chair in a massive bear hug. "Have you any idea what this means? The village finally has an awakened that isn't from the Luor family! And that awakened is my grandson!"

Not for long if you don't let me go.

It was at that moment Dallion discovered that victory also has its cost.

A MOTHER'S HAIRPIN

The more Dallion learned about awakening in this new world, the more its limitations became clear. For starters, it wasn't possible to use the ability at will. Although invisible, the stress awakening caused to the body was extreme. While mending in the awakened realm didn't feel too bad, once it was over, a day of light activity, or better yet, rest, was highly recommended. Dallion had discovered this the hard way when he had attempted to improve a broken chair shortly after the chief's trial. Not only was he unable to enter the chair's state, but he had fainted immediately after.

Upon waking up, the first thing he received was a sharp slap from his mother. The second was a long and detailed explanation of what to and not to do as far as awakening powers were concerned. Despite having her powers sealed away, she remained the daughter of an awakened and, unlike Dallion, had spent years studying theory before breaking through her first barrier. Interestingly enough, Dallion had no memories of the books she had used to gain her knowledge. In fact, he had no knowledge of seeing books anywhere growing up.

According to Gertha, awakening was divided into levels, with each level determining how many times per day a person could use the ability to improve an item without suffering harm. Doing more was possible, though it came with consequences, as Dallion had found out. That explained why the village chief hadn't followed up the trial with another task. Even he couldn't break the rules in such an obvious way. It was also considered sensible for a person to avoid improving items of a greater level. The reason for this wasn't apparent, but Dallion's mother insisted on it.

Skills and "traits" were a vital part of the awakened's life. The traits were representations of one's being, namely: body, mind, perception, and reaction. Body represented a person's strength and ability to heal. Mind was the person's memory capabilities and wit. Perception was the degree to which one perceived sights, sounds, smells, tastes, and touch. Finally, reaction was the individual's reaction speed. Normally, one started with three points on each, and was allowed to increase the value of one of them with each breakthrough, which also brought an increase in awakening level.

Dallion didn't mention he had received a bonus of two additional reaction points. He did, however, thank his good fortune for it. If he had fought the guardian with a reaction of three, the outcome would have been very different.

Gertha also spoke of two lost traits: magic and one other, the name of which had been forgotten with time. From her words, Dallion understood that incredibly few people awakened with magic, and those who did went on to quickly become nobles of vast importance in the large cities or even the imperial capital itself.

Skills, on the other hand, were much fuzzier. For one thing, there didn't seem to be any clarity regarding their type and number. Some, such as guard and attack, were obvious. Most people were offered one of them upon awakening, occasionally given the option to pick between both. Every now and again, less common skills would appear.

"I was offered music," Dallion's mother said with a sad smile. "It allowed me to see and create emotions for people. I could have brought cheer to the entire village, maybe beyond…but it was no combat skill."

Dallion felt a lump in his throat. To be given such a rare gift only to have it snuffed out by a jealous village chief, that was beyond cruel.

Do you miss it? he wanted to ask but knew he shouldn't. The answer was obvious.

"I better go help Dad in the field." Dallion attempted to stand up from his bed.

"No." His mother placed her hand firmly on his shoulder. "You're an awakened now. You don't have to work."

"That doesn't sound fair." That explained why everyone in the Luor family was so spoiled. "Besides, I don't mind helping a bit."

"What you must do is train." The soft tone of the woman's voice had become as hard as steel. "As an awakened, you're given a week to get used to your power. After that, the village chief will call you to perform another task." She clenched her fists.

Let me guess, Dallion thought. *Another tradition for the good of the city.*

The chief's ploy was so transparent. Not only had he monopolized the awakened in Dherma, but even then, he treated them as servants, doing what he saw fit.

A thought popped up in Dallion's mind. *Maybe it had started with good intentions.* There was some logic to having the gifted devote their skills to the village. The place was practically falling apart. Even so, there had to be better ways to do it.

"Now that Aspion has seen what you're capable of, he'll think of something more difficult to break you," Gertha said. "Your only chance is to be ready."

Seven days to prepare. With one gone, only six remained. Six chances to improve items and develop his skills. Dallion suddenly appreciated not having to help out with daily chores. Six days wasn't nearly enough.

"How do I increase my awakened level?" Dallion asked.

"You're not ready for that." His mother shook her head. "It takes months to reach the point of a breakthrough. The only thing you can do until then is improve the skills you have." She took a hairpin made of bone from her hair and held it in front of him. "And I'll help you do that. Use your skill as much as you can. It's not about defeating your opponent but getting comfortable with the skill you have."

Learning what I have.

"Did you see awakening markers using your skill?" the woman asked.

"Yes. They were like green footprints showing me where to step to avoid the guardian's attacks. I could also see the areas in which they aimed to hit."

"Mine were different." A sad smile appeared on the woman's face. "They were blue and…" The smile faded away. "It's been so long, I can't remember. I recall you had to follow through. You always gain an advantage if you do."

"I will." Dallion nodded, then reached out and grabbed the tip of the hairpin.

ITEM AWAKENING
The HAIRPIN is Level 1

Once again, reality changed, placing Dallion in a small room, this one smooth and white as if made of pearl. His buckler had appeared, strapped to his left arm, same as last time. Unfortunately, the clothes he wore were his "pajamas," or the medieval equivalent that passed for such.

This is awkward.

You are in a small room of bone.
Defeat the guardian to change the HAIRPIN's destiny!

"I know, I know." Dallion gently tapped on the rectangle.

As it vanished, a doorway emerged. If nothing else, that confirmed the notion that nothing bad could happen in the initial room. It was also apparent the room depended on the material the item was made of. Based on that logic, the room size had to be linked to the item's level.

"Guard skills, activate!" Dallion said out loud, raising his buckler above his head.

Nothing happened.

Okay, so they don't appear on command. He lowered his shield. At least there was no one here to see him. Taking a deep breath, Dallion walked through the doorway. Going by past experience, he expected to enter a room with an opponent. Instead, he found himself in a very short and twisty corridor branching off in three directions.

You are in a Labyrinth of DAMAGE
Reach the center of the labyrinth to repair the HAIRPIN.

Well, Dallion swallowed, *this is new.*

MENDING LABYRINTH

L abyrinths came in different shapes and sizes. The oldest was said to have been built in Egypt and so complicated, it was impossible to complete without the key. Dallion, for his part, had completed a lot of labyrinth puzzles as a child back on Earth. It was his passion, earning him several rewards, including second place at the regional Labyrinth Solving tournament. To be honest, though, it wasn't a large tournament and had quickly dissolved when he was in middle school.

This labyrinth was different from any Dallion had seen in a number of ways. For starters, its shape was highly irregular. There were no set straight lines, but no defined curves either. It was as if the labyrinth varied between the two based on its own free will. Several times, Dallion would start walking down a straight corridor, just to have it twist and curve the moment he backtracked. In other instances, he'd spend minutes walking in zig-zag fashion, only to find he had made five steps from the starting point.

That wasn't the most confusing element, however. Unlike what the floating rectangle had said, his goal wasn't to reach the center of the labyrinth, or at least not the only goal; he also had to repair it in the process. If anything, Dallion assumed reaching the center would end the repair progress, applying the changes to the item.

Repairing, as it turned out, came in different forms as well. There was the standard element: cracked walls with missing pieces scattered throughout the labyrinth; those could be repaired by placing the placing the piece in the correct spot. The real trick, however, was fixing the overall shape. As it turned out, walking along a corridor not only got him from point A to point B, it also allowed him to stretch, straighten, curve, or squeeze the path he walked on.

Like trying to make a wall out of jelly bricks.

The concept was simple. Executing it took some skill, a bit of luck, and a whole lot of persistence. Each time Dallion would repair a wall or lock a path in place, a blue rectangle would appear, informing him of the overall progress.

Labyrinth section mended!
Overall completion 96%

The first time Dallion had returned a bone "brick" to its spot, his completion was thirty-seven percent. He had painstakingly achieved a lot since then. Even so, or maybe because of it, the missing four percent infuriated him to no end. In theory, nothing stopped him from stepping through the archway at the labyrinth's center. After all, the goal was to practice his guard skills in combat, not repair the item itself. The completionist in him, though, kept nagging for him to reach the coveted one hundred percent.

"Where are you?" Dallion grumbled.

The first awakened trait he'd improve, given the chance, was his perception. Maybe then he'd be able to see hints that would help him mend things better. Now, he understood why his grandfather had been so tired after mending the table. While the process only took a moment in the real world, it involved hours of labor within the item itself, not to mention the mental anguish.

"It's not the walls," Dallion said out loud in the hopes that doing so would give him an idea. "It has to be the paths."

He had spent what felt like hours walking up and down, checking if any corridor could be changed. All of them appeared firm. Just to be sure, Dallion went through the labyrinth yet again, carefully looking for minuscule cracks or holes in the white surface. Just as before, there seemed to be none.

"Okay." He closed his eyes. "If it isn't the walls, and it's not the paths, is there anything that—"

He suddenly stopped as a bout of inspiration hit him harder than a revolving door.

I'm an idiot! Dallion rushed toward the center of the labyrinth.

There was one element he hadn't checked, something so obvious, he'd gone past it dozens of times without paying attention—the archway that led to the room beyond. From his trial in the ring, Dallion knew that stepping through would take him to the item's guardian, where the battle would commence. That memory had become associated with fear, instinctively making him stay at a distance from the arch at all times. It was almost like an annoying voice in the back of his mind, whispering danger whenever he got close. Now, Dallion's determination had outweighed the fear, and the whispers had faded away.

Upon reaching the center of the labyrinth, everything fell into place. Looking at the archway, the deformation was obvious. The keystone was so low that only a child could pass under it without hitting its head. Taking a step forward, Dallion pushed it up. The top of the archway gave in as if made of putty before finally locking in place.

Labyrinth fully mended!
The HAIRPIN is now flawless.

Dallion could almost hear victory music in his head. A reward would have been nice, but at least he had the knowledge he had repaired the item to a hundred percent. Beaming with joy, he stepped through.

Instantly, the walls of the labyrinth sank into the floor, creating a round hall.

COMBAT INITIATED

The familiar red rectangle appeared, along with the new opponent.

HAIRPIN GUARDIAN
Species: BLADE SPIDER
Class: IVORY
Health: UNKNOWN
Traits: UNKNOWN
Skills: UNKNOWN
Weakness: UNKNOWN

A white rectangle appeared above the creature. The guardian was very different from the one Dallion had faced before. There was nothing human about it. Rather, it was a mix between a Boston Dynamics robot and an avant-garde statue. The spider, for lack of a better term, was the size of a desk, entirely white—as if made of plastic—with eight blade-tipped legs, six eyes the size of golf balls, and a roundish body.

I didn't know that hairpins look like that on the inside. Dallion shivered. He could only imagine what a comb must be like. If this was any indication, combing must resemble having a centipede go through his hair several times per day.

Before he could say or do a thing, green strings filled the air, starting at the creature's legs and ending all over his body. A split second later, green footprints and shield markers appeared.

"Damn it!" Dallion dashed to the side.

The spider leapt forward. Faster and far more aggressive than the colossus, it attacked with a series of jabs while simultaneously running alongside Dallion. Having eight legs that could be used for movement and attack was an overpowering advantage.

Deep in his heart, Dallion knew his mother wouldn't give him a challenge he couldn't beat. He also remembered her words: It wasn't about achieving victory but learning what he knew. Right now, though, his only thought was to get as far away from the bladed menace as possible.

Follow the steps, he said to himself, twisting as if he were walking on a tightrope. *Follow the steps, and it'll be okay.*

Two of the spider's legs hit Dallion in the thigh.

MINOR WOUND
Your health has been reduced by 5%

A red rectangle appeared in front of Dallion. The pain was far less than expected. It felt similar to the annoying sensation of a pinprick or an ant bite. To Dallion's relief, the attacks didn't cause any noticeable harm, though they were still something he preferred to avoid.

The guardian attacked again. This time, Dallion evaded the bladed legs by diligently following the green guard markers. The moment he matched a full set of eight footprints and two shield positions, time slowed to a crawl.

"Now it's my turn." Dallion grinned.

MOTHER'S TRAINING

Time slow, as the name suggested, allowed a person to experience the passage of time much faster than everyone else. Games and movies illustrated that by allowing characters to perform actions within the fraction of a second while their opponents stood helplessly like statues. In practice, the experience was very different.

The time slow effects allowed Dallion to analyze the situation and make a better decision while not being under pressure. However, they didn't make him faster. He had his reaction trait to thank for that. At this point, it would have been easy for him to whap the bone spider on the head with his buckler and put an end the fight. Doing so, though, would gain him little.

So, that's what you were aiming for, Mom? Dallion smiled.

The bone blade spider was perfect for him to practice his guard skills. The creature was fast, agile, and dealt insignificant amounts of damage. Defeating it would be simple. Learning to consistently evade it, though, that was the real trick.

"Here you go, little buddy." Dallion gently shoved the creature to the side with his shield as if he were shooing a kitten off the kitchen table.

Time resumed its normal pace. The spider paused, visibly confused as to what had happened. Its eyes moved in all directions before focusing on its opponent once more.

"Come on," Dallion said, tapping on his shield. "Let's have another go."

The spider took a few steps back. Half of its limbs tapped the ground, preparing for its attack. Dallion could almost sense the guardian's intentions. This was no longer a simple fight; it was a challenge to determine who had more skill. There was a moment of silence, after which the spider charged.

The fight continued for hours. Letting go of his fear, Dallion lost track of time. Everything had become an enjoyable experience, almost a dance in which each side tried to outperform the other. Following the step and shield indicators had become remarkably easy. For every four successful sequences, he would mess up one. And it was through performing them that he noticed the advantages they provided.

Completing one sequence flawlessly caused time to slow. Completing two in a row, without attacking in between, made it stop completely, also allowing him to move a short distance away without stopping the time flow. The only rule was that Dallion could only move within the range of the flashing footprints that remained. Every subsequent sequence increased the distance. A few experiments determined that, while he could step anywhere so long as it was within range, doing so would break the sequence. Potentially, it was good for a one-off attack, but if Dallion wanted to compound his advantage, he had to follow the markers.

Despite Dallion's many attempts, he wasn't able to complete five guard sequences in a row. Sadly, that no longer was an issue of execution. It was his body that couldn't keep up or, more specifically, his "body" trait. On the fourth sequence, he could already feel resistance as if he were moving through syrup. Upon starting the fifth, his limbs just refused to move forward. Apparently, if he wanted to achieve more, he had to find a way to increase the level of his body trait.

"How about we call it a day?" Dallion asked, brushing the sweat off his forehead.

While enjoyable, it had been exhausting experience, and he had reached his limit. The spider, in contrast, seemed no different. There was no indication whether its stamina had decreased. Stopping its attack, the guardian paused for a few moments, legs tapping on the bone floor, then took a few steps back.

"I don't suppose you can forfeit the fight?" Dallion smiled.

The spider lifted two legs in the equivalent of a shrug.

"Didn't think so." Dallion sighed. "Well, let's do this."

On cue, the spider dashed forward. The creature, so fast and scary before, now looked like a snail slowly crawling forward. Dallion was able to clearly see all the spots the guardian targeted. The muscle memory gained from the hours of fighting let him evade the attack even without looking at the guard markers on the floor: two steps forward, one to the side, two jumps and a twist. As before, time slowed down; though, this time, Dallion didn't proceed with the sequence, choosing to slam his shield onto the creature.

AGGRAVATED STRIKE
Dealt damage is increased by 100%

Nice, Dallion thought.

HAIRPIN Level increased
The HAIRPIN has been improved to IVORY.
Your GUARD skills have increased to 3.

Suddenly, Dallion found himself back in his bed, holding on to the hairpin his mother had given him. There was a moment of disorientation while his mind got used to the notion he had returned to the real world. The moment that happened, sweat oozed from every pore of his body, drenching the pajamas.

"Careful not to overdo it." Gertha pulled the hairpin out of his hand. The object had become far more refined, polished and sharp with an almost pearl-like shine. "Awakening numbs fatigue, but the body still needs rest. I suggest you stay in bed for a while. Before that, get changed. I'll bring some fresh sheets."

"The guardians," Damion started. As he did, he noticed he was gasping for air. "The guardians, are they intelligent?"

The woman smiled.

"Only for the awakened. That's one of the curses we have to live with. Once you're awakened, you can never look at objects in the same way." She placed the hairpin back in her hair. "Those who are too softhearted see the agony of items no matter where you look. Those who are too cruel find joy in breaking things, only to imagine their guardians in pain."

It was no mystery in which category the village chief's family fell. Dallion distinctly remembered Veil breaking things a lot for no good reason. Now, he knew why.

"Rest a bit," Dallion's mother whispered. "I'll bring some food as well."

Taking a few more moments to catch his breath, Dallion got up and went to the yard's well for a wash. The state of the well tempted him to use his awakened skills on it, but reason prevailed.

Only once per day, Dallion told himself. Besides, there was no telling whether he could even handle something as large as a well. So far, he had only improved objects that could fit within the palm of his hand. Given there was so little he knew about the rules of awakening, it was safer to follow his mother's instructions and those of his grandfather when the old man bothered to give any useful advice. The elder seemed determined to let Dallion figure things out on his own. In the long term, that was probably the right way to go, but there were times when Dallion felt he could use some much-needed advice.

The next few days followed a cycle of rest, practice, rest, washing, as well as lots of eating. Dallion's Aunt Vanessa frequently came to visit, of course, each time "accidentally" bringing a small trinket with her. During the course of a conversation—regardless of topic—she would inadvertently mention she'd appreciate to have the item "adjusted."

The first such item was a simple handkerchief. Vanessa wanted it made into silk but reluctantly accepted fine cotton as a result. The second was a vase Dallion found too tacky for his taste but had no problem improving. As for the final one, the woman had brought a single copper coin. Upon seeing it, Dallion was impressed at the woman's ingenuity. Turning lead to gold had long been a dream of alchemists back on Earth.

In this world, that was a real possibility, at least for the awakened. Kraisten, however, had made it clear in no uncertain terms that his grandson was not to meddle with any metals, let alone copper. The message was received loud and clear since Vanessa had promptly left and hadn't bothered visiting the following day.

On the fifth day since Dallion's awakening, his parents reluctantly let him choose what to improve on his own. It didn't take long for him to decide on what exactly. He had taken the opportunity to go to the river at the edge of the village and take his younger brother with him.

"Are you sure, brother?" Linner asked. "There are lots of other things to improve. Or you can repair—"

"Nothing else needs improving. And I've already repaired everything in the house," Dallion interrupted.

For the most part, it was true. After Dallion had found that mending items didn't affect his improvement limit, he had gone on a mending spree, effectively repairing most of the smaller items in the house, as well as a pot, a pan, and a few of his father's tools.

Repairing things didn't improve his skills in any way, but it was fun, and Dallion liked items looking better.

"At your last birthday, I promised I'd improve the best pebble for you, and I'll keep that promise."

It had been a childish promise, made years before Dallion even appeared in the world. Given his little brother's constant support and admiration, it only felt proper that he finally got his birthday wish—an improved river pebble.

"You remember our deal." Dallion entered the river. "You choose the pebble, I improve it."

"Of course!" The child grinned and splashed farther in, searching for "the perfect" pebble.

Standing at the riverbank, Dallion couldn't help but wonder what sort of guardian he'd face. So far, he had fought metal, bone, cloth, clay, and wood. Stone was definitely going to be a first.

"Hello, Dallion," a female voice nearby said. Turning around, he saw the village chief's granddaughter, prominently wearing the metal ring he had improved for her. "Let's have a talk."

THE ARRANGEMENT

Seeing Gloria wasn't on the top of Dallion's list. After what he and his mother had been subjected to at the hands of the Luor family, he didn't want anything to do with them. The past him, however, had a somewhat different view. This was probably the first time Gloria had spoken to Dallion, and definitely the first she had sought him out. The problem was that she wasn't unbeautiful, earning herself a pass when it came to the arrogance and cruelty of the rest of the Luors.

"The ring suits you well," Dallion said.

"Oh, err…" Gloria paused. Possibly it was a trick of the light, but Dallion was almost certain he saw her face change color. "I'm not here for that," she snapped and hid her hands behind her back.

Similar to all Luors, her hair was platinum blonde, neatly combed in a braid over her shoulder. Her clothes were simple, yet elegant, improved at least twice and frequently mended. After spending so much time using his awakened powers, Dallion could tell at a glance when something seemed unnaturally perfect. The whole outfit was suited for the pages of a fashion catalogue and, admittedly, suited Gloria quite well.

Gloria Luor, as the name suggested, was the chief's second

youngest grandchild. An awakened, like her brother, she was granted a special status in the village. Rarely lifting a finger to help anyone, she spent most of her time at the mansion. According to the local gossip, Aspion had actively been searching for eligible suitors for her hand, with the aim of increasing his influence. There had been a few candidates, but the village chief had found them lacking.

"Is everything all right, brother?" Linner asked from the river.

"It's fine, Lin," Gloria answered in Dallion's stead. "I'm just here to thank your brother for the ring he improved for me."

Concern remained written on the child's face.

"It's fine." Dallion nodded with a smile, going with her lie. "You just find that perfect pebble, okay?"

"Okay…" Linner wasn't entirely convinced but still went back to what he was doing. Even so, he shot curious glances at the two every now and again.

"I used to be like him once," Gloria whispered as she moved closer to Dallion.

"Poor and afraid?" Dallion couldn't resist.

"Carefree and happy."

"Yeah, must be difficult living in luxury. Getting everything you wish for…" He shook his head in faux pity. "Must be really tough."

"I make my own clothes," the girl said with an icy hardness to her voice. "It's expected of me. But what do you know? You've only been awakened for five days."

"Well, it's been a breeze so far," Dallion lied. "Maybe this awakened thing isn't as difficult as your family makes it out to be."

"You think it's easy?" Gloria crossed her arms. "You were lucky with the ring! I don't know what skill you were given, but it's not going to be enough."

Dallion opened his mouth to say something, but the girl continued before a sound could leave his throat.

"In two days, you'll be called back to the house to help the

56

village," Gloria went on. "You'll be given an impossible task. Well, impossible at your current awakened level, at least."

That was a surprise. Dallion was fully aware the village chief had this planned for him, but he didn't expect Gloria would openly share it. The naïve part that was his past self thought she had done so out of the goodness of her heart. The part of him that had grown up on Earth knew better.

"And even if you miraculously manage that, in a week, you'll be called on again, and again, until you fail."

There were no two ways about that. The girl was absolutely right. No matter how hard Dallion trained, there was no way he could rely on chance forever, not after attracting so much attention. He had been lucky once, could be lucky a few more times as well, but, at some point, that luck would run out, and the fall would be all the greater.

"What's it to you?" Dallion asked.

"Does it matter?" Gloria gave him a smug look. "Can you afford to refuse any help at this point?"

The question further convinced Dallion she had come with something in mind. Strictly speaking, she hadn't offered any help, merely implied it, but he was right. The risk of ignoring her was greater than hearing her out. In the back of his mind, though, a small voice whispered this was an opportunity he might never again have.

"You're a level one, aren't you?" Gloria persisted. Clearly, she wasn't someone who was used to getting no as an answer.

Dallion didn't reply.

"Level ones only have one skill, and no matter how rare that skill is, it won't be enough for the upcoming task. Trust me."

You really think I can trust you? Dallion smirked on the inside.

A short distance away, Linner had gotten out of the river but still hadn't returned to Dallion. It was almost as if he no longer noticed the presence of Gloria or his brother.

"And you've decided to help me just like that?" Dallion asked. "For no reason at all."

"When do you think you'll reach level two?"

"It takes months of practice to reach a breakthrough point." Dallion recited what his mother had told him.

"Years," Gloria corrected. "And there's no guarantee you'll succeed the first time. However, there's also another way."

What?

This was the first time Dallion had heard of this. Given that he'd only been in this world for a week, it wasn't that much of surprise. Something in Gloria's voice suggested there was more to it, though, some kind of cheat that bypassed years of training.

"There's a way for you to achieve a breakthrough much sooner. With a bit of luck, you can become a level two and do it tomorrow," the girl whispered. "However, you'll have to decide if you're going to trust me or not."

The last time Dallion had been forced to make an instant decision was when applying for college. At the time, he hadn't been too thrilled by the prospect, wanting to enjoy another year of freedom before. His father, though, had given him an ultimatum: apply immediately or say goodbye to any associated financial support. Now, like back then, the choice was no choice at all.

"How difficult will it be?"

"Nothing you can't handle." Gloria stepped back.

"And I suppose I mustn't tell anyone else about this?"

"That would be best."

"You're not giving me too much of a choice." Dallion sighed theatrically. His performance seemed to have an effect, for the girl glanced away, partial guilt appearing on her face. "What do I have to do?"

"Meet me here at midnight tonight. Make sure no one finds out about this."

That sounded like a trap if Dallion had ever heard one.

"Okay." Then again, there were ways to spring a trap. "Anything else?"

"No." Gloria turned around. "Oh, and thanks for the ring," she added before hastily walking away.

Midnight tonight, Dallion thought. Things were getting interesting. Possibly *too* interesting.

"Brother, brother!" Linner rushed toward him now that Gloria had gone. "I found it! I found the perfect pebble."

"That's great!" Dallion grabbed his brother and lifted him into the air. Thanks to the awakened powers, the boy felt as light as a pillow. "Give it here," Dallion said as he put Linner back on the ground. "And let me do my magic."

As for tonight, I have the perfect plan.

MIDNIGHT MEETING

It was ironic that given everything that had happened since his arrival in this world, sneaking out of home remained the most difficult challenge Dallion had faced so far. Being in a strange world with weird magic abilities, one would have expected fending off monsters or exploring dungeons to be the most difficult to face. Trying to sneak out unnoticed of a two-room house with a squeaky floor proved to be an even greater feat.

Back in his previous life, this wouldn't have been an issue. With his parents working late most of the time, Dallion could walk out of the front door without an issue. Things were so easy that he didn't even have to bother to climb out of a window. Here, he had to work for it.

Using the footwork he had developed through his guard skills, Dallion leapt from spot to spot—repairing the board underneath before it could make a sound—until he finally reached the door. From there, it was a quick pull and twist so he could open the door, then squeeze through the crack before it shut back again. Unlike the village chief, Dallion's family could only afford a bar to keep it locked at night.

Better safe than sorry, a voice whispered in Dallion's mind.

Gloria had told him to be at the river at midnight. That was why Dallion was there two hours earlier. The first half-hour he had spent seeking out a good spot for an ambush, for lack of a better word. Considering how flat the terrain was, the best Dallion could do was find the least conspicuous piece of vegetation. Once he did, he hid there and waited…and waited…and waited.

Twenty minutes later, he bitterly regretted his decision to appear early. Waiting, unlike the version shown in games and movies, turned out to be an utterly boring process. Dallion didn't have a phone or book to pass the time with. The only thing he had was the skill to tell time by the night sky.

No one came at eleven, nor at eleven twenty, nor at eleven forty. Ten minutes to midnight, Dallion was so fed up with the whole thing, he just wished Gloria would appear with her surprise escort and get it over with. To his astonishment, that didn't happen. At midnight, on the dot, the girl arrived completely alone.

"Dallion," she said in semi-whisper, looking around. "Dallion?"

Throwing all caution to the wind, he left his hiding place and quickly went her direction.

Being the only thing taller than four feet, he was easy to spot. Even so, approaching from an unexpected direction made Gloria hesitant. Doubt covered her face, visible even in the faint light of the moons.

"What were you doing there?" she asked once Dallion got close enough.

"I got lost," Dallion grumbled. Judging by Gloria's expression, she didn't appreciate the sarcasm. "Anyway, I'm here. How do I improve my awakening?"

"You'll see. First, don't use your awakened powers for anything until I tell you."

That had to be the reason the meeting was at midnight. Smart, although she could have simply told Dallion about her plan.

"Anytime you're ready," he said after a while.

"We have to get there first." Gloria chuckled. It was nothing but a momentary smile under the moonlight, but it made her seem like a normal person for once. For a few seconds, one could almost forget she was related to the village chief.

"Where's there exactly?"

There was a long pause.

This is stupid, Dallion thought. "You'll be taking me there, right?"

A sudden reluctance became visible on Gloria's face, as if she were about to share the greatest secret in her possession. That made little sense since she was asked him here in the first place. A voice in the back of Dallion's mind urged him to give up on the whole thing and just go home. Clearly, she needed him more than he needed her, so if she didn't want to share what was actually going on, he might as well walk off.

"To a cave a short way off," Gloria said.

"Why didn't we meet there directly?"

"It's secret, all right? Only my grandfather's supposed to know about it. Once every year, he chooses someone in the family and takes them there in the hopes they'll awaken. Everyone is blind-folded so only he knows the exact location."

That sounded very much like the village chief. Even the members of his family were considered a threat. It was natural for him to monopolize a cheat that would grant him awakened powers faster than the conventional way, then use it to build up his family.

"That's how you awakened?"

"Yes." The girl nodded. "It's not something I'm proud of. But that doesn't matter anymore." She clenched her fists. "What matters is the future, and there isn't much time."

For the next half-hour, the two continued downstream along the river until they reached a rocky area. Every step filled Dallion with irrational dread. People weren't allowed to stray far from the village. There was constant talk of beasts and monsters roaming the area, ready to attack anyone who foolishly wandered into their domains. Thinking back, Dallion had never witnessed such events but was convinced that they occurred.

Large boulders emerged from the ground without rhyme or reason. Dallion vaguely remembered his grandfather telling him about the area. It was called Ogre Gorge and, ages ago, was said to have been the battlefield of two tribes of ogres the size of mountains. The fight had lasted for centuries, until all ogres killed each other, only their bones and shattered skulls remaining. The boulders sticking out of the ground were said to be scattered teeth. It was a charming story, if utterly unbelievable.

"It's not long now," Gloria said, walking through a cluster of rocks. "You can almost see it from here."

"No problem. One question, though. If you were blindfolded when you got here, how did you find it?"

"My awakening. When I was given the option, I chose to improve my perception. I remembered the sounds and smells on the way back."

Neat trick.

A cave emerged shortly later, digging into a boulder like a cavity in a tooth. Pitch black and barely large enough to let a person pass, it continued on for a few dozen steps, ending in a large underground chamber. The entire time, Dallion was forced to hold on to Gloria. After all, she was the one with the high perception. The only thing he could do in the situation was make sure he didn't fall or bump into anything.

As they ventured farther in the chamber, a warm glow emerged, covering everything in light.

"You can let go now," the girl said as she continued to the center of the area, where a small altar was located.

There were no words to describe the sight. The altar was dazzling with its simplicity. Unlike anything Dallion had seen in this or his previous world, it was perfectly monolithic, shaped like a simplified hex grid. Six pillars of hex-shaped crystal rose from the floor, surrounding a seventh. Gray light—a notion Dallion never thought could exist—shone through them, giving off a faint but unmistakable sensation of power, like a holy artifact low on batteries.

"What's that?" Dallion asked.

"An altar of the Seven Moons," the girl replied. "It must have been a shrine once, long forgotten and abandoned. Its power remains, though."

"Its power?"

"The Seven Moons are what gave humanity the power of awakening. They can also help us grow. When you improve their altar, you actually improve yourself." Gloria put her left hand on top of the central pillar, then turned around and extended her right in Dallion's direction. "This is how you'll gain your second skill."

THE AWAKENING SHRINE

You are in a small awakening shrine.
Complete the trial to improve your destiny!

E ntering the realm through another person was unusual, even more so than doing it one's self. There was no mental preparedness, merely popping up in an entirely new reality in the blink of the eye. Dallion wondered whether it was possible to have non-awakened enter the realms. If so, he could have other members of his family—maybe even his aunt—see what it was like being within an item. On second thought, though, maybe it was better not to experiment.

Unlike the awakened rooms Dallion had seen so far, this one was open. In fact, it wasn't so much a room as an open space with six columns in the middle. Bluish-white sky continued to the horizon above ground of gray rock. There was no sun that could be seen, although Dallion swore he saw the outlines of several moons in the whiteness above.

"It was like that the first time I came here as well," Gloria said a few steps away. "I spent hours looking at the sky."

"Why are we both here?"

This was the first time he had seen a living person in an awakened realm. Unusually, it had always been empty rooms, mazes, and item guardians. Having Gloria here, equipped with a long saber, was beyond unexpected.

"Shrines are different." She sighed like a teacher who had to repeat an explanation in class. "By improving them, you improve yourself."

Dallion kept staring at her as his mind tried to make sense of it all. On their own, each of the concepts was clear, simple, and understandable, but when jumbled together, nothing seemed to make any sense.

"The shrine is like you," the girl said extremely slowly, almost dragging every word. "If you complete a challenge here, it's the same as if you complete a challenge for yourself. After that happens, you can claim the reward it offers you as if it's—"

"I got that." Dallion's pride kicked in, forcing him to interrupt. "But why are there two of us? That's not supposed to happen, even upon reaching a breakthrough."

"The shrine allows other awakened to be invited for support."

Finally, things started to make sense. It also meant Dallion's idea of inviting others went out of the window. Maybe that was for the best. Also, Gloria's motives had finally become clear. It wasn't that she wanted to help Dallion, rather, she was in need of his help. Granted, it was mutual help. He was also going to get a free breakthrough as a result, and at a time he needed it.

"This isn't your first time here, is it?" Dallion asked.

"It's my fifth. The last time was two years ago."

That was quite a while ago.

"Why did you stop?"

"When I failed last time, the shrine suggested I find another awakened to help me." The girl gave Dallion a long, silent look. "Now, I have."

"There wasn't anyone else you could ask?"

"No one I can rely on. The awakened in the village are either old or part of my family." There was a pointed pause. "I don't want anyone in my family to learn about this. You hate my grandfather and have as much to lose if he found out you know about the shrine."

One could only be impressed by her logic and mercantile nature. It was obvious she had plans of her own that didn't involve the village chief, or anyone else for that matter. The moment she had approached Dallion had been meticulously calculated so he couldn't refuse. There was no doubt Aspion had prepared a task beyond Dallion's awakening level. Still, Gloria could have just come up to him with the offer earlier.

"What's the trial?" Dallion smiled. No point in being upset at what could have been.

"The previous tasks were combat, so probably the next will be as well." She evaded the question, then turned to her left and took a step forward. An arch formed between the columns in front of her, marked by the glowing number four.

Fourth trial? Dallion wondered. If so, that meant that the shrine was limited to six trials.

"Remember, we'll need to work together on this," Gloria said in a bossy fashion. "I'll focus on attacking the monster while you guard me."

"How come I do the guarding?" Dallion grumbled.

"You have the guard skills." She pointed at his buckler with her saber. "I have a perception of six. I knew what you could do the moment you improved my ring. Well, that and I asked the guardian."

"How come she talks to you?"

"Guardians can't speak, but after gaining a few levels, you can learn to communicate through gestures."

When people wanted to brag, they would often slip in a piece of useless information to attract the listener's focus. Gloria was no different, mentioning her perception skills, again, then stressing on the level in an attempt to impress. Dallion, in contrast, remained silent. He could easily have mentioned he had reflexes at six despite only being a level one awakened. There was still the option that he did, though, maybe after the trial was complete.

Shrine trial 4 chosen!
Prepare for combat!

The moment the two walked through the archway, all four columns that weren't part of the arch melted away. A strong gust of wind appeared out of nowhere, sending a wave of dust at them. Instantly, Dallion jumped in front of the girl, raising his buckler to keep the sand from hitting them.

The sandstorm kept building up for a while until, suddenly, it stopped. Dallion, however, took no chances, keeping the buckler in front.

"Are you all right?" he asked, glancing back at Gloria. The girl nodded.

Slowly, he lowered his shield. The landscape had changed completely. Gone were the endless barren plains, replaced by dunes of rusty sand as far as the eye could see. A large orange sun had emerged in the sky, scorching down on everything beneath.

"Did this happen last time?" Dallion asked.

"Sort of…" Gloria bit her lip. "There was a desert, but no storm."

"I guess this happens when you invite someone over. Any other surprises I should know about?"

"Can we just get this over with?" the girl snapped.

"Yes, your Highness." Dallion smirked, stepping to the side. "I'll get right to defeating…" His words trailed off.

SHRINE GUARDIAN 4

Species: DRAGON
Class: SAND
Health: UNKNOWN
Traits: UNKNOWN
Skills:
- SANDSTORM (Species Unique)
- UNKNOWN
- UNKNOWN
Weakness: EYES

A white rectangle had become visible a short distance away. The issue, however, was what could be seen beneath it. A massive beast —the size of a small commercial airplane—towered above Dallion, glaring at him with glowing amber eyes. It was everything one would imagine an eastern dragon to be: long, scaly, snakelike, with a massive head that could gobble up Dallion's house for breakfast. Upon seeing the two minuscule humans, the creature snorted, releasing streams of sand into the air from its nostrils.

"Err, Gloria?" Dallion asked in his quietest and most polite tone. "Was this the guardian you faced before?"

Speechless, the girl slowly shook her head.

"I didn't think so."

COMBAT INITIATED

DARUDE SANDSTORM DRAGON

"Darude!" Dallion shouted as he rushed forward, pushing Gloria to the side. He had already seen the giant green cone covering them both as well as the footprints telling him how to evade it. This time, though, there was also a set of orange footprints making their way to Gloria, potentially suggesting that was meant to protect her. Either that, or maybe the path was more dangerous. There hadn't been any new floating rectangles to provide explanations, so Dallion decided to follow his usual routine.

The days of training had allowed him to execute the guard action flawlessly—the series of eight steps was matched without issue. As before, time froze, only now a second series of paler steps emerged, along with hand positions.

So, guard skills can be used on others as well, Dallion thought.

Taking advantage of the adrenaline rushing through his veins, he grabbed Gloria in the air—following the instructions—then ran toward the edge of the massive green cone. Moments later, he found he had failed to leave its range on time.

Time returned to normal as a torrent of sand emerged from the dragon's mouth, blasting everything in its path. Dallion felt it brush against the sole of his foot, scraping off the lower part of his shoe, then continuing to the peel off part of his skin.

MINOR WOUND
Your health has been reduced by 5%

The pain was insignificant but served as a reminder not to take the dragon lightly.

"What are you doing?!" Gloria pulled away. That wasn't the reaction Dallion had expected, given that he had just saved her life, or at the very least prevented a massive health decrease.

"You're welcome," he grumbled.

"I was about to attack!" Gloria hissed. "All you had to do was—"

"Get back!" Dallion shouted as a large green circle appeared in the sand in front of them.

With a thundering sound, the dragon flew down, slapping into the sand and completely disappearing from view. Dallion had barely enough time to spot the defense markers when Gloria did a series of back somersaults, moving safely out of danger. Her technique was flawless, capable of putting Olympic medalists to shame. Dallion had never been a fan of gymnastics, but he knew excellence when he saw it. There was no way such a feat could be achieved through training. It had to be an awakened skill.

You don't have guard, he thought. *But you need it. Or maybe you only need me to be the distraction?*

Dallion stepped back just in the nick of time, saved by his high reflexes. The green circle burst in an eruption of sand as the dragon emerged. The fear was that the creature would attack in some elaborate fashion—possibly swipe its tail—making the impact area too large for Dallion to escape. However, no new green markings appeared.

"It's not going to attack!" Dallion shouted.

That proved to be more than enough for Gloria. On cue, she jumped in the air, rising parallel to the sand dragon, at which point she attacked. Her saber danced through the air, creating one giant motion blur. The movement was faster than Dallion could follow. The interesting point was that, other than her attacks, Gloria's speed was quite…normal, possibly even being as low as Dallion's own. Quite probably, this meant that she knew a second skill, which boosted her attack strikes, at least with a saber. Once the fight was over, Dallion planned to ask her about it.

"He'll twist around!" Dallion shouted as green lines appeared in the air.

Gloria immediately turned mid-flight, pushing away from the dragon with a gracious kick, only to land next to Dallion seconds later.

Wow.

He had been practicing for less than a week, and he could already see the results of his troubles. Gloria had had years to perfect her abilities, as did every other awakened in the Luor family. Given that—and the cheat to increase their awakening level—it was natural for them to be so arrogant. When it came to raw strength and skills, there wasn't anyone in the village who could compare.

"All clear," Dallion said as the dragon continued upward. They probably had ten seconds before the next attack. "How many skills do you know?"

"Two," she said in a smug voice, suggesting it was a big deal. "Help me defeat this, and you'll end up with two as well."

While that sounded good, it was easier said than done. Dallion's guard skill allowed him to protect himself, and Gloria, apparently. However, the attack had done next to nothing. Looking at the white rectangle above the creature, he saw its health remained at ninety-seven percent. If three percent was the average amount of damage Gloria could do, it was going to take over thirty attacks to take it down.

The dragon turned its head with a snarl. An enormous green cone—only visible to Dallion—emerged, covering Gloria entirely.

"Watch out!" Dallion shouted. "Sandstorm!"

This time, Gloria grasped what he was telling her, remaining in place. Several sets of footprint markers appeared. Two sets—both leading to her—glowed brighter.

So that's it, Dallion rushed forward. The glowing did, in fact, indicate the skill was for assisting someone else. It sounded logical, although a rectangle explaining it would have been nice. Interesting if there would be further marker changes in the course of the fight.

The options presented to Dallion were to rush straight for Gloria, then grab her and leap to the side—same as before—or do something a bit more interesting. The unorthodox option involved dashing up to Gloria, then using the shield to thrust her up beyond the edge of the cone, then dash-plunge out of its reach. That seemed visually attractive, but, more important, it allowed Gloria to follow up with an attack of her own.

Two steps, one turn, three more steps, and a semi-twist with the last, Dallion thought as he completed the sequence. The moment he did, time slowed, as expected.

"I'll boost you up," Dallion whispered, hoping she could make out his words. "Jump up from there and attack it. The weak spot is the eyes."

The moment he added the last, Dallion felt silly. Given that she could see the white rectangle, just like him, it was natural that she'd know the weakness of the dragon. If anything, it was likely thanks to her perception that he got to see all the additional information in the first place.

"Here goes." He completed the second sequence.

Dallion's hands moved through the air, thrusting the girl up just enough to escape the dragon's attack. As she thrust herself off the shield, a smile appeared on Gloria's face. She had understood the plan and now added a few touches of her own. Her body twisted in the air—still affected by the time freeze, making her move as if in slow motion, spinning the saber around her in a flurry of slashes.

Meanwhile, Dallion leapt forward as fast as he could. At this point, there was nothing further he could do except remain alive.

Time returned to normal. The stream of sand blasted past Dallion, hitting the ground with such strength, it created the sound of a small explosion. Simultaneously, Gloria's attacks made contact.

COMBINATION ATTACK
Dealt damage is increased by 200%

MODERATE STRIKE
Dealt damage is increased by 150%

Two red rectangles appeared in the air, stacking near the sand dragon's head.

OUT OF THE BOX

The sand dragon plunged into the sand with a splash, though not before Dallion could see its status rectangle. Seventy-nine percent of health remained—not bad for a single attack, although after all the damage bonuses, he had hoped for more. Without a doubt, this creature was beyond anything he had faced before. It was definitely stronger than a vase, or handkerchief, or even the metal ring the village chief had tried to seal his powers with.

"Careful!" Gloria landed a few steps away. "It's bound to come for another run."

"Right." He gathered as much. "How did you do so much damage?"

"My attack skills are at ten."

Ten? Dallion would have said that was ten times more than his own, but that would be a lie. He had no attack skills at all. If he had to face a creature of this nature on his own, the buckler wouldn't achieve anything. Come to think of it, although seemingly impressive, Gloria's skills were unusually low. If he had been awakened for as long as her, Dallion would have entered into the double digits, if not in the triple by now. All she had to do was improve minor items each day, every day for a year, and she would be well within the hundreds. That was, unless there wasn't some other reason to keep her this low.

"I don't see him anywhere," Dallion said as he looked around. There were no green markings in sight. "Think he ran away?"

"Guardians don't run away," Gloria said in an indignant tone, though she, too, looked about. "They shouldn't run away," she added moments later. "The whole point of them is to guard the item's wholeness."

"Maybe this one decided to hide? We're the ones who have to defeat him, so…"

Gloria glared at him. Dallion could almost hear her saying this was the stupidest thing she had heard in her life. No doubt she was searching for a better way to phrase just that. Before she could, a green zone appeared beneath their feet. Step markers soon followed.

"Damn it!" Dallion dashed forward. "It's beneath us!"

There was no way to avoid the attack. All visible escape footprints rose into the air, telling Dallion unequivocally that, even with his reflexes, he couldn't get out of range. What he could do, hopefully, was to end up in a safe enough position to minimize the potential damage.

"Grab on to me!" he shouted, reaching back toward Gloria. "When he emerges, jump!"

"What do you mean?"

Two sets of teeth the size of rocks emerged from the sand rising at both sides of Dallion and Gloria. The dragon was clearly smart enough not to try the same attack twice. After losing an eye in its first attack, it had decided to take a different approach, namely swallow his prey outright. That was a far more efficient method and reduced the chance of additional wounds. Yet even such a plan had its weakness.

"Jump!" Dallion grabbed Gloria around the waist.

There was a moment's hesitation, but she did as she was told, propelling both upward faster than the dragon.

So far, so good, Dallion told himself. The first step had gone according to plan. Now, the tricky part began.

It was all a gamble. Dallion's reflexes level allowed him to start an action faster than the shrine guardian. He only hoped Gloria's higher perception and overall level would allow her to notice what he was about to do at the moment that he did it. A moment's delay or hesitation, and the whole thing was over.

Time froze, only this time just in Dallion's mind. He saw the scene fold out before him, just as the dozens of ways everything could go wrong. Gritting his teeth, he let go of Gloria and twisted his body in the air. Once done, he raised the buckler against his chest, placing it between him and Gloria.

Please, figure it out, Dallion thought.

The second stretched for eternity as he watched her remain still, doing absolutely nothing. Had he misjudged her? Had she frozen up with fear? Or did he overestimate her out-of-the-box thinking? It was clear from the start that pulling off the plan was close to impossible in the best of circumstances. Given a choice, any choice, Dallion would have done something else. Unfortunately, this was the only series of actions that had a chance of bringing them victory, and he had hoped against hope the two of them could achieve a miracle.

At the very last moment, Gloria twisted in the air as well. Her knees pressed against her chest. Then, in one single moment, her entire body extended like a wound-up spring. The soles of Gloria's shoes hit Dallion's buckler right in the center, repelling both of them from each other like a pair of same pole magnets.

Yes! Dallion thought as relief and adrenaline filled him.

This was a reckless idea, absurd even and, somehow, it had worked.

Out Of The Box!
(+2 Mind)
Unorthodox thinking at a moment's notice!

A blue rectangle appeared in front of Dallion, only to be punched away. As much as he liked praise, he preferred to be able to see what was going on around him.

Just as he did so, he saw the sand dragon's giant maw rising in the space that had formed between Gloria and Dallion. The monster passed no more than inches away but, somehow, Dallion had managed to survive this attack. He could only hope Gloria had managed to do so as well. Given that she was lighter than him—or at least he assumed that to be the case—physics suggested she must have traveled a greater distance, putting her safely out of danger.

COMBINATION ATTACK
Dealt damage is increased by 200%

MODERATE STRIKE
Dealt damage is increased by 150%

A pair of red rectangles emerged, letting Dallion know his plan had succeeded. Not only that, but Gloria had managed to land in another hit. If things continued in this fashion, defeating the guardian was only a matter of time.

Sweet! Dallion grinned.

Another large chunk of life gone. The first thing he was going to do upon landing was to check the dragon's status rectangle. Before that, though, there was one minor thing he had to worry about—gravity. While the dragon's attack had missed him by a hair, the ground wasn't as merciful, slamming Dallion with a vengeance. Since it couldn't be considered an enemy, no guard markers appeared, leaving him to crash into it like a sack of potatoes.

SERIOUS FALL!
Health has been reduced by 20%

"Twenty for a bump?" Dallion groaned.

The pain had been less than he had imagined, almost as if he'd fallen on a pile of hay after a three-story jump. His pride, on the other hand, had suffered considerably more. The gamer in him grumbled he should have managed a flawless execution and not botched the landing in such a spectacular fashion.

A loud roar filled the air. Far above Dallion, the dragon had reached the peak of its ascent. The massive body twirled and coiled as the guardian thrust downward toward the sand. Normally, that would be a cause for concern. The lack of green markers, though, made it clear no attack was imminent.

"Dallion!" Gloria shouted as she landed a short distance away.

Unlike him, the girl had landed elegantly as a professional acrobat. On the other hand, the front of her clothes was covered in splashes of rusty blood.

I hope that comes out, Dallion thought as he waved.

"Are you crazy?" She rushed toward him. "Why in the world did you try something like that?!"

"It worked." Dallion shrugged. "It's not like you came up with anything. Besides, you got another hit. Now, all we have to do is repeat this a few more times and—"

"A few more times?" she interrupted. "Are you even listening to yourself? What would you have done if I hadn't reacted?"

"Lost my awakened powers along with you?" Dallion crossed his arms. He didn't like being talked down to, even from her. No, especially from her! The past him might have crushed on her, but the current one didn't…or at least not as much.

"Idiot! We can't lose our powers in awakening shrines."

"Then what's your problem?"

"My problem is that we still need to defeat him, and until you stop—"

The SHRINE Guardian has admitted defeat.
Do you accept his surrender?

A blue rectangle appeared, putting an abrupt end to the argument. Despite all the games he had played back on Earth, this was the first time Dallion had seen such behavior. In the MMOs he'd played, enemy bosses fought until they were defeated. In general, only players offered to surrender, confirming the notion that, in this world, guardians not only had a personality of their own but also enough intelligence to know when to stop a hopeless battle.

Two smaller rectangles appeared under the large one. One had the image of a hand giving a thumbs-up, the other had the thumb pointing down. Having seen enough movies about the Roman Empire, Dallion had a pretty good idea where this was going.

Walking up to the notification, Gloria reached for the thumbs-down rectangle.

"Hey!" Dallion caught her hand. "Why continue? We won."

"You came here for more skills, right? Defeating the guardian is the only way to guarantee that."

"We defeated it. Look, he surrendered."

"Fine." Gloria pulled her hand back. "I'm sure to boost my level. If you want to gamble with your future, go ahead."

Was killing the dragon the only way to gain a skill? Dallion couldn't be sure, but he definitely didn't want to keep on fighting the creature unless he had to. Continuing the battle would only become more difficult. Already, he felt low on stamina. Combining that with the fact that his adrenaline boost was wearing off, it made much more sense to accept a quick victory.

Dallion hesitated. This was his second big choice since he had arrived in this world. Ultimately, he tapped the second rectangle.

The moment he did, all three rectangles disappeared, and a series of new ones took their place.

A cold chill ran down Dallion's spine.

"Damn it..." Dallion clenched his fists. At that moment, it felt as if the powers that be mocked him.

CROSSROADS

You are at a crossroads.
Choose the item that will serve you best.

The dreaded message glowed in front of Dallion's face. Two smaller rectangles floated below it. One had had a realistic picture of a short sword—the exact same that had been in the corridor that had welcomed him to this world. The second picture was of a blacksmith's anvil...and that made Dallion's heart break in two.

From what Kraisten had said, crafting skills were quite rare, not to mention extremely valued. Getting one was enough to set up a person for life. Having one was enough to attract the attention of the Order of the Seven Moons, or the service guilds that existed in the big cities. The chance of getting crafting skill was said to be one in a dozen, maybe even less. Dallion had been indeed fortunate to get one, and after his first serious fight no less. Unfortunately, such a skill wouldn't serve him in battle and, at the moment, that was the only thing that counted.

"Why..." he hissed through gritted teeth.

"What's wrong?" Gloria's features softened as she glanced at him. "Didn't you get a skill?"

"I got a skill…" Dallion whispered. There was no point in sharing the entire picture. "I got attack."

Attack was considered the most common of the common. From what Dallion's mother and grandfather had said, half of all awakened started with that skill. And now he was forced to take it in the place of something as valuable as forging. Looking away, Dallion tapped on the rectangle with the picture of a sword.

ATTACK skills obtained.

"You jerk." Gloria frowned. "I was scared you hadn't gotten anything. Attack's just what you need. A bit of practice, and you should be able to pass Grandfather's trial. After all, it can't be as difficult as this."

"Right." Dallion struggled to hide his disappointment. His entire being shook on the inside. "Attack's just what I needed," he repeated. "It can't be as difficult as this."

You have broken through your second barrier.
You are now Level 2
Choose the trait that you value the most.

As before, there were four options to choose from: *body, mind, reaction*, and *perception*. Interestingly enough, mind had already increased from three to five on its own. Thinking back, Dallion remembered seeing something in the blue rectangle that had appeared during the fight. So, it seemed that achievements had practical significance in this world. The unexpected bonus made Dallion consider increasing mind further to six, or even boosting reaction to seven. Both were valid options, but spending a while thinking about it, he decided to improve his perception instead. As Gloria had shown, the trait could be quite useful for finding an enemy's weaknesses.

You have assisted GLORIA LUOR in her trial
GLORIA LUOR's Level has increased to 4.

A green rectangle appeared the moment Dallion finished with his choice. The surrounding desert disappeared in the blink of the eye, returning Dallion and Gloria back to the shrine cave. The reality shift came with the usual moment of disorientation, reinforced by the altar's light fading away, plunging them into darkness.

Unlike before, Dallion found he was able to see. It wasn't much —barely the outlines of the cave entrance—but it was far more than he could before. All this because of one point increase of perception. Awakening powers were more than scary.

"Come on." Gloria grabbed him by the hand. "We're done."

"Okay." Dallion took a step forward. The sole of his foot was still tingling as if it had been dragged along a rough concrete surface. Apparently, at the end of the day, some experiences from the realms bled through into the real world.

"Are you all right?" Gloria asked, noticing him limping.

"I shouldn't have kicked that dragon." He cracked a joke. "I'll be fine. How's it feel to be a level four?"

"It's fine."

The two walked in silence. Every now and again, Gloria paused for a few moments so he could rest a bit, then continue.

Various thoughts kept spinning in Dallion's mind, as if three different realities fought for space in his skull, none fully able to achieve dominance. A lot had happened in the last few days, but also nothing at all. The most disturbing part was that, until a moment ago, he thought he had awakening all figured out. The fight had made it painfully obvious how insignificant his knowledge was, not to mention how limited his skills were. Compared to a normal person, Dallion was able to achieve the impossible. That notion had further been boosted by his lucky victory over the ring guardian. Seeing a sand dragon and a level four awakened had sent those notions crumbling down.

I don't know a damned thing.

Even his past life experience—for lack of a better word—was little more than a set of vague memories, providing the barest of information about the world around him. That might have been enough for the past him, but not for someone with any sense of curiosity.

Thinking back, Dallion knew quite a lot about the village, the people in it, especially his own family, and precious little else. Try as he might, he could barely come up with the name of the village, let alone anything beyond. He knew there were cities in the country he was—by all indications a kingdom, or empire of sorts—filled with guilds and nobles, he knew there was a capital. There were indications the country was, or had been, at war... So many questions Dallion had been comfortable not asking. Before his awakening, there hadn't been any point. He was going to live and likely die in the village, never knowing what lay in the world beyond.

"Gloria," Dallion began once they left the cave, "have you thought of leaving the village?"

"Get free of my grandfather?" The girl let out a sad laugh. "All the time. But I know it's impossible."

Dallion arched a brow. That wasn't an answer he expected.

"Why not?"

"Even if he'd let me, what's the point? Life always seems better out there, but is it? My father tried it once when he was young. He didn't last a month." There was a deep sigh.

"Is it so dangerous outside?"

There it was again. There was no logical reason for Dallion to refer to the wide world as "outside," yet he constantly did it.

"I don't know. Maybe. However, it's harsh to anyone with

doubts. Look at my grandfather. He has skills, money, even connections with traveling merchants, and he still chose to remain here. If it was so good out there, wouldn't he have gone already?"

That makes sense.

"I've only known him to leave for a few weeks to visit nearby villages to discuss arranged marriages, then return."

There was a long pause. The girl looked up at the night sky. Dallion noticed the minuscule signs of sadness on her face—turned down corners of her mouth, slight wincing of the eyes, and her breathing becoming slower and deeper than a moment ago. Had these indications always been there? Or was it his recently improved perception that had given him an edge?

"Grandfather went to a city once," Gloria continued. "It was long ago, before my father was born. He doesn't talk about it, but when he has nightmares, he screams about it in his sleep. The others pretend it doesn't happen. They can't make out the screams, though. I could." Gloria looked back at him. "The city changed him. I don't know why or how, but it turned him into what he is now. One has to be crazy to go there. I know I won't, and unless you want to become like him, or join the Order of the Seven Moons, you mustn't either."

VILLAGE BOUND

S lightly over an hour had passed by the time Dallion and Gloria
reached the village. An unexpected feeling of guilt seemed to
have passed over both of them. Dallion could hear it like a voice in
the back of his mind, criticizing him for giving in to temptation and
taking a shortcut to leveling up. In addition, there was the fear what
the village chief would do to him if it ever became known he'd gone
to the awakening shrine in secret.

"Thanks for helping me," Gloria whispered. "But I won't be
doing this again," she added as if they'd committed some grave sin.

"Guess it was fun while it lasted." Dallion offered a smile.

The girl didn't reply. Instead, she turned around and leaped
away, doing a triple forward somersault. That was undoubtedly a
clear instance of bragging, but Dallion had to admit it looked
impressive. Being unable to do the same, he could only walk back
to his home.

Sneaking back in proved much easier than sneaking out. The
first thing Dallion did was to curse himself for being so inventive
that he barred the door from the inside when he had snuck out.
Other than the occasional wild animal wandering nearby, nothing
bad happened in the village itself, so he could have merely closed

the door. The voice in the back of his mind kept repeating that the village was the safest place there could be ever since he had awakened near the statue. Next time, if there was a next time, he'd take that into serious consideration.

The humiliating part was that with the windows shuttered—a tradition that had no logical reason—Dallion's only means of entry was to knock on the door and think of a plausible excuse.

Dallion's parents turned out to be sound sleepers, so it came to his younger brother to do the honors. The naïveté with which the boy opened the door without even asking was borderline surreal. Back in his previous world, the first thing children were told was not to trust strangers, and definitely not answer the door when alone. The worst part was that, according to Dallion's memories, he had been no less trusting than his brother.

"What are you doing up so early?" Linner asked with a yawn.

"I wanted to practice a bit."

Strictly speaking, that wasn't a lie. Of course, he added nothing about Gloria, the shrine, or the fact he had gained a second skill. Thinking about it still made Dallion slightly annoyed. If it wasn't for the village chief's insecure pettiness, he could have had a rare crafting skill. Then again, if it hadn't been for that pettiness, he wouldn't have learned about the shrine in the first place.

"I'm going back to sleep," Linner grumbled, half-asleep, then zombied off back in the house.

Dallion followed, closing the door behind him. The voice in the back of his mind made him bar it yet again.

The bed felt scratchier than before. The cloth was rough, every wrinkle felt like a sliver of fabric biting into his skin, and the grains of dust felt like pebbles.

I've become like the princess with the hundred mattresses, Dallion said to himself, then shivered thinking what Gloria had been going through. No wonder she upgraded all her clothes. With the perception she had, normal clothes probably felt like wearing barbed wire.

Morning came at the worst possible time. Just as Dallion started to doze off, his family walking about the house made the task impossible. With a yawn and a sigh, he got up and went to get washed.

Breakfast was the first moment of dread he faced. If a single point of perception was enough to make his eyes and skin so much more sensitive, it was expected to have the same effect on taste. Fortunately, it turned out that his mother's cooking had become tastier than before. As the morning progressed, more people came to the house.

A few neighbors were the first to drop by. Cracking jokes as usual, they grabbed Dallion's father for the start of their workday on the field. The usual gaggle of children soon followed. Too young to be given any real chores and too old to remain in the house, they spent several minutes staring at Dallion—or the newly awakened, very much to Linner's pride—then rushed out to play with Dallion's brother. Lastly, elder Kraisten Seene arrived.

"Hello, Grandpa." Dallion waved enthusiastically. The moment he'd been waiting for had finally come.

"You're in a good mood today." The old man smiled as he made his way to the dining table. "Is your training going well?"

"I've been keeping an eye on him," Dallion's mother said, bringing a mug of steaming tea to the elder. The aroma was pleasant, almost overwhelming. "He's been doing fine. If the Seven are willing, he'll be ready for tomorrow."

"That's all we can hope for." The elder put up a brave front, but Dallion could clearly see he was worried.

"Grandpa, there's something I want to ask you." He leaned forward. "Can you tell me something about the cities?"

"The cities?"

"Yeah. You mentioned that awakened with rare skills got to go there. I'm just curious what they are like."

"This is quite sudden." His features moved into a deep frown. "You've never been interested in that before."

"I wasn't awakened before."

"Right, right…" For a moment, it almost seemed the question saddened the old man. "Well, the cities are very different from everything you know. A lot of people are either awakened or related to one, and everything is made to reflect it."

"Are awakened a ruling class there?"

"Ruling class?" The elder laughed. "Yes, and no. The lord mayor running the city is always awakened, as are many of the nobles and guild masters. However, awakened also keep the city in order. Blacksmiths, carpenters, masons, even tailors can be awakened. In the cities, even the gift isn't always a guarantee for success."

"So, you've been in one?"

"Oh, yes. Many times. When I was young, I was much more reckless than I am now. I thought I could make a name for myself there…" His daze drifted away, looking at something Dallion couldn't see. "You're thinking of going there, aren't you?"

It would have been easy to say yes. Dallion wanted very much to go there. If the city was even a fraction of how his grandfather described it, it would be much closer to his old home than this village. Even so, he felt serious doubts, an almost dormant fear from his memories whispering that the cities were bad luck. Still, Dallion found it curious most people in the village were outright terrified by the prospect.

"I'm considering it." He chose the diplomatic reply.

"Considering is good. Just be sure that's what you really want to do. Sometimes, people go to the cities and find they don't really want to be there. A miserable life awaits those…"

Everything suggested there was more to the story. The elder, however, chose not to continue. Finishing his drink, he stood, gave Dallion a hearty tap on the shoulder, then left. It was almost as if he had guessed his next question and had chosen to leave before it was asked. That created something of a problem for Dallion, since he still wanted an answer. There always was the option to ask the remaining village elders, or even people from the Luor family, yet something told him the result would likely be the same.

Why doesn't anyone leave this village? Dallion wondered. By any logic, there had to be at least a few should have chanced it. Life here was as hard as it got. *Why didn't I want to leave it?*

It was said that an overabundance of coincidences always led to a hidden pattern. All one had to do was keep track and, eventually, the truth would be uncovered. Now that Dallion had noticed the unusual reluctance, he had set his mind on finding the reasons behind it. Until then, though, he had to prepare for the village chief's next awakened task.

PERSONAL SHRINE TRIAL

Increasing one's awakening status, as it turned out, had a considerable number of advantages. Apart from the increased perception and the new skill Dallion had gained, he found he could improve items twice per day without harm. The discovery had come completely by accident. The day after Dallion's adventure, he had been asked to improve an item. Out of habit, Dallion had done just that and…nothing happened.

Dallion improved the item in question—a decorative teapot his aunt happened to forget at his grandfather's place with a note describing its poor state—and only then realized this was the second time he had done so. The surprise was quite welcome, since it enabled him to avoid explaining what he had done that night. It also allowed him to improve things he wanted in secret, not to mention explore his newly found abilities.

The attack skill turned out to be exactly the way Dallion imagined it would be. Instead of green markers, he was presented with a series of red ones, suggesting where and how he should attack. More curious, the slightly heightened perception had caused weak spots and vulnerabilities to become visible on his enemy. Targeting one had resulted in instant defeat of the first guardian Dallion had faced. Only on the next, and final, day before the trial did he consciously try to avoid taking advantage of his skills in order to get some degree in training.

The experience in the awakened shrine had made him aware of how weak he actually was. Gloria, with her high perception and attack, would probably turn him into Swiss cheese in a serious fight, then start playing whack-a-mole with his inner organs afterwards. Guard skills and reflexes were a good counter but, at his low stamina, they were a limited resource, as Dallion had found when facing a cooking pot guardian.

The fight had left him drained of energy. On the positive side, the achievement had earned him much praise and thanks from his entire family, not to mention it had improved the taste of his moth-er's cooking even more. Even so, it didn't hide the fact that Dallion could barely crawl his way to bed.

Another obvious change was that mending had become far easier and more efficient. Labyrinth flaws had become apparent, allowing Dallion to fix several of them in a single pass.

In under two days, he had managed to achieve more than he had in the previous five, not to mention he had returned to a few pesky items he had left only at ninety-seven percent mended. Even with everything going on, his completionist mind didn't let him leave anything incomplete. If this were a game platform, he would have received a number of achievements by now. Secretly, he was still hoping he would. After all, actions in the awakened realm had provided him bonuses before. Unfortunately, there was no guide or sneak peak of what he had to do to earn those hidden achievements.

The night before Dallion's expected first official village task, a thought came to mind. Rather, the thought had lingered ever since the fight against the sand dragon, but only now he found the will to do something about it. Originally, Dallion had told himself he would never go through the experience—and subsequent guilt trip —of leveling up. When push came to shove, though, he'd had an epiphany: Being level two was nice, but being level three was better. With that in mind, he had waited for his family to fall asleep and, once again, snuck out of his house.

It wasn't difficult to find the shrine cave. Gloria had done a good job getting him there, following a series of landmarks. Thinking back, it was entirely possible she had done so deliberately for his benefit. Beneath her somewhat arrogant, and undeniably pretty, exterior, she appeared to be rather nice. A pity she had explained so little about the shrines.

As Dallion put his hand on the altar, he closed his eyes, wishing he'd be offered the forging skills once more. When he opened them, he was back in the realm of the shrine.

You are in a small awakening shrine.
Complete the trial to improve your destiny!

Yes!

So far, everything appeared the same, from the sky to the endless bare wasteland. At the same time, there were a few subtle details Dallion hadn't noticed before. For one, the moons above were much brighter, faintly glowing in the sky. There were seven of them in total, all of various colors and sizes. The blue one was the largest, shining with an intensity equal to that of Earth's. Most of the rest were pale blotches of color, and two were little more than a circle outline in a sky of white.

The columns also seemed more detailed, if identical. As Dallion took a step forward, an arch formed over the two columns in front of him. That wasn't the only change. A glowing Roman numeral one had emerged in the capstone of the arch, as had a rather solid stone wall blocking the way through it.

What's this? Dallion slid his fingers along the wall. It was very real and very solid. Hitting it with his buckler yielded no results, forcing him to move toward the column to the right. As expected, a second archway emerged, this one bearing the Roman numeral two, although it, too, was completely blocked.

Fear crept in. Had Dallion gone through all this trouble for nothing? Could it be that there was some other hidden requirement Gloria hadn't mentioned? That would definitely explain why she was so careless when sharing the shrine's location.

Anxious, Dallion stepped to the right again. An archway with the glowing number three emerged. Thankfully, the stone wall didn't.

The moment he did, a wave of relief passed through him. The archway was there, unblocked, along with the Roman numeral three on top. A wave of relief swept through Dallion.

"Phew." He whipped the sweat off his forehead. There was a way to progress, after all.

Curiously, he walked around the rest of the columns until all six archways had materialized. There were six of them in total, five of which had a number. The first two were blocked, leaving Dallion to choose from the third onwards. Remembering how challenging his battle against the sand dragon had been, he decided to step through the third.

Shrine trial 3 chosen!
Prepare for combat!

"Yeah, yeah." Dallion dismissed the rectangle. The novelty had long since worn off, turning the once mysterious glowing rectangles into common real-life pop-ups.

The surrounding landscape shifted although, this time, it wasn't a desert that had appeared but a tropical beach. Blue sky and sea continued for as far as the eye could see. Behind and to the sides, a modest cluster of palm trees formed a small but dense jungle. It was clear the fighting would take place in water…which wasn't ideal.

Dallion strongly disliked swimming and wasn't particularly

good at it. Even when he'd been pressured to go to the pool as a teen, he always gravitated to the shallow end.

"I'm here!" Dallion shouted, still on the beach. "I'm ready."

The guardian's reaction was immediate. A fountain of water emerged from the endless sea. Dallion braced himself, buckler and short sword at the ready.

"Hey!" a cheerful voice said. Its owner was not at all what Dallion had expected.

SHRINE GUARDIAN 3
Species: SLIME
Class: WATER
Health: UNKNOWN
Traits: UNKNOWN
Skills:
- SQUIRT (Species Unique)
- WATER SHIELD (Species Unique)
- BOUNCE (Species Unique)
Weakness: NONE

ENDLESS COMBO

ighting a creature with no weaknesses turned out less difficult than Dallion expected. Having to deal with a slime that shot "water bullets," on the other hand, was extremely vexing. The projectiles themselves weren't nearly destructive as Dallion imagined. They didn't cut through objects, nor did they explode. What they did was smart like a paintball pellet hitting bare skin.

"Damn it!" Dallion shouted as several more "shots" hit his shield.

One would have thought a shield would be enough protection. Initially, that had been true, but, with each minute, the impact pressure grew to the point Dallion felt pain in his arm each time something splashed on the shield. There was no denying it anymore, his physical weakness was starting to show. First thing Dallion was going to do after his next level-up was to increase his body stat.

Red and green markers appeared and shifted constantly, like a *Dance Dance Revolution* on difficult mode.

Following them wasn't an issue for the most part, but doing so on water caused certain difficulties. Despite Dallion's best attempts, his aversion to water was the reason for him stopping short of completing multiple sequences.

Several times, he tried to bait the guardian farther inland, only to get bombarded by a volley of water projectiles as a result.

"You really are annoying, you know that?" Dallion grumbled under his breath.

Simple tricks weren't going to help him win this encounter, so he resorted to the next best thing—brute force combinatorics. If there was one thing the point-and-click adventure games back on Earth had taught him, it was that every puzzle could be solved by combining every item with every other. The trick was not to get hit too many times in the process.

Forcing himself to step into the water, Dallion completed a full guard sequence. When time slowed to a crawl, he didn't attack as he usually did but proceeded to execute a second sequence, then a third. Only at the end of that, when the bonus was substantial, did he switch and go on the offensive.

Once he jumped to a perfect counterattack spot, a new series of markers appeared. Unlike the ones before, they were half green, half red. Both shield and sword markers were visible in the air, allowing him to perform several strikes on the slime. This was precisely the boost he needed.

"How about this?" Dallion attacked, slamming the guardian simultaneously with his buckler and the flat side of his sword.

COMBINATION ATTACK
Dealt damage is increased by 200%

Metal slammed against water which, unfortunately, had the consistency of wet concrete, causing the entire slime to jiggle.

The temptation to do another "squish" attack was enormous, but Dallion chose to continue as the markers suggested, twisting around the guardian and doing another slice attack. It was a good thing that he did. The attack didn't end, instead creating a new set of green-red markers, more elaborate than the last. When Dallion completed it—with quite a bit of difficulty—the process continued.

Endless combo, Dallion thought.

It stood to logic. It had been established that guard sequences continued up to the point that an action was done to break them. However, counterattacks were seemingly exempt from this logic, allowing him to deal some damage and still enjoy the time slow benefits.

The third sequence proved too much, causing him to fumble halfway through. Not wanting to waste any of the time freeze, Dallion performed another dual attack.

COMBINATION ATTACK
Dealt damage is increased by 200%

Another red rectangle appeared. Fortunately, this proved to be enough. The slime lost form, pouring back into the endless sea. Moments later, a green rectangle appeared, officially indicating the end of the awakening trial.

You have broken through your third barrier.
You are Level 3
Choose the trait you value the most

No skill rewards? Dallion thought.

Regret twisted his stomach like a football during practice. It was too much to expect he'd be offered forging skills a second time, but he had hoped to receive something new. Apparently, the only certain reward when leveling up was a free point Dallion had to assign to one of his existing traits.

The choice was all too familiar. Maybe for that reason, Dallion found himself going through some analysis paralysis. It was tempting to increase his perception, especially now that he knew how it helped him in real life. Mind was something he didn't think about. If there were any apparent benefits, he didn't feel them. Reaction, on the other hand, was something that would give him a definite edge. He had already seen that starting with a value of six had helped him achieve victory against the ring guardian. Increasing the trait to seven would likely be phenomenal. And, finally, there was body...

To be honest, it was the last trait Dallion wanted to improve. Being strong and muscular, while tempting, was something he thought he could achieve on his own through daily work and exercises. After all, he had managed to melt quite a lot of fat through item mending alone, not to mention that had also added a bit of muscle mass in a few areas. Was there really a need to invest in body?

What is the proper choice? he wondered.

Back on Earth, Dallion's father used to say that proper choice was the "educated comparison of known benefits and penalties." For the most part, it was clear what the other three traits provided. It could also be assumed that body would grant more strength and potentially stamina. Could he be certain without trying, though?

"Here goes." Dallion tapped the body rectangle with his index finger. Some things required decisiveness.

Awakening increased
Your ATTACK skills have increased to 5

The tropical island had vanished, replaced by the dark surroundings of the cave. Dallion remained there for a few minutes, thinking. Had he made the right choice? He didn't feel stronger, nor—if his clothes were any indication—had any of his muscles grown particularly. He could hope the effects of the new increase would become apparent when facing a guardian. Or maybe there was another way to check. For that, though, he had to get back home.

The way back went unnoticeably fast. The only thing Dallion had to be careful of was not to be seen by anyone, a surprisingly difficult task once he entered the village proper. While most of the people remained in their homes after dark, an alarming number would peek out of their windows at the least of noises. Dallion had noticed that when he went to relieve himself in the outhouse each morning.

Lacking internet, television, or even books, people had little else to fight boredom than to snoop about and gossip. There was every chance that Dallion's previous "sneak out" had been seen and secretly discussed. Thankfully, since none of them had actually followed him to the shrine, they had no idea what he was doing exactly. And even if they did, none of his neighbors shared any love toward the Luors and secretly backed him against the village chief.

Standing in front of his house, Dallion looked up at the sky. Several moons were visible between the clouds. As far as he could determine, about an hour remained until midnight—perfect for his small test. Bending down, he took a chipped stone from the ground and used his awakening powers on it. A split second later—or half an hour in the awakened state—the stone had turned into flawlessly polished granite.

"Cool." Dallion looked at the stone, then put it gently on the ground. The improvement hadn't been a mistake after all.

THE SECOND TASK

The entire village had gathered to witness Dallion's short trip to the chief's mansion. The atmosphere was noticeably different from last time. Then, everyone had accepted the fact he'd lose his gift and had remained in their homes. Now, there were sparks of hope in everyone's eyes as the first person to challenge the Luor family's awakened monopoly had appeared. Even the other village elders—awakened in their own right—had appeared to witness the spectacle.

The change of attitude was visible to the village chief's supporters as well. This time, the guards of Aspion's mansion had come personally to escort Dallion from his home. Their expressions were, in contrast to everyone else's, quite somber, as if they had been forced doing a task they particularly hated. The duo rushed Dallion through the inner courtyard, making sure to shut the door as quickly as possible behind him.

Where did all your spunk go? Dallion smiled to himself, looking at them. Past him had been absolutely terrified of them. Being a level three awakened, if it came to a fight, he could take them both without breaking a sweat.

Inside the mansion proper, the guards were joined by another pair of distant Luor relations, who took him directly to the main hall.

"Any idea what it'll be like?" Dallion asked casually. It was a slightly cruel thing to do given the fear written on everyone else's face, but he couldn't resist. After all, it was payback for the way they had treated him and his family.

The guards mumbled something beneath their noses. In truth, this was a new experience for them as well. In the past, awakened outside of the Luor family had only visited the mansion once.

The hall was as Dallion remembered it, though the people weren't. The chief's son and two oldest granddaughters weren't present. In their place was a dry, skinny man in his fifties, some woman in her thirties covered with a mask of makeup Dallion vaguely recalled to be the chief's niece, and a child of five.

So, these are the Luor awakened, Dallion thought. *Good to know.*

There were no obvious indications they had the gift, but, for those who knew where to look, the signs were everywhere. Apart from the aura of extreme confidence emanating from the people, none of their clothes were torn or dirty. The same could be said for every trinket, weapon, or piece of jewelry they had on them.

This was a clear show of force, the village chief's reminder that Dallion wasn't the only awakened in Dherma. Veil and Gloria were also prominently placed, suggesting their abilities were greater than the rest. Looking closer, Dallion noticed Gloria's clothes, while identical in design, were now made of silk, a recent improvement if he had to guess.

You increased your perception again, didn't you? He smiled.

"Well met again, Dallion the Awakened." The village chief smiled, leaning forward from his seat. "You've caused quite a stir. It's not often that one gifted is so…" the old man rubbed his chin, "…enthusiastic."

"One might say my horizon's been cleared in the past week," Dallion replied.

"Indeed, one might," Aspion hissed, maintaining his smile. "Which is why it is your duty to help the village. As you know, it's an awakened's calling to help others. Without that help, the village will crumble to dust and be swallowed by the wilderness."

Wait, what?

No one had told Dallion about this. To be more precise, there always were stories, but no one in Dallion's memory actually believed it to be literal. The Luors would often claim they were the ones keeping the city safe against the horrors of the wilderness. There was constant talk that, without them, buildings would break down and decay into nothingness to the point it would disappear in less than a single generation.

Even before awakening, Dallion thought that to be a metaphor of the Luors maintaining what little the village had. Only now had it dawned on him that everything was meant to be taken literally. Awakened actually spent effort mending and possibly improving everything within the city, reversing the process of entropy in this world. The chief's mansion was an obvious example, but thinking about it, all the vital buildings of Dherma had remained in perfect condition for as long as he could remember. Although not flashy, the village mill was in good shape, as were the barns, the kennels, the single bridge over the river... So many things constantly maintained that Dallion had taken for granted.

"You want me to repair a house?" Dallion's face turned two shades paler.

"Of course not." The old man let out a dry laugh. "A well."

That was a bit of a tall order. The well near Dallion's house wasn't much, and even it was bigger than any item he had improved. Given that it was just a mending, maybe there was a chance that—

"The village square well," Aspion added. "It has been a decade since anyone seriously mended that. In fact, your grandfather was the last person who attempted to repair it a few years ago. Sadly, he's no longer as young as he once was, and the job was quite lacking."

The village well? How the heck do I do that?!

At his current level, he could repair three stones per day at most. The well must have been composed of thousands. Attempting anything of the sort would take years.

"Something wrong?" The old man rubbed his hands.

Several members of his family grinned. His grandson was the most egregious example, his expression screaming, "Why don't you die already?" Only Gloria looked away, choosing to avoid Dallion's glance.

"Weren't you so full of energy just moments ago?" the chief pressed on.

"My awakening level doesn't allow me to mend all that. Maybe if I can help in some other—"

"Of course, it doesn't. That's why I'll help you." Aspion cracked his fingers. "I'll bring you into the awakened realm of the well. All you have to do is mend it. Simple, right?"

Having never done it before, there was no way Dallion could say whether it was simple or not. If the chief's past behavior was any indication, the difficulty would range from hard to impossible. Was that why he had gathered every awakened from his family? Dallion's success last time had already created ripples in the village, ripples the old man very much needed to straighten if he were to retain his unopposed rule.

"Sure," Dallion bluffed, a smile on his face. As his best friend in high school had said: When in doubt, always act like an ass. "When do we start?"

"We start immediately."

The village chief stood. With the confidence of a king, the old man strode past Dallion and out of the hall. The rest of his family followed, acting as a sort of entourage. Dallion was forced to join in near the end, a clear indication of his low status. On the positive side, he was at least close to Gloria.

"Did you know about this?" Dallion whispered with the faintest of breaths. A normal person wouldn't have been able to hear him, nor see his lips move. Someone with the perception of seven standing close would, though.

The girl gave him a silent nod.

"Why didn't you warn me, then?"

For a split-second, Gloria's face crumbled in sadness and shame. It lasted less than the blink of the eye, but enough for Dallion to get his answer. She had wanted to tell him, but something prevented her. Either the girl was a very good actress and had set him up, or this had been a last-minute decision by the village chief. Either way, Dallion was going to have a long talk with her once this was over.

WITHIN THE WELL

When the village chief appeared from his mansion, the entire crowd fell into a subdued silence. While not imposing in stature, an invisible strength emanated from the old man, crushing the spirits of everyone around. There was a sense that, despite everything he had caused to happen to the village, he was also the one who had kept it from destruction and, if he wished, he could use that same power against anyone who opposed him.

Almost immediately, everyone's glances fell to the ground. Even the Luor guards trailed a few steps back, trying to distance themselves from their leader.

The procession made its way to the side of the mansion, then continued toward the so-called village square. Dallion remembered his grandfather saying the spot used to mark the center of the village. Whether that had been true in the distant past remained unclear, but, at present, it was closer to Dallion's home than the central point of Dherma.

While by no means sophisticated or elegant, the well was the main source of water for washing and livestock needs. Most families had their own small wells to use for washing and drinking. Thinking about it, Dallion realized that everyone tended to avoid the river. There was no logical reason to do so, but ever since he could remember, Dallion's parents had warned him to avoid swimming there, and under no circumstances drink from it.

"Looking forward to it?" the village chief asked with sadistic glee, looking over his shoulder. "The entire village has gathered to witness your exploits firsthand, so better not disappoint them."

"That's a given." Dallion laughed. In his heart, though, he knew he was in deep crap.

Upon reaching the square, everyone stopped in perfect unison. The action was so sudden, it caught Dallion by surprise, causing him to bump into the person in front of him. Fortunately, that person turned out to be Gloria. Unfortunately, she didn't appreciate it one bit, giving him a discreet elbow in the stomach.

"Everything all right?" Aspion asked casually.

"It's all fine." Dallion kept the smile on his face. Gloria's elbow had caused him more pain than he liked to admit. It wasn't that it was particularly strong—Dallion had experienced far worse at the hands of guardians in the awakened realms. The spot, however, was specially chosen to knock out his breath rather effectively.

Good thing I improved my body, Dallion thought. Even so, it was somewhat embarrassing that his improved mind and reaction had failed to prevent the incident from happening in the first place.

"Come along," the village chief ordered in a loud voice. The old man placed his left hand on the edge of the well, then extended his right behind him. "Let's start this."

This felt rather familiar. Gloria had done the same when she had asked Dallion to help her level up at the awakening shrine. The difference in this case was that this wasn't a shrine, and Aspion wasn't a friend.

Given the circumstances, the normal thing for a person to do was run away. Dallion could forget about the challenge, the chief, the entire village, and just head off into the wilderness. With his level of awakening, he would definitely be accepted in a town or city, maybe hired as a guard of a traveling merchant. Unfortunately, the prideful voice in the back of his mind refused to let him. Dallion made his way to the chief and grabbed his hand.

AREA AWAKENING

The well disappeared, along with the village square and everything beyond it. Only Aspion remained in what had become a quite inhospitable place. As far as the eye could see, there was nothing but mountainous cliffs, rocks, and rivers. Gray clouds blocked all but a few rays of light, making it feel like a winter afternoon.

You are in the Land of WELL.
Defeat the guardian to change the land's destiny.

"Surprised?" Aspion sat on a nearby stone. "Area awakening is different from the awakenings you're used to. Items have everything set up for you to mend them, guiding you every step of the way. Here, you must work to achieve something."

"I have to build a labyrinth?" Dallion arched a brow.

The question must have been delectably stupid, for the village chief rubbed his hands together with such an expression of joy that one would have thought he'd won the national lottery.

"Build a labyrinth?" He laughed. "Something like that," he added, struggling to keep a straight face. "Actually, it was your grandfather who improved this very well ages ago. We were both young in those days, so we tended to be a bit reckless, pretty much as much as you are now." He bent down and took a stone from the ground. "No one has done anything since then. One awakened or other would mend the well now and again, though just enough to keep it from crumbling. Of course, nothing is stopping you from improving it to the next level."

The same old trap. This time, Dallion knew better than to volunteer.

"What do I need to do?" He looked in the distance. It didn't take long for him to notice the large mountains formed a wall marking the boundaries of the realm, an unbreachable ring that surrounded everything and prevented anyone from going farther.

"Depends on what you want to achieve." Aspion shrugged. "To mend the well, you need to kill all the creatures that have infested it. To improve it, defeat the guardian on top of the central mountain."

It sounded simple enough, which meant it probably wasn't. There had to be more. Of course, asking directly would either result in an outright lie or a hint so vague, it might as well be false.

"What about you, respected Chief?" Dallion added as much sarcasm in his words as he could muster. The reaction on the old man's face, however, suggested it had come out as flattery. "What will you do in the meantime?"

"Me?" Aspion scratched his nose. "I'll be waiting for you outside." He stood up. "Oh, and don't worry. Take your time. After all, time only flows on the outside."

With a snap of his finger, the village chief disappeared. The moment he did, a green rectangle appeared in his place.

ASPION LUOR has granted you the power to change the land's destiny.
Defeat the guardian to leave the Land of WELL.

He stared blankly. The chief's action was utterly despicable... and so predictable, Dallion was amazed he expected anything less. Of course, the old man would imprison him alone in this realm. The really scary part was that no one was going to notice unless Dallion completed the trial or was defeated and lost his awakening powers. He could stay here for months, even years, and not a second would pass for the village. As far as the crowd was concerned, he had just grabbed hold of the chief's hand.

"The Land of Well," Dallion crossed his arms. "I hope you're ready." Not only was he going to defeat all the creatures and vanquish the guardian, but, if it was in his power, he was also going to add a "the" in the rectangles' descriptions as well.

REALM MENDING

The realm turned out to be larger than expected. Initially, Dallion had decided to see whether anything would happen if he made his way toward the encircling mountains. Hours of walking later, there was no change. Given the distance, it was normal to suspect there wouldn't be an immediate difference after walking a distance that short. However, according to his improved perception, the only mountain that appeared to change size was the one in the center. Even spookier, the mountains behind it also remained the same height since Dallion's arrival in the realm.

If there was a way to escape this place, climbing over the ring of mountains wasn't it. The one thing the village chief hadn't lied about was that the only way to exit was to defeat the guardian...or fail trying.

"Kill the monsters, defeat the guardian," Dallion said.

His football coach in high school had said that shouting your goals out loud was already half a victory. The only thing Dallion felt right now was stupid. Even so, there was a sense of wonder in the air. Being in a new world gave off a feeling of adventure, just like the first time he'd gone to a mall or a retro-arcade. There was something magical about the newness of everything. Even the stones were seemingly perfect without chips or even scratches, as if they had been bought in bulk, then carefully shipped and arranged to this world.

Reaching down, Dallion picked up a small rock and tried to awaken it. Nothing happened. Apparently, one couldn't enter into a "deeper" realm.

Kill the monsters, he thought as he put the rock back on the ground. *But where are the monsters?*

Despite his heightened perception, he wasn't able to see any of the creatures Aspion had claimed to fill the realm. And yet, Dallion had a sense they lurked somewhere out of view. Potentially, that was a good thing. If the "monsters" were scared to face him directly, it suggested they were much weaker, relying on numbers and the element of surprise.

Adjusting his buckler, Dallion turned and began the long trip to the central mountain. The time he had wasted searching a way out had its effect. By the time he had reached the foot of the main mountain, the sun had already set. Darkness covered the realm, and with it, came cold and a deep sense of fear.

"There's nothing to be scared of," Dallion whispered. "I'm an awakened, they aren't."

From what little he knew about wildlife, nocturnal creatures were usually afraid of light and fire. That suggested the best course of action was to set up a campfire for the night. The problem with that was that Dallion had no way of making one. All around, there was nothing other than stone and water. Even if Dallion used his clothes and somehow managed to ignite them by making sparks, the flames wouldn't survive for long.

Undoubtedly, there probably was a chapter in some old scout's book describing how to ensure shelter in similar circumstances. Since Dallion didn't know it, he did the only thing he could come up with—curled up against a solid wall of rock, sword in one hand, his buckler covering up as much of his body as possible.

In time, fear gave way to cold, which gave way to exhaustion, and finally, drowsiness. After what seemed like an eternity, Dallion dozed off. As he did, the sound of running water slowly changed into a rhythmic drip. The sequence was strangely familiar...very close to that Nightcore song that had been so prevalent at the party he had been to before appearing in this world. Strangely enough, it was the only song he could remember of that faithful night. If he concentrated, he could clearly make out the rhythm, almost hear the laughter of his friends, smell the alcohol and vape smoke fill the air. It almost felt as if he could open his eyes and—

A loud roar ripped the mental image out of Dallion's mind. His reflexes acted on his own, jolting him to his feet. The dozens of hours spent training had buried several sets of movements into his mind and body, making Dallion twist just as green and red combat markers appeared. Like a skater, Dallion did a double axel spin, sword held firmly and extended outwards. There was a loud ripping sound as the blade of the weapon ripped through Dallion's attacker even before he saw exactly what it was.

A blood-freezing scream filled the air. For a split second, Dallion was able to catch a glimpse of a panther-like silhouette as it disappeared in a puff of smoke.

Realm section mended!
Overall completion 3%

A glowing blue rectangle appeared in front of him. Dallion quickly slashed it away, looking about for other enemies. There didn't seem to be any at the moment, but one thing was for certain, if there was one monster, there would be more.

So much for a quiet night's rest, he thought, his veins pumped with adrenaline.

Three percent mended. That meant there were at least thirty more creatures out there. Of course, that assumed the realm completion level had been zero to begin with. Thinking about it, Dallion quickly came to the conclusion he had found one more reason to hate calculus.

"As they say, when life gives you lemons…" he said to give himself a boost of courage, "…squeeze them in life's eyes. Time to do some mending!"

The clouds had broken just enough to let the blue moon's rays cover most of the mountain. Normally, Dallion would consider the view inspiring, maybe even suitable for a date. A dozen panther shapes farther up the mountain made him revise his statement.

That, as the saying went, wasn't good. For one thing, the creatures outnumbered him significantly. Also, they held the high ground, as every strategy guide, and meme, suggested was always better. Since Dallion didn't, the only thing he could do was rely on a sudden charge, which he did.

Red markers appeared, providing him with several attack options. It was interesting to know that each case depicted one single strike as being enough against these creatures. This was vastly different from Dallion's experience against guardians, but a very welcome one.

Gripping the hilt of his short sword, Dallion rushed on. Seeing him, three of the creatures broke off from the rest of the pack, rushing down toward him. The one in front leapt his direction, claws ready for the kill.

The footsteps turned red and green as the rest of the markers shifted about. Dallion barely had to glance at them while raising his buckler. His speed advantage allowed him to block the creature's attack with ease, the improvement in body helped him stand his ground, and his newly developed attack skill allowed him to deflect the attack with his buckler, then spin around and slash the creature while still in the air.

COMBINATION ATTACK

Dealt damage is increased by 200%

A red rectangle appeared as the first attacker poofed into nothingness. Two more beasts followed shortly after, only to be dispatched just as easily to the point Dallion felt almost bad for them.

COMBINATION ATTACK
Dealt damage is increased by 200%

COMBINATION ATTACK
Dealt damage is increased by 200%

"Is that all you've got?" Dallion asked, slicing the red rectangles with his short sword.

The panthers must have felt the same, for they didn't charge at him one by one, choosing instead to move closer together. In a single instant, all their movements synced as if a single mind controlled them. Even with the amount of adrenaline running through his veins, Dallion felt more than a bit of hesitation.

Realm section mended!
Overall completion 9%

A blue rectangle emerged, only to disappear immediately after.

"So, each of you is two percent?" Dallion asked, eyes locked on his enemy. Once again, red markers covered the ground.

THE PACK

Fighting a pack was different from fighting a group of creatures. An individual creature, even a strong and intelligent one, had one course of action. Thanks to the markers his skills provided him, Dallion could see that action and react in the most appropriate fashion. Whether it was one, three, or five panthers that attacked, he had the speed to protect himself, then counterattack, always resulting in an instant kill.

The pack had a wholly different behavior. Each separate creature was part of the whole, like an extra arm or leg. This went beyond mere coordination, so Dallion had to stop treating it as such. The fight had changed from a simple one-to-one encounter to a tactical clash of armies. The only issue, however, was that, unlike his opponent, Dallion had an army of one.

Four creatures split from the back, attacking all at once. The entire space around Dallion became filled with green markers, constantly shifting position as the beasts approached. At this point, skills were no longer enough to guarantee him victory. While all possible defenses were presented, the sheer amount of options was so great that it constituted no choice at all. Retreating, Dallion raised his buckler arm just as two of the panthers leaped at his face.

He barely had enough time to deflect them—using his force to lift-toss them above his head like pancakes—when the second pair rushed, taking advantage of his unprotected body.

"Back!" Dallion shouted, waving his sword wildly like a feather duster. The blade managed to slice through the leg of a panther, turning it into a cloud of smoke. At the exact same moment, a second creature took advantage to get in close and sink its teeth into Dallion's leg before immediately leaping back well outside his reach.

MINOR INJURY!
Health has been reduced by 5%

A red rectangle appeared in the air. The pain was nowhere near as intense as Dallion expected, but that didn't change the fact that they had succeeded in their attack, a painful reminder he wasn't infallible.

Angered, Dallion took a swing in the air after the escaping creature. Thinking a single hit would probably kill it only annoyed him further.

Defeated by a swarm of ants, he thought. Fear popped into his mind. For a split second, he imagined himself lying on the ground and defeated by well cracks. Definitely not a heroic way to lose his awakening, and almost as bad as losing a major battle because of a tooth cavity.

Dallion's senses quickly caught the sound of claws on stone. The two creatures he'd thrown off with his shield charged toward him from behind. Maybe that, too, had been part of the pack's plan, a triple attack disguised as a double attack. Not a bad move. Fortunately for Dallion, he still had one advantage they didn't.

Ignoring all skill markers, he turned around. His reaction speed allowed him to visualize the creatures before they could bite. One clean arc attack, and both were no more, poofing out like balls of smoke.

Realm section mended!
Overall completion 37%

A third of the enemies were destroyed. Any other day, he would see this as a good sign. At the moment, he was far too busy scurrying away from the pack to care. Waving his sword out of instinct, Dallion continued backward off the foot of the mountain. The pack sent a few of its members toward him, growling and barking as they did. There was little doubt Dallion had lost. The pack was superior to him, both in terms of numbers and tactics. All they had to do was keep the pressure up to the point he'd run out of strength. Against all odds, however, they suddenly stopped.

What the heck? Dallion blinked.

There was no reason for them to do so. Even if he were stronger in one-on-one battles, there were more than enough of them to take him down. Unsure what was going on, Dallion stopped as well. More and more creatures approached, forming one big mass of claws and teeth ten steps away. And yet, none dared move an inch further, as if they had reached some invisible line.

For almost a minute, Dallion stood there, breathing heavily, buckler raised, sword in hand. Only then did it dawn on him. The creatures were part of the mountain. Like the cracks in the mending labyrinths, the beasts were linked to a specific part of the well. They couldn't go beyond it, just as a crack couldn't leave the object it had formed on. The central mountain, along with its multitude of streams and rivers, represented the well, and the panther-like creatures were the cracks. As long as Dallion didn't venture into their domain, they wouldn't attack. That meant he could get some rest without fear of being devoured. Just to be on the safe side, he spent ten more minutes observing them, then walked farther away from the mountain, all the time keeping his guard up. To his relief, no one followed.

"Guess you feel pretty stupid?" Dallion shouted in a final attempt to provoke them. All he got in response were growls. Now that he knew he was safe, though, the sounds had lost their threat.

Pain suddenly kicked in. As the danger had gone, so had the adrenaline that had kept him going for so long. Exhaustion followed, hitting him like a foam pillow and almost bringing him down.

I'll just close my eyes for a moment, Dallion thought as he sat on the cold ground. *Just a minute or two.*

Next thing he knew, it was already morning. The clouds had cleared, letting warm rays of light cover the entire ground. Looking at the perfect azure sky above, Dallion did what anyone in his place would—grumble and cover his face with his buckler. His mind wanted to continue with the snooze. His body, on the other hand, had dealt with the exhaustion to the point it started noticing how uncomfortable the rocks beneath him really were. For ten minutes, Dallion tried to convince it otherwise but ultimately gave up. With a deep sigh, he stood, then stretched.

There was a slight stinging sensation still present in Dallion's leg. When he rolled up his trousers to check, he found there was no wound, but rather a series of purplish-red dots in the area the creature had bitten him. That meant that bites—at least from these creatures—didn't cause permanent damage. Even so, it was prudent not to charge at the pack next time. To win against such an enemy, he'd need a plan, and one that did more than rely on skill markers.

As Sun Tzu famously wrote, "If you know the enemy and know yourself, you need not fear the result of a hundred battles." Translated into the language of first-person shooter maps, that meant check out the terrain in search of good camping and ambush spots.

FOUL AIR HUNTING

The bright, cheerful light made Dallion gain a whole new appreciation of the realm of the well. The feelings of dread that had plagued him the previous day were all but gone, making the area a whole lot more welcoming. If it wasn't for the complete lack of plants or forest animals, this could easily pass for a rather pleasant hiking spot. Thinking about it, maybe this had to do with the creatures Dallion had killed last night. As the blue rectangles had pointed out, getting rid of a creature tended to mend this realm in the process, and that changed its appearance both in the real world and here.

I guess structures don't have mending labyrinths, Dallion thought.

The air felt fresh, the water from the streams—once Dallion found the courage to try it—tasted sweet, and the central mountain was a rock climber's dream. Dallion wasn't a rock climber, but he had watched enough YouTube videos to assume himself an online connoisseur. The increase of his "traits" made him think he had what it took to go up the face of a cliff. Reality quickly smacked the idea out of his head, showing him how little he had improved in that aspect. Apparently, a few points in body didn't a rock climber make.

The only way to proceed up was the old-fashioned way, searching for something approaching a pack and making his way along it. Faced with that prospect, Dallion chose to explore the mountain before that.

By midday, the fascination had started to wane. Despite spending hours walking about, including venturing in several caves, Dallion had yet to find anything of interest. Worse, the realm failed to provide anything remotely edible, which—as his stomach kept reminding him—started to be something of a problem.

On the positive side, there was no sign of the panther creatures, as if the light had made them hide somewhere. That was supposed to be a good thing, as it meant Dallion could enjoy some calm before sunset. However, in the back of his mind, there still was a nagging feeling something was wrong.

The guardian, Dallion thought. *All I need to do is to defeat the guardian. I don't have to mend everything to a hundred percent. Thirty-seven percent should be enough for a few years.*

Despite his attempts at logic, though, the gamer in him cried out in pain. A deep desire kept insisting he at least mend it halfway before giving up. Defeated by his own irrational desire, Dallion gave in and kept on searching.

The farther up the mountain he went, the warmer the weather became. More and more caves appeared, making Dallion lose interest in further exploration. So far, all of them had been exactly the same—dark and cold tunnels that led to nowhere. There were no clues or treasures, or even monster dens. That led him to the inevitable conclusion the guardian had to be on the peak of the mountain, where the final fight would take place.

By the late afternoon, Dallion had managed to reach the halfway point of the mountain. As he paused for some rest, two things became clear. There was no way he could climb to the top in one day and, come nighttime, he'd have to face the pack of cracks once more. Logically, that gave him a few courses of action. The first was to climb back down and face the creatures at the foot of the mountain, where he held an advantage.

It wasn't going to be easy, but he could kill a few panthers at a time, then retreat to safety, then repeat the process. With a bit of luck and a lot of effort, he would be able to mend the entire realm in a few days, possibly a week, then safely make his way to the mountain peak. Sadly, the lack of food would make each day progressively more difficult, grinding Dallion down before the guardian fight.

The second option was to follow the all-or-nothing philosophy and face the pack on the mountain itself. As long as he picked a good enough spot, there was a chance he would thin the pack enough for the creatures to scatter, then kill them off one by one. Potentially, he could try finding the crackling lair—if it existed—and take the battle to them.

Being a logical sort of person, at least when it came to games, Dallion decided to hunt for the lair. That way, even if he failed to find anything, he'd be left with a significant combat advantage.

After another few thousand feet up the mountain, Dallion stopped to take a rest. The sun continued with its descent, giving the realm several hours of light left. In a part of the sky, three of the seven moons were visible as pale circles, patiently waiting to shine.

"Find a beast's lair," Dallion said out loud. "If I were a crack in a well, where would I hide?"

The obvious answer was beneath the stones. He had often heard of people talking that it was the hidden cracks that were the most dangerous of all. Likely that was true, but in a world of awakened, that wouldn't hold true, especially when talking about a well. Given the state of the village, it was a wonder the village chief had anyone mend the well at all. In turn, that suggested there was no reason for cracks to hide, which meant there had to be clues revealing their location. He just had to know how to find them.

Dallion looked around carefully, examining his immediate

surroundings. Initially, there wasn't anything out of the ordinary, nothing but rocks and water. Soon enough, he started to see certain small discrepancies.

Thank you, improved perception. Dallion smiled.

While the overall state of the realm had vastly improved since the previous day, that was not the case for everything. Some of the rocks were darker and crumblier than the rest. Not only that, but a few of the visible springs Dallion had seen were far murkier than they should be. If his theory was right, a crackling lair would affect the state of both the rocks and water, leading Dallion to its location.

It took Dallion about an hour to find a cave in decrepit condition. The moment he entered, the smell of stale air and stagnant water hit him like a brick, forcing him to instinctively cover his nose. This had to be the place. Dallion drew his sword and cautiously went on.

The inside of the cave was pitch black. It was only thanks to Dallion's heightened senses that he was able to see the vague outlines of the walls. With that and some help from his short sword, Dallion was able not to trip as he walked.

For minutes, nothing changed. Just as Dallion started having second thoughts, a faint growl came from farther down the cave. It wasn't an aggressive growl, more like a snore in a cartoon show.

Finally, Dallion thought, gripping the hilt of his sword tightly.

There could be no doubt as to the source of the stench. Now, all that he hoped for was that he hadn't bitten off more than he could chew. Moments later, red footstep markers appeared in the darkness. He had just been given the opportunity to attack first.

HOTHEAD

The red footstep markers led to a large chamber, where they split into dozens of options. The chamber was more den than lair. The creatures had grouped in one giant blacker than black blob in the center, snoring away, surrounded by shallow puddles of water. Judging by the blob's size, there had to be about six cracklings there, possibly a few more. Considering it took one hit to kill a creature, by Dallion's estimates, he could eliminate three of them before they were able to respond. With a bit of luck, and if he used his skills adequately, there even was a chance he could take all of them out.

It was a risky move, potentially reckless given the lack of light…and that was why Dallion did it, charging forward without a moment's thought.

HOTHEAT!
(+2 Reaction)
Charging head on into dangers could be called brave, but it's not always a smart decision.

Dallion ignored the rectangle as he lunged, striking the blob indiscriminately with his short sword.

SNEAK ATTACK
Dealt damage is increased by 50%
Opponent's options to react are limited

He didn't stop, following up with his attack sequence. Red rectangles piled one atop the other, each indicating a successful kill. Three creatures had gone before the blob began to budge. Two more perished after it did. Only then did green markers appear.

Let's see how well you do this time. Dallion followed the green footsteps to safety.

The blob burst apart like a water balloon meeting a needle. Judging by the number of cracklings still alive, his initial estimates were way off the mark. Black silhouettes scattered throughout the chamber, quickly merging with the surrounding darkness. Even so, Dallion's other senses gave a rough estimate of where they were, not to mention the defense markers provided a few hints as well.

A heavy mass with claws clashed against his buckler, only to receive a quick jab before the red markers could appear.

The markers must be contextual, Dallion thought while hacking away at another enemy. The lack of contact told him that the creature had successfully evaded his attacks, retreating elsewhere in the chamber. Taking no chances, Dallion leapt to the side, moving to a safe wall of the chamber.

Based on how fluid his movement had become, having his reaction trait increase once more was a huge boon. However, the more he thought about it, the more he came to the conclusion there was no such thing as a tilted build in this world. While his reaction speed had given him an incredible initial boost when it came to fighting enemies, it wasn't as efficient when facing anything stronger. The truth was all traits were vital, not to mention they boosted the skills he had been given. Perception was necessary for the markers to appear, reaction was needed for him to execute them on time, body was a must for long fights requiring lots of stamina, and mind… Strictly speaking, Dallion had yet to figure out what that trait was for, but he had a feeling he'd be facing some limitation if he had kept it at three.

MINOR INJURY!
Health has been reduced by 5%

A sharp pain ran through his right arm. A creature successfully sank its claws in moments before dying. From what he could tell, three more remained—not overwhelming, but enough to make things difficult for him further on. Leaping back, Dallion waved his weapon to discourage any following attacks. In the darkness, he relied exclusively on markers. Fortunately for him, his opponents weren't smart enough to take advantage of his limitations. One by one, they charged at him, hoping to exploit a gap in his defenses. Dallion's adrenaline shot up. He didn't defend meeting each with a slash. Moments later, they stopped coming. Dallion waited for a while longer, bracing for any surprise attacks. None followed. Having suffered a wound, though, was a painful reminder that he still had a lot to learn.

Realm section mended!
Overall completion 55%

A blue rectangle appeared, marking the end of the fight. Now that it was official, Dallion had a chance to rest. In theory, from this point on, things were only going to get easier. To prove his point, a ray of sunlight shone through the ceiling, lighting up the chamber. The stench had completely vanished, along with all the grime and decay that had covered the surrounding rock.

"Tha-that's nothing," Dallion said, still running on adrenaline. "I can take you all!" He waved his sword, though not too energetically since his arm still stung from the wound. As before, there didn't seem to be any blood or torn skin, just an already healed scar covered with purple spots. Having some bandages would have been nice, possibly some disinfectant as well. Lacking either, he tore off part of the sleeve of his shirt, then went to the nearest puddle.

The water was crystal clean, just as he had predicted. To be sure, Dallion took a gulp. There was no trace of bitterness. Encouraged, Dallion drank some more, then proceeded to soak the piece of cloth.

Washing off the area of the wound, Dallion wrapped the self-made bandage over it. The scar covered a large mark on his forearm, though it didn't seem deep. A bit of pain was still present, but so long as he didn't exert himself too much, it was something he could live with. As for infection, there didn't seem to be any. In the realms of items, Dallion wouldn't even get an actual wound. Since this was his first time fighting cracks, however, he chose to be on the safe side and used organic methods to ensure it was completely disinfected. Not a very dignified approach, and one he wouldn't resort to had there been other people around.

I wonder if it'll leave a scar once I get out of here? Dallion mused. The only way to find out was to defeat the guardian and leave this realm. For that, he had to continue his climb to the peak.

Before leaving the chamber, Dallion sniffed about one last time. The air was clean, suggesting that if there were other creatures, they were hiding pretty deep. The only thing left to do now was go back outside and continue the trip.

Sunset had already begun by the time Dallion emerged from the cave. Warm orange light fell on the mountainside, contrasting with the dark blue cast by the shadows.

"Well played," Dallion said, admiring at the vista. "After a fight in stench and darkness, you give me this?"

Lying on the ground, Dallion closed his eyes. He didn't feel sleepy just yet, though a break felt good. His stomach gurgled, issuing its hourly complaint.

"Later," he told his stomach. At least there was enough water. If things got particularly bad, Dallion was going to resort to drinking in the hopes that would trick his stomach into shutting up. "There'll be lots of food later."

According to what he remembered from school, a person could survive for weeks without food. That didn't account for the pack of bloodthirsty creatures in the area, of course. If Dallion's calculations were correct, there were twenty-two of them left, nearly three times as many as he had fought in the cave chamber. A logical assumption was to assume that they were located in two or three dens deeper in the mountain. Come night, they would emerge and try to shoo him off their mountain or, failing that, attempt to devour him. Given the effort it had taken Dallion to climb this far, he wasn't sure which of the two options was worse.

"I'll get through this," Dallion whispered. "And once I do, I'll have a word with you, old man." He clenched his fists, thinking about Aspion. The village chief knew exactly what was in this realm and had imprisoned him here anyway, all for the sake of keeping the Luor monopoly of power. Things weren't going to work out the way he thought they would. Dallion was going to mend the well completely, defeat the guardian, and return to the real world with his awakened powers intact. And when he did, the whole village would see who was arrogant and who wasn't.

ONE OF MANY

As night fell, and Dallion prepared mentally for his inevitable battle against the pack, one thing became alarmingly apparent. While wounds didn't require medical attention, the pain and discomfort remained. Even after resting a bit, Dallion found the flexibility of his sword arm to be significantly reduced. An entire range of motions had become difficult to perform, making the completion of attack and guard sequences all the more difficult to achieve.

Even in its final moments, the annoying creature that had scarred his arm had managed to achieve its goal. That suggested that, even solo, it had continued to act as one of the pack. The question now was, what would follow?

Dallion focused his attention on the mountain above. Any creature coming from there would be more difficult to handle. With luck, he had already gotten higher than the remaining dens, granting him the high ground in all upcoming battles. As far as he could make out, there were no dark rocks or murky streams coming from above, but that was only true for this side of the mountain. There was no telling what could be hiding on the back.

Soon enough, the first signs of approaching enemies presented themselves in the form of faint cracking sounds, as if stones split beneath vast pressure. Given the nature of the creatures, it was inevitable they would be there, especially in the current environment. Despite all of Dallion's work, the realm remained fragile, and a large pack of cracklings in one spot was more than the rocks could take.

At this point, there were a variety of things Dallion could have done. He could have taunted the creatures to take advantage of the higher ground, he could have attempted to sneak up to them and take out several with a surprise attack. He could have also charged at them like the reckless hothead he was. Unsurprisingly, he did the latter.

"Darude!" Dallion yelled, gripping his short sword with all his might. He knew that the creatures wouldn't get the reference, but that was the closest thing he could think of as a battle cry and didn't want it to go to waste.

The beasts froze. Apparently, they hadn't experienced anyone charge at them in such fashion, let alone shout. The years of neglect —that were far longer in the realm of the well itself—initiated by the village chief had bred complacency. In all that time, nothing had challenged the creatures for the role of dominant species with the exception of the occasional underprepared awakened Aspion threw in there.

Dallion could almost feel the confusion that went through the beasts. For several moments, they hesitated. They stalled, providing more than enough time for Dallion to rush through their ranks like scissors through silk.

Realm section mended!
Overall completion 63%

The rectangle came as a surprise, although a welcome one. If all his fights could be like this, mending the well would be a piece of cake. The burning pain in his leg and forearm, though, disagreed.

Dallion tried to stop, but the inertia of running downhill proved too much. With the grace of a sack of potatoes rolling down a staircase, he went from one defensive stance into another, then, seeing it wouldn't work, turned sideways. His body, stronger than before since his awakening, was now able to counter the gathered force, albeit in a very unflattering fashion. It took a short while, but finally, he managed to come to a complete standstill.

Sweat and shame drenched his clothes. Good thing there wasn't anyone to see. If this had happened on Earth, he could have gone viral as part of YouTube's most embarrassing video clip compilations.

I'm definitely not doing that again, Dallion told himself. *Not until I learn acrobatics.*

COMBAT INITIATED.

A series of green lines—seven, from what he could tell—appeared all over the front of his body. The trial run was over. From this point on, the pack wouldn't let him have any more free kills.

Damn it!

Dallion spun around just in time to see four panthers heading his way. They used the same tactics as before: two attacking low, and two attacking high, while the rest remained waiting in reserve. This time, though, Dallion was prepared. He stepped to the right, his swing forming the figure eight, effectively slashing both leaping creatures while they were still in the air. The action caught the duo by surprise, leaving them completely unable to avoid the attack.

"Not so confident now, are you?" Dallion followed through by matching the red-green footprint markers to spin in place, then slashed at the remaining two ground attackers.

COMBINATION ATTACK
Dealt damage is increased by 200%

COMBINATION ATTACK
Dealt damage is increased by 200%

Two more enemies poofed into nothingness. In the span of several seconds, the pack had been reduced by four. Unfortunately, as impressive as the feat was, it didn't come without a cost. Two bolts of pain shot down his forearm, almost making Dallion drop his sword. His leg didn't feel all that better. From here on, he was going to have to limit his twists and turns.

Realm section mended!
Overall completion 71%

So, this is what status effects feel like in real life, Dallion thought.

There had been times back on Earth when he had wondered about the concept, mostly curious whether it would make an interesting video series for him to post. Like most things, nothing had come out of it. The few ideas he'd had were clichéd and contrived, causing him to quickly give up and move to whatever was the next craze. Now, when he experienced what it was life in real life, he didn't like the results at all.

Quickly picking up his sword, Dallion looked around. There was no sign of the rest of the pack. One would have thought they would have taken advantage of his weakness and charged at him together as they had done at the foot of the mountain. The fact they hadn't suggested there were some additional restraints that prevented them. That didn't make too much sense, but at least it meant Dallion would only have to deal of four of them at a time.

That meant there were only four waves left. Not an impossible task, though no walk in the park either.

Breathing deeply, Dallion held the sword as tightly as he could, waiting for the next attack. Moments turned to seconds, yet nothing came. Was it possible the rest had given up? If a guardian could do it, why not these creatures?

Cautiously optimistic, Dallion glanced over his shoulder, hoping to see a glowing rectangle. Alas, there was no such luck. Instead, out of the corner of his eye, he noticed a rather large black silhouette farther up the mountain. Initially, it looked like a trick of the light, a cloud shadow in the night, or just a figment of his imagination. However, as the seconds passed, the silhouette grew, acquiring the unmistakable form of a panther…a monstrously big panther. By the time it had come within attacking distance, Dallion wished he had run off the mountain.

"Aren't you a big one?" he asked. Interestingly enough, no green markers appeared.

Could this be the guardian of the realm? That would explain why the rest of the creatures had run away. The lack of white rectangle, however, suggested that not to be the case.

"Where's the rest of your pack?" Dallion asked.

His first reaction was to glance around, ready for a sneak attack. They had to be here, especially if this beast was their leader.

"Are you taking me on alone? That's noble of you. I don't suppose we can call it a draw?" It sort of worked in *Monty Python.*

The monster growled, but it was more than a growl, as if a dozen growls had merged into one. Without warning, eight pairs of eyes emerged in the creature's body, each followed by its own set of jaws underneath.

Dallion swallowed. The giant panther wasn't the leader of the pack; it was the pack! And it didn't look particularly pleased.

OUTCLASSED

Whoever said that the larger a creature, the slower its actions clearly had no idea what they were talking about. As Dallion found out, the pack-panther was not only big—roughly the size of an elephant—but it also had reflexes rivaling his own. The first time it attacked, Dallion barely evaded by following the guard skill markers that had appeared. What was more, the beast had no intention of letting him make use of his skill specials, interrupting him mid-sequence with consecutive attacks.

How did I get myself mixed up in this? Dallion wondered as massive claws swirled around him.

Ten minutes ago, it had seemed like a solution to defeating the pack had been found. The greater concern was not losing any health before the fight with the guardian. Now that he was engaged in a fight for his life, Dallion's only focus was to survive. All his plans and regrets had swiftly vanished. No longer did he second-guess his inner voice to pick attack skills when given the choice. If anything, he wished he could have had more time to get to learn to use them better.

"Let me attack!" Dallion shouted, slashing at the beast's paw.

There was a loud howl accompanied by a shearing sound. Half

of the paw fell off, disappearing in a puff of smoke. Moments later, a new one emerged as good as new. Apparently, simple attacks weren't going to do a lot. In order to achieve victory, he'd have to think up something new, and quickly.

Struggling to suppress the increasing pain in his leg, Dallion hopped several steps back. To his surprise, the panther didn't immediately follow. It was a minor thing, something that would likely have gone unnoticed before. However, that minor hesitation on the monster's part presented an opportunity, one Dallion couldn't afford to miss.

Green and red footsteps appeared, creating a path of attack toward the crackling: three-steps forward, a step to the side while using the buckler to defend against the inevitable paw slam, a crouch-twist, then finally, a slash in the beast's back. The sequence was rather complicated and would undoubtedly result in pain, but it was the only chance Dallion had.

Let's hope you regret this more than me. Dallion took a deep breath and charged.

The monster reacted just as the markers suggested it would, turning slightly toward Dallion, then attempting to slice him in half with its massive claws. The buckler met the paw head on, pushing Dallion back in the process.

Pain shot through Dallion's entire body. Both his arm and leg felt as if they had pins of molten metal drilled into them.

Push through the pain. Dallion gritted his teeth. *Crouch-twist,* he told himself, angling the shield so the attacker's remaining strength didn't affect him. The paw slid off, ripping the air above his head.

"Got you!" Dallion shouted.

The panther's side was exposed. An immediate attack was certain to cause significant damage, possibly enough to make the creature retreat a few steps. However, Dallion didn't stop following through with the sequence that led to the creature's back.

At that point, several things happened at once. Time went to a crawl, as it was supposed to, and a second set of red-green markers appeared, suggesting what the follow-up attack would be. However, just as Dallion thrust his sword at the creature, two new heads emerged. Both opened their jaws, moving in the direction of Dallion's arm. The entire thing was in slow motion, but even so, it was clear he had been caught off guard. A series of green lines emerged, linking the teeth to Dallion's sword arm.

Damn it!

That was the price of overconfidence. All this time, he had considered his enemies to be brainless mobs that did the same actions over and over again. As it turned out, they could form strategies and trick him straight into their trap. The beast had sacrificed part of its health but, in exchange, had gotten Dallion's attack arm. Without a sword, he had as much chance of winning as a dodo bird flying over the Atlantic.

Think!

Dallion's reaction was high enough for him to attempt something, though he had no idea what it should be. If he went through with his attack, both he and the monster would suffer serious damage. If he didn't, there was no telling whether he'd get another opening. Was this a time to be reckless or to exert caution for once?

Options played out in his mind. Some of them were better than others, but all required his full arm movement. If only Dallion hadn't gotten bitten, if only his body trait had been a bit higher, things would have been different. Now, he had to make a choice.

Crap!

If only he had a better weapon, or even two weapons, he wouldn't be facing such a dilemma. Back on Earth, it was said that only incompetent players blamed their gear. Dallion had no intention of doing that. There was nothing wrong with the short sword, even if he preferred something that could let him attack from a distance. For a moment, he considered changing hands, or throwing the sword and picking it up later. Neither of those options was particularly viable. Awakening had granted him a lot of abilities, but ambidexterity wasn't one of them, at least not yet. As things stood, he only had one sword arm and one shield arm...

A realization hit Dallion like a lightning bolt. How could he forget so soon? The sword wasn't his only weapon; he had the shield as well!

Mustering all his remaining strength, Dallion swung his buckler at the two heads while continuing with his sword attack. Timing was key. The tip of the sword sank into the panther's hide. The creature's heads opened their jaws, aiming to bite into his wrist, but before they could, the edge of the buckler hit the leftmost one on the side.

COMBINATION ATTACK
Dealt damage is increased by 200%

Both heads disappeared in a puff of smoke as Dallion thrust the sword in until its entire blade was buried in the monster.

An ear-popping howl shattered the air, forcing Dallion to jump back. A split second later, the panther did the same, doubling the distance between them.

"Thank goodness," Dallion managed to say, breathing heavily.

The pain in his body had subsided, replaced by numbness. Thankfully, the panther didn't seem to be doing all that better. The creature that had been only attacking up to this point took a defensive stance, glaring at Dallion with such ferocity, it could drill a hole through concrete with its gaze alone. That wasn't the only change. It was only now that Dallion noticed his opponent had significantly shrunk since the start of the fight. If he would venture a guess, he'd say the panther was about a third smaller than before, with far fewer eyes floating through its dark silhouette of a body.

Of course! Dallion thought.

Everything became clear now. The creature was the embodiment of the pack and, as such, shared all characteristics of the creatures that made it up. Each successful strike corresponded to the death of a pack member, and as the pack members diminished, so did the overall size of the enemy.

"Nice try, but it'll take more than that to defeat me." Dallion smirked. Finally, he'd gotten to use a cheesy line in real life. That filled him with a surprising degree of gratification, though not as much as seeing a way out of this.

Eight times, he told himself. *I just have to hit it eight times.*

"Darude!" Dallion yelled and charged.

The battle was far from over, and he had just regained the initiative.

FLAWED VICTORY

The panther leapt back. Already shaken by Dallion's previous attack, it no longer had the intention of taking on his charge head on. This proved to be to Dallion's benefit, who could now make use of the combat markers. Gritting his teeth, he followed the red-green footprints as best he could, ending it with a slash attack.

MINOR STRIKE
Dealt damage is increased by 10%

A red rectangle emerged. The strike was much less efficient than the previous ones but wasn't of major concern. Percentages didn't particularly matter when fighting these creatures. It had already been established that one hit represented one kill, and anything beyond that was lost.

Three new sets of paws emerged on the side of the panther, each striking indiscriminately. Maybe it was due to the adrenaline rush, but Dallion found them to be much slower than before. Evading them was no issue, even with his numb leg. If anything, the terrain presented a far bigger challenge than the creature.

Raising his shield, Dallion took a step to the side, then leaped back. Green footprints appeared and disappeared as he did, attempting to guide him better, but, at present, Dallion ignored them. As tempting as it was to attempt completing another sequence, doing so was becoming increasingly difficult, especially when retreating.

Letting out a loud yell, Dallion swung the sword in front of him. This wasn't meant as an attack but a means to intimidate the panther into retreating…and it worked. The monster, while still several times Dallion's size, leaped back a dozen feet, then stopped in place. It, too, was analyzing the situation, determining the best course of action to take.

How I wish I could read your mind, Dallion thought.

For a few moments, he even concentrated on the panther's head, as if hoping a new awakened ability would manifest. Given how everything else worked, it wouldn't be surprising if that was the hidden benefit of the mind trait. Alas, all that Dallion got from the experience was a mild headache.

That would have been too easy. He relaxed his eyes.

"You sure you don't want a draw?" Dallion asked.

A snarl indicated the creature hadn't changed its mind.

Perfect, Dallion grumbled internally. Right now, it looked more likely than not he'd win this encounter, but at a cost. The battle was going to leave him severely wounded and exhausted.

Holding his breath, Dallion charged forward. A moment later, so did the panther. Both had realized two things: the longer the battle dragged out, the more both sides would suffer and, given the present circumstances, the attacker held the advantage.

Two more heads emerged from the beast's body, turning it into a makeshift Cerberus. Meanwhile, Dallion did his best to follow the markers that would cause him the least amount of pain. The two clashed once again.

Following the advice of the markers, Dallion blocked the crea-ture's paw with his buckler, twisting to the side so as to take the weight off his wounded leg. Simultaneously, he weaved his sword in the direction of the panther's neck.

AVERAGE WOUND
Your health has been reduced by 10%

As Dallion sliced through two of the heads, the third managed to bite his forearm. There was no pain—the arm had already been desensitized by everything it had been subjected to. Unwilling to let things stand as they were, Dallion slammed the third head with his buckler. That proved enough for the creature to release its jaws.

Two sets of markers appeared around Dallion: green ones indicating his best course of retreat, and red ones, indicating the best places of attack. Once again, Dallion was presented with a choice. This time, though, he didn't even hesitate. At the last charge, he had already committed to an all-out attack, and he wasn't changing his mind now.

The sword moved about clumsily, hacking again and again. Under normal circumstances, any opponent would have easily evaded it, though not at this distance.

Just a little more, Dallion thought as he kept on attacking. This was the best, possibly only, opportunity he would get. With each successful attack, the creature got smaller and smaller until, finally, it broke back into two normal-sized panthers, both of which leapt away.

No! Dallion screamed on the inside. He was so close to winning this, and yet victory had slipped away in the very last moment. Any other time, he would welcome fighting two panthers. They were relatively small, straightforward, and unable to compose a real pack. However, in his present condition, even two were too much. Dallion's actions had become slow and sloppy.

Rays of moonlight shone through the cloud cover. Several of the moons peeked through as if to watch the final moments of the battle.

At least I have light, Dallion thought. Given everything he had been through, there was no reason for him to pay attention to such things, but still, he did. It might have been an illusion, but he felt slightly more energized than a moment ago. It almost seemed as if the moons granted him part of their power.

"Are you sure you don't want to surrender?" Dallion asked loudly. "There's only two of you left now."

Guttural growling was the only response he got. Twenty feet ahead, one of the creatures emerged, teeth bared.

So, this is your game? Dallion glanced over his shoulder. As expected, the other panther had circled round, placing itself in a position to attack from behind.

"If this is how you want to go…" Dallion raised his sword. "… you're welcome to try."

Time seemed to freeze, but not due to any ability Dallion had. For a moment, he tried to imagine all possible outcomes. In the end, it was all going to be a matter of instincts and reaction.

Good thing I increased that trait, Dallion thought.

The moment gone, both panthers charged. One would no doubt perish in the attack, but doing so would provide an opportunity for the other to take Dallion now.

Green markers appeared everywhere, constantly changing as the creatures grew nearer. Then, suddenly, they all vanished.

Dallion's body twisted as he performed a full circular slash with both his sword and buckler. Timed to just the right moment, the blade slashed through the creature in front, while the edge of the buckler slammed the one from behind in the head. The latter wasn't enough to kill the creature but prevented Dallion from receiving any additional damage until he finished it off by following through with the sword strike.

COMBINATION ATTACK
Dealt damage is increased by 200%

Realm section mended!
Overall completion 99%

Two rectangles appeared in the air in front of him.

"You got to be kidding me," Dallion said, looking at the blue completion rectangle. After that, he collapsed on the ground.

STARS AND MOONS

S tars. Until now, Dallion had never realized how much he missed them. Not the few pale dots he used to see back on Earth, but real stars, covering the sky like salt on a black paper napkin. Even the moons had brightened, emanating a crisp-colored glow. Lying on his back, Dallion raised his hand as if stretching to grab hold of a star. It was childish, but right now, he wanted to be a child, at least for a little longer.

The fight against the pack had exhausted him—more physically than mentally—to the point of collapse. He had suffered a few more bites, each costing him between five and ten percent health, and had seen things he wished he hadn't, but in the end, he had won. The giant beast had gradually been reduced to a normal-sized panther, which Dallion had sliced in two with barely any effort at all.

At that point, a blue rectangle had appeared, informing him that the realm had been mended up to ninety-nine percent. That was welcoming news, even if annoyed Dallion to no end. On the one hand, it confirmed that there wouldn't be any more fighting for the night, or at all, up to the point he faced the guardian. On the other hand, he was missing one percent.

The realm had also become much brighter after the fight. It

wasn't only the rocks and streams that appeared to have obtained a slight glow, but the air itself had become crisper, fresher. Dallion could feel an unmistakable sensation of joy with every breath. There was nothing like this on Earth, or even back in the village.

"The seven moons," Dallion said out loud.

What were they really? Deities? Sources of awakened abilities? Both? Dallion had often come across them mentioned in everyday talk, and still that was all they were, parts of phrases without further explanations. Everyone knew there was some order or religion based on them, just as everyone knew their monasteries were willing to accept anyone to join their ranks, even social pariahs, but that was all. It wasn't only that people didn't have answers; they didn't have questions either. Dallion barely had the faintest of interest, everything considered. All his efforts were entirely focused on getting him to level up and improve his skills, almost to the point of obsession. To be honest, until entering this realm, he hadn't given the matter any thought at all.

"I really need to live more and level less, don't I?" he asked the moons. To his slight disappointment, the moons didn't reply. Unfortunately, something else did, a nagging voice reminding Dallion that ninety-nine percent wasn't a hundred. Like a temptress, the voice insisted that, with a little bit of effort, Dallion could easily track down the final creature and end it to get the coveted hundred percent, earning him deep moral satisfaction.

Maybe tomorrow, Dallion thought, in part annoyed with himself about entertaining the idea. *Maybe after I rest a bit.*

The night passed quickly and painlessly. In the morning, Dallion felt completely refreshed. The pain had all but subsided, along with the hunger. It was almost surprising how comfortable sleeping on rocks felt after a fight. Then again, it was also possible mending the realm had changed its properties, making it far more welcoming.

Dallion stretched, then went to the nearest stream for a drink and quick wash. Done, he set off up the mountain once more. The nagging reminder of the missing one percent pestered him a bit longer but soon gave way to his determination to get done with the challenge and return to the real world.

If I come across it, I come across it, Dallion told himself and persisted on.

The higher he got, the steeper the mountain became. The easy path soon disappeared, forcing him to do some rudimentary climbing. It wasn't a pleasant process. His right arm still hurt a bit, though nowhere as much as it had last night. Thanks to his increased awakening traits, Dallion was able to climb up some easy cliff sections and keep on moving at a regular speed.

By early afternoon, he had halved the distance yet again. By his rough estimations, a dozen miles or so, separated him from the top. Normally, Dallion would pass such a distance in a few hours. Rock climbing, however, had never been his thing, so it seemed more realistic to think he'd get there by nightfall.

Alas, he didn't.

When the sun touched the horizon, the most difficult part of the journey remained. Sharp vertical cliffs and narrow ledges led to the top, forcing Dallion to make full use of his perception and reaction traits to move from one section to the next. By nightfall, he was fortunate enough to reach a small recess in the rocks, large enough for him to curl up for the night.

Dallion's recklessness urged him to keep going for the top, but his common sense told him it would be a terrible idea trying to climb in the dark.

"Tomorrow," he told himself. "I'll get there tomorrow."

This time, the nap was far less comfortable and considerably more hazardous. It reminded him of the mattress hanging off a cliff that was a popular meme back on Earth. Things seemed a bit less dangerous here, although Dallion didn't want to find out if falling off a cliff would result in him being thrown out of the realm with his awakened powers removed.

The following morning, he continued. Despite his initial enthusiasm, progress was slow and cumbersome. Lacking Gloria's skills, Dallion had to fight for every inch of cliff, at times taking hours to climb a few dozen feet. It was only in the evening that he managed, after a few slips and several dozen near falls, to pull himself onto the top.

Finally, Dallion lay on the flat peak like a steak in a frying pan. This whole endeavor felt more difficult than besting the panther pack. Now he understood why people held awakened in such high regard. Awakened skills made difficult things easy, replacing decades of rigorous training to achieve the same result. If Dallion had climbing skills, he might well have gone up the face of the cliff in less than an hour. With markers involved, it might have been even enjoyable.

"No pain, no gain." Dallion uttered the phrase his mother back on Earth used to say. "At least I'm here now."

Unfortunately, as vital as getting to the mountain peak was, it wasn't the end goal of the trip. There was still the matter of facing the well's guardian in order to escape the realm. Given how difficult the fight with the pack was, it was safe to assume the guardian would be no pushover. Come to think about it, there was no telling what exactly the guardian would be like. In the past, each of the beings shared characteristics of the item they represented. But what were the characteristics of a well? Mostly rocks and a bit of water? Or was it going to be the other way around?

Dallion stood up and looked around.

The top of the mountain was roughly the size of a tennis court, composed entirely of stone. There were no altars, thrones, columns, or anything else indicating a battle arena. What he could see, though, even in the moonlight, was a dark patch right in the middle.

Could it be? His heart skipped a beat. There was a chance he had found the final panther hidden in the realm.

ROCK AND CUB

Dallion rushed to the spot. There was a small hole in the rock, no larger than a punch bowl. In it, a small panther-like cub was curled up, sleeping. Sensing Dallion, the cub opened a lazy eye, then suddenly jumped up, hissing with the ferocity of a YouTube kitten.

"You're the last beast?" Dallion blinked.

He knew the creatures were bad, a representation of the cracks and decay on the well's surface. Killing it would be a good thing, not to mention earn him a hundred percent mending rate. Even so, he had mixed feelings about this.

"Hey, hey, little guy." He extended his left hand. As expected, the panther cub bit a finger. Also, as expected, the pain was so insignificant, it made the creature's efforts to fight cute. "Don't be like that." Dallion petted it with his left hand. A hundred percent or not, he wasn't harming this. "I'm not here for you. Just get back to sleep, okay?"

The suggestion made the cub pause. For several seconds, it remained still, reducing what little pressure it had on Dallion's finger. It was clear it no longer wanted to hurt him. At the same time, it didn't let want to go either. In the end, it reluctantly released Dallion's finger.

"That's right." He petted it on the head. "Just curl back up. I'll be gone soon, and you can get back to whatever snoozing."

Faint purring came from the creature.

"Yeah, yeah." Dallion laughed. "I don't suppose you know where the guardian's at?"

The cub tilted its head, then curled back in its spot, still looking at him.

"Guess not." That would have been too easy. "Anyway, get back to sleep. I'll deal with this on my own. Just, please, don't do too much damage when I'm gone. I know it's your nature, but maybe have the well last a decade or two before the next awakened comes to fix things?"

Dallion knew the chances of that happening were slim. In the end, a creature couldn't go against its nature. The crackling looked quite cute now. Maybe it even didn't want to cause harm to the realm. However, it would inevitably grow up and transform into the panthers that had attempted to kill Dallion.

Petting it one last time, Dallion turned around. He had hardly taken a few steps away when a series of mew-like squeaks filled the air.

Seriously? Dallion looked over his shoulder. The cub increased the intensity of its mewing, clearly indicating it wanted him to return. Being in a family that had three cats and a Labrador, Dallion was well-versed in the wants of creatures. This cub might well be a theoretical embodiment of damage in another world, but in many ways, it remained a kitten.

"Quit it," Dallion said. "You've had enough pats."

The squeaking continued.

"Fine." He went back to the cub and tapped the top of its head with a finger. "Serves me right for not fighting you, right?"

The purring resumed.

"Right," Dallion replied to his own question.

After everything he'd been through, the last thing Dallion imagined he'd be doing at the peak of the mountain was to end up playing with a panther cub. Paradoxically, the creature was better behaved than all the cats Dallion had and the vast majority of the ones he'd seen. Curling up, all it seemed to want was to be petted as it snoozed off. It wasn't attention it was demanding, but rather the sensation of affection.

"You've never been petted before, have you?"

Being a crackling, that was unsurprising. People rarely developed warm relationships with the damage in their homes and mountains.

As he kept on petting the creature, Dallion looked into the distance. The ring of surrounding mountains was perfectly visible, marking the end of the world. More freakishly, their height had also considerably increased, making them appear twice the height they were before Dallion had reached the top of the central mountain. Even with all the skills in the world, Dallion doubted he could reach their peaks, and even if he did, there was no telling what he might see beyond.

"This is one crazy place," he said. "And to think all this is just a well. Out in the real world, you're probably just a small crack in a stone, but here…"

Dallion's words trailed off. The cub had reduced in size. Still purring, parts of it would vanish into the night each time Dallion's hand passed over it. It was as if through his actions, Dallion was erasing its very existence. Alarmed, he stopped.

"Cub?" he asked.

The creature didn't respond, remaining curled up in a ball, its breathing slow and shallow.

What are you sad about? a voice asked in the back of Dallion's mind. *It's just a crack. It doesn't even exist. And even if it did, it's fading on its own. Better than having to kill it outright. At least it'll pass on happily.*

Dallion's hesitation subsided. Part of the sadness did not. Nonetheless, he went back to stroking the kitten. A short while later, it was gone.

Realm fully mended!
The WELL is now flawless!

The rectangle came with a large dose of bittersweetness. Dallion had fully mended the realm, which meant the village wouldn't worry about their water source. It also meant that the cub had gone.

Alternative Approach!
(+2 Mind)
Finding an alternative way to a problem always leads to choice, though choice sometimes comes with danger.

A philosopher, or someone with a lot of time, would have come up with a lot of questions on the topic. Were cracks alive? Or were they merely a representation of the well's inner pain and fears? Was getting an alternative approach a good thing or not? What was the meaning of it all? At present, Dallion had no interest in any of those questions. The faint curiosity he had was drowned by the voice in the back of his mind, complimenting him on getting a new achievement and the corresponding trait increase.

With the disappearance of the last creature, the dark patch beneath vanished too. Now, every part of the mountain was flawless, just as the blue rectangle had shown.

"Rest well, cub," Dallion said. He was just about to move away when part of the rock floor in front of him crumbled away, revealing a small hole.

COMBAT INITIATED

A red rectangle appeared. Dallion jumped back and drew his sword. By the time he did, the hole had grown to the size of a dining table. Perfectly round, it devoured everything around until it reached half the diameter of the mountaintop.

For over a minute, Dallion stood there, anxiously waiting for something to happen. Some guardians waited to be challenged, others—like the sand dragon—preferred to make a grand entrance. There was no telling what this one would do.

After another minute, curiosity and lack of patience shoved him to the edge of the hole.

"Hello?" Dallion peeked down.

As it turned out, the core of the mountain wasn't dark or empty. Blue shimmering water shone from the bottom, illuminating the shaft with soft blue light.

"A well." He laughed. "The arena is a well."

On cue, the water rippled, then shot up. Green markers emerged, indicating what position the shield was in would offer the best protection. Immediately, Dallion took a step back, following the markers to the inch.

The jet of water burst up to the sky like a truckload of Mentos had fallen into a cola lake. Dallion swore several of the moons were almost hit in the process. Moments later, the water fell back down, though, this time, a creature had emerged on the opposite side of the opening.

WELL GUARDIAN
Species: GOLEM
Class: STONE & WATER
Health: UNKNOWN
Traits: UNKNOWN
Skills:

- **GUARD**
- **ATTACK**
- **WATER JET (Species Unique)**
- **ROCK THROW (Species Unique)**
- **UNKNOWN (Species Unique)**
Weakness: TENDONS

Dallion swallowed. The golem wasn't terribly large. In fact, it was about the same size as the colossus he had faced a week ago in the ring. Polished ovals of stone formed the creature's head, hands, and feet, surrounded and held together by glowing blue water in the form of a body. In any game, movie, or miniature store, this would have passed as cool. Having one as an opponent was less so.

"Any chance you'd go for a draw?" Dallion asked.

The golem shook its head.

PROMISE IN A DREAM

"Huh?" The village chief blinked as Dallion let go of his hand.

That wasn't the only change that occurred. The well itself had gone through a serious transformation, doubling in size, as well as growing a small water fountain. There were two separate sections, each the size of a room, constantly filled with water pouring from large fountainheads in the form of lions.

Complete silence filled the square as people gazed upon the well in amazement. Gradually, whispers arose in the crowd. People terrified of the Luors were openly saying Dallion had done a better job with the task, even if it was in hushed voices. However, the person who appeared most amazed of all was Aspion himself.

How about that, old man? Dallion smirked.

He could almost tell what was going through the chief's head. Just like the ring, this was supposed to end Dallion's awakened powers, regardless if he had learned a second skill or not. It was no coincidence that, of all the structures in the village, Aspion had chosen this particular one. On the surface, it seemed in a stable, though, in reality, it was on the brink of collapse. The whole point was for the old man to get involved after Dallion's inevitable failure and crush the seed of dissent by showing the village owed its existence to him, and him alone. Now, that was no longer possible.

"I've improved the well," Dallion said loudly. "Thank you for giving me the opportunity to help the inhabitants of this village." He smiled, rubbing his success in the old man's face. "The well should be good for decades to come."

Dallion expected cheers, clapping, or any sort of excitement, if nothing else for the fact that getting water had become a whole lot easier. Instead, all he saw were tense smiles. What was more, the crowd wasn't looking at him but at the village chief.

"Good." The chief's smile didn't drop, although Dallion could clearly see it was fake. "I expected nothing less from the grandson of Seene. You've done quite well, bringing the well to its current state. It must have been quite a battle?"

"It was," Dallion lied.

Things had proceeded in an entirely different fashion.

Dallion's stomach growled. Days of hunger had accumulated despite only a second passing in the real world.

"Err, sorry about that." Dallion swallowed.

"You're hungry," Aspion noted. "To be expected after such a task. Come, this is a day of celebration! There will be a feast in your honor! I'll make sure that—"

"I wouldn't want to inconvenience the village chief," Dallion interrupted, doing the exact opposite. "You've already shown me so much kindness. I just want to spend some time with my family and get some rest."

Aspion's smile thinned. Had the standoff been anywhere else, Dallion would have been severely punished, possibly thrown in a dungeon—if the village had any—and left there for days. The presence of the crowd protected him. While all of them were terrified of the Luors, there was only so much abuse one could take. Punishing Dallion after he had not only mended the well, but also improved it, would have caused more friction than the village chief was prepared to deal with.

The old man had gone through too much trouble to make this a public event, as a warning to anyone who opposed him. However, that relied on Dallion failing. Now that he had succeeded, the chief couldn't deny his victory.

How do you like them apples, old man? Dallion smiled.

"As you wish." Aspion shrugged. "You are the hero of the day, after all. You have earned your rest. Go spend it with your family." He then briskly turned around, heading to his mansion, hurriedly followed by the rest of his entourage.

Half a minute later—once the entire Luor family was gone—the square erupted in cheers. Everyone wanted to be close to Dallion, wishing him the best, thanking and complimenting him on his success. It was as if he had become a superstar overnight. Unfortunately, none of them knew what such an achievement had cost him. Despite putting up a brave, even cocky, front, Dallion was exhausted, remaining upright on nothing but sheer will. His legs were shaky, ready to give out at the first step.

"I have you," Kraisten whispered, grabbing hold of his grandson. "Just stay up for a while longer. I'll take you home."

"Thanks," Dallion managed to say.

The next few minutes were a blur. Dallion watched as he was walked out of the square off to a building not too far away. The details were unclear. Rooms changed one after the other, each strange and unfamiliar, until he finally collapsed into a bed. The moment he did, all his sleepiness was gone as if it had never been.

Dallion opened his eyes. The room seemed familiar…the desk, the posters, shelves of books and comics, even a potato PC that was so old, it had trouble running most games in the last three years.

What am I doing here? Dallion wondered. This wasn't just some random room; it was his. Everything was arranged just the way he remembered it, which was to say it could use some cleaning and tidying up.

"Wow." Dallion rubbed his eyes. "That was some trip." *But it seemed so real.*

The awakening, the fights, even some of the villagers. He'd had long conversations with people, cracked jokes, even almost punched a few in the face. A pity that none of them were real. Some of them weren't bad. His "family" had been nice, and his "younger brother" was the epitome of joy and mischief. Even Gloria wasn't that bad in her own unique way.

"I better cut down on the parties." Dallion sat up. He didn't want to get kicked out of college on his first day. Besides…

He suddenly stopped. There was no way he could be here. Dallion had left his parents' house several days ago for college. He was supposed to be at the campus dorm.

What's going on here?

Uncertain, he went to the door and opened it. A faint sizzling sound drifted in the air, along with the smell of grilled cheese. Someone was cooking in the kitchen.

"Mom?" Dallion went forward. "Mom?" He entered the room.

There was someone at the stove, but it definitely wasn't his mother.

"Don't forget about your promise, okay?" a water-stone golem said, then flipped a cheese pancake. "One must always keep a promise."

"Okay." Dallion felt the urge to reply.

"Have you fully awakened?"

"I'm not sure." Had he? It was difficult to say. He felt that he had, but he also felt there was something missing.

"Better hurry up. I don't want to be stuck in the kitchen all day."

"Sure. No problem. Can I have one of those?" He pointed at the pile of cheese pancakes on the kitchen table.

"No. They're for after you awaken."

"Okay, then I'll—"

"Awaken!" the golem shouted.

Dallion jumped to his feet. His body was drenched in sweat. Breathing heavily, he looked around. He was in a simple room, one he hadn't seen before. Through the window, the sun set over the village chief's mansion.

"Dherma," he whispered.

He was still in the village. Strange that he would think of his life on Earth. Or rather, it was strange it had taken him so long to think about it. If someone ended up in an unfamiliar place, the first thing they usually did was try to find out how they got there, as well as how to get back. Dallion had done neither, rather going along the flow.

"Glad you're up," a voice said behind him. It was his grandfather. "It's time I told you a few things."

TYPES OF AWAKENING

"Here." The elder put a bowl of freshly baked potatoes on the table. "Your mother made these."

Dallion nodded, finishing the previous dish. He had been gulping down food with the speed of a vacuum cleaner for the last ten minutes and was only able to marginally reduce the craving. Up until today, he didn't think such hunger was possible. The experience in the realm of the well, though, had taken a lot from him.

"She sends you her best," the elder continued. "So do the rest. Even that favor hoarder— Chew better. Even awakened can choke."

"Mhm." Dallion replied, reaching for the potatoes. Back on Earth, he had strongly disliked them. Chips were as far as he went and, even then, he preferred to leave them unfinished. In this world, they tasted like the best thing ever, and would be even better if he could add a bit of salt and butter.

"You've increased your awakening level, haven't you?"

The question made Dallion freeze. All of a sudden, his appetite vanished, replaced by concern. Up until now, he had been convinced no one other than Gloria was aware of his secret. Clearly, that wasn't the case.

"Don't worry." His grandfather smiled. "It's a good thing. There was no way you could have completed an area improvement in your previous state with guard skills alone. What level are you now?"

"Three." He leaned back, leaving a half-eaten potato on the plate in front of him.

"Three? Not bad." The elder nodded a few times. "Skills?"

"Guard and attack." There was a moment's hesitation. "I could have had forging." Dallion paused again. "Why didn't you tell me about the tasks? You knew what the village chief would do and still said nothing."

"Didn't I? I thought I had."

"Everything you and Mother taught me were things I already knew."

Strictly speaking, that was only partially true. His grandfather was the one to show him how to mend things in the first place. Not only that, but he had described a few other skills as well. Without a doubt, he was at fault for keeping Dallion in the dark regarding everything relating to Aspion's practices, but without his help, Dallion wouldn't have been able to use his guard skill nearly as well as he had. On the other hand, Gloria had helped Dallion considerably more.

"You didn't tell me about the awakening shrines or the Order of the Seven Moons," he continued. "Even now, what are they exactly? Everyone keeps going how Aunt Vanessa wanted my parents to send me off to one of their monasteries, but no one knows why or even how."

"Is that the most important question you can think of?" the old man asked, then reached to take a potato from the bowl. "It's true, I haven't told you certain things, but there's a lot I can tell you now. Do you want to hear about the basic types of awakening?"

"Yeah, right." Dallion crossed his arms. "Sure, go ahead. Don't let me stop you."

"Don't be pissy when someone's doing you a favor." The elder pointed a finger straight at Dallion's face, making it clear he wasn't someone to be talked down to. "Look, I know it's all new for you, but you'll need a lot of help going forward, and you can't be picky about how you get it."

The outburst was sudden and completely unexpected. From what Dallion could remember, his grandfather had only done so decades ago, back when Dallion had been a child. Since then, the old man had never gone so far.

"The first type of awakening is called personal awakening," Kraisten continued, his tone back to normal. "No one knows exactly why it takes place, but it is said that through luck, genetics, or intense training, one could achieve their first level. That is the key to unlocking your powers, the first step to your inner realm. The more you improve, the larger your inner realm becomes. That's where your first skill is presented."

"Two," Dallion corrected. "I was offered two."

"I was offered three," the elder grunted. "Doesn't matter because you can only choose one. Through that choice, you're allowed to do other things, like awakening and mending items. Preferably small ones. That is the second type of awakening."

"I'm still waiting to hear something new."

"Each time you improve an item, one of the skills used increases. Also, if you're lucky, you can achieve unexpected feats, boosting your other traits. Have you done any of those?"

"A few." *So, that's something rare.* "I got one upon awakening."

There was a moment during which Dallion was tempted to talk more on the topic, but having to openly admit that his first achievement was "Reckless" wouldn't create a good impression. Instead, he moved on to something else.

"What about the shrines?" he asked. "I stumbled on one outside the village. They helped boost my awakening level."

"The shrines are a shortcut. They allow you to undergo a personal awakening without actually doing it. Depending on the shrine, you can boost your awakening level to five, ten, or twenty. Provided you complete their trials."

Dallion leaned forward. Things were starting to get interesting.

"The Order of the Seven Moons built them long ago. At one point, there were lots of them scattered throughout the land, but with time, fewer and fewer were maintained to the point they ceased to function. Most monasteries have them, but it takes years before a devotee can pass their trials. Also, they are almost always for internal use."

That was interesting. The one Gloria had shown him was a relic from the past. The shrine didn't look like a shrine in anything but name. What would it have been like centuries ago? Maybe the battle of the ogres was more than a myth, and they were linked to the shrine's destruction? Lucky that the altar had somehow remained intact.

"Just like standard personal awakening, there is no punishment for failure. If you don't succeed, you can always try again. That's not the case for item awakening. Fail there, and your awakening is locked away for good." The elder sighed. "And also worse."

"Worse?"

"Failure doesn't destroy the mind or the body. All skills and abilities you have gained remain, however. They'll continue to help you in everyday life, but you'll never be able to awaken anything else. Each time you try, you'll end up in your starting room, the doorway sealed off, a reminder of what could have been."

Chills went down Dallion's spine. He remembered how frightened and confused he was the first time he had appeared in the small, dark room. Being condemned to be locked there each time he tried to use a skill would probably be terrible.

"You never explained that to me before…"

"I'm explaining it to you, now," his grandfather sighed. "The third basic type of awakening is area awakening. It's like awakening an item, but the realm is different. It's larger, more elaborate. In many aspects, it's like you're in the real world, only it's a representation of the area."

"I know," Dallion said. "Mending was different. There wasn't any labyrinth."

"Mending *is* different," Kraisten agreed. "So is the number of guardians. The larger the area, the more guardians it has. Defeating each one increases the level of one skill." He then peeled off the skin of the potato he held and slowly ate it.

"And?" Dallion said after a while.

"And what?"

"Grandpa…" he sighed. "Is that all? How can I invite someone to help me improve something? When do guardians give up? How do I leave an awakened realm without defeating the guardian?"

"Quite a lot of questions.;" The man laughed. "Tell you what. Before I answer, how about you do something for me? Enter your awakening room and go as far as you can. Once you're done, come back here, and I'll tell you everything I can."

"That's it?" It sounded suspiciously simple. "What's the catch?"

"So young and so cynical. Just do it, all right?"

"Fine." Dallion stood up. "How do I enter my room?"

"The same way you awaken everything else. Just think of yourself as an object."

Yeah, right. This is the stupidest thing I've—

PERSONAL AWAKENING

Dallion found himself in a small room.

INSIDE ONESELF

W *ow. It really worked!*

Dallion was in an awakened realm and had entered it without having to focus on an object. The room was the same he had found himself upon awakening, or after his night of getting drunk near campus, respectively. The dull gray walls, the floor, the single doorway were as he remembered them. The only thing missing was the blowing blue rectangle. There was one major difference, however. There were two framed items on the wall—a buckler and a short sword. Each was on a separate wall, as part of a different section. On closer examination, Dallion saw a small plaque attached to each of the frames.

"Short sword six, buckler nine," he read out loud. The moment he did, a blue rectangle appeared in the middle of the room.

YOU ARE LEVEL 3

"Thank you for the obvious." Dallion laughed and tapped the rectangle away. "Any way I can see my traits?"

Sadly, the room didn't respond. After waiting for a bit more, Dallion tapped the rectangle to get rid of it and walked through the doorway. Initially, he expected to find himself in a corridor, like last time. Instead, he entered a small library. Rather, it was more an office than a library. The size of the room was similar to the one he had left, only this one had wooden shelves stacked with books all over the walls. A platinum-blond scribe in bright red clothes sat at a large wooden table in the corner, diligently writing with a large black feather.

"Hello?" Dallion asked.

The scribe didn't pay any notice to him, scribbling on a piece of paper in front of him. Judging by the chaos at the table, he must have been working for quite a while.

"I said, hello," Dallion repeated.

The scribe looked over his shoulder with bored disgust.

"Who are you?" Dallion asked. While the scribe looked harmless, he wasn't going to let some weird bureaucrat do whatever he liked in his awakened realm.

"Go back to your room," the scribe replied. "There's nothing for you to see here."

"Okay…" *I thought this was my room.* "What are you doing, though?"

"Are you blind? I'm working."

That made sense. And since the scribe was working, the only proper thing for Dallion to do was leave. However, his curiosity had other things in mind.

"Working on what?" Dallion moved closer.

Among the scrolls and pieces of paper, he spotted a map of the village. For the most part, everything was as Dallion remembered it, but now and again, there would be a structure out of place or even one that wasn't supposed to exist.

Dherma, Wetie Province? Dallion read. He knew Dherma was the name of the village. Strange that it remained so difficult to remember. Wetie was clearly the name of the province, yet Dallion couldn't remember hearing about it or the noble it belonged to. As far as he was concerned, nothing specific existed outside of the village. On the few occasions people acknowledged the existence of towns, cities, and even monasteries, they had done so in the vaguest possible way. Everyone agreed there were several cities out there, yet no one seemed to know how to reach them.

Standing by the table, Dallion reached for the map, only to get slapped on the hands by the scribe.

"Hey!" Dallion pulled his hand back. "What was that for? I just wanted to get a better look at the map."

"You don't need to know about the map," the scribe snapped. He appeared to be the same age as Dallion, possibly slightly shorter, and definitely a lot more annoying. "Don't you have things to do? Just let me work and go about your business!"

"Well, I just might!" Dallion yelled, then turned around and left the library.

See if I don't! No one talks to me like that in my own awakening room! I'll go now, but next time I come back, we'll have words!

Without warning, Dallion's surrounding disappeared. Gone were the dull gray walls, replaced by the small dining room of his grandfather's house.

"How did it go?" the elder asked.

For several seconds, Dallion sat there, unsure how to respond. Being pulled out of a realm on someone else's whim was disorientating to say the least. His mind jumped back and forth trying to figure out which was the real reality and which wasn't until finally fixing on his present environment.

"I found a library," Dallion said. "It wasn't there before."

"The more you increase your level, the more your domain will change," Kraisten explained. "New rooms will appear...although a library?"

"There was some annoying scribe inside," Dallion continued. "He said he was busy working and shooed me out."

"Why did you leave?"

The question puzzled Dallion, mostly because he wasn't able to think of any good answer.

"Because he asked me?" That sounded stupid. "It'll be different next time. Next time, I'll go and tell him exactly what I think and—"

The old man laughed. It was a deep, hearty laugh that filled the entire room and probably was heard by people outside.

"What's so funny?"

"You. I didn't expect your first experience with a limiting echo would be a scribe in a library. You must like books a lot."

"Nah." Dallion wanted to say he preferred to look things up online. However, that would make little sense to anyone in this world. For all intents and purposes, a library was as good a representation as any. "Not that much."

"It's different for everyone. The room is the metaphor of a person's innermost thoughts. In some cases, it's a library; in others, it's a bathhouse, a serene garden…" He waved his hand. "The only thing in common is the limiting echo that occupies it."

"Limiting echo? What's that?"

"Have some more to eat." The old man stood up. "I need to take care of something. I'll be back in a bit."

Usually, this was the point in horror movies that the person who uttered those words disappeared, never to be seen again. Sometimes, they'd leave a vague clue behind, or a bloodied piece of clothing. To Dallion's relief, his grandfather soon came back with a bottle of alcohol. Remembering the strong effect of the drink, Dallion quickly pulled back from the table.

"Want some?" the old man offered, to which Dallion vehemently shook his head. "Your loss." Kraisten took a swig from the bottle. "You've already noticed that people around here don't explain much. Everyone just seems to know enough to get along with their everyday life. Anything beyond that is ignored and quickly forgotten."

Dallion nodded.

"The only reason you've started to notice is because you've reached level three. The greater your awakened level, the more you'll start to notice, the more you'll start to question. Didn't it seem strange that up to a week ago you had so few questions?"

A week ago, I was a college freshman back on Earth, Dallion thought. Still, his grandfather was correct. The local Dallion didn't have any questions, dreams, or aspirations. He knew he'd remain in the village, grow up to work the fields as his father did, marry at some point—though definitely not to Gloria—have children, and watch the cycle continue. Paradoxically enough, through her selfishness, Aunt Vanessa had displayed the greatest amount of free will.

"That's because everyone in the village has a limiting echo in here." The old man tapped the side of his forehead. "Think of it as a voice that keeps you from asking important questions. Or all the times there's a voice in the back of your head telling you not to do something, like disobey Aspion, for example. Or even telling others things you know might help them."

"That's what's happening?" Surely, that couldn't be true. The more Dallion tried to wrap his mind around it, the more he saw the idea as absurd.

"You have your doubts?"

"It's…" Dallion stopped himself. "Is there a way you can prove this? I mean even—"

"What's the name of this village?"

"Dherma," Dallion replied instantly.

"Who's the ruler of the county we're in?"

Dallion couldn't reply. The name was on the tip of his tongue. He had used it dozens of times—everyone had—but, for some reason, he couldn't remember right now.

"That's what a limiter does, it limits your knowledge. Those who are awakened have a chance to see bits and pieces; they can even trick the echo in their awakened realm to allow them a glimpse of the things they know. However, until the echo is defeated, they'll never get the whole picture. And just as the average person won't talk about things, I can't tell you much more than you already know."

That was it, the mini-Eureka moment Dallion had hoped for. On the surface, his grandfather hadn't told him much, just a few scraps of information he could have figured out on his own. However, he had given him the key to unlocking everything.

That's why you kept repeating that you can tell me things now, Dallion thought.

"Who created the echo?" he asked.

"Who do you think?" The old man smirked.

The village chief. Apparently, that also was something his grandfather couldn't share openly. "How do I get rid of it?"

"To get rid of an echo, you must defeat it like any unwanted creature in an awakened realm. You'll have to get a bit stronger than you are now, though." The elder took another gulp of his bottle. "To destroy all the echoes, though, you need to defeat their creator. And for that, you'll need to break your first awakening gate."

LEVEL CAPPED

L ife slowly returned to normal after Dallion's first "village task." It was astonishing how quickly the joy and euphoria left everyone's consciousness, along with the actual events that had occurred. After a day, the only people who mentioned the improvement of the well were Dallion's parents. One day later, even they stopped, carrying on as if the well had always had its current state.

That wasn't the only change that had transpired. The Luors, so openly arrogant in the past, had essentially locked themselves in the mansion, rarely making an appearance. On a few occasions, Dallion had glimpsed Gloria venture outside the walls of the chief's house, only to be reminded by the guards she shouldn't be doing so.

If there was such a thing as the perfect status quo, this was it... except for Dallion. The conversation with his grandfather had opened Dallion's eyes, and now he couldn't stop seeing the discrepancies in everyone's behavior. Often, he'd deliberately ask questions that interested him—the Order of the Seven Moons, what was beyond the village, the state of the world—only to watch the conversation slowly drag on to the usual nothingness people spoke about. It seemed that, from the entire village, only he had retained his spark of curiosity.

As the days went by, Dallion kept using his awakening powers. Once most of the important items in his house had been improved—including the things that Aunt Vanessa happened to "forget"—he went on to helping out neighbors and family friends. It was through this fashion Dallion discovered there was a sort of level cap to all his skills. Apparently, once his guard and attack skills reached level ten, no amount of improving was able to increase them further.

Improving an area also seemed out of the question. When Dallion tried with a shed, the only thing he was able to do was improve the specific board he touched. Then, when he attempted the same with the wall of his house, nothing at all happened, as if he were touching air.

Asking his grandfather about it yielded no answers other than the usual, "I can't tell you right now." The only hint he was able to gain from the elder was that it was a good idea to keep leveling up and maybe something would happen.

In half a week alone, Dallion had made four attempts to complete the fourth trial of the awakening shrine, and each time, he had fallen short. The sand dragon—thankfully a quarter of the size of the one he had faced with Gloria—proved to be both faster and smarter on a tactical level than expected. It was like playing a sidescroller on highest difficulty with just one life. No matter how well Dallion did, there always came a moment he'd make a mistake and be thrown out of the challenge. In one instance, Dallion regretted being able to see the guardian's health. Losing when the enemy boss was at two percent life was probably the most gut-wrenching experience he'd experienced since the first time he'd had his heart broken in high school.

After Dallion's seventh failure, he felt he had reached his limits. The last few times had been abysmal. Not only didn't he reach his record of two percent, he had been eliminated while the dragon was at half health. If he had learned anything from his experience against the well pack, it definitely wasn't fighting dragons.

Midnight passed, granting Dallion three more attempts at leveling up but, after his series of failures, he was reluctant to try. Instead, he went back to the riverbank next to the village and lay on the ground. The stars shined above him, forming constellations he knew nothing about. No doubt there was a story behind each, possibly a local zodiac linked with the world's myths and legends. Until the limiting echo in his realm was removed, it was unlikely Dallion would learn about them.

"It's not easy reaching level four, is it?" a familiar voice asked a short distance away. Dallion instantly recognized the voice, although he was still annoyed at himself for not hearing her approach. If he had managed to level up and increase his perception trait, most likely he would have.

"Hey." She walked alongside him.

"Hey," Dallion replied, still looking at the sky. "It's tougher than I thought." With all his gamer experience from Earth, he thought he'd have won the battle days ago.

"You thought you'd manage in a week?" The girl carefully cleaned the ground next to Dallion and sat. "If it was that easy, I'd have done it years ago. Did you reach your skill limit?"

"Yes, I reached my skill limit." Part of Dallion was annoyed she was talking to him, though another was glad she had come here. "How did you know I've been going to the shrine?"

"I started going there the moment I learned about it. Why wouldn't you?"

That stood to reason.

"Also, you're bad at covering your tracks. Don't worry, Grand-father doesn't believe in perception. He thinks it's a useless trait. I guess that's why he finds me such a disappointment unless it comes to negotiations."

Surprise, surprise. The old man likes having his own lie detector when bargaining, Dallion thought.

191

"So, what happens now?" he asked. "Know any shortcut to help me reach level four?"

"Nope." Gloria shook her head. "You have to do it by yourself."

"No help? That's a bit mercenary of you."

Even in the moonlight, Dallion saw her cheeks change color.

"It's not like that! I've already reached level four, so the challenge is blocked for me, and there's no way we can handle the fifth one. If you're so stubborn about it, let's go try right now."

"Oh." Dallion hadn't thought of that, despite experiencing it himself. Quite likely this was the limiting echo's doing. The annoying little entity was finding new and creative ways to hinder his advancement. "Sorry, I completely forgot about that. Any chance I'd convince any of your relatives to help out?"

Gloria stared at him for several long seconds, then burst out laughing. That made Dallion feel better as well.

"Only you could ask such a thing. It'll almost be worth it seeing you try. My brother hates your guts, and the rest don't want to get on Grandfather's bad side. Not that they'll be any help," she added in near disgust. "They're happy to stay at level two and spend their lives improving trinkets and bossing people around."

"Your brother's level three?" For some reason, Dallion thought he'd be higher.

"He's a natural, so Grandfather doesn't want to get him to get too strong. If he knew about me, I'd probably be locked in my room." There was another long pause. "Sorry I didn't warn you about the well. I wanted to, but Grandfather would have found out and—"

"It's okay. You weren't the only one. It's everyone for himself, after all." That was a bit harsh, but Dallion wasn't in a charitable mood right now.

"I didn't get what I wanted either," Gloria said.

Experience back on Earth had taught Dallion two valuable lessons: to know when someone changed the topic to something regarding their problems, and to be smart enough not to interrupt when they did.

"Grandfather is marrying me off in a month. He said he found a suitable traveling merchant who had a son."

It would have been easy for Dallion to claim he was surprised, but the truth was that this was exactly the sort of thing he thought the village chief was capable of. The thought had crossed his mind the very first time he saw Aspion's family after awakening in this world. The man's granddaughters were clearly raised for one purpose, to be pawns for establishing alliances with people deemed important.

"When I improved my clothes for the third time, I hoped he would find me too valuable and reconsider." The girl looked at the stars. "It seems that was never an option. His mind is already made up. I'm not even sure I'll get to be married here or will be sent off."

"You don't have a say in the matter?"

"No one does. Grandfather has already found two candidates for my brother's wife as well. At least he'll get to stay here." The girl clenched her fists. "I'm the fourth highest awakened in the village, and I still can't—"

Abruptly, she stopped. As far as Dallion was aware, less than a second had passed, yet his keen perception noticed a stone on the ground next to the girl's fists had become far more polished than the rest.

"Sorry about this," Gloria moved her hand off the improved stone. "I just needed to talk to someone."

"Sure." *You did more than talk, didn't you?* "Don't worry. There's still a month. We'll figure out something."

No matter what it cost him, Dallion was going to do everything possible to find a way to defeat the village elder and destroy all of his echoes.

THE ECHO

"Brother, brother!" Linner shouted loud enough for half the village to hear. "Look what I got!"

The child never seemed to get tired, making Dallion wonder whether he was the only awakened in the family. If stamina was any indication, his younger brother definitely had him beat.

"Look!" Linner rushed up to him, holding a small scaly fish. "Isn't it great?!"

"Wow, that's a winner." Dallion smiled. He had no idea what fish that was and, in the back of his mind, a subtle voice whispered there was no point learning anyway.

Honestly speaking, the fish wasn't anything special. It was barely large enough to fit in his hand. His brother, however, looked at it as if he'd caught the greatest treasure there ever was. That was the thing about children; they didn't only enjoy the simple things in life, they enjoyed virtually anything.

"I know, right?! Dad helped me catch it!"

Translated, that probably meant their father was the one who caught it and only let Linner hold it after it was taken out of the net. Come to think of it, Dallion didn't have any memories of fishing either in this world or Earth.

"Mom promised she'd let me help her cook it! Want to watch?!"

"Oh, yeah?" Dallion asked with an indecisive smile. "You go get started. I need to do something, but I'll be right there."

"Promise?" The child gave Dallion a suspicious look.

Drat! "Absolutely. Do you doubt me?" Internally, he sighed. There was no escape now. He had condemned himself to a few hours of boredom sitting in the kitchen as Linner fluttered around, while his mother tried to actually get some work done. Then again, maybe it wasn't all bad. Dallion was in need of a break from his standard routine.

"Okay. Don't take long!" The child rushed away.

The joys of youth, Dallion smiled. A moment later, he entered his awakening room.

YOU ARE LEVEL 3

The blue rectangle greeted him.

"This is getting old, you know." He tapped it as he passed by.

It felt as if the room snickered at him, constantly reminding that he had failed to increase his level despite all the attempts. Today, Dallion was going to take a different approach. His grandfather had told him that he'd be at a disadvantage until he was rid of the village chief's echo. If so, this was a perfect time to do so.

Dallion took the sword and buckler from their frames, then went out of the room and walked into the library. The scribe was there, rearranging the books in the library.

"You again?" the echo snapped the moment Dallion crossed the threshold. "Go do something useful. I'm busy."

Dallion felt an overburdening desire to do as he was told. A voice in the back of his mind reminded him that this was a library and any fighting that took place here would do more damage than the scribe himself. The pressure was substantial. Every fiber in

Dallion's body urged him to step back. Gritting his teeth, however, he took a step forward,

"No!" he said firmly. "I'm not leaving! You are!"

The line felt so cheesy that Dallion was ashamed he'd even spoken it. Thankfully, it had the desired effect. The scribe, surprised at the unexpected defiance, turned away from the shelf so as to face Dallion.

"So, you want to fight, eh?" the scribe asked with a half-smile, which only increased the smugness of his tone.

"Not if you leave." Dallion raised his sword.

"A sword?" The scribe laughed. "Don't you know that the quill is mightier than the sword?"

The cliché felt like chalk on a blackboard. Dallion winced, then opened his mouth to voice a suitable reply. Before he could utter a word, dozens of green lines appeared from all over the room, all ending in his chest.

What the heck?

Dallion's reaction kicked in, but so did the dozens of quills that flew out of nowhere, darting at him like a barrage of arrows. As he leapt to the side, shielding his face with his buckler, green markers appeared with a slight delay, offering options for protection. Green footsteps soon followed.

COMBAT INITIATED.

Now, you tell me! Dallion rolled the table, then knocked it down. Scrolls and pieces of paper flew everywhere. Unfortunately, little changed. While the table provided a bit of protection, that only caused the quills to change trajectory, finding their way into Dallion's back.

QUILL WOUND

Your health has been reduced by 5%
QUILL WOUND
Your health has been reduced by 5%
QUILL WOUND
Your health has been reduced by 5%
QUILL WOUND
Your health has been reduced by 5%

Four red rectangles stacked up in the air.

Seriously?! Dallion rolled to the side. Less than a few seconds had passed and already he'd lost a fifth of his health, not to mention that he remained constantly on the defensive. The scribe had barely moved from his original position, observing the whole thing with mild, sadistic amusement. There was no white rectangle above his head, suggesting the echo would likely die in one hit. However, neither Dallion nor his skills saw any way of reaching the blond menace. Not a single red marker had appeared, and charging head on was likely going to transform him into a porcupine.

QUILL WOUND
Your health has been reduced by 5%
QUILL WOUND
Your health has been reduced by 5%

More quills poured down from above. At this point, there was only one thing left for Dallion to do.

"I'm leaving!" he shouted, jump-rolling toward the door. "I'm leaving!"

A few quills more followed, attempting to score a few more hits, but the brunt of the attack had stopped. The next thing Dallion knew, he was back in his house, looking at his brother running toward the kitchen.

Sweat covered Dallion's forehead, but that wasn't his main concern right now. As most people who'd gone through such an ordeal, he checked his body for wounds, trying to be as discreet about it as possible. The good news was that there were none. The bad news, it didn't look like he'd defeat the echo anytime soon. Based on the results of the attempt just now, it would be more likely that he managed to take down the sand dragon.

Stupid ranged attacks, he grumbled to himself. *Stupid cheating echo.*

Why did he have to have ranged attacks, auto targeting ones at that? Such skills were practically cheating. There was no way Dallion could win such a fight. Even if he charged at the echo, he'd get pincushioned by several dozen quills before he reached him.

"Dallion," his mother called out. The tone of her voice sounded urgent.

"I'll be there in a moment." *Might as well watch them cook. Not like I'll achieve anything else today.*

Just to be on the safe side, he took off his shirt to check for signs of blood, then put it back on and went to the kitchen. When he got there, he found both his mother and brother standing near the window, still as statues, looking at something outside.

"Is Dad back?" Dallion asked casually. "Did he bring more fish?"

"It's not your father…" Gertha said, her voice barely a whisper.

Outside, at the edge of the village, a small group of people approached. They were nothing like the locals or anyone else who had visited in the last ten years. All of them were dressed in green and yellow medieval tabards with chain armor visible underneath. The leader of the procession was a tall, dark-skinned woman riding a brown horse. From what Dallion remembered of his D&D sessions, she probably was a noble of some sort, complete with helmet, shield, and a suit of half-armor. She was also the first and only dark-skinned person he had seen in this world. As she drew closer, Dallion was able to see the crest on her shield: seven different-colored spheres on a black background.

"The Order of the Seven Moons," Dallion whispered.

THE ARCHDUKE'S ENVOY

The arrival of the soldiers was accompanied by the calm type of confusion Dallion had grown to expect. For the most part, the people seemed vaguely intrigued, just as someone would be if a distant relative suddenly showed up at the front door. On their part, the members of the Order had annoyed contempt written all over their faces. It was obvious they didn't want to be there.

"I am Dame Vesuvia, here by order of his grace Archduke Lanitol," the woman said loudly. It was impressive that her horse didn't budge an inch as she spoke, as if made of marble. "Who's in charge of this village?"

Several people set off in the direction of the chief's mansion. The rest remained a short distance away, whispering between themselves.

What are they doing here? Dallion wondered. As far as he could remember, this had never happened before. He had some vague recollection of a temple monk passing through a few years back, but never before that were there soldiers, and certainly not a noble. Eager to learn more, he took a step forward. As he did, his mother grabbed him by the arm.

"Mom?" Dallion looked at her, surprised.

"Don't go," the woman whispered, gripping his sleeve tightly.

"Why? What's the matter?"

"Don't go," she repeated.

Dallion was just about to ask what she had in mind when a sight outside caught his attention. The chief had made his way to the edge of the village and had used his awakened powers to do so. Only a blur had been visible before the old man appeared a short distance from the noble.

"I am Aspion Luor," the village chief said. His voice sounded twice as loud as it usually did. Though, compared to that of the dame, it sounded like a kitten trying to roar at a lion. "How may we serve the archduke's envoy?"

At the mention of the archduke, several of the soldiers smirked. Amusement covered their faces as they watched the verbal standoff unfold. The village chief was making an attempt to hold his ground. This was his domain, and he didn't want to appear weak, especially in front of outsiders. The dame didn't even seem to notice. She remained on her mount with the determination of one who would see the world melt into flames before showing any emotion. Just looking at her made Dallion feel cold chills run down his spine.

"A chainling has been seen somewhere in this area. We are to hunt it down and kill it." The dame's eyes narrowed. "How many awakened do you have?"

Awakened? Dallion's heart skipped a beat.

"Not many." Aspion's hand trembled. Conscious of the fact, the chief quickly hid it behind his back. "This is a simple village, Dame. Most of the awakened are old without the necessary skills to—"

"How many?" The dame's voice sounded like granite being squeezed into a cocktail.

The village chief wavered. Dallion watched him transform from the majestic, all powerful, undisputed ruler of the village into a weak trembling old man.

"A dozen," the chief whispered, looking down at the ground. "Close to a dozen."

"How many are fit for a hunt?"

"Two, maybe three…but—"

"Three." The dame audibly sighed. It was clear she'd hoped for more. "Arm them with what you have and get them ready. We'll be heading out within the hour."

"But it's not safe for them to leave the village. How will they accompany you?

"There's a cleric from the Order of Seven with us. He'll see to that. All you need to do is bring them here. And bring some provisions and hay. Enough to last a week."

"Yes, Dame." Aspion bowed even lower.

Wow.

To say that Dallion was impressed was an understatement. In his heart, he always knew the nobles had to be more powerful than the chief, but even he didn't expect such a difference. What he wouldn't give to have the ability to determine a person's level by sight. Maybe he could ask directly? After all, he had to be one of the three awakened. Most of the others were too old, too young, or unsuited for fighting.

"Dallion," his mother whispered.

The woman's face was pale with fear. She had known this would happen the moment the outsiders had walked into the village.

"Please, don't go," she insisted.

As much as it pained Dallion seeing his mother in such a terrified state, he didn't see himself having a choice. Leaving the village was dangerous, but it was better than being stuck inside, waiting for Aspion to come up with a task that could end up sealing Dallion's powers.

"I promise I'll be all right."

Gertha released her grip, letting her hand slide off Dallion's sleeve.

"I know you'll try." The woman forced a smile on her face, though tears still sparkled in the corners of her eyes. "Don't put yourself in danger."

Dallion nodded, then quickly rushed out of the house, joining the rest of the crowd as the soldiers made their way to the village square. In total, there were twenty-one of them, most equipped with swords—proper swords, not the oversized dagger Dallion had to use in his awakened state—and chainmail armor. Right at the back, there was a second, much smaller group clad in leather armor. Judging by their somewhat confused state and cheap clothes, it could be assumed they had been taken from other villages to help with the hunt. There was one person, however, who was dressed in a dark blue robe.

That must be the cleric if I'd ever seen one, Dallion thought.

The hood kept the person's face hidden, making it impossible to tell anything about him. The only other thing that stood out was that, unlike everyone else, he didn't seem to have any combat gear whatsoever.

"Hey, you!" one of the soldiers shouted at Dallion. "What are you looking at?"

"I'm an awakened," Dallion replied. Despite the impressive fashion in which the soldiers had arrived, he still had some pride left.

The soldier didn't even pause to reply, only snorted with a shake of his head, then kept walking. Unperturbed, Dallion did so as well. A spark of arrogance had lit up in him for some reason, pushing him to show he was no worse than anyone here, with the exception of the dame, of course.

"What about you?" he asked loudly, short of yelling.

"It's not worth it," a large red-haired man in worn leather armor said. "You'll be traveling with them for a while. Best not get them mad this early."

If there was someone who could be described as a walking red bear, this man definitely was it. Not only was he one length taller and two wider than Dallion, but his head, face, and arms were covered in bright red hair, as if he had implanted a furry crimson hoodie in his skin.

"Name's Havoc," the man said.

"Havoc?"

"Long story. My parents had a sense of humor. Others didn't approve of it much. How about you?"

"Dallion. Dallion Seene."

"Dallion." Havoc made a serious expression. "Guess your parents had a sense of humor as well. What's your level?"

"Three." Saying that out loud made Dallion feel instant regret again that he hadn't managed to defeat the sand dragon. "You?"

"Used to be more, but I'm down to four now."

Dallion gaped. *Levels could decrease?*

"Long story. Anyway, a piece of advice, never pick a fight with a soldier. You'll end up regretting it. Also, stay away from him." The man glanced at the cleric. "You never know how humorous the Seven are feeling."

AMONG MONSTERS

As time passed, interest in the soldiers began to wane. While the children and some young adults remained on the edges of the village square, most had gone back to their everyday chores. Bread, fruit, water, and what little other provisions the villagers had were brought to the soldiers, only to be accepted with such reluctance that one would think they were doing the locals a favor. Some could barely hide their disgust, treating the food as if it were manure.

Even the dame's horse had snorted loudly when it had gotten a whiff of the hay. A quick glance from its owner, though, and it diligently ate what it was offered.

"Fill all flasks and water sacks," Dame Vesuvia ordered as she splashed some water on her face. Unlike her troops, she didn't seem in the mood for food, water, or even rest. A few steps away, the cleric stood silently like a shadow defying the sun.

Dallion—once he had revealed he was one of the awakened—had been placed a short distance away and told to remain quiet. Soon, he was joined by the remaining two "volunteers." It was no surprise that Veil—the village chief's grandson—had been selected. However, Dallion didn't expect Gloria to be sent along as well.

"You're all I got?" the dame asked. For once, there didn't seem to be annoyance in her voice but rather a hint of regret. "Names?"

"Gloria Luor," the girl was first to reply. "The chief's grand-daughter."

"Veil Luor." Her brother puffed up his chest in an effort to impress.

"Dallion Seene," Dallion added in the end. "My grandfather's one of the elders."

"Hereditary ones." The dame nodded, then moved closer. "Skills and levels?"

There was a moment of silence. Veil and Gloria had been brought up knowing not to share details of their abilities with anyone outside the family, and certainly not in public. On his end, Dallion didn't have any desire to have the village chief learn what he was capable of.

"Two threes and a four," the cleric said a short distance away. His voice was dry and scratchy to the ear.

"Who's the four?" the noble asked, showing the barest hint of interest.

The cleric pointed to Gloria, earning her an impressed nod from the dame and a face of utter disbelief from her brother. Dallion was left with mixed feelings. On the one hand, he would have preferred to be the target of attention. On the other, he was more than willing to let that pass as long as Veil's humiliation lasted longer.

"I've got attack skills and body at ten," Veil quickly said.

As much as Dallion hated to admit it, that was outright impressive. Even with a single skill, that much power ensured he'd be able to fight nonstop for days. Back on Earth, he would have been an MMA champion, at least.

"And you?" Dame Vesuvia asked Gloria.

"Attack and athletics at ten…" The girl hesitated. "Perception at five…"

"Seven," the cleric corrected. His hood turned to Dallion. "Attack and guard. Reaction at eight."

Thank you for letting me speak, Dallion grumbled internally.

"Single focus bumpkins." The dame sighed, then went to take a seat on the edge of the well. "I guess that's all I could expect from a place like this."

"Could have been worse." The cleric clearly shared her view. "At least they've reached their cap."

"Do any of you have experience fighting?"

Veil crossed his arms with a confident smirk. Even Dallion felt somewhat insulted by the question. Of course, they were experienced in fighting. The fact that each of them had increased their traits to such a level should have been enough. Dallion alone had defeated over a dozen guardians, not counting his experience in the well.

"Actual fighting?" the dame clarified. "As in against other people?"

"I've gone hunting many times." Veil gave Dallion a quick glance, which screamed, *I'm far better than you, scum*, as if he'd said it out loud. "I've killed deer, boar, sometimes wolves."

"And you two?"

Gloria shook her head.

"I caught a fish with my bare hands once?" Dallion cracked a joke. The lack of response told him it had been the wrong move.

"So, none of you have actually fought," the dame said firmly. "Not even between yourselves?"

"Grandfather doesn't allow fights between awakened," Veil said with a semi-grumble. "I could have, though. I can take on anyone here if you'd like."

"I don't have the time for games. We'll be fighting for real. If you mess up there, you'll end up dead. If you don't mess up, maybe you'll be lucky enough to get away with a few scars and most of your body parts intact. You'll be given an emblem and a dartbow.

Guard both with your life because, if you lose it, you might as well be dead. Now, join the others."

The speech wasn't particularly inspiring, but it got its point across. If there had been any doubts the three of them were in the "weakling" category, they were now gone. One glance at the soldiers' weapons was enough to show that their equipment had been improved multiple times and mended to perfection. The silvery gleam suggested the level of each being well above seven, possibly more.

"What level do you think they are?" Veil whispered as they made their way to the non-chain-mailed group of soldiers on the other end of the square.

That was an unexpected shift in behavior on his part. For the first time Dallion could remember, the blond's anger and arrogance had vanished. One would almost be tempted to say he and Dallion had grown up together, if not outright friends. Being told there was a high chance of dying tended to do that to people. From this moment on, all three of them were members of the same village—nothing more, nothing less—and, as such, they had to stick together.

"Seven, maybe eight," Dallion replied.

"Eight…" Veil whistled. "I can't even imagine what it's like to be eight."

"Double digits," Gloria said. "They're all double digits."

"Don't be stupid," her brother snorted. "There's no such level."

"That's what they are."

"Grandpa told us there's no level beyond nine. Are you calling him a liar?"

"No!" the girl snapped back. "That's what I see when looking at them. All of them are double digits…"

Just great. We've joined a group of monsters, Dallion thought. He, too, couldn't fathom what someone of that level was capable of. If what Gloria said was true, it was no wonder the dame was so disappointed in their skills.

This changed things considerably. As much as Dallion wanted to shine and rub it in to the Luors, and by proxy, the village chief, his instincts for survival kicked in. As the dame had said, this wasn't a game anymore. The only reason he could think that they had been asked to join a group whose skills surpassed them by a factor of ten was to serve as cannon fodder; and if that were the case, it meant they were highly expendable.

"We must stick together," Dallion whispered. "During the hunt, we watch each other's backs. As long as—"

"Hey, Dallion!" A shout filled the air as Havoc waved to the trio as he approached. "Welcome to the volunteers. Don't worry, it's not as bad as it sounds. Keep your heads low, and everything will be fine."

"So, this hunt isn't as dangerous as the dame made it out to be?"

"Oh, it's dangerous all right, but we won't be the ones on the front lines. As long as they don't pick you as a scout or lure, you'll be just fine."

"Yeah." Dallion laughed despite the sudden pain in his stomach. One trait was needed to make a good scout, and Gloria had it at level seven.

AWAKENING FAILED

"Here's your emblem." The cleric handed Dallion a pendant on a silver chain. The trinket was circular, composed of an unfamiliar pale blue metal and had six small gems of different colors placed so as to form a perfect hexagram. "Wear it all times, don't lose it."

The materials alone were probably worth more than the entire village and everything in it. Dallion could see how a less scrupulous person would be tempted to grab a few pendants and run off to enjoy their ill-gotten gains. As the metal touched his skin, a sudden warmness enveloped him, feeling like a summer breeze.

"What does it do?" he asked.

"It makes sure you don't get blocked if you lose an awakening fight," the cleric explained. Judging by his bored expression, that had to have been a common question. "Here's your dartbow." He handed what appeared to be a hand-sized metal crossbow. "Don't lose it, and don't use it unless fighting or training."

"I'm not even sure how to use it."

Dallion examined the weapon. It was comfortably light and smooth to touch. No strings, springs, or cogs were openly visible; just a metal frame, a simple trigger, and a small limb. It was difficult to imagine the device was capable of shooting anything, even if it had bolts. The craftsmanship, though, was exquisite, incomparable to anything Dallion had seen in the village.

"You'll have your first training after nightfall. Until then, you'll just carry it."

"No, I mean, I don't know how to use ranged weapons."

This response made the cleric pause. Moving a step closer, he removed his hood, revealing a very pale head completely deprived of body hair. Surprisingly, he didn't appear remotely old, but rather closer to Dallion's own age. Red eyes stared forward, sending chills through everyone who saw them.

An albino? Dallion shivered. This was the first time he had seen one outside of games or movies, and it made him feel uneasy.

"You have guard and attack skills," the cleric said, as if that was an explanation within itself.

"That's right. But I've only been using a short sword during my awakening trials. I didn't even know you could get a crossbow…" His voice slowly trailed off.

"The items don't matter. Hasn't anyone explained this?"

"Well…" *Funny story about that.* "I guess not. There was a lot to do, so—"

"Items in the awakened state aren't real. They're the reflection of the skills you've obtained. The sword becomes whatever weapon you take inside."

"Nope, it doesn't. I tried taking a pitchfork, and all I did was—"

Before Dallion could finish, the cleric grabbed his hand. The surroundings instantly disappeared, replaced by a stone courtyard stretching into the infinity.

PERSONAL AWAKENING

What the heck? Dallion jumped back.

His instinct was to reach for the sword, but the weapon was nowhere to be found. Instead, a dartbow was holstered on his side.

"Draw it," the cleric ordered.

Dallion hesitated. It was clear he was in an awakened realm, but why wasn't he in a room? This didn't look like an area, and it definitely wasn't the usual room he started in. The closest thing he could compare it to was the inside of an awakening shrine.

"Draw the weapon," the cleric repeated.

"Right." Dallion did as he was told.

The weapon looked slightly different in the realm. A metal string had appeared, connecting both sides of the limb, transforming it into an actually functioning weapon. In addition, a single bolt was placed on top, making it resemble a miniature crossbow of sorts.

Dallion moved it about. The weight felt slightly off as if it were made of plastic or aluminum. One would be tempted to call it a toy if it wasn't for the sensation of power it gave. For some reason, just holding it was enough to create a feeling of invulnerability.

"Aim at me." The cleric took a step back.

"Are you sure? I haven't used one of these before."

The cleric sighed, then gestured to Dallion to go ahead.

Okay, then.

The moment Dallion raised the dartbow, a series of red markers appeared. Two footprints had formed near his feet, indicating what stance he should take, along with a line from the tip of the bolt continuing forward like a laser pointer.

That was new. Dallion moved the weapon about. It was just like the cones he saw when guarding against attacks, only reversed. There were no words to describe the sudden sensation of power that came with ranged combat. If he felt powerful just by holding it, seeing the markers made him feel like a deity.

No longer would Dallion have to dance about in order to attack an enemy. There would be no need for him to be cautious while approaching, making it possible to take on dozens of enemies in seconds. If he'd had this when facing the pack, he would have annihilated it the moment he came across them.

The realization was soon dwarfed by the greater one: Awakened skills were in fact groups. It was so obvious, and yet Dallion had never thought about it. It didn't help that his grandfather was incapable of explaining a single thing.

"Aim." The cleric was starting to lose patience.

Dallion did so. The moment the red line touched the cleric's shoulder, he suddenly froze. The part of him that was from Earth felt a deep reluctance to move the aim marker to the cleric's head. The logical part of his mind told him there was no danger, that the pendant would protect the albino from the bolt. Even so, there was a voice in the back of his mind screaming for him not to do it.

Stop limiting me, Dallion thought.

This was the limiting echo's doing. It had to be. All Dallion had to do was let go of his fears and get on with it. Before he could, the cleric drew a dartbow of his own and fired an arrow straight at Dallion's chest.

COMBAT INITIATED

TERMINAL WOUND
Your health has been reduced by 100%

Two red rectangles appeared in unison.

AWAKENING FAILED

"What the?!" Dallion leapt back, only to trip and fall onto the ground. He'd just been cast out of the awakened state by a single shot. This wasn't a fight; it was someone swatting a fly. Just how strong was the cleric?

Laughter abounded, mostly coming from Veil.

"You're no longer playing games." The cleric pulled his hood back up. "Get some training. Improve, or you won't be coming back from this."

"What did you do?" Dallion asked, but the cleric had already turned away.

Why didn't any guard markers appear? They had always done so when he was under threat, even when half-asleep. This was the second time they had delayed, to the point Dallion didn't have a chance to react.

"You showed him." Veil approached, highly amused by the scene. "Maybe teach me how you did that, okay?"

Dallion looked around, trying to make sense of his surroundings. To his surprise, Veil helped him up, then walked him to the others.

"Don't worry, we've all gone through this," Gloria whispered. "It takes a bit getting used to."

"He's the only one who fell on his ass," Veil snorted. Clearly, he wasn't going to let that go anytime soon.

"He was fast." Dallion swallowed. "I barely saw him attack."

"That's what it's like fighting a double digit. Good thing we'll be in the back."

Normally, that would be a relief. If the soldiers were even half as strong as the cleric, they would be unstoppable. And yet, the archduke wouldn't have sent such a large number of awakened if the threat they had to deal with wasn't even greater. If a cleric of the Order could do that to Dallion, what was the creature they were hunting capable of?

"Pack up and get ready!" Dame Vesuvia shouted. "We're leaving! Volunteers, follow the line!"

BASIC TRAINING

W alking turned out to be far less fun than expected. Initially, the trio was fascinated by everything around them as if they had stepped across an invisible barrier at the village limits, earning themselves a taste of freedom. As time passed, the sense of wonder faded. The grass was just as green, the wilderness was vast and empty, and the roads nearly nonexistent. The entire village began to look like a small bubble of civilization in an endless sea of nothingness.

Another interesting thing, as Dallion found out, was that the group wasn't exactly from the Order of the Seven Moons. Rather, they were a small squad of soldiers from the archduke's army, whose job it was to eliminate "nuisances" in his domain. According to the whispers, they, too, had been volunteered for the task and were not too happy about that fact. The mysterious cleric was, in fact, the only representative from the Order, as he made clear on several occasions. Dame Vesuvia was a different matter altogether. From what Havoc had shared, she was first and foremost a noble, but had spent some time at the Order's cathedral in the province's capital to earn the rank "initiate." That came with a large set of privileges, as well as her own personalized emblem.

Dallion had no idea what exactly "personalized" meant, though he suspected it was more than having a different appearance. The one he was given supposedly allowed him to be protected while walking throughout the wilderness. It wouldn't be far-fetched to assume the dame's granted her some magical powers as well.

Come evening, the group paused for a rest. On Earth, the process would have involved putting up tents, building a large campfire, as well as setting up guard patrols to protect the area while the rest slept. Here, the dame let everyone know they had half an hour to eat and rest before continuing. What was more, Dallion, Gloria, and Veil were told they would have to undergo basic training at that time as well.

"You three," a bulky soldier grumbled. "Gather 'round."

Clearly, he was the one volunteered to be their trainer. Other soldiers were doing the same, splitting the "draftees" into groups by village. Now, for the first time, Dallion saw how few they really were. As part of the crowd, he'd felt they were a force to be reckoned with. In reality, only five villagers had offered their awakened —not a lot for something as large as a province.

"Grab on," the soldier said, extending his right arm.

"What's your name?" Dallion asked.

The soldier blinked, paused, then narrowed his eyes. "Why?"

"Since you'll be our trainer, I thought we should know how to address you."

Several waves of emotions passed through the soldier's face. The only ones that Dallion was able to catch with his perception level were surprise, wonder, and a split second of gratitude.

"Kalis," the man replied. Clearly, no one had called him a trainer before. "I'll just be showing you the basics. A word of advice, don't get your hopes up," he quickly added in a harsher voice. "Let's go."

ITEM AWAKENING

Once more, Dallion found himself in an unknown space. This time, it was similar to a training room. Weapons and target dummies were scattered about in an almost chaotic fashion. Kalis was also present, as were Gloria and Veil.

A blue rectangle emerged but was quickly waved away by the soldier before anyone could read the specifics of the realm.

"It'll take us a few days to find the chainling," Kalis began. "That gives you about ten training sessions at most, so don't waste them! Have any of you used a dartbow before?"

"Naturally," Veil said in a smug fashion, looking sideways to Dallion.

I really hate you, you know. Dallion gritted his teeth.

"I haven't." Dallion raised his hand. "Other than when I got it…" That had been a bit of an embarrassment.

"It's simple. Aim and squeeze the trigger. Your attack skills will handle the rest. Just keep one thing in mind. Out there, you won't get to see any markers. You'll have to rely on what you've learned." The soldier waved a finger at Veil's face, almost drilling a hole in his nose. "No shortcuts! Got it?"

In response, the blond drew his weapon in one move and shot a bolt right in the head of a nearby training dummy.

"Like that?"

One had to admit Veil was quite good at it. Maybe he didn't have the perception of his sister or the reflexes of Dallion, but he had spent a large part of his bored life fighting, in and out of awakened state.

"Passable," Kalis turned to Gloria. "Can you match that?"

Calmly, the girl aimed and fired two shots. Both bolts hit the same target, burying themselves an inch on either side. Having good perception had its advantages.

"Not bad. Where did you learn to use a dartbow like that?"

"Family heirloom," Gloria replied.

"Fair enough. How about you?" Kalis asked Dallion.

There was no response. It was abundantly clear Dallion had never held such a weapon before now.

"Just try to hit the target, okay?" the soldier said.

Deep breaths, Dallion told himself as he went into position. There was no way he was letting himself be outdone. Gripping the weapon as tightly as he could, he aimed just above Veil's bolt and slowly squeezed. The projectile darted out almost instantly, hitting its target dead on.

"Darude," Dallion whispered beneath his breath.

"Okay." The soldier nodded a few times. "You're not a lost cause after all. At least I won't have to explain the boring stuff."

"Training is over?" Veil frowned. "I was expecting something a bit more challenging. Can't we get a moving target at least? Or fight against each other?"

"Who told you training is over?" The hard edge in the Kalis' voice made all three of them freeze in place. "I just said we'll skip the boring stuff. The real training starts now."

All weapons and target dummies vanished in the blink of an eye. A large cage emerged at the far end of the room. Only darkness was visible inside, as if the cage contained the night sky.

COMBAT INITIATED

"In one minute, the cage will open," Kalis said with a wicked smile. "It's up to you three to survive for five minutes. Those who don't won't get any food. Use any skills you have."

"That's it?" Droplets of sweat appeared on Gloria's forehead. "Don't we get any advice?"

"Work together, don't get cornered, and try not to die too fast."

"What if we kill it?" Dallion asked.

There was a moment of silence. All eyes turned toward Kalis. Everyone wanted to know the answer, though no one other than Dallion dared to ask the question. There was no doubt achieving such a feat would be difficult, but with three people, it was theoretically possible. It wasn't that long ago that Dallion and Gloria had defeated a vastly superior sand dragon by working together, and that was before either of them had ranged weapons.

"Kill it?" The soldier laughed. "Kill it, and I'll give each of you a silver coin."

It wasn't the level increase Dallion had been hoping for, but a silver coin was nothing to sneeze at.

"You're on." Dallion cracked his neck. He had one huge advantage the soldier hadn't taken into account—he had a buckler and the skills to use it.

PRACTICE GUARDIAN

PRACTICE GUARDIAN
Species: UNKNOWN
Class: UNKNOWN
Health: UNKNOWN
Traits: UNKNOWN
Skills: UNKNOWN
Weakness: UNKNOWN

The cage burst open, releasing the darkness within. Black strands whirled through the air, giving form to the unknown creature. This was the first time Dallion saw a species depicted as "unknown." Even when his perception was low, the white rectangle still gave the species' name and class. In this case, it was as if the creature had somehow surrounded itself in a shroud of invisibility that even the awakening state couldn't pierce.

The smoke swirled and twisted, gaining a semblance of a form that shifted from one state to another. This was the calm before the storm. All three trainees came to the same realization in less than a second and reacted in an entirely different fashion. Gloria used her acrobatic skills to leap back as far as possible, holding the dartbow tightly in front of her. Veil, being an attacker, shot three bolts at the silhouette. As for Dallion, he took a defensive side-stand, raising his buckler just enough to cover the upper part of his torso.

Where are you? Dallion kept his eyes on the creature, waiting for the defense markers to appear. He knew the creature would attack—anything that had to be kept in a cage had to do so given an opportunity—and yet, it chose not to.

Three black strands emerged from the silhouette, grabbing hold of the bolts before they could hit their target. Dallion swallowed. This wasn't a good sign. Two glowing red eyes emerged in the darkness, followed by a series of sharp blue teeth...very large blue teeth.

Green markers appeared, though they weren't usual markers. In the past, defense markers had always indicated where the creature was about to attack, yet this was the first time Dallion was given a choice between three completely different targets. Three green lines started from the creature's mouth, linking it to Dallion's left leg, Veil's right arm, and Gloria's throat.

The range was rather large for hesitation, larger than anything Dallion had experienced before. At the same time, the lines were extremely precise, focusing on their targets like lasers.

"Look out!" Dallion shouted, realizing the situation.

It had to be a pack creature. That was the only thing that made sense. Within seconds, it was probably going to split in three and attack each of them.

Set off by the shout, the creature reacted. All three lines disappeared as the black silhouette leapt forward, ignoring Dallion completely, heading straight for Veil. The speed was such that the blond barely managed to shoot one more bolt before blue glowing teeth sank into his throat.

FATAL WOUND
VEIL LUOR's health has been reduced by 100%.

A red rectangle appeared just as Veil poofed out of existence. By now, he was probably back in the real world, contemplating a day without supper. That wasn't Dallion's main concern, though. Two new sets of defense markers had appeared.

"Gloria, get here!" he shouted, aiming at the creature.

The moment the red pointer touched the monster's back, Dallion squeezed the trigger. The bolt split the air, almost as fast as a bullet, and just as all the ones before, it failed to reach its target. This time, the creature jumped to its left, avoiding the attack with ease.

Dallion shot again, then again, and again. Bolts flew along the trajectory line like a stream, each missing by a few inches each time. It was almost as if the creature toyed with Dallion while directing its attention toward the real threat—Gloria.

The girl seemed to be perfectly aware of that, for she continued to retreat. It wouldn't be long until she ran out of room. Once that happened, the creature would finish her off and go for Dallion.

Time appeared to slow as Dallion's mind went through the options. He didn't have the speed to take the creature in a close combat attack, and all of his ranged attacks were easily avoided.

I need more time, he thought.

Maybe charging could end up being the solution? He didn't need to kill it himself, just cause a good enough distraction for Gloria to do so. With her perception level, she'd easily be able to locate the beast's weak spots and fire at them.

Just give up, a voice whispered in the back of his mind. *There's no point in trying so hard. This isn't the real thing, it's just an exercise. No one will get hurt. At most, they'll skip a meal.*

That much was true. There wouldn't be anything lost if Dallion just gave up. And even if by some miracle he managed to defeat the guardian, what would happen? A silver coin sounded like a lot, but it wasn't going to let him buy anything he couldn't already get. At best, it would be several seasons until a traveling merchant passed by.

"No!" Dallion shouted. *I'm not giving up!*

The creature snarled, its jaws moving throughout its body to snap in the direction of Dallion. Unfortunately, that couldn't constitute a distraction. He had to do something else, and fast.

Dallion glanced at his weapon. Given it was made of a metal he knew nothing of, he wouldn't be able to improve it, even if it were possible to enter another realm. The rules on that were pretty clear, but they also gave Dallion an interesting idea. There was one option he hadn't tried.

Please, work. Dallion grabbed his right hand with his left.

REALM LINK

A green rectangle emerged. More importantly, a doorway formed in the nearby wall. This definitely wasn't what Dallion had in mind, but he took what he could get. Caught by surprise, the practice guardian leapt away like a cat seeing a cucumber.

"Get ready!" Dallion shouted and removed the buckler from his arm.

I want to do a defensive attack, he thought.

A single set of green and red markers appeared: a dash of footsteps forward, followed by a twist, and release of the shield, just like throwing a discus. Dallion had never thrown a discus in his life. He had barely seen it done at the Olympics. Now was the time to try it out.

Without hesitation, he ran forward. His feet matched each step perfectly. Two sequences later, time came to a stop—a real stop, not just a trick of his mind. Four steps more, and Dallion held the buckler as the marker in the air indicated, twisted, and released it at the precise moment. The shield split the air, following a trajectory toward the beast's head. The attack didn't stop there, though. One more set of markers remained—red markers indicating the optimal spot from which Dallion could shoot his dartbow. Dallion did just that.

Time returned to normal, along with a loud *thump* as the buckler struck the monster in the head.

DAZED EFFECT
??? has been dazed.
???'s actions will be performed at 50% speed for the next ten seconds.

Best choice of first item ever, Dallion thought.

The bolt once again missed its target, as Dallion suspected it would, but it didn't matter. The distraction had been long enough for Gloria to join the fight.

COMBINATION ATTACK
Dealt Damage is increased by 200%

CRITICAL STRIKE
Dealt Damage is increased by 200%

MOMENT OF GLORY

The creature let out a blood-freezing roar as it leapt away from Gloria. Without the status information, there was no telling how much health it had remaining, but the damage was obvious. The beast's movements, although still impressively fast, were hesitant, as if it had to think twice before performing the simplest action.

"The left side!" Gloria shouted as she leapt off the ground, doing a wall run that would have put the majority of Earth movies to shame. "Shoot at its left side!"

On cue, red markers appeared on the relevant side of the creature, perfect targets for Dallion to take advantage of. Bolts filled the air, coming from both sides. This time, every second one hit its mark. While most of Gloria's were deflected by a cluster of black strands emerging from the creature's morphing body, Dallion's weren't.

Just a little bit more, Dallion thought. As strong as the creature was, it wasn't invulnerable. For a moment, he caught a glimpse of his buckler. The small shield was on the floor, less than a brief dash away. With a bit of effort, Dallion could run past the creature and grab it.

A new set of green markers appeared. Only one option was given, a dash to the spot where Gloria would land. From there, he was expected to protect her with his own body, taking the brunt of the creature's attacks. It was interesting that the guard skill remained functional even when Dallion didn't have his shield. Unfortunately, it didn't provide any way to retrieve said shield.

There were several pros and cons to the situation. If Dallion were to follow the markers, he'd give Gloria a chance of victory at the price of him losing his supper. It could be said this was the logical thing to do. Her skills were far better suited to the situation, not to mention she'd had more practice with the dartbow. On the other hand, Dallion could reclaim his shield and try a repeat of his attack. This could potentially create some short-term tension between him and the girl, though nothing that couldn't be resolved later. Besides, a silver was nothing to laugh at, and who knows, maybe he'd even impress the rest of the group?

The decision merited a few seconds' consideration, which Dallion did while rushing toward Gloria. Upon reaching her, the only conclusion he'd come to was another question: *Why not both?*

"Stay behind me!" Dallion grabbed her in a hug-like embrace, then turned his back in the direction of the creature. There was no way his body could match the sturdiness of a buckler but, for all intents and purposes, it would hopefully be enough to cushion one blow.

To Dallion's surprise, Gloria also had a plan. Initially, she moved in lockstep, allowing Dallion to position himself between her and the creature. At the same time, she took the dartbow out of his hand. Since he wasn't going to use it, Dallion let her have it.

The girl's action didn't end here, however. Instead of waiting patiently for the creature to slash Dallion out of his awakened state, she extended both arms on either side of him. Each hand held a dartbow, and each was aimed at the creature's head. Moments later, four bolts flew forward.

MULTI ATTACK
Dealt damage is increased by 400%

CRITICAL STRIKE
Dealt Damage is increased by 200%

Talk about damage. Dallion smiled. With so many multipliers, there was no way the monster would last for much longer. In a worst-case scenario, Gloria would slowly bleed it out, running, jumping about, and firing the occasional bolt. A pity he wouldn't see it happen.

GUARDIAN DEFEATED

I stand corrected, Dallion thought.

Next thing he knew, he was at the camp again. He, Veil, and Gloria were all still holding the soldier's arm, who now looked at them with an entirely different expression. He was obviously pleased with their victory. Even more, he was impressed.

"I could have gotten him." Veil moved his hand off with a grumble. "Let me have another go. I'll get it this time!"

"You only get one go in real life," Kalis snapped. "You get bread for supper. Mess up next time, and you get less."

Veil let out a faux laugh, trying to appear that such things were beneath him. Dallion could clearly see the blond was furious at his defeat. It was written all over his face.

"You'll get a silver," the soldier said to Gloria, making her blush slightly. "Good speed, good approach, keep it up."

The girl nodded.

"And you…" Kalis pointed at Dallion. "…you get to eat your supper."

"What?" Dallion blinked. The realization that he wouldn't get a reward felt like a sharp slap on his face. "Why? I was alive when

233

the creature was killed!" *Standard team victory, yo!* Any multi-player game would agree. "Why don't I get a silver?"

"Because you're reckless and dumb as a brick in winter!"

Dallion raised a finger to say something, then suddenly stopped. A brick in winter? What did that even mean?

"You triggered your awakening," the soldier said.

"Yeah? We all did."

"No. You triggered your awakening, and through that, linked it to mine. Have you any idea how reckless that is? You're not even fully awakened! You've no idea how to protect your awakening room, and yet you opened the door for anyone to go inside! What if I had made my echo go in there? You might as well give back your pendant and save us all some time and agony."

Dallion didn't say a word. It had seemed a good idea when fighting the beast. In truth, it was the only idea he'd had. Looking back now, it wasn't his best. Kalis was absolutely right. Doing something without knowing the consequences was worse than doing nothing at all.

"Look," the soldier put his hand on Dallion's shoulder, "you got the right idea. As the only one with guard skills, creating opportunities for others is what you should do, but not at the expense of yourself. A guard who's dead isn't much of a guard."

"I understand."

"That's good. Enjoy your food, then get some rest."

Typical soldier behavior. It was obvious even to Veil that Kalis was somewhat proud of their achievement, yet he never voiced that sentiment. Instead, he turned around with a stern expression and started walking away.

"One question," Dallion asked before Kalis got too far away. "How many killed the chainling echo on their first go?"

"Chainling?" The soldier looked over his shoulder. "That wasn't a chainling. That was just a strand-lynx cub. A chainling is something it's better to see just once, or even not at all."

BELT BUCKLE MEETING

Walking, training, food, and rest; those were the activities associated with the hunting party, as the soldiers called the group. There was nothing glorious or special about it. The only thing that made them different from troops on Earth was the ability to condense everything other than walking in three neat thirty-minute segments. It turned out that sleep in an awakened realm was just as adequate as the real thing, provided one didn't do it for more than a real time week.

Dallion found the notion fascinating in its simplicity. Up to now, he had never thought of using his awakening powers in such a way. His mother and grandfather had insisted the real world was for sleeping and the awakened state was for training. Of course, back in the village, everyone had time to spare. Here, time was a luxury the hunting party didn't have.

The group kept marching day and night. Every morning and evening, the cleric would have a discussion with Dame Vesuvia, then point them in a new direction. Everyone else would follow without hesitation. There was no indication any of them used a map, and even the few instances Dallion was close enough to overhear the conversations, no specific region names were mentioned.

Meanwhile, the training continued. Three times per day, Karis gathered the group and had them face a new echo. There was no offer of rewards, just observations, instructions, and the occasional smack on the head. To Dallion's annoyance, he got smacked about as often as Veil. Gloria, on the other hand, had yet to be punished. It was almost unbelievable that the "spoiled" girl whose leading focus was perception could be such a good fighter.

Veil had also shown incredible improvement. Two training sessions were enough for him to find the monster's pattern and start using his force efficiently. What was more, he had started relying on Dallion for defense. The hatred between the two had slowly been put on pause, replaced by rivalry, with each trying to outdo the other. Initially, it was a foregone conclusion—Dallion had two skills, not to mention that his speed gave him a vast advantage. However, Veil had quickly caught up and surpassed him using brute strength alone.

Looking at him, Dallion could see the effects of having a high body trait. The blond was stronger, faster, and more vigorous by far, only focused on one specific thing. At the start of the trip, Dallion had mistakenly seen him as a hammer. Now, he viewed him as a precision scalpel that focused its attack at a single point with extreme force.

On the third day, things changed. Word spread that the trail of the chainling had been found, indicating they could catch up with the creature in the next day or so. This prompted a reorganization of the hunting party. The volunteers were moved from the back to the middle. Dame Vesuvia remained in front, with the cleric nearby. No one was allowed to venture far from the group, and all eating was to be done while walking. Rest and training, while maintaining their normal length in the awakened realms, were reduced to ten real time seconds.

"Hey." Veil approached Dallion as they walked. "I want to ask you something."

Dallion nodded and waited. Seconds passed, continuing up to a minute and, the entire time, the blond remained silent.

"Well?" Dallion asked, slightly annoyed.

"Not here."

That was all Dallion needed to know. Apart from the obvious, training had taught him one other thing, how to invite or be invited in an awakened realm. Without another word, he grabbed Veil's hand.

ITEM AWAKENING

You are in a small metal room.
Complete the trial to improve the BELT BUCKLE's destiny!

"Seriously?" Dallion gave Veil an amused look. "A belt buckle?"

"It's the first thing I thought of, okay?" Veil snapped. "What's wrong with it?"

"Nothing, just…a belt buckle." He shook his head.

"Anyway, you heard about the chainling, right? We'll probably get to fight it soon. Maybe tonight."

"I doubt it. Havoc said it'll still be a few days."

"What does he know?" Veil frowned. For some reason, he and the orange-haired giant hadn't gotten along very well. "Also, that doesn't change the facts."

"The facts?"

"We're trash. We're worse than trash. We're weak trash."

Despite Veil's obsession with repetition, Dallion had to admit he was right. In the entire hunting party, there was only one level two. All the other volunteers were threes, with a few notable exceptions. That was part of the reason Gloria got special treatment—better food, more detailed training instructions and, on one occasion, a chat with Dame Vesuvia herself.

"If we're to do anything, we need to get stronger."

"Veil, we're in the middle of nowhere. It's not like there are many people who'd be impressed with—"

"I'm not talking about impressing people! I'm talking about surviving!"

In a person's life, there were many instances in which their opinion about something was completely changed from one single event. In the case of Veil, this was that event. A simple clarification had made Dallion look upon him in a way he never had before. In the past, he had always thought of Veil as a bully, someone who looked at the weak with disdain and enjoyed humiliating them. Even the recent rivalry hadn't been enough to change Dallion's mind. However, there was another side to Veil as well—he wanted to protect people.

"Everything counts in large amounts. We might be useless trash shooting needles from the back lines, but every bit stronger we get will help." There was a long pause. "I can't let Gloria do this alone, and I think you can't either."

Wow. When you go, you go deep.

"I'll try to break through to the next level," Veil continued. "I think you should do the same."

"How? I've been trying to do that for days! Besides, it's not like there's an awakening shrine anywhere nearby."

"The cleric. He was able to tell our levels just by looking at us. Maybe he knows of a way I could become level four as well."

"Maybe…" *Why didn't I think of this?* "It'll probably be danger-ous, though. I don't know about you, but getting to level three was a pretty rough fight."

"Of course, it'll be difficult! That's what I'm telling you for! Weren't you supposed to be the smart one?!"

The smart one? Local standards had to be quite low, especially given most of the good realizations Dallion had made were in hindsight.

"Anyway, I'll either get there or I won't. That's not the point. You need to find a way to get stronger as well. If not through the cleric, some other way. Got it?"

"Got it."

"You better." Veil smiled. "I'll kick your ass home and back if you don't."

THREAD OF SMOKE

There was no way of telling whether Veil succeeded or not. In the course of the day, he approached the cleric, then walked back to the volunteer group without a word. Dallion suspected that a longer conversation had taken place in an awakened realm, possibly accompanied by a trial. No one had shared the results of the outcome, but based on Veil's expression, they probably weren't too good.

So much for getting to level four, Dallion thought. That didn't change their previous conversation, though. Dallion had to become stronger before they ran into the beast. The only question was how. Given the training regimen, there was no time for further awakenings, so Dallion couldn't improve objects for personal practice. Furthermore, thanks to Veil's blunder, Dallion didn't think asking the cleric was a good idea anymore. Not to mention things weren't all that good between him and the albino.

Ever since the "practice session" with the dartbow, the cleric seemed to resent Dallion for no clear reason. At first, the youth thought it was all his imagination. It wasn't like the cleric was particularly talkative or close to anyone. However, with time, more and more clues stacked up.

Asking for help from Gloria wasn't an option either. By order of the dame, she had been moved farther to the front of the group along with the sole other level four. When Dallion tried to find out the reason for this change, he had been told to shut up and keep walking. Not the most trust-inspiring reaction one could hope for.

"Don't worry." Havoc approached. "She's in better hands than the lot of us."

"What do you mean?"

"She's a four. Parties tend to protect those. At least more than us losers." The large man laughed. "Shouldn't complain too much, though. Could have been worse. We could have been twos." He looked over his shoulder at a scared boy of fifteen, who constantly stared at the ground as he walked.

"What happens to twos?" Dallion asked.

"Nothing much. The soldiers won't go out of their way to save them if things get bad. Then again, you can't be sure about anything during hunts. What happens happens, so why waste time worrying about it, right?" He gave Dallion a pat on the back, almost knocking him to the ground.

A few steps away, Veil snorted, though didn't voice any comments.

"You know a lot about hunts," Dallion grumbled.

"You live a long life, you pick up a thing or two. Also, this isn't my first party."

"Oh?" This sparked Dallion's interest, but not only his. Veil, along with another few people within earshot, casually moved closer, trying to listen in on the conversation.

"It's no big deal." Havoc shrugged. "Every few years, some bad beastie starts causing problems, and some unfortunate squad or other has to go and kill it. Most of the time, it's the hunters who deal with it, but I guess the nobles can only trust mercenaries that much."

"If it's that often, how come we've never heard about it?"

Dallion asked, wondering if the events of Ogre's Gorge had been the result of a hunt. Having two tribes of monsters completely wipe themselves out was way too convenient to be true.

"It's inevitable to happen, even in the middle of nowhere. I guess you've just been lucky so far."

"Does that mean—"

"On guard!" Dame Vesuvia shouted.

The hunting party reacted immediately, springing into action like a well-oiled machine. The majority of soldiers spread out, forming a circle, while Kalis, along with the other trainers, went to their respective groups, giving out dartbow bolts and strings.

"You've got five shots," he said as he shoved the bolt pack in Dallion's hands. "Make them count."

"What's going on?" Dallion whispered.

Kalis looked him in the eyes for several seconds, then gave a pack to Veil.

"Don't get yourselves killed," he added.

Dallion felt shivers down his spine. No further explanations were necessary. The group had finally found what they were looking for.

The bolt pack was made to fit the dartbow perfectly. Dallion watched as people around him clicked it into place with one swift action, after which they placed the string to the sides of the weapon's limb. Silently, he did the same.

Five shots...not nearly as many as he'd used in training. Both he and Veil had been generous with the number of shots, often using the weapon as a repeater gun. Only Gloria had tried to be more conservative, only shooting when she absolutely had to. Given the strict limitation, Dallion doubted she'd manage to do much better either.

"Don't waste your bolts!" Kalis shouted for all to hear. "Shoot only if your life is in danger! Don't charge, don't try to help us, and don't break the circle!"

More clicks followed, as the group prepped their weapons, followed by silence. Dallion stood, trying to see over the circle of soldiers. With the exception of a few hills nearby and a chain of snow-covered mountains in the distance, there was nothing remarkable in the area, just cold grassy plains continuing on and on.

There has to be something, Dallion thought. *A city, a village, or even—*

Then he noticed it—smoke in the distance. Little more than a black thread, it rose into the sky, originating from relatively close by. Dallion rose on his toes to try and see more, but Havoc grabbed him by the shoulder, slamming him back down.

"Don't," the red-haired man whispered. "You'll see it soon enough."

The entire group fell silent to the point that steps, even the occasional movement of chainmail, could be heard.

"How close is it?" Dame Vesuvia asked, drawing a two-piece sword. Back on Earth, the weapon would be pegged as a cheap movie prop and mercilessly ridiculed and laughed at. Here, its power radiated even from a distance. The two blade halves—shaped like a tuning fork—were never meant to be the cutting part; they merely held the real blade, created from what could only be described as hardened air.

The tension was so thick that one could cut it with a knife. For the first time since he was there, Dallion stared at his own mortality. He wasn't the only one. Not only the volunteers, but the soldiers, who were otherwise more annoyed than bothered, gripped their weapons tightly, focused on what was before them.

Slowly, the cleric stepped further away from the circle. His steps almost echoed in the utter silence. A dozen feet later, he stopped and pulled back his hood. For the briefest of moments, Dallion thought he saw bloody cracks form on part of his exposed skin.

"It's not here," the cleric said. "This is just the aftermath."

Internally, Dallion let out a sigh of relief. It seemed he was going to live one more day.

"It's half a day away," the cleric added, pulling his hood back on. "Fifteen hours at most. It did its thing and moved on."

"By the Crippled's luck! That's the last thing I needed!" The dame scowled. "Did it heal?"

"Maybe. I'll need to check the spot to know more. Either way, if we don't hurry, it'll get stronger."

"You're sure it's not hiding?"

There was a long pause. Dallion, like many others, held his breath. He didn't know the specifics of the conversation, but his imagination did a pretty good job of filling in the blanks.

"It's nowhere near," the cleric replied after a while. "I'll go and check the spot. Then we—"

"No," the dame interrupted. "We all go. I'll need you close in case we lose the trail again."

"We can't waste time, Initiate. I'll go see. You need to continue on its trail. If it finds more health bags, you might not be able to take it down."

"That is not your decision to make, Cleric!" The woman's voice had a force behind it that could make steel snap. Dallion felt as if a gust of wind had hit him in the chest. Judging by the reaction of the people nearby, he wasn't the only one.

"Yes, Initiate." The cleric bowed. "By the Seven Moons."

"By the Seven." The dame sheathed her sword. "Double march forward!" she ordered. "Heavy troops in front, volunteers in the back! Keep your eyes peeled and don't stop until told to!"

THE CARAVAN

The source of fire turned out to be the remains of several wooden wagons. As the hunting party approached, Dallion was able to see more details of the scene, and just as Havoc had predicted, he wished he hadn't. People and beasts of burden were scattered on the ground, charred or ripped to pieces, sometimes both. The remains of two large wagons lay smoldering, most of their wheels bashed off. Whatever beast had done this, it had to be fast, strong, and extremely bloodthirsty...just like the practice guardian Dallion had faced so many times in the last few days.

"Any survivors?" Dallion whispered, turning to Havoc, who was tall enough to get a better view.

The large man shook his head.

Not too far away, Gloria vomited on the ground. The smell of living remains, tolerable for Dallion and the rest of the volunteers, proved too strong for her.

Dame Vesuvia raised her hand, indicating for the group to stop. Shortly after, she continued on her own a few feet farther. Her trusted horse attempted to resist, but a slight pull of the reins let it know that the noble wouldn't tolerate disobedience.

"It's not here," the cleric said in a partially told-you-so voice.

"I want lookouts!" Dame Vesuvia shouted. "Three pairs. If you spot anything, come back here! The rest of you search the remains. I want to know exactly what happened here. Volunteers, help in!"

Six soldiers rushed off in three directions as ordered. The rest relaxed their guard and dispersed throughout the area. With fewer people in one spot, the degree of devastation was far more visible. The group that had been slaughtered had been large, possibly larger than the hunting party itself. Over a dozen bodies—or the pitiful remains of such—could be seen in the vicinity alone, with more clustered further away. Quite a few of them had weapons, though there were also those who didn't, suggesting that the group had been traveling with an armed escort.

"You two." Kalis pointed to Dallion and Veil. "Come here!"

Dallion's stomach churned, but he obeyed. Veil didn't seem to have such an issue, for not only did he go to the soldier without hesitation, but he glanced over a smoldering corpse nearby.

"Soldiers?" he asked, bending down to relieve the corpse of the sword in its hand.

"Mercenaries more like," Kalis replied, then removed the black rag that had once probably been a shirt of some sort. A glittering locket appeared, hanging around the body's neck. Surprisingly, other than a bit of blood, it didn't seem damaged in any way. "Merchant emblem!" Kalis shouted. "Foreign."

Fighting the discomfort in his stomach, Dallion moved closer to get a better look. The emblem seemed similar to the one he'd been given, but it was also different. Instead of six gems, it was composed of three metal rings, one within another. The outmost one was made of bluish silver, the middle one appeared to be gold, and the innermost seemed like red copper.

The discovery caused some commotion. Soon, other soldiers yelled to confirm that they, too, had found similar emblems as well.

"Merchant caravan," the dame said with an unusual amount of

dislike. "Where do you think they were going? There aren't any trading cities this far south."

"They don't need a city to trade, Initiate," the cleric said, causing Dallion to glance at him over his shoulder. "Especially if it saves them some coin."

"Black market trading?" Vesuvia didn't seem convinced.

"As you yourself said, there's nothing this far south. The chance of anyone stumbling on them by accident is next to none. A perfect place to exchange illicit goods, or something more blasphemous."

"Slaughtered by a chainling during a secret meeting. It would have been poetic if it wasn't so serious."

"The Seven only protect those who accept protection," the albino reminded.

"Find what they were carrying. If it's something the chainling can use, I want to know."

The cleric nodded, then moved away. Dallion tried to see where he was going but was suddenly interrupted.

"Hey, give me a hand," Veil said, bringing Dallion's attention back onto the corpse. "Grab his boots and help me turn over."

"What's that for?"

"I want to check something without having him break up in my hands."

Imagining the colorful event made Dallion's last meal roil. Even so, he had no intention of backing out. If he were to face the chainling, he'd see far worse.

As the duo turned the body around, a new series of wounds emerged, two dozen incisions tearing through the dead man's clothes, each as if made by a dagger.

"I knew it." Veil smiled. "You can let go."

"What is it?" Dallion asked.

"He wasn't bitten and then burned. He was burned because he was bitten. It's just like the thing we've been training against."

"I don't remember any of that."

"That's because you never got seriously bitten. When the creature bites deep, it feels like fountains of flames bursting through you. I thought it was part of the training, but it looks like it's the real thing as well."

There were so many questions Dallion didn't want to ask. Not mentioning this during all their training discussions was one thing. Knowing what getting burned from within felt like was outright disturbing. Thinking back, there had been rumors the village chief was merciless, punishing the members of his own family if they became too uppity. Surely, though, he wouldn't go that far against his own grandchildren…or would he?

"A chainling can do that?" Dallion asked.

Things were becoming more and more complicated by the day. Dallion looked around. Kalis had gone off to show the merchant emblem to Dame Vesuvia. Everyone else was a fair distance away, although, at their awakened level, they likely had the perception to hear anything said.

"If the chainling does that, being in the back rows won't be very safe either," Dallion whispered so only Veil could hear.

"I guess." The blond didn't seem worried in the least. "It's not like there's much we can do. I'll go check if there's anything left in the wagons. Lend a hand?"

How can you be so blind?! Dallion wanted to shout. Veil was behaving as if someone had removed his common-sense gland. Why couldn't he understand what Dallion was trying to say? If the chainling could turn people into a flamethrower, then standing behind one would make things more dangerous, not less. At least in front, one could do something to evade. Being stuck in the back only doomed them to a terrified existence, waiting for the inevitable. It would be better if they deserted the hunting party and took their chances in the wilderness alone, instead of—

Dallion didn't finish that thought. Rather, a new one had popped into his head.

Why am I so terrified? he wondered. The danger was real, he could see that, but that couldn't be the reason he was getting more and more frightened by the day. Ever since the initial victory against the practice guardian, he had been acting more and more cautiously to the point he was afraid of trying anything new.

"Afraid…" Dallion whispered. *There's no reason for me to be so afraid. Unless I'm not actually the one who's terrified.*

Taking a deep breath, Dallion took his dartbow out of its holster. A moment later, the scene of carnage vanished.

LIMITING ECHO

D allion took a deep breath. Entering the library in his awakened realm became more difficult each time. When his grandfather had told him about it, he'd been curious. The second time, he'd been cautious. Now, after the scribe echo had tried to kill him with feathers, he was outright terrified.

Clutching his emblem with his left hand, Dallion forced himself to cross the threshold. The instant he did, he felt the weight of two mountains on his shoulders.

"So, you decided to come back." the scribe said, arms crossed. The table had vanished, replaced by an even larger desk just as messy as before. "Didn't have enough last time?" He raised a finger in the air.

Dallion knew perfectly well what would follow. Dozens of voices filled his mind, yelling for him to get out as quickly as possible. Pain, terror, regret, all piled on him like a wall of bricks. In that single instant, Dallion felt like a small defenseless animal being driven in a corner. The only means to escape was to run back out through the door while he still had the chance.

No! He gritted his teeth. *I have to get stronger. I have to be able to face a chainling. I have to…*

"Still here?" The scribe sounded somewhat surprised.

"Y-yes!" Dallion managed to mutter. "I-I-I think there's something y-you should know."

"Is that so?" The echo took a step closer. "Tell me, before I kick you out and—"

Dallion didn't let the scribe finish. Drenched in sweat, he raised his dartbow and took one shot right at the echo's chest.

"Huh?" The scribe didn't even react. There was a single *poof*, after which the scribe vanished, along with the crushing atmosphere of the room.

That was it? Dallion blinked.

Now that it was over, it was so anticlimactic, it felt disappointing. Moments ago, Dallion had imagined an entirely different scenario involving quills darting at him from all sides and running about the room in an effort to evade them. The faithful shot that had killed the echo was aimed to be nothing more than a provocation to the things rolling. Dallion had been absolutely certain it would be evaded. Not that Dallion was complaining. Getting rid of the echo's burden made him feel like on the first day of spring break.

I've been living in fear of that?!

The mist of terror left Dallion's mind, replaced by dozens of questions and a thirst for answers. There were so many things he wanted to learn, hundreds he wanted to try.

Suddenly, dozens of the pieces of paper that cluttered the room crackled. Minuscule flames flickered along the edge, quickly eating through them.

The map! Dallion rushed to the desk. He remembered there was one hiding among the papers written by the echo. That was something he knew he couldn't lose at any cost. As he brushed them off, something caught Dallion's eye.

You're never to leave the village.
Going to the cities is bad.

You'll never survive there.
Stay in the village where it's safe.

Those and many more phrases covered the pages burning up. Each had been an order, a whisper in the back of Dallion's mind, telling him what to do and what to ignore.

"That's what's been keeping me in the village?" Dallion looked at the pieces of paper crumble before his eyes. Morbid curiosity tempted him to read through all the scribe's notes just to see how much damage the echo had done. Common sense made him focus on more important things.

Here we go! Dallion brushed off the burning papers, revealing a large map. This likely represented all Dallion's "local" knowledge about the world—not much judging by the many blank spots, but at least it was a start.

Apparently, the world was of a late medieval type, following an evolved feudal model. The Tamin Empire—of which Dallion's village was part of—was said to span half the world, although Dallion had serious doubts that was true. The Wetie province was one of the several major areas ruled by an archduke. In this case, Archduke Lanitol.

Dallion knew next to nothing about the noble, but his grandfather had told him enough of the noble ranks to know that the title put him one step beneath the emperor himself.

The village of Dherma, along with another handful of villages, was located in the southwest reaches of the empire next to a whole lot of nothing. The village itself had been founded by the Imperial Knight Sir Kaan generations ago during one of the empire's waves of expansion. It had been of minor significance even back then, so it had come as no surprise that after his death, the domain would be left to utter neglect.

Lacking an owner, the land eventually entered the domain of Count Priscord, who had no interest in it whatsoever and let the villages fend for themselves. Ever since, the local villages had been self-governed.

That explained a few things. For one, Dallion now knew why the village chief was so obsessed with echoing everyone and keeping them from leaving the village. If the people learned what was out there, a lot of the younger generation would have left to seek their luck and fortune elsewhere. Such an option threatened the Luor monopoly of power.

Dallion looked at the library of books. There were quite a few of them—knowledge of the world, knowledge how to live, even some interesting myths and folktales he'd heard as a child. All that knowledge was now his, along with the questions it brought.

Time to go back. Dallion closed his eyes. When he opened them again, he was back in the real world. From the perspective of everyone else, no more than a second had passed. The soldiers were still examining the dead bodies, grouping them in piles. If nothing else, the dame had the intention of giving them a proper burial before continuing with the hunt for the chainling.

"Dal!" Veil shouted from the remains of a wagon a short distance away. "Look what I found!"

When did I become "Dal"? "Be right there," Dallion yelled back.

Making his way to Veil, Dallion noticed the soldiers didn't seem to be interested in any of the weapons or valuables scattered about. In contrast, they were very eager to collect the merchant emblems. Kalis, along with another soldier, kept count, making sure that the number of pendants matched the corpses.

"Look what I got." Veil pulled out a sword from a nearby the wreckage. It was massive, at least four feet long, with a two-hand hilt. The ease with which the blond held it with one hand made the weapon look like a movie prop, but Dallion knew he couldn't lift it on his own. "Sky iron." Veil tapped on the side of the blade. "I think I'll keep this."

"Sure, if they let you have it." Dallion shrugged. He was a tiny bit envious, but after experiencing the awesome power of ranged combat, he wasn't losing any sleep over a sword, especially one he couldn't lift at his present level.

"Battlefield law—finders keepers." Veil swung the sword about, doing a perfect butterfly swing. "Besides, it's not like they'll give me any of their weapons."

"Guess not." Dallion nodded. "Anything else good in there?"

"Nothing much. Check if you want."

"I'll do that. You better go have a word with Kalis about your sword. If you tell him about it on your own, you'll have a better chance of keeping it."

"Right." Veil's smile vanished. "That's actually smart."

"Yeah, yeah." Dallion laughed. At the same time, he also felt pity. If the village chief had put a limiting echo into Veil's realm, a lot of simple things would probably seem complicated.

"Dal? You okay?"

Dallion looked over his shoulder. "Yeah. Why?"

"I don't know. You seem different somehow. You were all shivering a moment ago, and now you're more like you were after your awakening."

"Well, I guess I am." Dallion smiled. "I just decided to stop being afraid."

MERCHANT TOMBSTONE

T he bodies were buried without much fanfare. After everything of importance was taken from them, Dame Vesuvia had them all gathered at one spot and left the rest to the cleric. Dallion thought there would be something similar to a service, but he was vastly mistaken. Apparently, in this world, everyone accepted that the "Seven Moons" controlled every aspect of life and death, so the dead merely had to be returned to them in the most expedient fashion.

The cleric approached the pile, placed his hand on the ground, after which the earth itself opened and swallowed them. That didn't seem like an awakened power. If anything, it was closer to magic.

A clay tombstone emerged, marking the place and giving a very brief description etched on the surface.

Merchant Caravan
Killed by chainling
Year of the Seven Moons, 1205

"We move on," the dame said, turning her horse around. Shortly after, the hunting party was on the march again. The group's formation changed again. Dame Vesuvia, along with the strongest soldiers of the group, were in front leading the way while the cleric had joined the volunteers in the back. At first, Dallion thought the albino was sent here to be safe but, after a while, he realized the obvious— he was protecting them.

With the limiter echo gone, Dallion could remember the details of the Order he had heard back in Dherma. It was said that the Seven Moons granted the gift of awakening to the inhabitants of the world back during the days of the seven races. The Order was established later, to guide the chosen and protect the world from chaos and destruction. Since then, it had spread throughout the known world, helping people, advising rulers, taking care of those no one else would. Their monasteries were open to all, granting them sanctuary from pursuit, food, and—if they wished—knowledge, and the ability to join their ranks.

Everyone should have been happy that someone of that stature had joined the hunting party, yet from what Dallion had seen, they felt uneasy in his presence. Other than the noble, Veil was the only one who had dared get close to him. Even Havoc and the soldiers kept a safe distance.

"Just look at him," Gloria hissed under her breath as she glanced at her brother. "Just because he found a sword doesn't mean he's anything special. He should have given that thing away, not argued to keep it."

"He didn't exactly argue."

More likely, it was a stubborn pleading that had earned him the right to keep the weapon. The cleric was largely to thank, or blame, respectively. It was through his order that the blond was allowed to use the weapon for the time being.

"Can he use it?"

"Oh, I'm sure he's already tried. Even back home, he'd be the one trying out all sorts of weapons in his awakened state. Mother was proud, but Father despised him for it."

Of course, he would, Dallion thought. The chief's son hadn't managed to awaken. Being the linking generation between two awakened, while not one himself, must have been quite shameful, especially for someone of the Luor family. Even among the villagers, it was no secret he was viewed poorly even by the rest of his family, a fact he tried to hide through a combination of feasts and animal hunts.

"How are you?" Dallion asked. "Soldiering on?"

"I'm fine." Gloria raised her chin. "I'm a level four. I have a better chance of surviving than any of you."

That wasn't what Dallion asked, but he nodded nonetheless. Even with his meager perception, he could see her tenseness.

He changed the subject. "What do you think of the chainling? Definitely tougher than the thing we fought in practice."

Gloria went silent. For half a minute, she didn't say a word, walking on, eyes on the ground.

"There's no beating it. The dame could probably survive the fight, maybe the cleric, but none of the rest of us will." Each word was uttered in a whisper so faint, only Dallion could hear it. "The rest of us are walking to our own slaughter."

"Gloria…"

"There's no hope. The only reason I'm sticking to the group is because it'll be even worse if I run off. The soldiers know it, even the other rejects know it."

"Gloria, we're not rejects—"

"And how could it be any different? We're village-bound, we were never supposed to leave Dherma. Nothing protects us here. Nothing…"

It was obvious Gloria still had an echo, and its grip over her was getting stronger. The emblem Dallion had received had initially reduced the echo's influence, but fear had somehow reactivated it. Now, there was only one thing Dallion could do to help Gloria get stronger.

PERSONAL AWAKENING

This was the first time Dallion had invited anyone in his awakening room. It was far easier than he expected, though strange nonetheless. Thankfully, the blue rectangle displaying his level was nowhere around.

Gloria blinked several times, then froze, then finally shook her head as if rinsing the fear off her hair.

"You've got an echo, don't you?" Dallion asked.

The blonde girl nodded.

"Everyone has," she replied. "Usually, I can negotiate with it about things, but the last few days…"

"Yeah." Dallion put his hand on her shoulder. "Ever since the chainling got close. You don't have to put up with it. With the dartbow, you can just shoot it and—"

"I know you're trying to be a friend, but you're ignorant."

For some reason, the words stung.

"An echo guides and protects. If I destroy it, I'll be left on my own. You can't always charge at things head on. Sometimes, you need to pause and think a little."

"It worked out so far."

The worst part was that Dallion had no way of knowing whether Gloria was right or it was the echo weaving a web of lies to protect itself.

"Also, you won't be alone. I'm here. If anything happens, I'll take care of it. Just like we did in the awakening shrine."

"This is more serious than an awakening trial." Gloria's voice softened a bit. "Here, we can actually die."

"Only if we let it happen. We've been doing pretty well in training lately. And that was just three of us. There will be a lot more."

"The caravan had a lot more. Look what happened to them."

"Not all of them were awakened," Dallion lied. There was no

way to know for sure. So far, only part of the weapons had been special, but that was far from a guarantee. "You don't need an echo to help you. Once you get rid of it, the world will be a whole different place. Trust me on this."

Gloria didn't say a word. The struggle was written all over her face. She wanted to believe him, but also didn't dare to.

"You can trust me on this. Here." He put his dartbow in her hand. "Use this. Just like you did to get my silver coin." When in doubt, resort to humor. "I'll be waiting here."

"No." Gloria pushed the weapon back in his hand. "I need to do this alone or not at all. If I'm to be the group's scout, I can't rely on others."

The pair left Dallion's awakened realm.

AMBUSHED

G loria didn't say a word after returning to the real world. Her panic had subsided, but there was no telling whether the talk with Dallion had calmed her down, or she was simply good at hiding things. Not too long after, the group slowed. Gloria was called by the dame and sent off with another soldier to scout on ahead. Everyone else was ordered to stop and rest—a real rest, not the awakened replacement they had done so far.

The volunteers, feeling they might not get many chances after this, took the opportunity to relax a bit. The soldiers, on the other hand, were tenser than ever, keeping their eyes peeled. Interestingly enough, Havoc was also quieter than Dallion remembered him.

"What happened?" Veil whispered.

"Huh?

"I saw you with my sister. What did you talk about?"

"Oh." *Worst time to get overprotective, Veil.* "She was a bit stressed out, so—"

"What did you talk about in your awakened realm?" the blond interrupted. "Did you think I wouldn't notice? We've been training like this for days. Of course, I'll know when you pull something off like that."

That was untypically smart of Veil, so much so it had caught Dallion completely off guard. It wasn't that he had anything to hide —at least not in this instance—but rather he didn't expect to get caught by Veil, of all people.

So much for being discreet, Dallion sighed internally.

"Well?" Veil pressed on.

"We were talking about echoes."

Since Gloria knew about it, Dallion assumed that her brother might as well. And it turned out he was right. Veil's expression lit up in surprise before quickly darkening. If Dallion was to guess, unlike the rest of Dherma village, the Luors were told of this minor inconvenience to their lives.

"Your grandfather put one in every person of the village." There was no malice in Dallion's words as he said that. "I got rid of mine and told her to do the same. She didn't seem ready."

"Idiot," Veil snarled, making it impossible to determine whether he was referring to his sister or Dallion.

"How did you get rid of yours?"

"Get rid of it?" Veil snorted. "The echo's no problem. He tried bossing me around when I was young, but that was years ago. I beat him up when I was eight. After that, he's behaved. Now, he helps me when I need to figure things out."

An unexpected approach, without a doubt. Dallion could almost imagine the scene. Apparently, if someone was all brawn and adrenaline, playing mind tricks wouldn't take. If anything, this could well be the single case in the entire village in which the echo was more miserable than its host.

"Anything else?" Veil asked.

"No, nothing much. Why the sudden concern? We agreed we need to get stronger and getting rid of the echo definitely does that." *Well, maybe not in your case.* "It's not like you managed to reach level four."

"I did."

Dallion's smirk vanished. That was an answer he didn't expect.

"What? When? You didn't say anything after your talk with the cleric, so I thought…"

"I got it done on the first go." Part of Veil's natural smugness shone through. "It wasn't even difficult."

"But you were ready to chew someone's head off. I saw your face." *And I wasn't the only one.*

"That wasn't because of the trial." Veil glanced around, then moved closer. "It was what the cleric told me." He added in an even softer whisper, "He said that even with that level, we won't be able to escape our prison."

"Our prison?" An interesting choice of words. Could it be he was talking about the village? Or was there something else in play? "What did he mean by that?"

"No idea. All he said was—"

"Look out!" Havoc yelled, then grabbed Dallion and Veil by their shirts and pulled them back just in time to avoid a flaming wagon wheel that came crashing down from the sky. A wave of fire burst, throwing everyone nearby to the ground.

"Chainling!" someone yelled.

Dallion felt the heatwave, along with the weight of Havoc on top of him. The large man's armor was scorched, letting off the familiar smell of burned leather. Battle instincts kicked in. All the hours spent fighting the echo made Dallion react. Before he knew it, he was back on his feet, dartbow in hand. It was only at this point he noticed something was missing—there was no buckler on his left hand.

"You okay?" Veil stood, offering a hand to Havoc.

"Watch the sky. There might be more." Havoc let out a groan. "Can't believe it got my leg! That's what happens when you get bumped down to a three."

Chaos erupted. Soldiers ran forward, forming a defensive line.

Half the volunteers were in shock, the other half looking wildly about for other flaming projectiles in the sky.

This was the point a rectangle would appear, warning Dallion of imminent danger, along with a whole range of defense markers. At least, that was what would have happened if this were an awakened realm.

Only now did Dallion realize how easily he'd had it in the past. Fighting in a realm was structured—there many tools to aid him, each providing options with absolute certainty. It was more like playing a strategy game. Here, he had to rely on his gut and senses. Thankfully, those had improved quite a bit as well.

"Can you fight?" Dallion asked Veil.

"I'm fine," Veil replied, holding a sword in one hand and a dartbow in the other. "Where's Gloria?"

"Up ahead. Let's go get her."

"Are you crazy?" Havoc shouted. "There's a chainling out there. You won't last a minute against it."

"Is it safer here?"

As if on cue, another flaming wagon piece landed, this one half a dozen steps away.

"Besides, we don't need to fight it. We just need to find Gloria." Next to Dallion, Veil nodded. "Let's go."

"Wait!" Havoc tried to get up on his feet, but the pain in his broken leg made him crash back down. "Damn it!" he yelled, fighting the pain. "Listen, the weak spot is in the chest, right below the throat. Got that? Below the throat!"

"Got it." Dallion caught a glimpse of an abandoned dartbow nearby. Whoever its owner was, they were either dead or in no condition to use it.

Grabbing it quickly with his left hand, he rushed forward. In the distance, more flaming balls of fire appeared in the sky, but that wasn't an issue. Dallion's only concern was Gloria. The rest could wait.

RUSHING UP

It didn't take long for Dallion to dash past the protective line of soldiers. All the training he had gone through with Kalis had gotten him accustomed to the point he could almost see the guide-markers without them being there. His body strafed and swirled almost on its own, passing by people and obstacles alike. Of course, it was a plus that no one actively tried to stop him. The skilled soldiers had the goal of keeping the chainling from reaching the heart of the group. They weren't concerned with people getting out.

"To the left," Dallion shouted as he turned. Behind him, Veil followed.

While not as nimble as Dallion, the blond's physical development allowed him to keep up with ease. With his body trait, he could easily overtake Dallion at any time. Doing so, though, would leave him without direction.

"You sure this is a good idea?" Veil asked as a burning yak splattered on the ground no more than fifty feet away.

"Game theory." Dallion grinned, running on. In truth, it was more a case of "gaming theory," but the logic held true. "The hunting party and the chainling must be evenly matched. So just as we're afraid of it, it's afraid of us. The entire reason it's shelling us with chunks of burning wagons is to cause enough chaos so it can run in for the kill. The soldiers know that, so they're standing their ground."

"Shelling?" Veil asked, confused.

"Throwing things at us," Dallion corrected himself. There were still some phrases that the people of this world wouldn't make sense of.

An entire wagon roof appeared in the sky, flying directly toward Dame Vesuvia. The woman didn't budge. Remaining on her horse like a statue, she raised her sword and waited. When the mass of flaming wood came near, she performed a single strike, slicing the threat out of existence.

Whoa! Dallion thought. Would he ever be able to reach her level? Even from this distance, he could tell the strike wasn't one, but a multitude of attacks, moving faster than his senses could perceive. He had only been able to catch the slight unnatural blur, but not the actions themselves.

"There's no way I can do that," Veil said. He, too, was impressed, though, clearly, he had a much higher opinion of himself. "What if the chainling throws that at us?"

"It won't. It won't even notice us. Do you pay attention to ants when fighting a boar?"

The example made Dallion weep on the inside, but it was simple enough for the blond to grasp quickly. The explanation ran the risk of Veil starting a fuss about being compared to an ant, but thankfully, he didn't.

"Chainlings are monsters," Veil said instead. "There's no way they're that smart."

"Oh, it's smart." Dallion knew just as much about chainlings as Veil, which was to say only what he'd been told since joining the hunting party. Even so, the way the beast behaved made him come to certain conclusions. "It saved a few of the caravan wagons to use against us. Also, it let us track it down so it could ambush us."

"How are you even getting all that?"

"Think about it. It's been hunted for a week at least and, suddenly, now it starts leaving tracks? The cleric said it had regained strength by killing the caravan, so how come it's easier to track now?"

"It's overconfident?"

"Only something smart can be overconfident." Dallion grinned to himself. "And if it was, wouldn't it take us head on instead of making it seem it's running away? It's been waiting for us. Gloria, acting as a scout, forced it to tip its hand. Seeing her, it knew the rest of the group was nearby, so it started throwing things at us sooner than it thought. That's why now's our chance to go find her and get her safely away before the beast and Dame Vesuvia get really serious."

All that was speculation on Dallion's part, but he felt it to be true. The last time he'd been so convinced was when facing a MMO dungeon boss with a guild. The guild master hadn't listened to him despite being his best friend, resulting in a total wipe of the party. A few weeks later, Dallion had come across a YouTube video using his exact strategy.

Still, he'd come to the conclusion far too easily. Getting rid of the echo was one thing—Dallion had felt like he'd broken free from a full body plaster cast—but the way the ideas had popped into his head at a moment's notice was next to surreal.

Maybe this is the benefit of the mind trait? Dallion wondered. *The ability to think on my feet and come up with ideas faster than the average person?*

It was a good assumption and definitely something to keep in mind when Dallion reached level four.

"Just trust me, okay?" he said.

Dallion expected some sort of verbal confrontation from Veil or, at the very least, an attempt at sarcasm. Instead, all he got was an approving grunt. Veil had accepted him as a leader, at least for the time being.

Based on the trajectory of flying objects, Dallion had a pretty good idea where the chainling was located. The precision with which it managed to target the dame specifically, suggested that it had an unimpeded line of sight, or some other way to scope the area. In turn, that suggested Gloria couldn't have gone too far ahead.

"We need a good vantage point," Dallion said, heading up the nearest hill. Since the caravan, Dame Vesuvia had opted to focus on speed rather than anything else, choosing the flat space between hills to catch up faster. The chainling had predicted that and used the group's tactics to set up an ambush. What about Gloria, though?

Dallion felt a lump in his throat. Relying on her perception, the girl had probably come to a similar conclusion and gone in search of the highest vantage point in the area. That would have suggested she had dashed up the hill Dallion was on. However, if that were the case, why wasn't there any sign of her?

The farther up Dallion got, the more concerned he became. The game logic he had spouted a moment ago seemed all but hollow now. What if the chainling hadn't attacked the main group directly but eliminated the scout first? Or even worse, what if the dame had no intention of using Gloria as a scout but as a lure?

She's fine, the part of Dallion that had spent its life in this world insisted. *She's got to be fine.*

Pressing on, Dallion sprinted the last few hundred feet. Upon approaching the top of the hill, his heart sank. Gloria was nowhere to be seen. Instead, there were several large patches of charred grass and debris all around.

Damn it! He clenched his fists.

The chainling had targeted her after all.

"Why are you here?" a dry voice suddenly asked.

PREPARATION

The cleric emerged out of thin air. One moment, he wasn't there; the next, lines of his silhouette appeared, gradually getting filled like a paint-by-numbers picture. If there had been any doubt in Dallion's mind that the cleric had magical powers, it was now completely gone. Only magic could achieve what he'd just witnessed.

From what Dallion had been told, the magic trait was one of those believed to have been lost to the world, or at least to humanity. Those born with it were supposedly treated as national treasures. To be in the presence of such a person, one couldn't help but kneel in awe. Still, there was something that didn't match up. No one revered the cleric in any way. He was avoided, possibly even feared, but he didn't look like someone commanding the authority a magic user was supposed to have.

Surprise was replaced with relief as another form gained opacity. A step away, Gloria emerged from the air and, by the looks of it, didn't seem remotely hurt.

"I asked you a question," the cleric repeated, not in the least amused.

"We came to see what had happened with the scouting party."

Dallion kept his cool. "And to weaken the chainling so Dame Vesuvia could kill it."

The last comment created enough interest for the cleric to remove his hood. Cold red eyes stared into Dallion's, making him feel like an ant under a magnifying glass on a hot summer day.

"You aren't lying," the albino cleric noted. "You're also stupid."

"Forgive me, but didn't you come here for the same reason?" Busted, Dallion grinned on the inside. To be honest, he didn't expect for the albino to be here. If anything, his place was next to the dame.

Apparently, the albino thought the same thing, for his expression changed.

"What's your plan?" the cleric asked.

Dallion blinked. That was kind of sudden. In his mind, he had imagined a long and complicated oral argument, with dozens of points and counterpoints. Then again, arguing on a battlefield close to a chainling wasn't something anyone desired. Every moment here came at a risk, which begged the question, why hadn't the cleric invited them to his awakening room?

Oh, crap! Dallion shivered at the realization. Out of all the possibilities, only one was likely. Doing so would put them at an even greater risk. Now it became absolutely clear why Kalis had freaked out to such an extent when Dallion had linked his awakening room during their first training session. The chainling had the ability to enter the rooms of others, which meant it was an awakened beast as well.

"The chainling is still wounded," Dallion began. "If it wasn't, it wouldn't bother with long-range attacks. It's also fast enough to kill anything that's close." Or so the state of the caravan suggested. "However, it can't focus on two things at once."

The cleric remained silent.

"I'm guessing it's next to impossible to flank the creature."

"Definitely impossible for you."

"So, we don't try. Instead, we charge straight at it."

"What?" Veil gasped.

If stares could drill holes, Dallion would have been Swiss cheese by now. It wasn't only the cleric who was skeptical of such an approach, but Gloria as well. Dallion could see her frown of disapproval, along with a hint of embarrassment for being acquainted with him. Only Veil gave the idea some actual thought, wondering whether he could pull it off or not.

"We don't need to kill it; just wound it," Dallion quickly added. "That would be enough for the dame to finish it off."

There was a long moment of silence only broken by the sound of another piece of burning wagon slamming a short distance away. Dame Vesuvia had decided to shorten the distance between her and the creature, causing it to become more aggressive in its approach.

"It's now or never," Dallion urged. Maybe it was because of the echoes, maybe it was part of this world's society, but from what he had seen so far, people rarely bluffed. And that was something he could take advantage of.

"How do we wound it?" the cleric asked.

So far, so good, Dallion thought. He had gotten them to listen. Now the complicated part began.

"You can make us invisible, right?" Dallion turned to the cleric.

"Don't rely on that. The chainling doesn't need eyes to see us coming."

"That's not to hide us. It's giving us a bit more time. Veil, you're good at throwing things, right?"

"Maybe?" the blond said, suspicious of the question.

"When we get near, I want you to throw your sword at the chainling's head. Aim for the eye. Can you manage that?"

"I can hit a target from a hundred feet," Veil boasted.

"The chainling will easily deflect it." Gloria crossed her arms. "Just like the practice guardian did in training."

"I know." Dallion smiled. "I'm counting on that. So, everyone ready to go?"

A series of nods followed. A plan had come together—a very risky plan, but even if half the things said of the chainling were true, this remained the best option Dallion could think of. That, as well as the dame taking it on her own. Either way, it was time to act.

"Follow me!" Dallion rushed forward.

The rest soon followed. Dallion could hear the steps of Veil and Gloria as they ran close behind him. The cleric's presence had vanished, as if he had deserted them. The semi-transparent quality that Dallion's legs and arms had acquired, though, suggested he was nearby.

The group reached the top of the hill, then continued down. Seconds later, Dallion got his first view of the chainling. All this time, he had speculated as to the nature of the creature: large, small, scaly, bony, furry. Each whisper he'd heard added a new element, making it grow in size and ferocity. From experience, Dallion knew there was no way for all the rumors to be true. However, even he wasn't prepared for the sight that emerged.

Standing next to a half-wrecked wagon, setting objects on fire and hurling them in the air, was…something. There was no way to consciously describe it, as if the creature was a void given silhouette form. It had an elongated body with several legs—the number changing each time Dallion tried to count—at least a dozen tails, and a single eye the size and shape of a bowling ball.

When the creature's leg came in contact with an object, the object instantly became part of it, then burst ablaze, moments before it was hurled in the distance. It was as if the creature was throwing parts of itself at the main force of the hunting party. Dallion's stomach churned as he imagined what might happen if any part of the chainling came in contact with him. Maybe he was a bit overly optimistic about this.

We're in deep crap now, Dallion thought.

BATTLEFIELD MODIFICATION

Dame Vesuvia charged on her stallion. A large group of soldiers followed on foot. What little remained of the volunteers was long forgotten. Neither as disciplined nor as prepared as the main force, they had suffered the greatest number of casualties, purely focusing on staying alive.

This was going to be the final confrontation. The chainling realized it as well, for it spun around, gathering as much of the wagon remains as it could, then threw them all at the incoming group like an artillery barrage.

Looking at it from a distance, Dallion was able to appreciate not having to be the one leading the charge. He was also relieved at the ease with which the dame pierced the wall of flame. There was nothing flashy he could see, no glowing lights, or materializing shields...the woman just passed through as if walking through a sheet of paper.

"Veil, can you hit it from here?" Dallion asked. Even if the chainling wasn't looking their direction, Dallion had gotten far closer to it than he would have liked.

"No. Need to get a bit closer."

That wasn't the answer Dallion hoped for. They were still about a hundred feet away. According to his theories, the chainling was unlikely to pay attention to them until it had dealt with the greater threat. The concern was that their involvement could quickly change its mind.

"When Veil throws the sword, grab my hand," Dallion shouted. "You too, Cleric."

"Why? What are you thinking?" Gloria asked.

"Later. When I tell you, I want you to aim for its throat. Don't shoot until I say so."

"Okay, but why—"

"Do you have your dartbow?"

"Yes, I have it, but what—"

Before Gloria could finish, a loud *pop* filled the air. It was just like the pop of the balloon, sudden, sharp, though not overly loud. It was accompanied by a radical change in the chainling's appearance. Spikes appeared all over its smooth silhouette like a porcupine shedding the skin of a snake. The new form was larger than before, darker, sleeker, covered by what could be described as an external skeleton of metallic bones.

Oh, damn! Dallion didn't need to be versed in local biology to know exactly what had happened. He had done the exact same in the last week. The creature had increased its awakening level, and that was bad for everyone involved.

"Veil, do it now!"

"I can't be precise from this distance."

"You don't have to be precise! Just aim for the head!"

With a grunt, Veil leapt into the air. Letting go of his dartbow, he grabbed the sword with both hands and spun it around mid-flight as if it were a throwing hammer. Two revolutions later, he let it go.

As the sword made its way toward the chainling, Dallion held his breath. The moment of truth had come.

"Cleric, stop the invisibility!" Dallion shouted. "Gloria, aim!"

The girl's arm appeared out of nothingness, holding a dartbow.

With perfect precision, Dallion put his hand on top so his pinkie finger barely touched the bolt while still holding his own weapon.

"Everyone, grab hold!" Dallion extended his free hand.

In normal circumstances, no one would have obeyed his command. The play was reckless to the point that even a five-year-old would notice. After running for about a minute, pumped up on adrenaline, though, instinct proved stronger than logic. Dallion felt two sets of fingers grab on, touching the flesh of his hand. To his surprise, a third hand grabbed hold of his neck. Someone was aware of his plan and was going ahead with it.

I hope I'm not wrong.

At that point, the sword hit. There wasn't any blood or anything spectacular. The tip of the blade struck the side of the chainling's skull, cracking the bone just before bouncing off. The creature stumbled, pushed to the side by the force of the blow, but quickly regained its footing. The head with the large single eye turned around to take a good look at its attacker.

Got you. Dallion smiled.

"Shoot!" he shouted.

The instant he felt the bolt release, Dallion did what he had planned all along.

ITEM AWAKENING

Everything disappeared. Dallion found himself in a rather large hall. Gloria, Veil, and the cleric were all there. Thankfully, the chainling wasn't.

The BOLT is Level 15

What the heck?! What exactly had gone into the creation of this bolt? Dallion could barely improve an item up to level five, and that was only if he started from utter junk.

You are in a large metal hall.
Defeat the guardian to change the BOLT's destiny!

"This was your plan?" Gloria all but shouted. "Getting us here so we could improve the bolt?!"

"Pretty much." Dallion grinned. Something suggested Gloria wasn't taking this all too well. Actually, the only reason she wasn't outright furious was that she was still trying to wrap her mind around the idea of it all.

"Have you any idea what it takes to improve sky silver?"

"No, but I'm about to…" This was the first time he had heard the term.

"Sky silver is one of the most stable elements there is! Why do you think weapons are made of it? If it was normal metal, anyone could turn the weapon to rust the moment it touches their skin."

"Oh." That actually was a pretty neat trick. Dallion had to remember it for later. Not that he had the skills to modify metal yet.

"Did you seriously think this through?!" Gloria crossed her arms. Her face was red with anger.

You look cute when you're angry, part of him thought. "Yes, actually. I suspected the bolts had to be solid enough so they'd take down the creature we're hunting."

Gloria frowned, refusing to acknowledge his logic.

"That's why we won't be improving the bolt. We'll just modify it."

"Modify?" Veil arched a brow. "Isn't that the same as improving?"

"Is mending the same as improving?" Dallion asked.

The question made both Veil and Gloria go *hmm,* though only Veil made the sound out loud.

"If we can mend things of a greater level, we can also damage them to some extent?" Dallion turned to the cleric. "Also, the bolts aren't made of sky silver, only the tips are. The rest is common metal. That's what we'll be changing."

"You want to modify the metal shaft of a bolt?" For the first time, there was a softer tone in the cleric's voice. Dallion could tell he was intrigued by the idea, possibly eager even.

"Precisely! And you're going to help."

ROCKET BOLT

Walking through the bolt was different from what Dallion expected. While sharing a lot of similarities—the starting point, the guardian room, the mending maze—each item had its own set of peculiarities. That was true not only for the appearance of the realm, but for all those who inhabited it as well. The guardians tended to be a reflection of the item's owner, or owners.

Gloria's ring guardian was strong, but also fair and kind, those of the items in Dallion's home were simplistic, but encouraging, and the rocks he had taken from the river were a little wild. However, it was the mazes that were the greatest difference. Each had a different shape, incorporating the item's true form and, as Dallion had found out, there was a direct connection between the damage on the outside and that in the labyrinth.

The labyrinth of the bolt turned out to be a tower composed of multiple smaller labyrinths placed on over the other. Initially, there wasn't even an indication. The starting room led directly to the guardian arena. Yet, when Dallion had shot at the connecting archway with his dartbow, the archway had transformed into a stairwell, moving the guardian room to the top.

"How did you think of this?" Veil asked, impressed.

"It's something my mother told me," Dallion replied.

To be honest, he hadn't given the matter much thought thanks to the echo, not that he had many opportunities to do so up until now. The entire time in the village had been spent learning skills basics in preparation for Aspion Luor's tasks. Looking back, Dallion was almost annoyed at the time he had wasted doing mundane things instead of experimenting and pushing the limits of his skills.

"She said that some people liked to damage items for the fun of it."

"Well, I've damaged a lot of things," Veil said with pride.

Dallion felt like shaking his head. Some things never changed.

"I've never done it from the inside, though. I'd just chip off a part of the thing, then go into the labyrinth to do more damage."

"Well…" *I'm not touching that topic.* "Since they are connected, you can do it on the inside as well. You just need to know the exact spot. Having some perception helps."

That shut Veil up as he darted an annoyed glance at his sister. Noticing it, Gloria raised her chin in a smug expression. Typical sibling rivalry at its best.

"What is your plan?" the cleric asked.

"It's simple. All we have to do is cause enough damage on every third floor so that the bolt holds together, but the bolt is on the brink of shattering. When the chainling grabs the shaft of the bolt, the tip will continue."

The only reaction Dallion got were blank stares. No one seemed to see the significance of what he had just said, and yet it was so obvious. Dallion had seen that in lots of videos. It was the same principle with arrow heads…more or less. Even in a low-tech medieval world, this principle was supposed to be known. Even the Romans back on Earth knew the principle. Maybe he wasn't explaining it right?

"Look, the bolt is already in flight. All we'll do is just break it up a bit so that the chainling can't stop it. At worst, it'll get sprayed by metal fragments. At best, we can kill it on the spot." Dallion paused for a moment. Maybe the last bit was pushing it too far. "With luck, we can wound it for Dame Vesuvia to kill off quickly." That sounded much better.

"So, we need to bash up parts of the labyrinth?" Veil was the first to break the silence.

"Only some floors, and not all of them..." Dallion started to have doubts. Not about the plan, rather he was unsure what the effect of giving Veil free rein to destroy things would be. "You and Gloria to the top. The cleric and I will start from the bottom."

"I don't get it." Veil shrugged. "No prob in smashing things up, though. Coming, sis?"

Gloria gave a Dallion a long stare, then just sighed.

"I hope you know what you're doing," she said, then followed her brother.

"There really is no downside," Dallion shouted as the siblings started their climb up. "Just don't break too much, okay?"

Part one of his plan had started. Originally, the next part involved them doing the same at least twice more, once for each of the bolts he was about to shoot and, if they were lucky, a few reloads more. They weren't going to be happy about it, but better a few days of grumbling alive than a calm death. The cleric was a huge, unexpected bonus. Dallion never imagined he'd join in or that he'd have magic. Now, the odds of this attack being a success had increased exponentially.

Seconds passed. Dallion calmly waited for Veil and Gloria to climb up and get well out of earshot.

"Any reason we have to wait?" the albino asked.

"Shh!" Dallion rose a finger, still looking up.

"I can stop sound just as I can stop light."

"Oh..." Now, he felt stupid. "Right. I didn't think about that. Can you heat things up as well?"

"Heat, freeze, harden, soften... What exactly do you know about magic?"

"I know a bit."

Unfortunately, it was mostly through games, cartoons, and roleplay sessions back on Earth. The truth was that until just a few minutes ago, he hadn't heard a spell described, let alone seen one. Dherma wasn't the place where magic was a vital topic, and the few questions he had on the subject were quickly subdued. Despite that, Dallion was convinced that his knowledge from Earth had to count for something. After all, magic was nothing but a set of principles—common principles, even.

"Know any good spells?" he asked.

"No."

The word was said with such a lack of emotion that Dallion suspected something to be off.

"While the Seven blessed me with the power of magic, I have proven unworthy to attain the skills to use it adequately. I can only affect change in items and areas. If I knew spells, you and I wouldn't be having this conversation."

"Because you'd have killed the chainling on your own?" Dallion felt the urge to take several steps back. Even with his perception of four, he could spot bitterness in a person, and the cleric was definitely bitter.

"Because I wouldn't have been sent on this mission at all. Who do you think improved the initiate's blade?"

Dallion didn't answer.

"When people like me fail at what they're supposed to do, they get punished. A true mage wouldn't allow a minor noble like her to clean their shoes, let alone address them so casually. A true mage wouldn't even be bothered about a minor nuisance at the edge of the empire. And, yes, as you said, a true mage would destroy a creature like this with the snap of a finger."

The tension in the air could be felt. Dallion felt tempted to make a wisecrack in an attempt to cool things down, but looking at the cleric's expression, there were serious doubts that would end up going well.

"And now that you know how much I know about magic," the cleric continued, "what is it you want me to do?"

Ouch. Bitter and passive aggressive.

"Any chance you can make the bolt invisible?"

"It wouldn't matter. The chainling would still see it."

"Any chance you could heat up part of the bolt's shaft? Heat it up to a melting point?"

"Easily. Why?"

"I want to make the bolt into a rocket."

The cleric's expression shifted. At first, it hardened, as if he was being mocked. Then it softened so much that Dallion felt he was being pitied.

"A rocket is a…" *How the heck do I explain the idea of a rocket?* "The idea is that if you suddenly heat up part of something in a specific shape, it will…make it fly faster?"

During his life, Dallion had heard a lot of terrible explanations, but they paled in comparison to what he had uttered just now. Trying to simplify something complex that he took for granted sounded like drunken gibberish.

"Err, I mean…"

"I know what a rocket is," the cleric interrupted, saving Dallion from his misery. "How do you know, though? Other than the Order and the imperial family, only a handful of nobles know the secret. Are you saying you know a way that would change a dartbow bolt into a rocket?"

"Maybe?" *What mess did I get myself into now? Maybe having a limiting echo wasn't all bad after all?* "I mean, it should. This one is sort of a test. We have a few more shots to get it right. No big deal, right?" He let out a fake laugh. "At worst, it'll—"

"How old are you?" The cleric narrowed his eyes. "In true years."

"True years…" Dallion hadn't heard the term before. "Twenty-two." Give or take.

"Twenty-two. You're still a child."

So are you, buddy, Dallion thought. *Relatively speaking.*

"You know a lot for a person your age." The faintest of smiles appeared on the albino's face. "What exactly do you need me to do?"

THE CHAINLING

Labyrinth section damaged!
Overall completion 37%

"One more to go," Dallion said in an attempt to cheer up the rest of the group.

Whatever enthusiasm for the plan there was had long vanished. There was a certain degree of repetition after which even the most otherworldly activity becomes tedious routine. At this point, everyone—Dallion included—just wanted to get it over with. Fifteen floors…five of which had to be damaged in a very specific fashion. If there was a definition of poor man's crafting, this was it.

So far, all the sections had been modified according to specifications, including the cleric's temperature adjustment. Dallion wasn't completely sure that a sudden heat source within a bell shape would create the equivalent of an explosion, although, according to his internet knowledge, it was supposed to. Having something heat up so much almost instantaneously had to have the same effect. Either way, they would soon find out.

The final labyrinth was located just under the bolt's guardian chamber. While Veil was destroying certain walls of the labyrinth with alarming speed and efficiency, Dallion peeked. As expected, the guardian wasn't there.

"How certain are you this will work?" Gloria asked.

"Fairly certain," Dallion lied and instantly regretted it. For a moment, it had slipped his mind that the girl was a walking lie detector. "Somewhat certain," he corrected himself.

Gloria's expression remained unchanged.

"Hit or miss, we must be ready for what's to follow," Dallion went on. "Once we return to the battlefield, stay close. I might need you to modify my other two bolts."

There was a loud groan.

"I'm just saying."

"If things get bad, I'll take care of things," the cleric said with a pensive expression. "You just run and don't look back."

"What about you?"

"The Seven won't allow me to get killed."

That wasn't encouraging. Dallion had no idea if the deities even existed. For all he knew, they might have been metaphors, although one had to admit the number of moons and their colors was more than a coincidence. If they were indeed just planets, their reflected light was supposed to be the same.

If you really exist, please, help me pull this off, Dallion thought, hedging his bets. There was a four in five chance that his plan worked. Given what the dartbow was capable of, there was a fifty-fifty chance that the modified bolt hit the creature in its weak spot. Even if it didn't, there was a sixty percent chance that fragments of molten metal were sprayed all over its body. In the end, all they had to do was distract the creature long enough for Dame Vesuvia to engage it.

"Veil? How's it going?" Dallion asked.

"Final punches, Dal." A loud slamming sound echoed

throughout the room. Dallion had no idea what Veil had done to be able to break metal, but he was glad for it. "Ready. What do we do now?"

"Now, we exit." Dallion took a deep breath. This would be the first time he'd go from a calm state to an intense sprint. "Everyone ready?"

All but the cleric nodded.

Good enough, Dallion thought and left the bolt. Pain hit him like a sledgehammer as, in his mind, he accelerated from zero to fifteen miles per hour in zero seconds flat. It would be funny that awakening was the only instance in which the phrase could be used properly…if it wasn't for the shock he experienced.

All plans of modifying two more bolts went out of the window as the shock made Dallion stop after several steps and empty his stomach contents.

I feel like I'm dying! he wanted to shout, if his body would let him.

A loud roar filled the air, sounding like a cross between a lion and a rusty chainsaw. Despite the pain, Dallion looked up. Against all odds, the bolt-rocket operation had been a success. It would have been nice if he had seen the bolt in action but seeing gushing black from the chainling's chest was the second-best thing.

"It actually worked." Dallion smiled. "It really actually worked."

COMBAT INITIATED

Huh?

This wasn't supposed to happen. Rectangles weren't supposed to appear in the real world, but it was right there, clear as day. Instinctively, Dallion looked at his left hand. There was no buckler there, just the second dartbow he held.

As terrifying as this was, however, a realization soon kicked in, making Dallion's blood freeze in his veins. There was only one creature on the battlefield that would want to fight with him, the same creature that had awakened powers.

Craaap!

Dallion jumped back. Both dartbows raised in the air, though no marker lines appeared. It was at that point the chainling reacted. In a second, it moved from its position to a step away. Several of the ribs were fractured, sticking to the body like pieces of broken porcelain. At this distance, the only course of action was for Dallion to shoot. As he squeezed the triggers, a paw emerged from the chainling's body, thrusting forward.

That was fast, Dallion thought as he flew back.

All the fear and concern evaporated from his mind as he considered this to be his final moments of existence. It wasn't so much surrender than a realization that was completely and utterly helpless. There was nothing he could do anymore. He was out of tricks and options. Given what the creature was capable of, he couldn't even awaken in a piece of his clothing to hide.

It was fun while it lasted, and despite the failure on a personal level, the group was more likely to succeed. Dallion had managed to distract the chainling. Heck, he had even wounded it. Now, Vesuvia and the cleric would have a much easier time. At least Gloria and Veil would get back safely to the village, and who knows? Maybe they'd be able to change the chief's mind on a few things.

The village chief… That was one of Dallion's main regrets. He had hoped to have a one-to-one with the old geezer.

And just when I got rid of the echo too. Dallion tried to laugh. *You're lucky, old man. I would have taken you in a minute. Five at most.*

The pain spread through Dallion's chest. There wasn't anything extraordinary about it. It felt very much as if he'd been hit with a pipe or club. If the caravan bodies were any indication, it was clear

292

what would happen now—flames would burst through Dallion's body, burning him beyond recognition, after which—

With a loud *thump*, Dallion crashed onto the ground. A few more seconds passed, and he was still there, out of breath, in pain, but very much alive. Just then, the combat rectangle vanished.

THE LOSS

The chainling jumped away from Dallion just in time to avoid a series of glowing red knives that flew its way. A second series of knives followed, making it retreat even farther. Initially, Dallion wondered why a creature as powerful as the chainling would be afraid of such weapons when he saw them melt into puddles of molten metal upon touching the ground.

Magic, he thought. Clearly, he wasn't the only one with out-of-the-box ideas.

"I told you to run," the cleric said, a short distance away. A pair of knives glowed in his hands. That was both impressive and unexpected. If anything, Dallion thought of him more as a quarterstaff fighter.

The cleric had barely made his move when another party arrived. Emerging out of thin air, Dame Vesuvia swung her weapon at the chainling. Faster than the eye could follow, her sword struck the creature's skull, sinking in at least half an inch. A bit farther and it could have split the chainling's head in two. Sadly, the monster's bones rivaled the durability of any armor. The force exerted on it was enough to push the entire creature back but not cut through.

Realizing her strike failed to achieve its goal, the dame proceeded with another attack, this time from the side. Watching her, Dallion felt like a level one guardian of a cheap wooden bowl. He could occasionally recognize some of the attack patterns, as he had a pretty good idea of at least some of the skills she used, but they were on an entirely different level. Saying that she used attack skills was like comparing a condor to a butterfly. The instant leap, the multi-attack, the disappearing and reappearing act; those were all things the markers had helped Dallion do in the awakened state. Dame Vesuvia was doing them in the real world with practically no effort at all, not to mention there were a lot of other elements that verged on the supernatural.

For a moment, it seemed as if there were three arms with three swords attached to Vesuvia's shoulder. A triple attack. Dallion had never seen one before, but the slight blur around the outlines of her arms told him it was the extreme speed creating that illusion. Just witnessing it was incredible! It defied imagination, the laws of physics, and almost reality itself.

Blades split the air, making their way to the target. The majority were evaded with ease, but a few managed to land.

Dallion blinked. An attack had hit its target? And not a rocket propelled ranged one either. That could only mean one thing—the chainling was getting weaker.

"Shoot at it, you idiot!" Gloria shouted from behind.

Snapping back to reality, Dallion reloaded his dartbows. He wasn't the only one. Several more bolts flew at the creature, followed by a charge of soldiers with swords. Considerably slower than the dame, they flashed in and out of existence, following the same movement technique awakened guard skills offered.

The main force of the hunting party surrounded the chainling. They were followed, at a distance, by the rest of the volunteers who, like Dallion, shot bolts in their own attempts to contribute to the battle. Their attacks were disorganized and random, to say the least, but even they were starting to score some hits.

Everything was moving so fast that Dallion couldn't keep up. The dame and the beast had transformed into a series of afterimage blurs shifting from spot to spot in the nearby area. The speed was such that he could no longer follow the specifics of the fight, only able to catch an occasional "frame" of one side landing a blow on the other's defense.

That's what a true awakened is.

"Keep your guard up!" Dame Vesuvia shouted, her words slower than her actions.

Several soldiers tried to pull back but were too late to avoid the black paw that emerged from the creature's body and slashed right through them. Initially, it looked like a few rips on their tabards. A ball of flame followed, engulfing three people, then knocking them to the ground.

Neither the massive chainmail armor nor the cleric's emblem had done anything to save them. The single chainling attack had left three dead, and things were just getting started.

"Keep the line!" Vesuvia ordered. "Large spread."

I couldn't have stopped that. Dallion stood. Both his dartbows were loaded now, but the chainling was moving too fast for him to target it. Looking over his shoulder, Dallion got a glimpse of Gloria and Veil. They were moving in toward him—the least safe thing they could do.

"Stay there!" Dallion rushed toward them. As much as he wanted to be the hero, he knew he didn't stand a chance. It was a miracle he hadn't ended up dead along with the soldiers. *I owe you one, Cleric.*

"This is wild." Veil smiled, looking at the fight with absolute admiration. "Only a noble can do that."

It was impossible to disagree. For every five strikes the chainling blocked, Dame Vesuvia managed to get one in. Slice by slice, it was being pushed back. Each jab, each faint cut weakened it, though not to the extent that it would give up and die. Four more soldiers burst into flames.

"She's weakening," Gloria said.

"Come on," Veil snorted. "She's winning. Just look."

"I am looking," the girl hissed. "And I'm telling you she's getting weaker. Her hits aren't landing as well as they did at first. And the soldiers are incompetent."

The words were harsh but ultimately correct. Only the cleric was of any use. When he ran out of throwing knives, the albino took his staff and switched to melee combat. His actions were by far not as impressive as those of the dame, though he still managed to keep from getting hit and, on occasion, strike the chainling.

"They're not that bad." Veil crossed his arms moments before another one burned up. This universe definitely had a wicked sense of humor. "Don't look at me! I didn't cause it." The blond stepped back defensively.

Think! Think! Think!

Dallion focused on the fight. From what he was seeing, he agreed with Veil that the dame would most likely win…but could he leave it at that? If there was a chance of failure, he had to think of something. At this point, the more reckless, the better.

"The chainling can't change the weapons, right?" He turned to Gloria.

"What?"

"Sky silver. Things made by it can't be changed through awakening, right?"

"Well, it might be possible in theory, but it's extremely difficult. That's why they forge them instead of trying to improve them. Much faster that way."

"In that case, I have an idea."

Without warning, Dallion rushed straight toward the battle. Vesuvia and the chainling kept flashing in and out from spot to spot, slightly slower than before. Both were focused on their immediate opponent, pretty much ignoring everything else.

"Cleric!" Dallion pointed his dartbows forward. "Help me modify two more bolts!"

It has to work! It has to!

"Just two more hits, and we can take the chainling down!" Dallion yelled as loud as he could.

The quarters of the surviving soldiers glanced in his direction. For a single moment, their curiosity bested years of training, diverting their attention to see what the commotion was about. So did the chainling.

For a split second, it turned its head toward him, its giant eye meeting those of Dallion. It would have taken a moment for the creature to reach him and slice his head off. And it clearly wanted to, especially after what Dallion had done to hurt it. Before it could, Vesuvia thrust her sword deep in its throat.

"You lose." Dallion smiled. The creature was highly intelligent, as he suspected, and it also held grudges. Now, the grudge was gone, along with its life.

A NAME OF HIS OWN

"You're lucky you aren't part of my troops," Dame Vesuvia said sharply. "Rushing toward a chainling with that level of training. If it wasn't for the cleric, you'd have been a pile of charred flesh."

Dallion kept quiet. He'd only been part of the hunting party for less than a week and already he felt like some things never changed. After the fighting was over, several people had received praise from the noble as well as some monetary rewards. It came as no surprise that Gloria was among the group, although Dallion was somewhat annoyed Veil was considered praiseworthy as well.

Ironically, it was all thanks to Dallion that the blond had earned his reward. Rushing to help a fellow volunteer and throwing a sword at the chainling were viewed in an entirely positive light. In contrast, the only reward Dallion got were several earfuls of complaints. Then again, things could have been far worse.

Eleven soldiers had been killed during the fight, as well as five volunteers, crushed by the flaming debris. That composed roughly half of the party. Among the survivors, a third had sustained injuries, some quite serious.

"What did you think you could achieve?" the dame asked.

I've already achieved what I wanted, Dallion wanted to say. Common sense, though, kept his mouth shut.

"There's a saying where I come from." Vesuvia narrowed her eyes. "Luck goes to those who least deserve it."

Dallion tried not to snort in laughter. As sayings went, this one was pretty bad. Not to mention he didn't consider himself excessively lucky. Surviving a recklessness charge was no doubt fortunate, but everything else considered, he wasn't even supposed to be here. If it weren't for him suddenly appearing in this world, he was on the track to be starting college and experience a blissful life of learning and partying. Instead, he ended up in a forgotten medieval village with a mini-tyrant set on sealing the powers of everyone who wasn't immediate family. Not to mention Dallion had effectively been "drafted" to hunt some unknown monster with the ability to set people and objects on fire. Yes, lucky indeed.

"You better not be expecting any reward," the dame said.

"I'm not, ma'am."

The woman arched a brow.

"I mean, milady," he corrected himself. Nobility titles were all so confusing.

"Good. Go get some rest. We're heading back in the morning. Real rest."

"Yes, milady." Dallion bowed slightly, then stepped away.

Real rest. Considering where they were, he wouldn't have minded sleeping in the awakened state. The only person who had anything close to a sleeping bag was the noble herself. The soldiers used their chainmail as pillows and their tabards as blankets. Just looking at them made Dallion feel terribly uncomfortable.

With a silent sigh, he made his way back to the nearest fire. With the hunt over, and half of the party dead, everyone had dispensed with the division. Only the wounded received special treatment and, given that Dallion didn't have any visible marks on his body, he wasn't considered in need of healing. Interestingly enough, Havoc wasn't either. The large man had recovered remarkably fast considering what had happened. His mood had improved quite a bit when he'd seen how many of the volunteers had survived, especially finding that Dallion and his crew were all right.

"Dallion!" Havoc shouted. "Come here. Saved you some ale. Wasn't easy." He kneed the unconscious Veil next to him. It was pretty obvious what had been going on, though it was impressive that the blond had drunken himself to a slumbering pile on the ground. "He would have gulped all of it down if he could. Good thing he's such a lightweight."

Given the strength of spirits in this world, it didn't come as a surprise. Dallion could get intoxicated by the smell of the fumes alone.

"Where's Gloria?" Dallion looked around as he sat.

"Off to do her business somewhere." Havoc didn't elaborate. "So, how did it go?"

"Is there anyone in the camp who didn't hear?" *It's not like it's that far away.*

"Oh, we heard. But that doesn't answer my question. How do you think it went?"

"Not great, not terrible." Dallion shrugged. "I'm starting to get used to the shouting. I don't see the reason for it, though."

"Oh, boy. You really don't know anything about the world, do you?" The large man shook his head. "That's the good thing about living in a hamlet; it keeps you safe from the bullshit going on. You probably think that being awakened is a big deal, right?"

"That's what I've been told. Repeatedly."

"Well, it isn't. It's just an ace in the sleeve. Good to have, but it won't get you anywhere if not used properly." Havoc moved closer. "You're a peasant," he whispered. "The dame is a noble and a member of the Order. Treating you as an equal for no reason is out of the question. Compliments can only be given through shouting and grumbling. The fact that you're being yelled at means they see potential in you, possibly enough to treat you as an equal one day."

"You think that's possible?"

"They say the only way to walk up the hill is by having money, skills, or lineage. That's a lie. What either of those would get you is to join the ranks of high society. You'll be able to talk to the right people, maybe even help to make an important decision now and again, but you'll never be a noble. However, here's the catch. In order to become a noble, you must first join the "polite society," and that comes with its own rules. You're not a merchant, and you don't have the lineage, but after what I saw right now, you might have the skills. You've a long way to go, though. Before anything, you must fully awaken. Then you must make a name for yourself. After that, who knows?"

Make a name for myself, Dallion thought.

That had a nice ring to it. Way better than college. Only now did it dawn on Dallion that there was a whole world out there ready for the taking. He didn't have to go back to the village. He could ask the dame to become a soldier or, if not, accompany the group to some city. The village elder couldn't stop him now. With the echo destroyed, he had no power.

"Keep in mind that the higher you climb, the more dangerous you'll get. See him?" Havoc glanced at the cleric. Since the battle, the albino had been tending to the wounded. The "insignificant" amount of magic he had seemed to work pretty well on minor wounds. "He was born with magic, so he thought he'd rise in the world. He got a lot of attention when he was fifteen, enough to get him a decade of prison and his name removed from existence. He was lucky the Order took him in. Others weren't."

Damn! Not for a moment had Dallion expected the cleric to have been in trouble. Havoc, sure. The bear-like man just screamed convict. His knowledge far exceeded his awakening level. The cleric, though…

"He was forbidden to use his name?" Dallion asked.

"No, his name doesn't exist anymore. It was taken out of every book and mind. No one could remember it, and even if they did, they'd never be able to utter it." Havoc's voice got darker. "Anyway, enough dark thoughts. We're supposed to celebrate." He shoved a half-empty waterskin in Dallion's hands. "Drink up. There's no telling when you'll have the chance."

"Yeah, sure."

A name of my own. Dallion took a sip. *Is that the way to go?*

THE TRIP BACK

The mood on the way back was very different from what it had been getting there. The farther the party went, the happier and more relieved the volunteers became. People smiled, joked during food breaks, even started sharing things from their lives. It was as if a great weight had been removed from their shoulders.

The soldiers, in contrast, became more and more cranky. For them, each step took them closer to the crowded, smelly barracks of their garrison.

Training had also changed focus. A day ago, the volunteers grumbled each time they had to face a personal guardian. Now, they chased after soldiers hoping to learn a few good tips that would set them apart from the people back in their villages. Veil was especially enthusiastic. There wasn't a day he wouldn't spend practicing —in and out of awakened state—with the goal of achieving level five. The cleric had made it publicly clear that Veil didn't have what it took, but that had only made the blond double his efforts.

As for Dallion, he still hadn't made up his mind. He would constantly think about it, putting off the decision for the next day. Kalis had attempted to convince him to join a city guard. His prep talk was very different from Havoc's. Only positive things were mentioned: rights, salary, prestige, training, assurances they wouldn't go hunting chainlings all the time.

Naturally, he was going to have to start from the bottom—possibly the equivalent of a stable boy—and move up at his own pace. The only guarantee was that he'd receive the means and the training to get there, nothing more. The offer was quite good, but Dallion felt unconvinced.

On the third evening, Havoc and another of the volunteers were dropped off. Dame Vesuvia had decided to pass through the villages based on proximity. Dherma was second on the list.

Goodbyes were said, promises made. Even Veil had reluctantly muttered something that could pass as a compliment. Dallion barely knew Havoc, but the experience made him feel as if they'd been together for months. The same could be said for other people in the party. From experience, however, he knew everything would be forgotten in a week. People would get back to their daily lives, as would Dallion.

"You're drifting again," Gloria said, joining him a short distance away from the main camp.

"Sort of." Dallion kept looking at the stars. "Don't you have anything to discuss with the dame?"

"The dame prefers talking to her horse." Veil joined in as well. "At least then there's an intelligent conversation going on."

"Idiot." Gloria sighed.

"So, what have you been up to, Dal? Plotting some wild plan?"

"No." Dallion opened his hand, revealing a smooth piece of marble. "I was making a gift for my brother."

It was an ordinary piece of rock, but it made Dallion think of simpler times. When he first awakened, a polished pebble was viewed as a treasure. The pride on his parents' faces could not be described, as for his brother...the child was on cloud nine, as if he'd received the local equivalent of a next gen console.

Shiny marble, Dallion thought.

"Hmm. How far did you improve it?" Veil asked. "Level five?"

"Six." With a bit of effort, Dallion could have possibly reached seven. The dartbow and the emblem gave him a tremendous advantage unavailable to him before.

"Not bad." Veil whistled. "I'll have to up my game. What do you think?" He nudged his sister. "Can you get anything that high? Other than clothes, that is."

"You should ask the cleric to reach level four," Gloria changed the topic without warning. "You have the skills for it."

"Yeah, you're the only one who's still a three. Don't shame the village."

"I don't think your grandfather would approve."

Everyone went silent. Both Gloria and Veil felt the need to look away. The sad truth was that, despite what they had gone through, things would return to normal once they returned to the village. Even if both of them had dealt with their echoes, no one else in the village had.

"You can run off, you know," Veil said after a long silence. "We'll think of something. Heck, we can say you died a hero killed by the chainling. Isn't that far off?"

Gloria gave her brother a warning glance.

"What? It can work. Grandad won't chase after him in the city. He hates those places. It'll be much easier for him to pretend that it's true and—"

"Will that change anything, though?" Dallion asked. "Life in the village is crap. Even you know that. Everyone is half awake in a gray never-ending dream. The only difference between you and my parents is that your dream has a bit more color in it." *Also, you didn't have your power sealed like my mother.*

"Dallion," Gloria whispered. "Don't do this."

Dallion just smiled. He had delayed his decision up to now, but he finally had made up his mind. Going to the city and making a name for himself was definitely something he wanted, but before that, there were a few loose ends that needed tying up.

"He's not joking." Veil's expression had become deadly serious. "Grandpa won't be happy about this. If he asks me, I'll have to fight you."

"Yeah, you probably would."

"You'll lose."

"I don't think so." Dallion smiled. "Did the dame let you keep your sword?"

"Yeah?" Veil arched a brow.

"Well, then it'll be a fair fight."

"You maniac." Veil laughed. "A fair fight, eh? Better remember that when I pound you into the ground."

"Idiots." Gloria turned around and walked off toward the camp-fires. Clearly, she didn't share the humor.

Would I have to fight her as well? Dallion wondered.

As things stood, she presented a greater challenge than Veil. Fighting against brute strength was one thing, against precision and acrobatics was a different matter.

"Don't worry. She's always been like that." Veil shook his head. "Still thinks she can chase her dreams. That's the real reason she's the family's little princess. Almost as reckless as you. The worst part is that she believes things can actually change. As if a medal from the dame would make Grandpa change his mind."

"Won't it? The dame is a noble, so—"

"That won't matter. Grandpa already has plans for her. He has plans for me as well. I've learned since I was a kid, the more you struggle, the more difficult it will become."

"Can't you leave the village?"

"We aren't like you, Dal. The moment you came for your acknowledgement, I knew. You became different after you went through your awakening. Grandpa saw it too. That's why he'll never let you go. When we return to the village, we'll no longer be friends."

"Don't bet on it." *I've become quite greedy, Veil. I'll settle things in the village and go to the cities, and I'll do it while keeping you and Gloria as friends!*

HOMECOMING

"**R**eturn to your village with the archduke's thanks," Dame
Vesuvia said with the dignity of a bored city official.

Just like at the previous village, there was no fanfare, no trum-
pets or speeches, not even any medals of recognition. The only
reward was a purse of coins for the village chief, given to Veil. The
notion that the chief had gained more out of this than everyone else
combined burned Dallion up inside. What calmed him down was
the knowing there wasn't anything much to spend the money on
until the next traveling merchant arrived. There was a nice irony to
the whole thing: through his isolating the village from the rest of the
world, the village chief had ensured he could hardly buy anything of
value he didn't already have. In a way, he had built a prison for
himself.

"Return the gear that was given to you and return with the
Seven's blessings," the dame finished, then slowly rode off,
followed by most of the group, leaving only the cleric behind.

You could have at least waited a minute, Dallion grumbled
internally.

"Dartbows and emblems," the cleric said.

Gloria and Veil handed theirs over without hesitation. Dallion did, with fifty percent hesitation. It would have been nice to keep the emblem. With it, the village chief would have no hold over him —Dallion could fail a thousand times in an awakened state, and he couldn't have his powers sealed. Just holding it filled him with power.

"I don't suppose I can keep this as a reward?" Dallion asked, looking at the pendant in the palm of his hand. It was just a piece of jewelry, a decoration like a game achievement back on Earth…and, at the same time, it wasn't.

"No." The cleric grabbed it. "Emblems belong to the Order."

"Well, it was worth a try." Dallion let out a forced laugh.

"You two head back," the cleric said to Veil and Gloria. "I have something to discuss with Dallion."

First name basis? That was either extremely good or positively terrible.

Dallion didn't know whether to feel honored or worried. The Luor siblings were of a similar opinion, for they left with as little as a wave. It was better for everyone that way. For one thing, it avoided the awkwardness of meeting the village chief. As far as the Luor family, and the village itself, were concerned, they were still supposed to hate Dallion's guts.

"You never said who taught you how to make rockets." The cleric pulled down his hood.

"It's a long story." Dallion smiled. Not this again. "I just copied something I heard. It was lucky it worked at all. A lot of things could have messed up."

"No, it wasn't luck." The cleric put a dartbow in Dallion's hand. "Emblems belong to the Order, but weapons don't. It's common that some get lost or damaged, especially when fighting something as dangerous as a chainling."

No way! You're giving me a dartbow? That's almost as good as getting an emblem. Actually, it was better! A ranged weapon would give Dallion a short-term advantage no emblem ever could.

"Yeah, lost." He nodded, unable to keep the grin off his face.

"No bolt clip, but that shouldn't be a problem while in the awakened state. Keep it hidden when you enter your village."

"You don't need to tell me twice." Dallion tucked it under his shirt. "Won't you get in trouble?"

"Who am I to go against the initiate's orders? Besides, the hunt was a success. In the eyes of the archduke and the Order, that's all that counts."

"Well, I don't know what to say. Thanks."

Judging by the albino's nod, that much was enough.

"Can I ask something?"

"Ask."

"What is your name?" Despite knowing it was a sore topic, Dallion had to know what having one's name erased really meant. Bracing himself for an angry outburst, he waited.

Several seconds passed in silence.

"Cleric," the albino replied at last. "My name now is Cleric. It was meant to serve as a reminder where I belong."

"Cleric..." using a title instead of a name felt weird, also incredibly harsh, "take care."

"Thank you, Dallion." The cleric pulled his hood back up. "Blessings of the Seven." He walked away.

A few moments later, Dallion went his own way, heading toward Dherma. He could barely contain his joy. Part of him wanted to rush back home and show everyone what he'd received, as well as mention he was the one who had killed the chainling, of course. Sadly, he couldn't do any of that. The agreement between Dallion, Veil, and Gloria was that all actual events during the hunt be kept secret. As far as everyone was concerned, it was Veil who had done the most, while Dallion had cowered in fear somewhere behind. It wasn't flattering in the least, nor was it fair, but it was practical.

Okay, time to head home. Dallion took a deep breath and walked on.

The village seemed in a far worse state that when Dallion had left. Objectively, that wasn't true. Everything remained in the exact same state as it had been a week ago. The influence of the limiting echo gone, it was apparent what an actual dump the place had become. Back when Dallion was a child, the houses had been in much better shape and didn't have to rely on awakened being forced to mend them.

"Brother!" Linner rushed at him. The boy's energy and enthusiasm appeared to be among the universal constants. "You're back!"

"Hey, Lin!" Dallion scooped his brother from the ground and put him on his shoulders. Ever since he had improved his body trait, the child had felt as light as a feather. "How have you been? You behaved well, I hope?"

"Of course!" Lin grinned. Dallion knew that was hardly the case. His brother was a constant handful. "So, what happened? Were there monsters? Did you fight a lot?"

"How about we leave that for a bit later, okay?" Dallion laughed. "I'm sure Mom and Dad also want to hear."

"Okay…but don't take too long!"

Dallion's parents greeted him in a much more reasonable way. His mother, visibly relieved at his safe return, managed to hold back her tears. Meanwhile, his father itched to give him a bear hug, only deciding against it since Linner was on Dallion's shoulders. As it turned out, sometimes carrying one's brother came with unexpected benefits.

"Where's Grandpa?" Dallion looked about.

"He and the other elders were called to the chief's house when the young master Veil arrived," Dallion's father explained.

Young Master Veil? Reality smacked Dallion in the face. Here, every member of the Luor family was viewed as nobility.

"We were scared you hadn't survived," Dallion's mother explained. "Bless the young master for telling us you're coming. He even gave us a copper coin to celebrate the occasion."

Giving my own reward to my family as charity? Dallion knew it was the only way his family could get anything out of the situation, but even so, he couldn't help but feel slightly insulted.

"Yeah, he's all heart. Did the chief call for me?"

"No." Dallion's mother shook her head. "The elder convinced him to delay that for tomorrow. You have today to spend with us."

"Great. That means I'll get to hear everything that happened while I was gone. And also, I'll tell a few stories of my own."

"Yaaaay!" Linner yelled with joy from Dallion's back.

And when we're done talking, I'll go do some practice with an old friend.

SAND DRAGON'S RETURN

The day passed in the medieval equivalent of partying, similar to when Dallion first awakened. There was lots of food by local standards, a healthy number of people, as well as lots of talk and laughter. However, it also seemed different. Lacking the echo, Dallion felt the fakeness of it all, as if he had been put in a TV drama in which everyone played their own roles. The smiles seemed fake, the questions seemed shallow, even the people's reactions appeared predictable, almost rehearsed.

Dallion's mother was the only exception. Only now was he able to see her actual degree of sadness. When he left the village, he thought she was just being quiet. Now, he could see the truth beyond that.

"What happened to the beast?" Dallion's father asked. "Did you skin it?"

"Others did, not me."

Dallion had long since stopped correcting the changes in the story. There was no point. The echoes had done their task, changing the perception of events in real time.

The massive hunting party became a group of neighboring villagers, Dame Vesuvia had been demoted to the sister of the village chief who had gone mostly as an observer, while the Luor siblings had done all the work. As for the chainling itself, it varied between a boar, bear, or a really large wolf. In the eyes of Dallion's family and neighbors, Dallion had done nothing but assist the Luors with a local nuisance just outside the village.

"I liked the story with the monster better," Lin pouted. For some reason, he was one of the few who remembered the original story. Maybe it had to do with his age or the child really had an active imagination.

"Yep, the creature was a great monster." Dallion winked. "And tomorrow, I'll tell you about it more, but now I must go out for a bit."

"Go out?" All the cheer suddenly stopped as everyone stared at him. "What do you mean, son?"

"Oh, I just wanted to walk about the village a bit before I went to bed. Nothing to worry about. I feel as if I haven't been here for so long that I want to get to know it again."

"Right, right." The large smile returned to his father's face. "Yeah. I remember when I first went on a hunt to catch a boar, it felt like I'd been gone for days."

Most likely you were, Dallion thought, keeping the smile on his face. *You probably went to a neighboring village but have forgotten. I'll make sure you remember soon.*

From what Dallion had learned during the hunt, Dherma was the only village to have self-isolated itself. Other villages, while still run tightly by their local chiefs, hadn't gone to such lengths to erase all notions of the outside world. As far as Dallion could tell, it used to be common visiting other villages in the area. For the last two decades, such a luxury was only reserved to a few of the Luor family.

"Yeah." Dallion let out a clumsy laugh. "Leave some food for me? I might have another bite when I come back."

"Of course." Dallion's mother nodded. "Just…take care of yourself, okay? It's after dark. I don't want you to come back too late."

You suspect something, don't you? "Sure thing, Mom." Dallion got up from the table. "Lin, I promise to tell you more stories tomorrow. Okay?"

"Yay! Thanks, brother! You're the best!"

"That's what big brothers are for."

With a smile and a wave, Dallion quickly left the room. Once outside, he could finally let out a sigh of relief. At least he didn't have to pretend anymore, and if all went well by tomorrow evening, no one else would have to pretend either.

Making sure that no one was watching, Dallion made his way to the river and out of the village. From there, he sprinted to the cave of the awakening shrine. The entire way, he wondered if he'd find Gloria there. The girl was good at sneaking out of her home just as much as he was. Unfortunately, when Dallion entered the chamber, he found he was the only one.

Maybe it's better this way, Dallion thought, even if he didn't feel so. *It would only have led to complications.* He placed his hand on the altar.

SHRINE AWAKENING

The green rectangle emerged, along with the expected changes around him.

You are in a small awakening shrine.
Complete the trial to improve your destiny.

"I'm back," Dallion said out loud, tapping the blue rectangle that had subsequently appeared. He had no idea what would happen, but he just felt like doing it.

The awakened space of the shrine felt simplistic compared to the gyms he had been training at. The difference was more than apparent. This was a low-level awakening shrine that didn't even reach double digits. Even so, there were a few levels to be obtained here.

Dallion took the dartbow from his holster, then turned around and walked toward the pair of columns in front of him. A very familiar archway with the Roman number four appeared.

Time to see how much I've improved. Dallion stepped through.

Shrine trial 4 chosen!
Prepare for combat!

Sand dunes formed around him as far as the eye could see. All that remained was for the sand dragon to appear.

"Darude, sandstorm dragon." Dallion chuckled to himself. Back when he had helped Gloria defeat it, it had seemed like such a vast achievement. Since then, he had made many attempts to best the guardian on his own, none of them successful.

SHRINE GUARDIAN 4
Species: DRAGON
Class: SAND
Health: 100%
Traits: UNKNOWN
Skills:
- SANDSTORM (Species Unique)
- SANDSWIM (Species Unique)
- SANDWAVE (Species Unique)
Weakness: EYES

A white rectangle appeared over a sand dune. Moments later, the massive form of the sandstorm dragon emerged. The monster glared at Dallion, massive eyes gleaming with the confidence of one who had remained undefeated.

"It's me again." Dallion smiled. "Fancy another attempt?"

The sand dragon roared, filling the surrounding air with fine dust.

COMBAT INITIATED

Dallion didn't waste time with poses. Following the ranged attack marker, he aimed at the dragon's eye and squeezed the trigger, then again and again. Three bolts shot, hitting their target with deadly accuracy.

CRITICAL HIT
Dealt damage is increased by 150%
CRITICAL HIT
Dealt damage is increased by 150%
CRITICAL HIT
Dealt damage is increased by 150%

Why didn't you block or evade? Dallion wondered. His initial shots were only meant to provoke the guardian so Dallion gained an advantage for his following attack. Instead, he had actually dealt damage? Well, he definitely wasn't going to put this to waste. Without hesitation, he aimed at the other eye and shot three times more.

CRITICAL HIT
Dealt damage is increased by 150%
CRITICAL HIT
Dealt damage is increased by 150%
CRITICAL HIT
Dealt damage is increased by 150%

The dragon let out another roar. Dallion quickly shielded his upper torso with his buckler. Instead of attacking, however, the guardian dropped to the ground like a giant sack of potatoes.

You have broken through your fourth barrier.
You are now Level 4
Choose the trait that you value the most.

A green rectangle appeared.

"Err, okay?" *This is ridiculous!*

The dragon that had seemed like a brick wall, stressing out Dallion for days, had been killed with six shots just like that? How could this happen?

"I guess this might take less time than I thought…"

THE FIFTH TRIAL

COLLECTED
(+2 Mind)
Being calm and dispassionate often helps in difficult situations,
although there's such a thing as overthinking.

The rectangle was unexpected, bringing a smile to Dallion's face. Achievements were always a joy to have. Other than the sense of personal satisfaction, they always came with a stat boost, mind in this case. The explanation text was weird, though. There was no telling whether this was flavor text or actual hints were being presented. It didn't help that Dallion already had earned the titles of Reckless and Collected, creating a potential existential paradox. Would the two qualities cancel each other out? Or would they complement each other in some strange and peculiar way? Hopefully, time would tell.

Dallion didn't have to wait for long. The moment he tapped away the rectangle, the standard leveling choice emerged before him. Just as before, four options were presented, although the values had significantly grown since the first time he had appeared in this world.

Dallion's mind had grown to an astonishing nine. If he ever managed to get back home, he wouldn't have a problem with any exams for the rest of his life. Reaction—which was his prize trait—remained at eight, while body and perception were equal at four each. As tempting as it was to increase mind to a full ten, Dallion hit the white rectangle that symbolized perception. He had seen the advantage it could have in combat, especially paired with a ranged weapon.

Once the choice was made, the sea of dunes vanished, replaced by the columns of the shrine's awakening area. Becoming a level four was a cause for celebration in itself. Dallion had achieved in a few weeks what others in the village had spent years on. At this point, he could call himself equal to Gloria and Veil, but that wasn't enough. The village chief remained stronger. If Dallion was to successfully challenge him, he had to up his game as well.

Dallion took a step to the right. A new archway formed—archway number five. Dallion had no idea what he would find there. Before joining the hunting party, he had tried entering out of sheer curiosity, only to find an empty sky. Maybe the awakening shrine didn't consider him ready to present him with its next trial? If so, would it now?

"Let's see what you have for me." Dallion stepped through.

Shrine trial 5 chosen!
Prepare for combat!

Dallion's heart skipped a beat. This was it, the final level of the shrine, if his grandfather was to be believed. Given the jump in difficulty between the third and fourth test, Dallion expected something terrifying.

Taking a defensive stance, he braced himself for what was to come. Unlike the previous locations, this one was hidden by a thick white mist.

What could the trial be? Dallion wondered.

The third one was related to water, the fourth to sand, which could be either earth or fire. That suggested that the fifth one had to be...

"Oh, crap."

As the mist cleared up a bit, Dallion found himself standing on top of a large cliff. At that point, he realized the mist he had been looking at all this time wasn't mist...it was a cloud.

A strong breeze swept through the area, revealing more of the surroundings. The cliff turned out to be a chain of sharp mountain peaks connected to each other through a series of thin, windy paths. The ground wasn't visible. In fact, Dallion wasn't sure there was ground, just an endlessness of sky and clouds above, below, and all around.

Good thing I have a ranged weapon. Dallion went to the nearest edge and looked down. Fighting anything here with a sword and buckler would have been next to impossible. Or maybe it was impossible. If "attack" was a group of skills, maybe the shrine was built to ensure that a person had experience in all kinds of attack skills, ranged included.

A series of hawkish cries filled the air.

Birds, Dallion thought. *It has to be birds.*

Logically, that was the only thing that made sense. Every trial guardian so far was linked to the surrounding environment. In a wide-open space, the obvious choice was to have something that could fly—eagles, harpies, maybe even some type of winged dragon. Whatever it was, Dallion was ready for it.

Taking a quick look around, Dallion went back, looking for a path up the mountain peak he was on. Given how high he was, he had no intention of attempting to climb, although if there was a safe route, getting access to the high ground was preferable.

COMBAT INITIATED

A red rectangle emerged, marking the start of the trial. With no time to climb, Dallion directed his attention toward the vast space around him. Scattered clouds were still covering most of the sky, making it difficult to spot any enemies. Or rather, they might have made it difficult if he hadn't improved his perception trait.

It took less than a second for him to spot several black outlines beneath a cloud surface. This was the first time in Dallion's life that he saw an actual flock of eagles emerge in the distance. Each eagle was the size of a man with a wingspan at least eight feet long. Without hesitation, Dallion drew his dartbow and took aim.

As suspected, a series of attack markers appeared on the targets. Dallion moved the red point emerging from his dartbow until it lined up with a target marker, then shot a bolt.

With a screech, one of the eagles dissolved in a puff of feathers, disappearing. Several more soon followed, shot out of the sky with extreme precision. At this distance, most people would be hard pressed to see the target at all, but thanks to Dallion's attack markers and improved senses, hitting them felt as easy as playing a computer game. In some aspects, maybe that was what awakening was? In a very magico-fictional fashion, of course.

Less than a minute later, the flock had been reduced in half. Initially, there was a moment of silent rejoicing on Dallion's part, but soon it was replaced by concern. There had been over a dozen hits so far, and yet not a single rectangle to show for it.

Dallion lowered his dartbow. The flock of eagles continued rising, completely disinterested in his presence. That was mildly curious, though definitely not as surprising as what followed.

Without warning, a giant hand of stone appeared from beneath the clouds a short distance away and grabbed one of the mountain peaks. Another hand followed, and another, and another. A giant statue emerged, dispersing the clouds with its mere movement.

What's going on? Dallion blinked, unable to look away at the monstrosity emerging. It was as if he faced the Statue of Liberty, or rather, her slightly bigger sister.

SHRINE GUARDIAN 5
Species: GRAND COLOSSUS
Class: GRANITE
Health: 100%
Traits: UNKNOWN
Skills:
- QUAR ARM ATTACK (Species Unique)
- EARTH SHAKER (Species Unique)
- STONE CUTTER (Species Unique)
Weakness: EARS

Now it became clear why no one in the village had completed the fifth trial.

FIGHTING A MOUNTAIN

F ighting a mountain on top of a mountain...

Dallion shot two bolts at the head of the giant colossus as quickly as the dartbow would let him. There had been a time, back on Earth, when he had wondered what it would be like playing the main character in *Shadow of the Colossus*. Now that he had his wish, he deeply regretted it.

Size really wasn't considered a factor in the awakened state. Dallion had fought large creatures, enormous creatures, large creatures that could become enormous upon merging in a group, and now gigantic creatures. The challenge limitation made so much more sense now. Without a ranged weapon, there would be no way to defeat the guardian, although maybe Gloria might have a chance with her acrobatic skills.

"If I don't get any new skills at the end of this combat, there's no justice in this world!" Dallion shouted in the hopes the shrine would take note. That was a problem for another day, though. At present, he still had to actually defeat the colossus.

Bolt after bolt hit the giant head, only to bounce off or sink in the stone of the guardian's face like a fashionable piercing.

According to the large white rectangle above the guardian's

head, the weak spots were supposed to be the creature's ears but, so far, Dallion had received no indication that was the case. Maybe the goal was to shoot into the ears? That made sense, even if it complicated the task to the extreme.

Suddenly, the guardian lifted its upper left arm. A massive green cone surrounded Dallion, along with part of the mountain behind him. Immediately, he reacted by sprinting toward the ledge path that connected to the next peak. It was this complete lack of hesitation that saved Dallion from certain defeat.

With one strike, the giant hand sliced the mountain in half. Its speed was vastly superior to what Dallion expected it would be. Apparently, just because a creature was large didn't mean it was slow.

"D-a-a-a-a-m-n i-i-i-t!" Dallion shouted, running along the ledge. He had no idea how he was keeping his balance, and he didn't care.

Red markers appeared as he ran, indicating the angle at which he had to hold the dartbow to hit his enemy. Dallion took full advantage of them, not even looking in the direction of the guardian as he squeezed the trigger. The situation was so desperate, he even considered throwing his buckler at the colossus if that would help increase his chances. As things stood, a tiny shield wasn't going to be much use for defense anyway.

Think! He glanced at the colossus.

The recent attack had removed most of the clouds, revealing the creature's upper torso, as well as several peaks in the area.

Dallion knew there was a way to defeat the colossus; otherwise, the awakening shrine wouldn't have allowed the trial to take place. The answer wasn't brute strength, so it had to be agility and precision.

Taking a close look at the surrounding environment, Dallion saw the peaks were connected along an arc. More than likely, they formed a ring round the guardian. Another interesting fact was that, despite the colossus' speed, it remained in exactly the same position, still facing the peak that he had just destroyed. The answer was to run to the side of the head and shoot a bolt inside the ear. The only problem was that, in order to do that, Dallion had to avoid the guardian's four arms.

"Maybe if I whirl the dartbow while I shoot, I'll get the bolt to curve?" Dallion asked out loud, hoping it would trigger a glowing rectangle to appear. Unfortunately for him, it didn't.

It was an absurd concept, but considering the logic of this place, it might well turn out possible. One attempt later, it became obvious that some things remained impossible even in a realm of magic. The bolt just flew on into the distance, unaffected by the amount of effort Dallion put in.

Upon reaching the second peak, Dallion raised his shield, expecting the guardian to react. To his surprise, there was no immediate attack. The massive face had turned slightly, looking at Dallion with a faint smile.

Of course, Dallion thought, annoyed at himself. He was facing a sentient entity, not a robot that repeated a set of instructions. All the guardians he had faced so far had been sentient. Why should this one be any different?

Mental images of the surrounding area formed in Dallion's mind as he continued to search for possible solutions. He could evade the next attack, then try to leap onto the colossus' hand. If he had acrobatic skills, he might even succeed to run to the guardian's head. Another option was to keep shooting at a distance in the hopes the bolts would wear the creature down, or possibly provoke it to move closer.

Two green cones surrounded Dallion. Quite sneaky on the part of the guardian, and it would have ended up fatal if Dallion hadn't expected it. Rushing forward as fast as his legs would take him, he managed to escape to the next ledge path. The sound of shattering rock filled the air as a second peak crumbled to rubble beneath the clouds.

There was no way to defeat something like this! There wasn't even a way to reach a stalemate. Eventually, Dallion would be left out of strength—or out of mountain peaks to run to—and then the guardian would squish him like a bug. And to think he thought the sand dragon was a challenging threat.

"How can I defeat a giant as tall as a mountain?" Dallion asked out loud while running.

Surprisingly, the answer came to him moments later. There was no guarantee it was the right answer, or even a particularly good answer, but something told Dallion it was worth the risk. All he had to do was reach the next peak.

"You're not fighting fair, you know!" Dallion shouted. "How about some fair play? Take a handicap or something!"

Maybe it was the adrenaline rushing through his veins, or maybe it was his imagination, but Dallion could have sworn he saw the colossus shrug.

"Overpowered, cheating jerk!" he grumbled as he kept on running.

It didn't take him long to reach the next peak. The guardian had politely allowed Dallion to get there safely...or maybe he was just toying with him. Either way, things were going to be different this time.

Personal awakening, Dallion thought and put his left hand over his mouth.

A doorway emerged in the mountain's face just ahead. This was what Dallion was waiting for. Linking awakening states might be bad, but when in an awakening shrine, there was nothing to worry about.

"How about this, you lump of rock?" Dallion shouted as he jumped into his awakening room.

THE PERSONAL ARENA
You Are Level 4

The rectangle illuminated the room. Never had Dallion been so glad to be in this small, dark space. Finally, he could catch his breath without worrying a ten-foot hand would slap him on the head…along with the rest of the mountain.

No wonder the soldiers treated all the volunteers differently. Compared to the "fully awakened," they probably were like kittens in a tiger's den. Thinking back, Dallion had been way too overconfident in his abilities. The limiting echo created by the village chief had made him think he was incapable of anything. Destroying it had created the notion that Dallion could do no wrong. The current challenge had quickly rectified this flaw, displaying the inadequate level of his abilities.

"I can't believe I charged at a chainling," Dallion said, lying on the floor.

Dame Vesuvia was right. He had been incredibly lucky. If the chainling hadn't been wounded, if Cleric hadn't been there to protect him, or if there hadn't been a group of double-digit awakened, he might very well have ended up dead and charred to a crisp.

Remaining idle for several seconds, Dallion glanced about the room. A number of changes had occurred. For one thing, it was slightly larger than before, and smooth walls replaced the previous medieval look, not to mention that his "ornaments" had increased. In addition to the sword and buckler, there now was a dartbow placed on one section of the wall, right beneath a plaque reading ATTACK SKILLS.

That was an interesting twist. It showed that Dallion had a choice of what weapon to use in his awakened state. Granted, there was no point in giving up the dartbow. However, there was something else he could do.

Dallion stood up and went to the attack area and took the short sword from the wall. Then he took the dartbow as well. The sword disappeared from his hand, appearing back on the wall. So much for dual-wielding, although maybe when he became fully awakened, he might be able to do that.

There were doorways in the room: one leading to the mini-library where the echo had previously resided and another linked the room to the mountain realm of the fifth trial. Dallion could see the colossus glaring at him from the distance.

"I bet you feel stupid, don't you?" Dallion crossed his arms. A mischievous voice in his brain dared him to move a few steps closer. The more reasonable part of him decided to delay that option for a bit. A short rest after all that running and jumping wasn't such a bad idea. Besides, if this room had changed so much since him reaching level four, maybe other rooms had as well?

Taking the buckler from the wall just in case, Dallion left the entry room. A hall formed outside, almost identical to the "corridor of judgment" he'd seen upon first awakening. The library room now was wide open just across. Dallion gave it a brief glance, but his interest lay in the corridor itself. Dartbow and buckler at the ready, he ventured on.

As he walked, torches consistently flared up and went out based on how close he was to them. Every few steps, there were a set of columns in the walls, as if dividing it in sections. Finally, the end emerged in the form of a bolted wooden double door. When presented with something unknown and potentially dangerous, Dallion did what virtually anyone else would: put his ear to the door's surface and started to listen.

For seconds, nothing happened. Even with a perception of five, there was nothing to be heard on the other side. Normally, when a door was barred, there was a reason for it, either keeping something in or keeping it out. Dallion knew he wasn't the one being kept in, but he also knew this was a shrine trial.

If nothing here could harm me, why not take the chance? Dallion asked.

Did it work that way, though? He was assuming quite a lot. The last few times he had made a similar mistake, he had ended up regretting it. Even so, it didn't look like he had any other options this time around. He clearly didn't have the skill or weapons to fight a mountain, so maybe there was something beyond this door that could help him even the odds?

Gently, Dallion removed the wooden bar. Taking a deep breath, he then opened the door with a single swing, then rushed in, aiming the dartbow forward. The new room was large and round, sharing characteristics of the gym that Kalis had trained Dallion in.

"So, this comes with level four?" Dallion lowered his weapon.

All in all, it was a nice place, though not nearly as nice as others he'd seen. There were no targets or practice dummies, just a wide-open space surrounded by stone walls.

COMBAT INITIATED

Three sets of green footprints appeared on the floor. Dallion didn't hesitate, rushing back. The moment he did, a figure emerged in the center of the arena.

That, in itself, was unusual. What was even more unexpected was that the figure was a guardian...a colossus guardian that looked remarkably like the one that had been smashing mountains a moment ago. The only difference was that this one was only seven feet high.

What the heck? Dallion shot three bolts at the guardian's head. Two of them were caught by the colossus' spare pair of hands, and the third bounced off its head without leaving a mark.

The creature glared at its attacker, then threw the bolts back at him. They were slow enough to deflect but proved that the colossus had both high speed and intelligence.

"What are you doing here?" Dallion kept his guard up. Maybe this was what Kalis had warned him about? Linking one awakened room to another allowed things to move between both. No, not things, creatures. "Did you follow me?"

The guardian frowned. Out in the mountain realm, it had shown nothing but smug smiles. Here, cold fury emanated from its expression.

"Or maybe I brought you here?"

Cool! Dallion thought. If he could bring guardians here to fight, his chances for victory improved considerably. Of course, it also meant he had to be careful what he brought here. In any event, he had to learn much more about what it was to be an awakened before he did this again. Before that, though, he had a guardian to defeat.

"How does it feel to be a fraction of your former self?" Now it was Dallion's turn to smile.

COLOSSAL COMBAT

Fighting the colossus with a dartbow and buckler turned out more difficult than Dallion expected. The more he tried to increase the distance, the more the guardian shortened it. Not to mention that for every shot that hit the guardian, three were deflected, and even half of those that weren't didn't deal any actual damage.

Why didn't your ears remain big? Dallion grumbled internally as he followed the markers to avoid yet another attack. To make things even more tense, the guardian—deliberately or not—performed multiple attacks, forcing Dallion to break his guard sequence mid-way.

After minutes of unsuccessful attempts, Dallion decided to resort to the good old methods of dealing with colossuses—a buckler to the head. The action was more out of desperation than anything else. It was half-expected to be easily blocked, similar to the standard attacks. To his surprise, though, the shield hit the stone head with a loud, resounding *clang*.

SURPRISE ATTACK

Dealt damage is increased by 50%
Opponent's options to react are limited

There was no way that could pass as a surprise attack, but Dallion had no intention of arguing. Taking advantage of the colossus' momentary daze, he rushed along the defense markers. Good thing too, for just as he finished the first set, the guardian began its next attack.

"Too late," Dallion whispered. The advantage gained from the first guard sequence helped him comfortably avoid the next, which in turn allowed him to complete another full defense set, then another, and another.

By the fourth, pressure had started to creep in. Thanks to his improved body trait, Dallion was nowhere near exhaustion, though he still had to be careful not to overdo it. At this point, he could already move a significant distance away between time-freezes, to the extent he could put himself in a good enough position to shoot at the colossus' ear from point-blank range. However, he decided to push on. The evasion sequence was much more complicated than before, following a pattern Dallion hadn't seen.

Step, step, jump, whirl, bend, twist left, he said to himself as he did it.

Colossus' arms struck left and right, each missing by inches. A moment of hesitation appeared in Dallion's mind but was quickly ignored as he gritted his teeth to match the final green footprints. The moment he did, time completely froze.

ESCAPE TRIGGERED
If you wish to end combat and leave the realm, smash the window

"There's an escape option?" Dallion gasped.

That changed everything! It pretty much meant he could leave a battle unharmed and didn't even have to rely on an emblem. The guard skills were unimaginably good! If people knew about this, they would probably not choose anything else.

Of course, being able to take advantage of this option required a person had the skill, speed, and endurance to complete five guard sequences in a row. It was by no means an easy task but, even so, an obvious cheat.

Dallion looked around. Green footsteps continued to cover the floor. By his speculation, the moment he took a step anywhere, the offer would end, and he'd return to his battle. However, given that there wasn't a timer anywhere on the rectangle, Dallion could also remain still for a while to catch his breath and rest.

His weakness is his ears, Dallion thought, doing his best to look over his shoulder at the guardian. Given the standard time freeze his guard skills provided, it was possible for him to jump into position. However, before he did, a question came to mind. What bonuses did attack streaks get? With green markers, it was simple. Following them would slow time, allowing him to get into a better position for a counterattack, or continue until the escape option became available. Red markers only allowed him to reach a point to perform the optimal attack. Even when using ranged weapons, all he got was a laser sight marker and that was it. Could it be that he needed to increase his level before anything became available? Now was a good moment to find out.

"Here goes," Dallion whispered.

Twisting his body in a hundred-and-eighty-degree leap, he jumped from green marker to green marker until he was a few feet away from the guardian. From this angle, the colossus' ear was perfectly visible. It also had a deep red marker on it.

The weak spot! Dallion thought.

It wasn't exactly what he had set out to find, but he wasn't going to complain. If his perception had been better, he wouldn't have had such a tough time. That explained why Gloria was so good at hitting the training guardian back in the hunting party. With her perception, she could easily see all the weak spots, and maybe more.

Taking advantage of the time freeze, Dallion aimed. When the two red dots aligned, transforming into bright orange, he squeezed the trigger.

CRITICAL STRIKE
Dealt damage is increased by 150%

The rectangle had barely appeared when Dallion shot a second bolt. To his surprise, that hit as well. It was exactly like with the sand dragon. Two more critical hits followed before the guardian managed to jump back.

It appeared that after each successful hit, the target lost the ability to react for a fraction of a second. Thinking about it, the same must have occurred dozens of times during battle, but Dallion had been focusing so hard on the guard sequence type of bonus that he had never noticed. Attack bonuses were far more subtle, at least for now, relying on hits, not the sequence of markers leading to it.

Good to know, Dallion thought as he retreated from the guardian. Looking at the white information rectangle of the colossus, the being's life had considerably dropped, reaching seventeen percent. A few more hits, and Dallion would be the clear victor. Given the new combo, it was pretty much a foregone conclusion. There was nothing the guardian could do but prolong the inevitable.

"Want us to stop here?" Dallion asked. "There's no point in going on. You can't win."

The colossus frowned, although not moving from its position. That was good. At least Dallion wasn't going to face a sudden charge again.

"I know you can give up," Dallion continued. "I'm not sure what the difference is, but it'll still get me to advance."

There was no reaction.

"I really have no problem repeating my attack. I just thought that a surrender would be better."

The features on the colossus' face softened. The guardian lowered its arms, then slowly walked toward Dallion in a relaxed fashion. If this were anywhere else, Dallion would probably have performed his combo attack and finished his enemy off. Since this remained an awakening shrine trial, though, he decided to take the chance and lowered his dartbow.

Step by step, the colossus approached until it stood in front of Dallion. At this distance, one could appreciate how formidable it actually was: seven feet of solid granite with four arms and the speed of a cheetah. Two of the colossus' hands moved up, covering its ears completely.

Dallion swallowed. Had he tipped his hand?

Another of the guardian's hands extended forward.

"You want us to shake on it?" Dallion wondered. "Sure, why not?" If he had decided to trust the creature, he might as well go all the way.

With next to no hesitation, Dallion shook the hand, or did as much as humanly possible—it was a piece of stone, after all.

"Thanks." Dallion smiled.

**The SHRINE Guardian has admitted defeat.
Do you accept his surrender?**

A blue rectangle appeared.

"Yes," Dallion said as he pressed the corresponding rectangle with his free hand.

No sooner had he done so, the guardian disappeared in a cloud of particles, along with the rectangle. Moments later, a new one appeared.

You have impressed the SHRINE guardian with your behavior! The Colossus has granted you a future boon.

PATH TO FULL AWAKENING

There was nothing glorious in the way Dallion had become level five—he hadn't bested the mountain, nor had he achieved a bone-crushing victory. Not too long ago, he would have considered a surrender a fake win. Now, though, he was remarkably pleased with the result. Reaching this level had proved to be far more difficult than he had expected. It definitely wasn't as simple as computer games back on Earth had made it out to be. Now, finally, he almost had what it took to challenge the village chief. Only one last step remained.

When given the choice of which trait to improve, Dallion had chosen body. Despite the clear advantages of a single focus of development, being balanced seemed to be the key. At least at this point, he wouldn't be worried about losing due to low stamina.

Done, Dallion went back to his starting awakening room. The gateway to the shrine was still there, although it no longer led to the mountain realm but the circle of columns instead. That wasn't the only change. Dallion's room had also grown to the size of a meeting hall. A pity it remained so empty. Having two weapons and a buckler in such a vast space was quite noticeable.

"Time to go for broke." Dallion took a deep breath and left the room.

The moment he did, all six columns shimmered a bright blue. Five of the archways were completely blocked now, leaving only one open. There was no number indicating the number of the trial, nor were there any symbols or any other indications of what one might expect. Was this part of the trial? Now was the moment to find out.

Ready for anything, Dallion walked through. To his surprise, the environment around him remained the same. An altar emerged from the ground, similar to the one that was present in the shrine back in the real world. Moments later, a light blue figure appeared behind it.

"Hello, Awakened." The figure shifted, taking the appearance of a woman dressed in a combination of long cyan robes and metal armor. If there was a way to describe her, it was a cross between the Greek goddess Athena and a Valkyrie. "Congratulations on passing the first gate on the path of greatness."

"Thank you." *It was nothing much.*

"One last task remains before your full awakening," the woman continued.

"Bring it on! I'm ready." Dallion puffed his chest, then mentally froze, realizing he had become like Veil. The realization sent cold chills down his spine. Some things were too horrible to imagine.

The woman narrowed her eyes.

"This task is unlike the ones you've done until now. There will be no enemy to best, no beast to capture, no puzzle to solve. Now, it is time for you to face the thing people fear the most."

"Err, before that, can I ask a question?" Instinct made Dallion raise his arm as if he were back in school. Thankfully, the woman found that acceptable enough because she nodded. "Who are you?"

The question was so clichéd that Dallion expected a sarcastic response at best. However, the features on the woman's face shifted in surprise.

"You are the first to ask me that in quite a while," she said in a pensive voice. "Sadly, that is not an answer I can yet give. Pass through the gate, and you'll find out." Her fashion of speaking changed drastically. For that single moment, she sounded like an ordinary person, not the over-the-top fantasy persona she had built up herself to be. "Instead, I shall tell you what you'll gain should you complete this test."

Strictly speaking, that was a clear bait and switch. Dallion didn't mind, though. There was something about the woman that made him feel at ease, a sense of shelter, calm, and hope. Just looking at her made all his questions seem insignificant.

"If you complete my test, you'll become a full awakened and gain the power to improve awakened areas, as well as create echoes of yourself."

The spark of curiosity flashed, burning through the sensation of calm that surrounded him.

"I can make echoes of myself? Does that mean I can place them in the heads of others?"

The woman's expression suddenly changed. Thanks to his perception level, Dallion was able to see the scorn written all over her.

"That is not what they are meant to be." The woman's voice had become as sharp as glass. "No more questions. Good luck in your test."

With that, the woman disappeared, transforming into blue mist that scattered in the air. Whoever she was, she definitely didn't appreciate the question. Still, Dallion couldn't help but wonder about her relation to the shrine. Could she be a goddess? A guide meant to help the awakened achieve their full potential, or at least become fully awakened? Or maybe just the magic equivalent of a hologram built in every awakening shrine? Either way, it was clear the village chief was doing something he wasn't supposed to.

"That old man really is a jerk," an oddly familiar voice said.

Without warning, a new person appeared across from Dallion on the other side of the altar. The concerning part was that the new person was also Dallion.

"Huh?" Dallion blinked.

"What?" The other Dallion shrugged. "We're both thinking it. It won't matter much after I challenge him. Everything will return to normal when that happens."

"Yeah, but...who're you?"

"I'm Dallion." The second Dallion laughed.

"*I'm* Dallion!" Dallion said.

"In a way, yes. You're my echo."

Your echo? Dallion thought.

There was no way that could be possible. Dallion was the real one. He remembered fighting through the sand dragon and the grand colossus to get here. Surely, he was the real one and the other him was the echo. In that case, why was the echo so confident?

Dallion took a step back and carefully examined his other self. The clothes, the weapons, the buckler...everything was a perfect copy down to the scrapes he had received in his last fight. Was this the test? Was he meant to defeat his echo?

"You are the echo," the second Dallion sighed as if reading his mind. "This new power will definitely take a while to get used to."

"What? Aren't you the echo?"

"Okay, let's play this game." The other Dallion crossed his arms. "If you're not the echo, how come I can read your thoughts and you can't read mine?"

That was a good question...a very, very good question. As much as Dallion struggled, he wasn't able to come up with an answer. The logic was ironclad, but it had to be false. There was no way for him to be the echo! Or was there?

DALLION'S ECHO

The prospect of being an echo of himself terrified Dallion. As much as he was certain he was the real him, there was just enough doubt to breed fear. If he was the original, nothing stopped him from leaving the awakening shrine. The echo would remain here—or alternatively vanish—and he would get back to challenging the village chief. However, if he turned out to be the echo, then attempting to leave would make him disappear.

"Yeah, it's a tough one." The other Dallion nodded. "Don't know what to suggest, man. If you want, I can leave. That way, you'll stay here."

Or vanish, Dallion thought. "What's the name of my first pet back in—"

"Alabaster, though it was my mom's poodle and not my own." The other finished the sentence. "Look, I can read your mind. Asking questions won't get you anywhere. Even if I am the echo, I'll know the answer as soon as you do."

That was hardly fair! If there was mind reading, it had to go both ways. Dallion moved to the altar. It was a solid piece of multi-colored crystal, identical to the one in the cave chamber, save for the wear and tear. Poking it revealed nothing useful. It would have been far too easy if that had revealed the truth.

"So, must we fight each other?" Dallion asked.

"I guess?" The other shrugged. "She didn't tell us much. Maybe we just have to prove who is who."

"How about a truce?"

"I thought about that, but would that help?"

"I don't know. Maybe if we shake hands, something will appear, or we'll merge in one or something."

It was a strange idea but, given everything, not the worst Dallion had come up with. The other him apparently agreed, for he approached Dallion and offered his hand. Taking a deep breath, Dallion shook the hand and...nothing happened. Both were there just as before. There was no glowing rectangle, nor any spectacular light effects.

"So, what's Plan B?" the second Dallion asked.

"Don't you have any ideas?"

"I'm not the one who needs convincing what I am. I thought it would be better if you come up with your own plans. It's not like you can keep them a secret from me."

The logic was flawless, just as Dallion would have come up with...although the other him was wrong about one thing. He would have trusted an idea that hadn't come from him, so long as it was a good idea.

How to prove he wasn't someone else? This sounded very much like a paradox puzzle. Strictly speaking, there was no way to prove a person was who they thought they were. Dallion had watched enough movies on the subject to be sure of that. If he were back on Earth, maybe the wonders of technology could compare his genes with that of the other Dallion and come to a conclusion. Lacking that, though...

"What if we both leave at the same time?" Dallion asked.

"That way, no one would know what to expect until it was over," the other said.

Dallion appreciated the other him approving of the idea, although he didn't like the air quotes his counterpart made when saying "no one."

"How do you plan on defeating the village chief?" Dallion asked suddenly.

"Huh? Same way you're thinking of doing it."

"Just say it, please. I can't read your mind, remember?"

"Fine, fine." The other Dallion sighed. "I'll do it in the morning when everyone is out there to see. It has to be public; otherwise, he might try to chicken out. Probably, he'll have me fight Veil first. Not Gloria, though."

"And if you have to fight her?"

"All depends on what happens, I guess. I won't hurt her, but I won't let her win either."

"That's a really bad plan."

"Hey," the other Dallion laughed, "it's your plan as well. It's not like we've got many options here. This isn't a medieval duel or something. The old man tried to kill us half a dozen times." He waved his hand. "Okay, not kill us; he only tried to seal our awakened power. You know that if he manages that, it'll be back to having an echo in the head." He tapped the right side of his temple.

Dallion shivered at the prospect. Now that he knew exactly what the scribe was and what he could do, having to bear one again was slightly terrifying.

"Anything else I missed?" the other Dallion asked.

"Guess not." *Drat!*

"Let's go, then."

Dallion waited a few more moments, then slowly made his way toward the arch he had come from. Every step, his fears increased. He felt he was the real one, and he definitely didn't want to disappear. What if refusing to find the other him resulted in Dallion being trapped in the shrine for all eternity?

Reaching the threshold, he stopped. Somehow, the dartbow had found itself in his hand. The other Dallion was only a step away. It would be so easy for him to ensure he would be the one getting out. A single shot and—

"Hold a sec!" Dallion shouted, taking a step back. "I have it!"

"You're going to shoot me," the other said in a cold voice, buckler raised high. "That's really low, you know."

"No, it's not." Before the other him could react, Dallion squeezed the trigger.

MAJOR WOUND
Your health has been reduced by 50%

A red rectangle appeared. Sharp pain came from Dallion's leg. However, he didn't mind it. Rather the opposite; he felt relieved. Putting the dartbow back in its holster, he looked at the other him, a smile shining through his pain.

"I didn't say which of us I'd shoot," Dallion said. "But you knew that, given that you can read my thoughts and all."

"Yeah, I knew." The other nodded. "All part of the test." He walked back to the altar. "Good thinking. An echo can only survive one shot. Good thing you upped your body. Dartbow bolts are serious business. Next time you're in doubt, just bang your head in the buckler. Safer that way."

"Right." At least now he knew exactly how much damage a bolt did. "Were you in on it from the start?"

"Duh. I might be your echo, but I wasn't made by you. How else could I guide you? Besides, breaking the fourth wall would have been weird. Now that you know what an echo is, it's okay. No hard feelings, right?"

He sat on the altar, waiting for Dallion to leave.

"Oh, right." The echo laughed. "The thing about mind reading. Echoes always read the thoughts of their creators, not the other way around. We have to know what we're supposed to be, after all."

"What will happen to you when I leave?"

"What happens to old memories? They're always out there somewhere."

The explanation didn't suit Dallion.

"Don't worry about it," the echo said before Dallion could voice his question. "It's magic." It winked. "You still have a job to do. If I'm gone, it's up to you to deal with the old man, remember? That's something we both want."

OLD PROPOSALS

The shrine altar remained dim after the test. Dallion made several attempts to get back inside, but to no avail. At one point, he even tried to mend the shrine, hoping to trick it into letting him in. That, too, was unsuccessful. As far as the awakening shrine was concerned, he had overextended his welcome.

While some more explanations would have been nice, the experience had made Dallion reach certain conclusions. For one thing, the shrines were only the first steps to awakening. They provided a little help—more hints and references—but not much in specifics. It was like trying to operate a secondhand television set without a user manual.

It was tempting to assume the village chief had hoarded the manuals—or whatever the local equivalent was—but judging by the overall state of things, it was more likely that it had been lost ages ago. At some point in the past, the Order of the Seven Moons must have had a monastery here, aimed at helping the awakened in this part of the world. Something had made them abandon it. Dallion strongly suspected the ogre battle in the area was more than a legend.

Awakened fighting giant mountains… The notion was scary as

it was fantastic, although Dallion had done just that not too long ago. If the colossus could be a mountain, then so could the ogres. Or wilder yet, maybe they had walked about in the real world, and it was the awakened who had defeated them?

Focus, Dallion told himself. He had more than Dallion could handle right now without worrying about roaming monsters.

"Thanks for all the help, Seven," Dallion said to the ceiling. "I promise to make good use of what you've taught me." *By kicking the village chief's ass,* he added in his mind.

Adjusting the dartbow under his clothes, Dallion left the cave. The stars were much brighter when he came out in the open. The single perception level he had increased made him feel as if he'd entered a whole new world. Sadly, it also came with a strong dose of itchiness.

Stupid clothes, Dallion grumbled. At his current level, improving them would be easy, though not recommended. He couldn't risk running out of awakening potential, even if he now could improve five items per day. To think that initially he could only do that once per day. Looking back, Dallion couldn't imagine how he had survived with such limitations.

The closer he got to the village, the more insistently his stomach rumbled. Going through two level-ups, even if the first could hardly be called difficult, had left its toll. Dallion felt like he could eat an entire feast, along with the table it was on. Hopefully, there would be some scraps waiting for him.

There was no one in the village streets when Dallion approached his house. All the people had gone indoors, likely under the influence of the chief's echoes. Dallion spent a while looking around just to be sure, then quietly sneaked into his house. The door had been left unbarred, eliminating the need for him to consider alternative means of entry. What was more, he found the table had already been set up with food.

Sweet! Dallion sat down and started eating.

The food tasted better than ever. It was just lettuce soup, fresh bread, and baked potatoes, but to Dallion, it felt like a feast. As he started eating, a door creaked open. Glancing over his shoulder, he saw his mother at the doorway.

"Does it taste well?" the woman asked.

"Definitely." Dallion smiled. "I really don't know how you do it, Mom."

"It helps having high perception." Dallion's mother made her way to the table and sat across him.

Dallion blinked. This wasn't a topic his mother spoke about often.

"It's all right." Gertha smiled. "Even echoes have their limits. Maternal instincts have a way of convincing them to loosen their hold." She took a piece of bread from the table. "Also, the village chief has a lot to feel guilty for."

"What do you mean?"

"The things your grandfather told you…not all of them are true. I know you've suspected as much, but it isn't his fault. There are things preventing him from helping you. Things he can't share…"

"I know." Dallion had already had the long talk with his grandfather. He would be having another now if the village chief hadn't called all the elders to his mansion under a fake pretext.

"The story you heard about me losing my powers also wasn't exactly true. It wasn't a lie…not exactly, but there were things omitted that made it false." The woman took a deep breath. "I didn't get tricked into improving the ring. Rather, that wasn't the only reason. Aspion always had grand plans for me, but it was an agreement with my father that kept them from acting on them. The two had made a vow to the Moons. My grandfather wouldn't meddle in the way Aspion ran the village and, in return, the village chief wouldn't harm my grandfather or anyone from his line unless provoked. All that changed when I awakened. Knowing how rare music skills are, Aspion offered me to join his family by marrying his son. That was the only loophole in the agreement. If I became a Luor, I was no longer just part of my grandfather's line."

That was very lawyerly of the village chief. It also explained why he hadn't tried to fight Dallion directly. If it hadn't been for the vow, Aspion could have easily sealed off Dallion's powers at any point. No attempts to give him tasks beyond his ability or locking him in an area domain from where he didn't have the level to exit. One direct fight, and Dallion would have been done for. As it had been made clear during the hunt, a multi-level gap was impossible to fill.

"I refused," Gertha went on. "And that is when he made his second offer."

Dallion couldn't say a word, listening intently to every word his mother said. His mother was offered to marry into the Luor family? He hadn't even considered the possibility. The entire notion seemed so medieval, it was beyond comprehension.

"He took a metal ring and told me it was to be my wedding ring," Dallion's mother continued. "It was up to me to choose, either I put it on and have him turn it to bronze, or I could improve it myself and give it to anyone I wished. It was painfully obvious it was a trap, but the echo made sure I didn't see that. I was young and had just enough of pride and arrogance to think I could manage on my own." The woman stopped, looking away.

That bastard! The chief had offered her a choice between two impossible options. Either choice was bad and, even so, Dallion's mother had been strong enough to choose the option she wanted. Ever since he could remember, Dallion had seen her somewhat sad, but also happy. Or was she? If she hadn't lost her awakened powers, it was a given she would have left the village, but that also meant Dallion and Linner never would have been born...

"I just wanted to tell you that I'm proud of what you've achieved." She smiled, looking back at her son. "I won't tell you what you must and mustn't do but, please, follow your heart. Don't get dragged down by others. Life is too wonderful to be bottled away for someone else's sake."

"I understand."

His mother smiled. "Thank you," she whispered. There was nothing left to add.

CLASH WITH THE CHIEF

There was something different in the air when Dallion woke up. Not long ago, he had dreaded this day, desperately trying to defeat the sand dragon and move beyond level three. The notion that he could reach level five or even get rid of the limiting echo in his realm were ludicrous to say the least. Now, not only had he achieved both, but he looked forward to what was to come, the day that everything would finally be settled.

The house was eerily empty, which was odd even if it was an hour after Dallion normally got up. Nonetheless, he went to the kitchen to get some breakfast. Looking among the pots, he found one with freshly steamed potatoes, as well as a small bowl of fresh butter. Good thing it hadn't gone bad. Considering the village didn't have any refrigeration technology, fresh food had to be consumed fast.

Taking his time, Dallion peeled the skin off several potatoes and put them on a plate. Halfway through, he added the butter on top, as well as a pinch of salt, before returning to the peeling. A pleasant smell tickled his nostrils. There was nothing better than potatoes. Pity he didn't give them as much respect back on Earth.

"Nothing better than food early in the morning, eh?" a voice asked nearby. There was no need to turn around to tell who it was.

"Morning, Veil," Dallion said as he kept on peeling. He'd heard the chief's grandson approach, although he had to admit the blond had gotten better at sneaking. Being a level four had its advantages. "Want a bite?"

Veil looked at the steaming potatoes, then shook his head.

"Nah, Grandpa's mad as it is. Eating with the enemy will only make things worse."

"I won't tell him if you don't." Dallion took a bite. Delicious.

"Maybe afterwards…if you're still in the mood."

The warning was clear. Just as Dallion had prepared for a fight, so had the village chief. After recent events, he had little choice. Even with all the echoes, people still considered him a hero. While none of them remembered the nature of the monster he had faced, the "boar" he'd fought became more and more vicious with every telling. It didn't help that the Luor family had desperately tried to place the focus on Gloria and Veil being the ones to thank for its defeat. At the end of the day, Dallion had also been there, and he had also come back alive. It was only a matter of time that his role became as important as those of the Luors involved.

"Can I finish this, at least?" Dallion asked with his mouth half-full.

"Always stuffing your face." Veil sighed. "You never change. Just make it quick, okay?"

Way to ruin breakfast. Dallion chomped down on several more potatoes, then wiped his hands with the closest cloth within reach. Not the most elegant way to finish a meal, but everything considered, it would have to do.

"Okay, let's go." He joined Veil.

The entire village had gathered in one part of the village. Dallion expected that to be the main square, or the chief's mansion.

Instead, Veil took him all the way to the other side of the village, where nothing but a few abandoned houses remained.

That was slightly confusing. There was nothing of importance there, only fields of wheat and potatoes stretched into the distance. What purpose could the village chief have in calling Dallion there? Was he going to ask him to improve the fields?

As he approached, Dallion saw the crowd was separated into three groups. There was the Luor family, standing tensely near one of the abandoned houses. Gloria was among them. The girl put on a brave face, making it seem that she enjoyed being there. With his current perception level, however, Dallion could tell she was faking it.

A short distance away, seated on makeshift wooden chairs, was the village council: Dallion's grandfather, five more elders, as well as Aspion Luor himself. With the exception of Kraisten and the village chief himself, everyone else seemed bored to the extreme, as if they'd seen it all before and couldn't wait to get back to somewhere warm and comfortable.

The last group was composed of the common people, waiting quietly for the announcement to take place. There was no joy in any of their faces. Sadly, there was no spark of hope either. Dallion's family was among them as well.

You definitely pulled out the stops, old man. Dallion frowned. *All the better.*

"Dallion." The village chief stood up from his seat. "So good to have you back. My grandchildren have told me a lot about how you helped in the hunt of the…boar." The old man's smile widened.

"No prob." Dallion forced a smile of his own. Without the echo, the chief's attempt at oratory seemed pathetic. How would anyone fall for something so obvious? "Glad to have helped."

Aspion's smile faded somewhat.

"As is the duty of any awakened," the chief continued, "and

while you've just returned from a glorious occasion, we must get back to your obligations to this village."

"Let me guess. You want me to repair that building?" Dallion pointed to one of the crumbling structures.

"Two of them," Aspion corrected. "You were away for over a week, so you have two obligations."

"Two weeks, huh?" Dallion rubbed his chin. "Guess there's no arguing with math. I'd have to say no, though."

"Huh?" The chief's expression froze. This was the first time anyone had refused an order in decades.

"Don't feel like it." Dallion shrugged. "Don't get me wrong. I'd love to help in some other way. Maybe do something everyone in the village will appreciate not just a few families."

"Oh?" Aspion's smile had vanished completely. There was no point in keeping up appearances at this point. It was clear Dallion had gotten rid of his limiting echo, which he couldn't have done if he was as weak as before.

"Actually, that was a lie. It's something everyone except you will appreciate." Dallion narrowed his eyes. "I'm taking you down, old man."

Dallion dashed forward. His speech and actions had caused enough confusion for everyone present to zone out for a moment. Right now, the chief's echoes worked overtime trying to suppress the fact that someone had refused a direct order. All Dallion needed to do was take advantage of those few moments to complete his attack. A single punch would likely be enough to send the old man flying. Regardless of the chief's level, his skills were capped. At best, he was as strong as Veil.

Step, step, twist, twist, slam, Dallion thought. It was just like hitting someone with a buckler on the head after a guard sequence…only without the actual buckler.

Time seemed to freeze. With every step, Dallion saw potential attacks. A frontal approach would be the most expected, so he chose to go with something else. Following the defense sequence he had been repeating dozens of times in the awakened realm, he dashed past the village chief.

"Got you, old man!" Dallion attacked with his fist.

THE VILLAGE WITHIN THE VILLAGE

A *n awakening area?*

Dallion stepped back. The chief still stood standing in front of him, eyes glaring with hatred. The village itself, though, had changed. The crumbling structures had not only miraculously repaired themselves, but had grown to the size of towers, drifting apart from one another.

You are in the land of DHERMA VILLAGE
Defeat the guardian to change the land's destiny

The realm of the village? Dallion wondered.

He had suspected there might be an awakened area that encompassed the entire village, but he hadn't expected it to be like this. In many aspects, the realm resembled the real world. If Dallion didn't know better, he'd think he was in some neighboring land. Everything seemed so lifelike, just different. There were vast fields, forests, mountains, even a large lake visible. Interestingly, there also were massive structures, ranging from small stone and wooden forts to what could only be described as a palace several miles in the distance.

"You think you have the guts to challenge me?" the village chief asked. He had also changed. A scabbard with a large sword hung from his waist, and—to Dallion's horror—a double-sized buckler was visible on his left arm. "It's your funeral. I only wanted for you to know your place," the man continued through clenched teeth. "All you had to do was to accept my authority and do as I asked, and you would have kept your powers. I would have even let you marry into the family, but, no, you had to make a scene."

"Marry into your family?" Dallion frowned. "Like my mother did?"

"She could have if she knew what was best." Aspion narrowed his eyes. "But, no, she had to be selfish to the end. Just like you. That's the problem with your family—selfish, every last one of you. And selfish people need to learn that the good of the many outweighs the good of the few."

"Wow, that's rich coming from you." Dallion wanted to take out his dartbow and shoot the village chief on the spot but managed to keep his calm. There would be time for that later. For the moment, there was no point in showing his trump card until he saw what the old man had up his sleeve.

"Your grandfather said that once and look at him now. Do you see this?" The village chief opened his arms as if showing the realm around him. "This is the village. My village."

"Looks a little rundown, if you ask me."

As if on cue, a guttural roaring sound came from the nearby structure. Thanks to his perception, Dallion managed to catch a glance of several ink-like creatures hidden inside. The creatures were very much different from the beings in items, or even in the well. They looked more sophisticated, even if barely equipped with rough loincloths and crude weapons. It was almost as if Dallion had stumbled on a lair of real-life goblins hiding in an abandoned building.

"It takes dedication to keep the village from crumbling."

Aspion ignored the creatures altogether. "Something you would have noticed if you had looked. Do you think that buildings remain upright on their own? Have you seen anyone repairing them?"

Actually, I have, Dallion thought.

There had been several instances when his father had to repair the roof on his own after a particularly fierce storm. There had been no assistance from the elders or the Luor family, no awakening magic, just a lot of effort and elbow grease. Of course, as a result, part of the roof still leaked to this very day.

"I'm the one who maintains everything! I'm the one who keeps you all safe! I'm the one you should be thankful to."

"Getting a bit upset there, old man." Dallion smirked. Normally, he was against such behavior, but the village chief deserved it. "The only reason you've remained in power is thanks to your echoes. Without them and your family, you're nothing."

"Oh?" A wicked smile reappeared on Aspion's face.

The moment he saw it, Dallion knew he was in trouble. He had tried to be too cool for his own good, and now there would be consequences. He could only hope he would be stronger than them.

"You're just a child." Aspion laughed. "For a moment, I was worried you might actually cause trouble, but now I just realized you know nothing!" He took a step back, then drew his sword. "You've no idea how I got to control the village, do you? You think the title was passed down just like that?"

The ground rumbled, slightly at first but, with every moment, it became more and more noticeable, as if an invisible giant made his way toward Dallion.

"A village realm is different from a building realm. Yes, you've destroyed my echo, improved the well, and even gone up a level or two. You're not in control of a realm, though. And do you know why?"

Dallion didn't like the sound of that. Tense, he kept looking around for the source of the rumbling. His senses screamed it had to be nearby, yet he still was unable to see it.

"In order to improve the wider realm, you must defeat all guardians in the area." As Aspion spoke, the ground behind him rose. "The village has five guardians in total, each corresponding to a vital part. To gain control of the realm, though, more is required. You need sacrifice, dedication, and the commitment that you'll be here when the realm needs you."

A few steps away, the ground had changed into a small hill. Massive arms of dirt emerged from both sides, giving the hill humanoid features.

Being an avid gamer, Dallion had heard the hills have eyes, but in this realm, they also had arms, legs, and a massive spiked club.

"But most important of all." The chief's expression lost any trace of humor. From here on, he was about to take Dallion's challenge seriously. "To gain control of a realm, you must defeat the key guardian and make him accept you as his master."

COMBAT INITIATED

A red rectangle emerged.

VILLAGE GUARDIAN

DHERMA VILLAGE GUARDIAN
Species: GOLEM
Class: EARTH
Health: 78%
Traits: UNKNOWN
Skills:
- ATTACK
- GUARD
- ACROBATICS
- ATHLETICS
- EARTH SHIELD SKIN (Species Unique)
Weakness: NONE

The guardian was not at all what Dallion had expected. The fact that there would be one entity responsible for the entire village was beyond comprehension. *One single entity was responsible for all this.* No wonder its health was at seventy-eight percent. The state of the village probably corresponded to the state of the guardian.

It was an interesting coincidence that he also was a golem

similar to the guardian of the well. The similarities, however, ended there. This guardian was far larger and, by the looks of it, less sophisticated than the stone golem, not to mention remarkably quiet. While the village chief had done all the talking, the golem had remained surprisingly silent, as if waiting to be given orders.

Just my luck, Dallion thought. He had to face the chief and his pet golem.

"It's hardly a fair fight." Dallion took a step back. "Maybe I should get a golem of my own?"

"There's no such thing as a fair fight," Aspion said in an icy tone. "A winner must know what to use in order to win. Didn't the noble tell you that?"

The village chief adjusted his buckler, then without warning, charged. Green markers appeared around Dallion. Three sets of defense markers, three attack paths the old man could use. It was almost like fighting the practice guardian.

"You're right," Dallion whispered. *I want to defend and attack.*

The color of the markers changed. Dallion drew his dartbow as he rushed forward. Calmly, he shot three bolts in the directions of the chief's attack paths, while continuing toward the third. It was a tactic he had developed in the hunting group with Veil and Gloria. Ironic that it would be the one he'd end up using against their grandfather. Moments later, he shot another bolt for good measure. The purpose of the attack wasn't to earn Dallion the win, but to see how the village elder would react.

With a twist of his buckler, Aspion deflected the bolts with ease. That much was to be expected. He had decades, possibly centuries, to practice his guard skills, compared to Dallion's weeks. That wasn't a concern, though. During Dallion's practice with Gloria, he had quickly found the buckler's limitations. No matter what he did, the right foot always remained unprotected.

A smile appeared on Dallion's face. Holding his breath, he aimed at the spot the attack marker said the chief's right foot would be, then squeezed the trigger. The bolt flew through the air, as if in slow motion, focusing on its target.

Got you! In his mind, Dallion could already see the red rectangle appear, informing him of the hit. Just a few more moments and the village chief would be severely injured, not to mention have his mobility significantly impaired. Just as the tip of the bolt was about to pierce the foot, however, the old man disappeared, shifting its location.

Huh? Dallion blinked.

The arrow continued its path, drilling into the soft ground. Before Dallion could figure out what was going on, a green shield marker appeared inches from his left shoulder. Instinct and pure luck made him react, twisting his body so to position his buckler in the position suggested…right in time to save him from the sword thrust that pushed him several steps back.

"You've got some skills after all," the village chief said, breaking his attack. Somehow, he had appeared a few steps away. "City guard standards must have gone to the Crippled if they're freely handing out dartbows," he grumbled. "Normally, you'd have to earn one of those, and the first rule was to learn to use it properly."

Guard skill benefits, Dallion thought, trying to rationalize how he had missed an obvious show. It had to be. There was no other explanation for this. Now, he finally understood what all his opponents had felt in the past. The skill was extremely beneficial to use, as he had done so quite often. When the shoe was on the other foot, though, it seemed painfully unfair.

"You probably thought you're such a big shot knowing two skills?" Aspion waited in place.

"That's one more than most people I've seen so far," Dallion lied, all the time keeping an eye on the earth golem.

"Guard and attack, the two most common skills. The dame won't make you her dog with just that." There was unmistakable bitterness in Aspion's voice. "Your grandfather had mastered three in the first month alone. And he wasn't the only one. Did you think that the title elder was just for show?"

"It's not the skills, it's how you use them." Dallion shot three bolts, then rushed forward. All he needed to do was hit the chief on the head with his buckler. It wouldn't be an elegant move, but it had served him well. Before that, however, he had to provoke the old man to do counterattack.

The first two bolts were deflected in quick succession. The village chief then avoided the third, preparing to meet Dallion with an attack of his own.

Green and red markers appeared.

I have you now, Dallion thought. This time, he didn't attack. Instead, he followed through, following the series of defense footprints until the jump ability was triggered. One quick leap, and he was on the other side of the village chief. Looking at the old man, it was so tempting to shoot a bolt right off. It was virtually impossible for the chief to react on time, let alone deflect it. However, that wasn't the goal. In order to get this right, Dallion had to follow through.

Twist, twist, forward, forward...

A second defense sequence was complete. Then a third, and a fourth, and a fifth...

ESCAPE TRIGGERED
If you wish to end combat and leave the realm, smash the window

Victory at last! From here on, there was no way for the village chief to do a thing. Dallion could leave the realm here and now, or he could jump to the old man's blind spot and attack. Either way, he would—

ESCAPE OPTION CANCELLED.

A new green rectangle popped up, putting an end to the time freeze. What was more, Aspion didn't seem remotely affected, or even impressed. His sword held low, he gave Dallion the look a chess master would give a toddler. Amusement and pity twinkled in his eye as if saying, "You've just learned to the move the pieces."

"Nice trick you've picked up," the old man said. "But nothing can exit this realm without my permission. You would have known that if you'd bothered to ask."

"As if you'd have told me." Dallion took a step back, raising the buckler in front of his chest.

"I'm not talking about me. I'm talking about your grandfather."

OFFER REJECTED

"My grandfather?" Dallion hesitated. Most of the things Dallion had learned about awakening were from his grandfather. He knew there was a lot the old man couldn't share because of the limiting echo, but was it possible there were details he could have mentioned and chosen not to?

"He was the one who first obtained control of this area," the village chief said. "I guess he's not as reliable as you thought."

"Yeah, things like echoes tend to get in the way."

At the moment, Dallion's concern was how to continue the fight, rather than any information his grandfather might have kept from him. Without the escape option, he couldn't make use of his ultimate surprise attack. To make matters worse, the bonuses of his entire defense sequence had been completely negated.

"You're not leaving here unless I let you." The village chief took a step forward.

He doesn't know what I was aiming to do, Dallion thought. That meant that, unlike the echo in the last trial, the old man couldn't read Dallion's thoughts. That gave him a chance. All Dallion needed to go was to trigger the escape option again but, this time, instead of trying to escape, take advantage of the time freeze and attack Aspion before the man canceled the option. The moment was only going to last fractions of the second, but in that time, the village chief would be vulnerable.

"Give up," Aspion said. "You don't even suspect your worth. The people need the awakened. So long as you don't oppose me, you can stay in the village. If you join my family, you'll never need for anything."

Options flickered through Dallion's mind. Direct attacks might not be good enough, but what about a ricochet shot? Combination attacks were a thing. If a melee attack could be combined with a defense action, why not a ranged one as well?

"As long as you promise me, I won't even ask you to admit defeat. No one can see what's happening here. In the real world, you'll continue with your attack, and I would think of some nonsense about your bravery proving you suitable for my grand-daughter. My echoes will take care of the rest."

"Anything so long as I don't cause a ripple?" Dallion tested his theory, discreetly aiming at the buckler with his dartbow. It only lasted a fraction of a second, but Dallion was able to see the red line bounce off the metal surface like a laser off a mirror. Part one of the new plan had gone without a hitch. "What if I want to leave? Go to a city? I heard they are the places to be."

"We all have to make sacrifices. You'll stay here. Whatever you want will be brought to you. Merchants like the awakened. Several members of my family earn their keep by improving an item or two each time one of the traveling peddlers passes by."

"I see. What about him?" Dallion pointed at something behind the village chief.

It was the oldest trick in the book. No one on Earth would have fallen for it. However, this wasn't Earth. Whether through habit or curiosity, Aspion turned around to look. And that was the precise moment that Dallion went on with the second part of his plan. Taking advantage of his high reactions, he angled the buckler in such a fashion so a shot would hit his target, then squeezed the trigger.

The bolt bounced exactly as the line suggested it would. The only time Dallion had seen anything of the sort was when playing virtual billiards. That was only part of the plan, though. A single attack, even if successful, wouldn't amount to much. Moments after firing the shot, Dallion sprinted forward.

Aspion turned in time to deflect the bolt at the very last moment. The action, though, had been close enough to trigger the appearance of a series of green markers.

Here we go again. Dallion held his breath. *Step, step, turn, step, twist…*

The pattern was easy to follow. Dallion went on segment by segment. The village chief didn't seem to catch on, continuing with his attempts to slice Dallion with his sword. Several times, the blade passed within inches of his face, a scary, yet surprisingly invigorating experience that only made Dallion more determined.

ESCAPE TRIGGERED
If you wish to end combat and leave the realm, smash the window

Finally, the rectangle appeared. Dallion didn't even bother waiting, immediately leaping to a spot on the side of the chief. From there, it was one simple swing to do one of his golden classics— shield to the head.

"Sleep tight, old man." Dallion grinned.

A loud ringing noise followed like metal hitting on metal.

There was a moment of confusion. Could it be that the village chief had a head of steel? Or maybe being awakened for so long had caused him to gain abilities Dallion wasn't aware of. As it became obvious, the answer was very different. Dallion's buckler had clashed against nothing else but the chief's shield, resulting in the unusual noise.

"How?" Dallion asked, leaping back.

"I told you, you're just a beginner in this." There was no hatred on the chief's face, only disappointment, and possibly even pity. "Even the gifted need time to develop. You were lucky being selected by the hunting party, but nice weapons and a one-week training course aren't enough to defeat me."

Without warning, Aspion jumped in the air. The action was elegant, precise, almost graceful. Looking at it, Dallion had the distinct feeling he had seen it before…only last time, it was Gloria who had performed it.

"You're good at combining your skills, just as your grandfather was." The chief landed back on the ground a short distance away. "But there's only so much you could do with attack and guard. I can do that as well, but also combine them with acrobatics." He leapt forward, swinging the sword as he did.

A series of green lines appeared on Dallion, changing location faster than he could keep up. There was no avoiding such an attack. The only option was retreating while deflecting what he could with his buckler.

MINOR WOUND
Your health has been reduced by 5%
MINOR WOUND
Your health has been reduced by 5%
MINOR WOUND
Your health has been reduced by 5%
MINOR WOUND
Your health has been reduced by 5%

Red rectangles stacked on top of each other. The attacks continued like a whirlwind of swords. This was no normal combo; it was something the village chief had trained to do. Halfway through, he paused, letting Dallion take a breath.

One single attack, and he had already reduced Dallion's health by a fifth.

"Last chance," Aspion said. "Give in or lose your powers."

"I think I'll pick option three." Dallion gritted his teeth.

"Suit yourself."

WEAK SPOT FOUND

In reality, fighting was never supposed to be fun. The awakening state had made it feel too much like a game. There was next to no pain, fatigue was slowed, and wounds were reduced to a floating notification rectangle. And still, the more rectangles piled up, the more scared Dallion became. He always knew the chief wasn't only for show—being able to keep every other awakened in check took some doing—however, even he didn't think things would be this bad.

The village chief's skills were a match for Dallion's. In addition, he also had Gloria's level of acrobatics and a variety of ways to combine them. Mixing acrobatics with swordsmanship was impressive enough. Adding buckler moves was astonishing.

Spin attacks, defense push jumps, corkscrew slashes... Dallion had to defend against each of them, and not always successfully. The defense markers and his out-of-the-box thinking were only able to do so much. When the amount of health reduced reached fifty, he started thinking of alternatives.

Escape was obviously out of the question; however, running away in the realm itself was a possibility. At the very least, it was going to give him some time to think of a better plan.

Deflecting the latest series of attacks, Dallion shot two bolts at the village chief, then dashed away through the fields. The new body level had done wonders for his speed, but just to be on the safe side, he took a few more shots over his shoulder.

Don't look back, he told himself. Looking back was only going to slow him down. He had other senses to rely on that. From what he could make out, Aspion was way back, not engaging in the chase.

That, in itself, was both strange and alarming. If Dallion was in the chief's place, he'd take full advantage of the momentum and swoop down after him like a hawk. Either that or send the earth golem. Why hadn't he, though? Come to think of it, the golem had been a silent observer this entire time. Dallion was pretty convinced the chief was telling the truth about him being in control of the realm, as well as its guardian. It shouldn't have been an issue for the old man to bark a few orders and have this whole fight over with. After all, he himself had said that there was nothing fair in war. If provided with such an overwhelming advantage, why wasn't he using it?

You can't use it, can you? Dallion thought. Rather, the chief couldn't use the guardian against its will. Most likely, he could use it to put up a show, or even for defense, but the guardian had a mind of its own and had decided not to take part in all of this. However, that didn't mean Dallion couldn't.

"Feeling tired, old man?" Dallion shouted, turning toward the lake. "Better not strain yourself. Would be embarrassing to pull out your back at your age."

A series of distant footsteps suggested the village chief had taken the bait and chased after him. For someone who spent a lifetime provoking people into making bad decisions, he was surprisingly thin-skinned.

If only Dallion had acrobatic skills, he could have jumped and fired a few bolts at his pursuer *Matrix* style. On the positive side, at least the village chief hadn't watched those movies, or Dallion would have been in serious trouble.

"Running won't save you," Aspion shouted from behind. "No matter where you go, I can tell where you're hiding."

"I'm not trying to hide! I just want to see how good you are at swimming," Dallion bluffed. He could only hope the chief didn't know about his fear of water. "If I swim across the lake, will you be able to catch me, then?"

Dallion slowed slightly, then turned around and took a few more shots. The bolts were easily evaded, but it was a relief to know the old man wasn't particularly fast. If anything, he was pretty much at the level Dallion had been when joining the hunting party. That was interesting. For someone who ridiculed perception and mind as useless skills, the chief didn't seem to have a lot in his body trait, or any of the rest for that matter.

By rough estimations, the lake was about fifteen minutes away—too far to run in one go. The better solution was to—

A wall of green appeared around Dallion. Faced with this, he instinctively jumped back, protecting his upper torso with the buckler while also shooting a bolt. The green disappeared just as the village chief appeared in the air, less than a few feet away. The sneaky old man had just taken advantage of the previous two bolts to make use of the guard skill bonus jump. He had also added something new.

The sword clashed against Dallion's buckler, shoving him to the ground. A series of other strikes followed. This time, it was Dallion's turn to evade. It was pure luck he was able to complete a full sequence, allowing him to jump away to safety.

"Not bad." The chief smiled. "A pity your grandfather couldn't see you now. Or maybe it's better this way. He would have been so disappointed with how things turned out."

"You're one to talk." Dallion breathed heavily. Even with a

body level of five, fatigue had started to creep in. "Seems to me like you're projecting."

"You know nothing! You're just like all the rest once they awaken! You get a bit of power and think everything is possible. I'm here to show you that it isn't!"

The village chief removed the buckler from his arm. The shield burst into dust and disappeared. An archway appeared behind him. There was no mystery about what had happened—the chief had linked to his own room. The unusual part came later as a new buckler appeared, this one with a sharp serrated edge. That wasn't good. Dallion's own buckler had done considerable damage when used in battle. An improved version was likely to finish him in three hits or less.

I should try shooting his right foot again, Dallion considered frantically. *Or maybe go for the left shoulder?*

Either was an option, but both seemed futile. Still, it was better than nothing. Before a second had passed, Dallion raised his dartbow and sent out a bolt.

CRITICAL HIT
Weak spot found!
Dealt damage is increased by 200%

Dallion blinked. The village chief had raised his shield to protect his shoulder, while the bolt had hit his foot. Apparently, he wasn't invulnerable after all.

THE CHIEF'S AWAKENING ROOM

Surprise appeared both on Dallion's and the chief's faces. Neither expected the attack to work. If anything, the village chief was surprised even more. Freezing up, he glanced at his foot, refusing to believe he'd been wounded. The bolt was there, sticking from his foot, even if there was no blood.

"You can't know this," Aspion whispered. "You don't have the level for this skill."

His entire body trembling, the village chief threw his sword on the ground. The weapon disappeared into thin air. Moments later, a doorway appeared less than a few feet away. In every aspect, it was similar to the archways Dallion had seen in the awakening shrine. However, he felt it was something more—a link to Aspion's awakened realm.

Still looking at his foot, he reached out forward. A new weapon appeared in his hand. It was twice as large as the one before, its blade made up of a series of triangular pieces fitted together. There was little doubt the attacks from this would be by far more devastating than a standard sword, yet the village chief didn't attack yet, as if still trying to wrap his head around how he had been hit.

The confusion lasted for several seconds. Dallion took the

chance to act. Up to now, his plan had been to reach the lake and make use of the well guardian. If this realm was a representation of the village, the lake was supposed to be the well, and if that were true, the water golem could potentially help him. The village chief had just presented him with a far better opportunity. In his anger to acquire a superior weapon, he had linked his personal realm to the village realm. Doing so, though, had given Dallion the option to enter it.

You've no idea how to protect your awakening room, and yet you opened the door for anyone to go inside! Dallion remembered Kalis' words. The soldier had been furious when Dallion had used that method during the practice rounds. Of course, back then, Dallion hadn't fully awakened. Now that he was, he might as well take the battle into the chief.

Without hesitation, Dallion rushed toward the archway. The village chief didn't even try to stop him, still mesmerized by his wound. Deciding not to put all his eggs in one basket, Dallion fired another shot as he leaped into the opening. The bolt split the air, aimed at the chief's shoulder. Before reaching his target, though, the old man twisted to the side. Dallion shot two more bolts. Before he could see the results, his surroundings disappeared, replaced by a dim hall. With a loud *thump*, Dallion landed on a hard stone floor.

"Damn it!" he whispered. He had been so close. If the chief hadn't snapped out of it, the battle could already have been won. On the other hand, he was fortunate to have landed a shot at all.

Based on his experience in the awakening shrine, the bolt should have reduced the chief's health by half. Considering the critical hit bonus, the old man likely had twenty-five percent left. Another hit, or even a smack with the buckler, and Dallion could well be the victor.

Where are you? Dallion wondered, looking around.

There was no sign of the chief. Following the rules of this place, only enemies appeared in the arena. The realm owner was likely to be waiting in the starting room. That gave Aspion home advantage, but at least Dallion could rest assured there would be no golem to face.

The arena itself was much more elaborate than Dallion's. While the floor was made completely out of stone, the walls had a number of decorations on them—sets of decorative armor, paintings depicting fight scenes, even a few portraits of what looked like the village chief in his youth. The general facial features remained unchanged, although there was no doubt the years hadn't treated the man well. Come to think of it, the portrait looked far closer to the scribe echo in Dallion's domain.

"Nice crib." Dallion went to one of the armor sets.

A lot of modern artists would have gone crazy about it back on Earth. The armor was made entirely of pressed paper, like a delicate papier mâché. The set itself depicted a cross between Norse and Greek design. "Roman Viking" if Dallion was pressed to come up with a name. Interestingly enough, the only weapons were those in the paintings.

Makes sense, Dallion thought. It wouldn't be very smart to give weapons and armor to anyone who just came here. The display was meant just to glorify the chief.

Talk about self-centered.

Since the entrance from the village realm had vanished, Dallion made his way to the only door in the hall. It was as large and ornate as everything else here. Dallion expected it to be barred from the other side. However, after a quick try, it turned out not to be. That was somewhat careless on the chief's part, or maybe a trap?

The corridor leading on from the arena was very different from Dallion's. It was wide, well-lit, and covered with a long, if somewhat crude, carpet. A few hundred steps farther, doors on the walls became visible. All of them were set in pairs facing each other, and all seemed to be chained shut. Dallion tried cracking one open just to peek inside, but the large metal chains were too tight. The most he was able to do was to move a door half an inch before giving up.

Okay, so maybe this isn't the nicest place, he thought.

After three sets of doors, finally, a pair of "normal" ones appeared.

Left or right? That was the question. Dallion had spent hundreds of hours pondering that question when playing video games. Experience had taught him that when in doubt, turn right, which was exactly what he did.

The room he entered turned out to be the chief's awakening room. It was considerably larger than Dallion's, with several sections covered with weapons and armor. Just looking at it suggested the chief had to be at a level nine at least.

Dallion swallowed. He hadn't expected such a vast difference. Based on the conversations he'd had with Gloria and Veil, the chief wasn't supposed to be more than a level five. Had he been hiding his strength all this time?

Slowly, Dallion moved to the "attack section" of the room. Twelve weapons were framed on the wall, including a dartbow similar to the one Dallion had. In addition, there were five swords of various shapes and sizes, two sets of daggers—placed one over the other—three clubs, and a morning star. It would almost have been impressive if all but two swords weren't chained to the wall.

"You're not supposed to touch those," a deep metallic voice said from behind.

METAL THORNS

allion briskly turned around, shooting a bolt at the source of the voice. The bolt split the air, then bounced off a massive iron breastplate, then continued to a different part of the room, where it pierced the wall like a pin.

This in itself was alarming, though not nearly as alarming as the person—or rather, the entity—Dallion had attempted to shoot.

Standing a few feet away was nothing short of a metallic construct composed entirely of pieces of armor. One could almost call it a living suit, though even that description was off. Most disconcerting of all was the hollow helmet that seemed to stare into Dallion's eyes.

"Those are not to be used," a hollow voice came from the inside of the armor. "You cannot put an end to the punishment."

"Punishment?" Dallion asked.

The entity before him had to be an echo. Dallion could tell that much—there was no rectangle above it—but not an echo he had seen before. It didn't resemble a person or creature, but instead, it was just air and steel. The thought of firing a bolt inside through the hollow opening beneath the helmet came to mind, though Dallion decided against it. This was one case he didn't want to recklessly charge forward.

"You're not the chief." Dallion lowered his weapon.

"You aren't either. Amusing that little Aspion would allow someone in his awakened room. Are you here to help him? You definitely lack the skills to do so."

"I'm not here to help him." *I'm also not that weak, you know. Wasn't being a full awakened supposed to be a big deal?*

"You're not?" The suit of armor tilted its helmet. "Are you a child of his? Or a rival?"

"Nope, and nope." Apparently, whoever created the guardian wasn't particularly good at hereditary traits. "Someone who's about to kick his ass." Not the best phrase to drop, but suitable given everything else.

"An enemy." The voice sounded amused, although it was difficult to tell since the armor completely lacked a face. "In that case, you're welcome. I'm not allowed to help you against him, but I'll make sure he doesn't go beyond the imposed limitations."

"Okay. What are his imposed limitations?"

"Awakening level restriction, skills use restriction, skills focus restriction, ability focus restriction, realm limitation," the suit of armor enumerated. "That's all I can tell you. You're welcome to look around, just don't touch anything that's been restricted."

Dallion blinked.

"That means anything that has chains around it," the suit of armor explained, then simply left the room.

Definitely an unexpected turn of events. To think the person who had subdued an entire village with his echoes would, in turn, be limited by an even more powerful one. Yet, who had created it? As far as Dallion knew, suits of armor couldn't be awakened. Although, given his limited knowledge on the topic, it was better not to come to any premature conclusions. Either way, it had to be someone powerful, possibly at the level of Dame Vesuvia.

Making sure the echo wasn't around, Dallion reached for one of the weapons on the village chief's wall. Metal thorns emerged from the chains, piercing his hand.

AVERAGE WOUND
Your health has been reduced by 10%

"Ouch!" Dallion quickly pulled his hand back. The echo wasn't kidding. Ten percent just for touching a weapon he wasn't supposed to? That was definitely one way to ensure the limitation held. Good thing the chains on the doors outside weren't as harsh.

Unpleasant, but that didn't excuse the chief. As the saying went, there always was a bigger asshole to deal with. Aspion's arrogance had made him meddle with the wrong person, and this was the result. Although…the awakening level restriction sounded very much like what Havoc had gone through. The large man had mentioned that he used to be a higher level but was reduced to a level three.

"Old man?" Dallion shouted. There was no response.

That was odd. Where could he be? Dallion looked at the doorway. One unchained door remained in the corridor. Taking a deep breath, he headed toward it.

One shot, Dallion said to himself. One shot was enough to win, then this awakened realm would be sealed, and the chief wouldn't cause problems for anyone anymore.

Carefully, Dallion took hold of the door's handle, then opened it with one swift action. The moment he did, a green shield marker emerged in front of his face.

"Damn!" Dallion raised his buckler right in the nick of time. A loud *clang* followed as another buckler pushed him five steps back.

SHOCK EFFECT
Your movement has been reduced by 10% for two minutes

Attacks' effectiveness reduced by 50% for two minutes

Seriously?! Dallion shot a series of bolts while retreating into the awakening room. Even in such circumstances, the old man kept on being a nuisance.

"You pest!" Aspion shouted. "I won't let you ruin everything!"

MINOR WOUND
Your health has been reduced by 5%
MINOR WOUND
Your health has been reduced by 5%

The attacks were remarkably fierce, even in the tight space of the corridor. The effects of the shock attack had made Dallion's actions sluggish. Despite the guard markers and his best efforts, defending himself was becoming more and more difficult. The only option was to move farther and farther back into the chief's awakening room.

"You dare enter my awakening room?" Aspion shouted while pressing on with his attacks. "You shouldn't have seen this! I'd only have sealed your power, but now I'll—" He suddenly froze.

"Yes?" The armor appeared out of nowhere. "What would you do now, Aspion?"

Well played, echo, Dallion thought. Whoever had placed it in the chief's awakening room must have hated him a lot to have their echo interfere in such a way. Dallion had just been given one last chance. It was up to him now to use it.

Closing his eyes for a second, Dallion went through the possible attack options. So many attack options, and so many of them useless. Direct attacks were risky. They would come with guard marker warnings, allowing the chief to block or evade them easily. Even a ricochet would be risky...or maybe it wouldn't be.

That's it. Dallion opened his eyes.

"Watch out!" he shouted, then twisted around and shot at the armor's helmet.

The suit of armor didn't try to evade the attack, remaining perfectly static as the projectile ricochet inside of it. The village chief's eyes widened with surprise, astonished by what had just happened. However, his astonishment didn't last long, for Dallion didn't stop. While the dartbow remained fixed on the suit of armor, he crashed into Aspion and shoved him right into a chained weapon framed to the wall. The old man's entire body writhed in pain—the protection had done its thing.

"Darude," Dallion whispered. *Got you at last.*

FINAL OFFER

"You lose." Dallion kicked the chief's sword out of his hand. Instantly, the weapon vanished from the floor and reappeared on the attack skill wall.

This could hardly be called a fair fight. Dallion had resorted to many things to gain the upper hand but, finally, it had paid off. The terror of Dherma village, the person who had sealed the awakened skills of his mother, the tyrant who had echoed every person in the village, had finally lost. At this point, even a sharp kick was enough to reduce his health to zero. If anything, it was a wonder the old man hadn't lost his abilities altogether.

One more hit, Dallion thought. One more hit and all the limiting echoes would be gone. The village would return to normal, and even—

"No!" Aspion raised a shivering hand in front of his face. "Don't do it! You don't understand!"

"I'm sure I don't." Tyrants were just like bullies. The moment they lost, they started coming up with excuses to defend themselves.

"It's not what you think! I just wanted to protect you all. This was the only way!"

"Yeah, yeah." Dallion aimed at the chief's torso. A hit anywhere would do the trick. "I'm sure the echoes were for their protection as well?"

"That was the only way to make sure no one had anything to do with the cities. You've never been there! You have no idea how dangerous those places are!" The chief moved up slightly, only to be reminded by the dartbow that Dallion wasn't inclined to listen. "Just because you've defeated me doesn't mean you're a match for the awakened in the cities! Your grandfather was like you. He thought being gifted gave him an advantage. Instead, it made him a target."

Grandpa? That gave Dallion some pause. Thanks to his perception, he could tell the village chief wasn't lying. Was it worth hearing him out, though? The goal of the entire exercise was for the old man to keep his awakened power.

ASPION LUOR has admitted defeat.
Do you accept his surrender?

Dallion stared at the blue rectangle. Apparently, people could surrender as well so long as they were in their own awakened rooms. Dallion considered learning how to do so at some point. It seemed like a useful ability to have.

"What happened to my grandfather?" Dallion asked. There was no way he would accept a surrender without getting some answers. This way, he could be certain the chief would keep his promise, and depending on what he said, Dallion was free to refuse.

"Dreams, arrogance, and aspirations, that's what happened," Aspion spat. "When he awakened, it was considered the greatest day in the village. He had tried so many times before, all of them unsuccessful. His parents had all but given up, but the idiot was stubborn. No one believed he could make it, then when it happened, he said he had been offered three skills."

That sounded about right. Dallion remembered his grandfather telling him he had three skills to choose from. The elder also implied he had gotten to learn them as well.

"Attack, guard, and forging," the chief continued. "I was so envious at the time. Not only had he beaten me by one, but he had acquired forging skills, while I only had acrobatics. It was the difference between day and night. No wonder everyone flocked to him."

"That's why you hated him?" Dallion interrupted. He had seen too many anime to know where this was going. "You despised the fact that the village chief preferred him to you, so you—"

"Of course, the chief preferred him! The chief was his father!"

Dallion blinked. That was unexpected. Trying to think back to his earliest memories of this world, he couldn't recall that being mentioned. As far as everyone was concerned, the Luor family had been in control of the village for generations. Although, if both Aspion and Dallion's grandfather had been in their teens when the change happened, no one of the younger generation would know. As for the people who had been alive at the time, the echoes had probably made sure they forgot the truth of things.

"And I didn't betray him. I was his friend." A note of sadness crept in. "The fact that both of us had become awakened only made us closer. And that is when he shared his dream." The chief paused for a while, then moved a bit, sitting comfortably on the floor. "The awakening had made the village too small for him. In a matter of weeks, the things that had seemed fun before tired him. We'd spend the days improving what we could throughout the village. We even made a competition of it. When that became old, we snuck out to the old temple to level up in the awakening shrine."

Dallion's throat went dry. So far, the story sounded somewhat familiar. He and Gloria had pretty much done the same. She had been the one reluctant to leave the village, while Dallion had kept inquiring about the cities. If circumstances had been different—if Dallion hadn't been in the chief's crosshairs, and the limiting echoes didn't exist—he could have even convinced her to join him on the outside.

"His father forbade it, but that didn't stop Kraisten. I used my awakening skills to break into the mansion and find a way out without anyone noticing. Then, one day, he asked the question: what do you think the cities are like?"

Scary. That would have been exactly what Dallion would have done if he were in his grandfather's place.

"And what did you say?"

"What could I say?" The chief let out a dry laugh. "I knew nothing about the cities. All I knew was that I'd work in the village for the rest of my life. However, I wasn't the only one who was there when he asked. My sister was as well."

Dallion's pulse hastened. Now he definitely knew where this was going...

ASPION'S STORY

Memory Fragment

DHERMA VILLAGE, FORTY YEARS AGO

"Have you ever wondered what it's like?" Kraisten asked from the top of the village bell tower. The place had been declared out of bounds ever since it had nearly crumbled in a storm three years ago. Unknown to most, Kraisten had used his awakening power to mend it months ago. Now, it was only the outside that looked decrepit; on the inside, the structure was as strong as granite.

"The cities?" Aspion shrugged. "Probably boring. What could they have there that we don't?" He crossed his arms. "Besides, it's not like we can get there."

"Uncle Ferion went to join the count's guard last harvest," Kierra said. She was the only one of the group who wasn't an awakened, though she tagged along either way.

"Idiot." Aspion smirked. "He was recruited. Big difference. Recruits don't go there because they want to. And it's not like he liked the place or anything."

That much was a lie. While their uncle had been recruited, he had sent several letters back to the village, including a pouch of copper coins and shipment of high-grade lumber. The mere fact that he had enough to hire a traveling merchant to travel all the way to Dherma showed that being a guard paid well.

"I'm thinking of going there." This wasn't the first time Kraisten had said something of the sort. In the last several months, the only conversations the three had been having were about awakening, doing on trips outside the village, as well as the cities. This time, though, there was something different in his voice. Anyone could tell that his mind had been made up.

"Right," Aspion whispered.

He wasn't like his friend. As the son of the village scribe, it fell on Aspion to take over from his father. Writing was considered a rare gift, almost as rare as awakening, so his fate was set since birth. Neither awakening, nor having a sister who was a better scribe than him was able to change the will of his father. In that respect, the man was as unshakable as Kraisten's father had been.

"If I find a way. Will you two come with me?" Kraisten asked.

"Sure," Kierra said almost instantly. Aspion, however, hesitated.

They had all heard stories about the cities. Going there meant a new beginning, all ties with the village severed. As an awakened, they would be looked after and, with luck, they might even reach a moderately high position. As an awakened forger, Kraisten would be snatched up by an artisan's guild on the spot. Thanks to his two skills, Aspion could potentially find work as a guard. Kierra, though, had nothing. If she didn't awaken, she would have to be left behind.

"Aspion?" Kraisten nudged. "It's not like you to be humble."

"And it's not like you to be reckless," the blond snapped. "At least it didn't use to be. You've changed a lot since your awakening."

"I suppose so." Kraisten smiled. "You know how it is. Once you unlock the room, there's no turning back."

"No turning back…"

Aspion's awakening had been drastically different. For him, he had gone to the village awakening spot—as he had been doing every year on his birthday—then suddenly felt the power of the Seven Moons bloom inside of him. There was nothing spectacular about it. He had remained the same person he had always been, only this time, his parents were much prouder of him…and also all sorts of relatives had come asking for favors. People Aspion couldn't even remember reminded him how much they had supported him ever since he was a baby. It was all lies, of course, but instead of admitting that, his father was all too happy to show off the abilities of his son by improving small trinkets whenever asked.

In Kraisten's case, the change had been dramatic. Always quiet in the past, he had suddenly become wild and reckless. In the first week alone, he had broken more rules than Aspion could think of. It had been fun—the tricks they'd played, the dares they'd gone through with, the secret trips to the awakening shrine. Lately, though, Kraisten's obsession was becoming dangerous.

"Why do you want to go to a city so much? It's not like it's bad here. The way things are going, your father will step down in a few years. That will make you the village chief."

Kierra laughed. Even with Kraisten's awakening, it was difficult to visualize him as chief. It was an unimaginable thought, yet Aspion knew firsthand what the chief's plans were. He had used his increased perception to listen in on a conversation between the chief and his father. Apparently, the old man had been bitten by Crippled spawn and was already starting to show signs of the illness. In a few years, he would barely be able to walk without help. After another five, he wouldn't be able to get out of bed.

"It's not a few years," Kraisten whispered, his expression darkening. "My father told me he'll make the announcement on my birthday."

Aspion and Kierra stared. That was far too soon. It also meant the chief's health was worsening faster that he'd thought.

"So, what are you going to do?" Aspion asked the question. "Run for it?"

"No. There's another way. The question is, will you join me?"

"Of course, he will," Kierra said before Aspion could reply. "You're friends after all."

"Sis…" Aspion wanted to tell her that she wasn't included in the invitation but couldn't. He wasn't certain if there was anything going between her and Kraisten—the two hadn't been particularly close in the past, but lately, he had started seeing things. Maybe it was all in his imagination, or maybe it wasn't. "…don't speak instead of me. I can give my own answer."

"Well?"

"Of course, we will." Aspion sighed. "I didn't want to be a scribe anyway."

"Good. In that case, level up as much as you can. I'll need you at full strength by the end of the week. After that, we'll walk out of the village." Kraisten smiled. "All of us."

With that, the conversation ended. With a nod and a wave, Kraisten climbed down the tower, making his way back to the village chief's mansion. Kierra followed shortly after.

"You coming?" Kierra looked up at her brother.

"Go ahead, I need to think about something."

"Okay. See you at home."

Aspion closed his eyes for a moment. When he opened them again, the bracelet on his left arm had changed from bronze to copper. Anywhere, this would have been seen as a great feat. However, he still couldn't catch up to Kraisten.

What are you planning? Aspion wondered. Whatever it was, it had the blond worried.

ASPION'S STORY – DHERMA VILLAGE

Memory Fragment

DHERMA VILLAGE, FORTY YEARS AGO

I t didn't take long for the plan to be revealed. The very next day, the village chief made an unusual announcement, or rather, it was more of a challenge. Should his son manage to improve the level of the village, he would be allowed to leave and head for the cities in the count's domain whenever he wanted.

The idea had surprised nearly everyone, though not Aspion. He had been the one who had told Kraisten of the significance of improving area domains. With settlements being rare, especially on the frontier, every advancement was regarded as a service to the local noble and required him to offer a boon as payment. If Kraisten were to improve the village awakened area, the count had no choice but to invite him to the city and offer a reward. In turn, the village chief had no choice but to obey the orders of the count.

Without a doubt, it was a good plan, though Aspion didn't think that his friends would be as reckless to try it. Improving an entire village was nothing like improving items, or even separate structures.

By noon, the entire town had gathered in front of the chief's mansion, waiting to witness the miracle. Kierra was there as well.

"Wow. Didn't expect so many people to gather," Kraisten said from the roof of the building.

"What did you expect?" Aspion laughed. "A level three settlement is practically a town."

"I thought you told me that towns started at five."

"Three is halfway there." Aspion shrugged. "It'll be more than most of the dumps in the area. From what my father says, most of them are twos. Improving Dherma will put us on the map."

"That's the plan."

"How are you going to do it anyway? Leveling up an area isn't a joke. It takes more than just being a level five."

"I know." Kraisten smiled. "That's why I have you."

AREA AWAKENING

You are in the land of DHERMA VILLAGE
Defeat the guardian to change the land's destiny

This was the first time Aspion had been in an area realm. It seemed very much different from he expected. It was much larger than an item's awakening room, larger even than the realms in which the awakening shrine trials had taken place. Also, there was a lot more color in it, not only the muddy brown that seemed to comprise everything in the real world, but actual vibrant colors. It was as if the Moons had drained all the colors of the village and poured them into the realm.

"So, this is it from the inside?" Kraisten crossed his arms. "Looks better than the real thing."

A large, keep-like structure was beneath them. It was the realm's representation of the chief's mansion. While definitely larger than everything else, it was poorly kept. Goblin creatures were visible hiding behind walls and edges, peeking at the duo with fear and aggression in their eyes.

"Cracks," Aspion said, drawing his short sword. "We don't need to fight them. If we defeat them, we'll just mend your place."

"Not fight them?" Kraisten drew his own sword. "Where's the fun in that?"

"We're here to defeat the guardian. Fighting anything before will just weaken us. Besides, who's to say we won't be making the guardian stronger?"

That stood to reason. It wasn't exactly "the enemy of my enemy" logic, but everyone could see how a wounded guardian would make for a weaker opponent. However, that didn't seem right. Despite the overwhelming logic, even Aspion could see that.

"Just one building," Kraisten said. "We improve that, and then we fight the guardian. Are you with me?"

Every fiber in Aspion's body screamed for him to refuse. Instead, he nodded.

The single improvement battle turned into two, then a dozen, then a hundred. As soon as the pair cut up a pack of goblins, Kraisten would lead them to another keep nearby, where they would do the same. It wasn't that fighting the goblins was easy. After their initial shock was gone, the creatures had started fighting back with both viciousness and imagination. It was only due to Aspion and Kraisten's teamwork—and the awakening markers—that they managed to emerge victorious.

Days quickly turned to weeks. Aspion would use his knowledge to find something that could pass as edible in the realm, while Kraisten used his forging skills to transform the metal ores at hand into superior weapons. In a way, it was almost as if they had already left the village and gone on an adventure, with one giant difference: in the awakened state, health never restored. The wounds they would receive slowly piled up, making them weaker and weaker. By the time they had mended three-quarters of the village buildings,

Aspion's health had been reduced to sixty percent. As for Kraisten, he had fallen to less than fifty.

"It's time to stop," Aspion said one evening as they sat around the campfire. "We can't mend the entire village. Three-quarters isn't all bad."

"It's not all of it," Kraisten replied, lying on the ground, eyes closed. "We'll finish the rest tomorrow."

"You've been saying that for days. It doesn't make it less false," Aspion grumbled. "The goblins are getting smarter. If we keep wasting our health on them, we won't have enough to challenge the guardian."

"And you happen to know where the guardian is?"

"Yes," Aspion lied. "Well, no, but that's not the point. We have to focus on finding him and keeping our health high until we do. What's the point in reaching him at twenty percent health?"

"We'll be fine. You worry too much. We've got better weapons, good armor, plus the element of surprise. We'll mop up the rest of the goblins, then find the guardian."

To Aspion's surprise, everything happened just as Kraisten had predicted it would. The next few days were spent cleaning out the remaining keeps, something they had done with relative ease while only receiving one additional minor wound. Then, on the fourth day, once the last goblin had been reduced to smoke, the village guardian emerged.

Aspion's fears had also turned out to be correct. The guardian was an earth golem, though neither he nor Kraisten had expected to face anything this huge. The monster towered thirty feet above them, holding a club of petrified wood as big as the bell tower they'd hang out at in the real world. For once, even Kraisten had to admit his friend had been right. Saving up more health would have been the wiser move. Then again, wiser didn't automatically mean better.

The fight had lasted over an hour. Combining their skills and attacks, the pair slowly chipped away at the golem's force. Some-times, Kraisten would blind it. Others, Aspion would use his acro-batic attacks to distract the monster enough so that his friend would have an opening. Percent by percent, they toiled until the Kraisten made the final blow—a five percent critical strike that crushed the guardian to pieces, but which also reconstructed him into a whole new version of itself.

It was both that had fought the guardian, but since Kraisten had landed the final blow, he was to become the domain ruler. However, since he wasn't particularly interested, he'd offered the creature an alternative. He would remain the realm's ruler, but only if Aspion had an equal authority within the realm, as well as out of it.

The offer was unusual enough to merit the appearance of a green rectangle, informing them it had been accepted. The next thing Aspion and Kraisten knew, they were back in the real world, standing on the roof of the village chief's mansion. As far as everyone was concerned, less than a second had passed, but in that fraction of the moment, Dherma had grown twice in size. The size and state of the buildings had changed as well. They were taller, sturdier, as well as perfectly flawless, as if they'd just been built.

"We did it," Kraisten whispered.

However, the village wasn't the only thing that had changed. After months of traveling and fighting, the two boys were also different from what they had been before.

ASPION'S STORY – DRAFTED

Memory Fragment

DHERMA VILLAGE, FORTY YEARS AGO

N ews of the leveling of Dherma spread throughout the entire county. Within days, an envoy of Count Harlow came to the village to mark the event. A celebration never before seen in the village was held, bestowing the title of vice-knight on the village chief. According to the new status, the village was allowed to become an official trading post where caravans could stop.

The people responsible for the area improvement were declared heroes, as well as given ten coins of silver each, traveler's emblems, and permission to enter any of the count's cities. The reward was enough to make any person happy, but Kraisten wasn't content. Despite Aspion's best efforts, the only thing his friend wanted to do was leave the village as quickly as possible.

"Why are you being so stubborn?" Kierra asked. "It's not like it's the end of the world. Kraisten only wants to go to the city for a few weeks. After that, he'll be back."

"You don't know what you're talking about," Aspion grumbled. "It's not like I'm stopping him."

"That's a lot of crap, and you know it." She crossed her arms.

"He won't go without you. And I know you well enough to see that you want to go as well but are refusing just because we're asking you."

That wasn't true at all. Aspion didn't want to go because he knew that, if they went, Kierra would come along. Two emblems and three people. Walking through the wilderness between settlements would be dangerous, even if Kierra had awakened, let alone now. However, that wasn't the only reason. The people from the cities terrified Aspion. He had only seen a few so far—the small number of awakened that had ever visited Dherma—but all of them had an air of frightening power around them. It was more than just being awakened. He had seen them be capable of impossible feats even in the real world.

"I'll think about it," he replied.

"When you say that, you really mean no."

"I don't want to spend my life there, okay?!" Aspion snapped. "If Kraisten wants to spend the rest of his life there, he can do so without my help."

"No one's talking about living there! It's just a visit. A few weeks at the most."

"You don't know him as well as I do. He doesn't want to go there to visit. He wants to go there to stay."

The argument continued for several more hours. The more Aspion tried to convince his sister to drop the topic, the more insistent she became. If there had been a way to use his awakening powers to make her to shut up, he would have. In the end, Aspion gave up. The very next morning, the three of them left the village.

No one saw them when they left. As much as Kraisten liked to be in the spotlight, he also wanted to be sure no one would try to stop him. Aspion and his sister did the same, taking clothes, food, and a few essentials before sneaking out of their home and joining him.

It was said that only the lucky and those with protection could cross the wilderness without any harm. Beasts, monsters, and cultists serving the Crippled Star roamed the land between domains. Only the Order of the Seven Moons and the traveling emblems were able to provide protection. It was decided between Aspion and Kraisten that they would let Kierra have one of the emblems while they took turns wearing the other.

The first few days passed slowly. Every time there was an unexplained sound, Aspion would tense up, gripping his short swords, ready for a fight. A fight, though, never followed. All that he'd get were a few ridiculing remarks from Kraisten, much to his annoyance.

After a week, the fear had given way to boredom. All the chatter had died down, all the things that could be said were said so many times that they became pointless repeating. The sleep and emblem switching schedules were known by heart, even the few hunting attempts couldn't break the monotony. Despite everything else that was said about the wilderness, it remained a deadly, yet boring place. On several occasions, Kierra tried to ditch her brother to spend some alone time with Kraisten but knowing that would be too much of a risk, Aspion didn't let her.

Eleven days were needed for them to reach the first town— Nerosal. By any imperial standard, it was small, barely worth the mention. To Aspion and his sister, though, it seemed enormous. The city walls were at least six stories tall, continuing for as far as the eye could see. Inside, hundreds of buildings, taller than those in Dherma, rose in dense clusters, more intricate and well-kept than a jeweler's brooch. For once, Aspion thought there might be some truth in Kraisten's words.

Sadly, just as the city was majestic, so were its prices. A silver coin was only enough to last them a week in a second-rate tavern. Even when pooling all their funds together, it was clear they wouldn't last over a month. In a way, Aspion was glad, as that meant that they might have to leave in a few weeks after all. However, even he had to admit falling under the town's spell.

Everything was so much better than in Dherma. The shops alone had more than any traveling merchant he had seen. The food was better, the clothes didn't feel like sawdust, and everyone seemed free to do anything they wished.

Finding work had turned out to be surprisingly easy. After learning that Kraisten had forging skills, he was quickly snatched up by the local blacksmith guild. Aspion had to spend a few days asking about, but ultimately, he was hired at a mending shop. The work wasn't the most interesting—ten hours of mending per day—but at least it paid well, and he had gotten a proper weapon to do it with. All in all, things were looking well.

"You know," Aspion said, sitting at the town's main fountain one evening after work. "This place isn't that bad."

"Told you," Kierra whispered to Kraisten.

"Shut up," Aspion mock grumbled. "Okay, you were right. It was worth it coming here. Not that I ever saw myself as a full-time mender."

"It's just temporary. There are better things in store."

"Easy for you to say. I heard you were promoted to journeyman. The whole neighborhood was making a big fuss about it. Guess that head of yours isn't only for show."

"Shows what they know." Kraisten smirked. "They made the offer, but I turned them down. There's a faster way to get noticed." He paused for a few moments. "There's talk of a war stirring up. Count Harlow has joined Count Priscord in supporting the claim of the archduke's second son. If they are successful, they'll become the most important nobles in the realm."

"The war won't bother us. Nerosal's far too insignificant to get involved, thank the Seven."

"Yeah…" Kraisten paused. "Thing is, I went to the local barracks and asked to join the count's army. And they accepted."

ASPION'S STORY – DEEP REGRETS

Memory Fragment

NEROSAL TOWN, FORTY YEARS AGO

I t was said that joining the army was the fastest way to a noble title. All it took was to be noticed by the right people and, soon, miracles could happen. The catch was that the chances of promotion were directly proportional to the danger involved. Joining the city guard in peacetime was a pretty decent gig. The only things one had to worry about were local riff-raff and the occasional hunt. Normally, it would take years to advance in rank. Joining in wartime was an entirely different matter.

Under normal conditions, Aspion wouldn't have even considered such a course of action, but the chance of earning a noble rank attracted him like a moth to a flame. What was more, from what Kraisten had found, Count Harlow wanted to be certain of his victory, so all soldiers—recruits included—would be granted access to a ten-level awakening shrine. The offer seemed too good to be true and, sadly, it was. Joining had been the first mistake.

In less than a week, Kraisten and Aspion had improved from an awakened five to double digits, while Kierra had managed to join the ranks of the awakened and risen to a level five. For a brief period of time, life seemed good. Everything was exactly as Kraisten had said it would…until the actual fighting began.

When the second son of the archduke announced his claim for his father's title, Harlow and Priscord's troops launched an attack on the non-loyal counts in the region. However, as the soldiers soon found out, their enemies had been expecting them. A war that they had been assured would be over in weeks dragged for months and longer. Seasons changed, as did orders, but the fighting went on.

Each day seemed worse than the last, though not for Kraisten. The man had proved to be a military genius, winning battles considered hopeless. Aspion and Kierra were there as well, following behind, but soon, it became obvious they couldn't keep up. The shadow of their friend was too large.

Half a year after the start of the war, a new opportunity emerged. Kraisten had been offered the chance to become a division commander and, along with that, to earn the title of knight. The only condition was that he capture the Warzen stronghold. That had been the second mistake.

Seven attempts had been made to take the stronghold, and none of them successful. Kraisten, however, had a plan.

"I won't lie to you, it will be risky," Kraisten explained to his soldiers. "Before we start anything, we'll need to go hunting. The weapons we currently have won't do a thing, so we'll have to go bigger."

"Just how big are we talking about, Captain?" Aspion asked. He knew how low morale was, so he took any chance he got to try and lighten the mood.

"As big as it gets. And then some."

Laughter filled the tent. While most of the people were still tense, the joke had created a momentary semblance of calm.

"To win this, we must get a chainling."

The laughter suddenly stopped. There wasn't a person alive who didn't know the significance of what had been said. Chainlings were monsters of the Crippled Star. Their only reason to exist was to kill and corrupt anything they came across. Killing one was difficult enough, catching it was impossible.

"Not to worry, that's the easy part," Kraisten continued as if nothing had happened. "We must then climb up the cliff side of the stronghold until we reach the base of the walls. There we must release the chainling and make sure it goes inside. Once it's there…" the man smiled, "…we'll become the heroes of the war."

Seldom were scarier words spoken. Three dozen people stared at Kraisten, wondering whether to believe their ears or not. They had seen him do the impossible, yet this was too much, even for him.

"I told you, it won't be easy. And I understand if anyone doesn't want to take part in this. However, there's no other way."

"How do you think we'll get a chainling, Captain?" one of the soldiers asked.

"I'll take care of that, don't worry. As I said, that's the easy part. You lot, better focus on the rest. The stronghold area will no doubt be watched. You could be pulled into an awakening duel at any point. I expect you to win if we are to succeed. Remember, if one person fails, the whole thing will go tumbling down, and we won't get another chance at this. Clear?"

Grumbles of acknowledgement filled the tent. The prospect of failing in an awakening fight managed to keep the fears of the chainlings at bay. No one knew how exactly Kraisten planned to catch the creature, and no one cared. It was bad enough they were going against the teachings of the Seven. So long as all ended in victory, they were willing to turn a blind eye.

Bit by bit, the soldiers left the tent until only Aspion and Kraisten remained.

"You handled them quite well," Aspion said. "A bit over the top, but it's certain they'll follow your orders. Now, tell me the real plan."

"That is the real plan. It'll take a chainling to destroy that place."

"Are you serious? Those things can't be controlled. And even if they could, where will we catch one? The last chainling was seen years ago. And even if one was roaming about, it would take weeks to find it. It simply can't be done."

"You surround yourself with books yet have so little imagination." Kraisten smiled. "We won't be hunting a chainling. We'll be making one."

A flash of light blinded Dallion for a moment. After he blinked, he was back in Aspion's awakening room.

"What the heck?" Dallion took a step back, still aiming the dartbow at the village chief. He had no idea what had happened just then. It was as if he had lived through a memory, so intense and so real as if he'd just been there.

"Painful recollections," the old man sighed, pointing to the suit of armor. "A gift that came along with that. It keeps reminding me what was, the choices made before everything went wrong. Each night, I hope I'm done with them, but it never stops." He closed his eyes. "The nightmares never stop."

SEALED DESTINY

"You were friends with my grandfather?" Dallion asked.

It was difficult to believe. After everything the village had been subjected to at the hands of the chief, it seemed ludicrous. And yet, there was no denying the memory he had seen.

"I was." Aspion spat out the words with disgust. "He craved attention and, in the end, he got it. The Order of the Seven Moons doesn't like people meddling with the Crippled Star, but that's nowhere near as bad as what your grandfather did afterwards! He—"

A bolt bounced off the floor inches from the chief's leg.

"I think you should shut up now." Whatever the past was, whatever reasons the old man had, he had done too much harm. There was no way he would get away with it, although maybe he didn't deserve to be condemned to the fate he had put upon others.

The surrender rectangle was still there, conveying the offer. All Dallion had to do was to accept, and he would have won.

"If I accept the surrender, will the echoes disappear?" Dallion asked.

"Yes. It's the same as if you've won the battle," Aspion replied, keeping an eye on the dartbow.

"I wasn't asking you." There was no way Dallion could trust anything the man said.

"No," the armor echo replied. "You would gain control of the village area, but the echoes will remain. You can make your own and send them to fight them, but you'll need time to learn how. Based on your skills, it'll take you half a decade at least."

I should have known. Dallion frowned. Even at the end, the old man tried to pull a fast one. Maybe there was good in him at one point, maybe he was his grandfather's best friend and even helped him achieve his dream. All that was gone now. Aspion was nothing more than a shell of his former self, twisted with hate, anger, and a lust for power.

"What if I shoot him?"

"Aspion's power would be sealed. All echoes he's created will disappear, and the village of Dherma will lose its area owner."

Seemed straightforward enough.

"Wait!" Aspion reached out. "Don't! I can still help you! There's a lot you don't know! Your grandfather can't tell you, but I can! Become village chief, take my mansion if you wish, just don't seal me."

"Did you give my mother that option? Or me when you imprisoned me in the well?"

"Imprisoned?" Aspion's eyes flashed with rage. "You call that imprisoned?! You have no idea what the word even means! I was imprisoned in a realm for twenty years for what your grandfather did! No food, no water; nothing but mist, fear, and hunger! I won't allow anyone to go through that, even if I have to create a thousand limiting echoes!"

Dallion pulled the trigger. The surrender rectangle evaporated into the air, disappearing in a cloud of glowing blue smoke. Other parts of the room soon followed—small things at first: weapon frames, room corners, the occasional spot on the wall. As the seconds went on, more and more sections turned into smoke. So, this was how an awakening room was sealed? It was not at all what Dallion had imagined.

"Sorry, old man, I just can't let you—" Dallion stopped.

The village chief had frozen motionless on the floor, not even blinking.

"Hey, you okay?" Despite himself, Dallion moved closer. Part of him was ready for another dirty trick, but none followed. The chief was completely out of it.

"That's what happens when someone loses the connection to their awakening room." The suit of armor moved closer. "It'll all seem like a dream before waking. The next time he tries to go here, it will be all gone. The only thing he'll be able to see is a small, empty room."

"You are level one," Dallion said. He would be lying if he didn't admit feeling a grain of pity. If there was any truth in the memory, Aspion had been good once. Maybe in his own way, he did what was best to keep the people of Dherma safe? "Will he remember what happened?"

"He'll always remember. That's part of his punishment. I could make the memories less vivid. Or I can increase them. As the one who sealed his power, you've earned the right to choose."

Dallion nodded. The village chief had been right about one thing, there were scarier people out there. Whoever had done this wasn't joking around. For one thing, the echo had been in Aspion's awakening room for decades.

"Numb them." Dallion walked away. As he did, parts of the village chief turned to smoke as well. "He was terrible to everyone around him as an awakened, but maybe as an ordinary person, he could find some peace."

"I very much doubt it." The armor shrugged. "But it's your call. When he goes to sleep, he'll no longer have night terrors."

"Thanks. What happens to me now? Do I need to find a way out of here before everything collapses?"

"If you want. Makes no difference. Once the awakening realm crumbles, you'll be back in the real world."

"Sounds a bit anticlimactic."

The suit of armor laughed.

"Any chance you'll tell me who you are or what the old man's crime was?"

"No."

"Thought so." Dallion looked at the room. Most of the walls and the entire ceiling had turned into smoke, making the floor feel like a piece of ice in a boiling pot of water. "Anyway, thanks for the help. See you around."

"You better hope not," the suit of armor whispered before the last solid fragment of the village chief's realm was gone.

ASPION LUOR's destiny has been sealed

Time stopped, then continued again. In a blink of the eye, Dallion was back in the outskirts of his village, flying through the air toward the village chief.

Crap! He had totally forgotten about that. All the fighting in the awakening realms had made him lose track of where the battle had started.

Putting in all the effort he had, Dallion twisted himself in the air, narrowly avoiding a direct collision with the chief. That had to be the clumsiest approach ever. It was only thanks to Dallion's guard skills that he managed to find his footing.

Immediately, he jumped back, expecting the village chief to take advantage of the situation and counterattack. Instead, the old man fell to his knees.

Utter silence filled the air. Not even the wind dared make a noise. The entire population of Dherma—hundreds of people, young and old—stared at the scene, unable to believe their eyes. It wasn't only the common folk, it was the elders, the guards, even the members of the Luor family who looked around as if they were seeing the world for the first time.

Dallion smiled in relief. He knew exactly what they were going through, the sensation of life without a limiting echo.

THE GLORY OF LUOR

E ver since he had first awakened in this world, Dallion had imagined defeating the village chief and freeing Dherma from his tyranny. Of course, back then, he couldn't even remember the name of the village, or pretty much anything else of significance. If he hadn't been from Earth, he might not have remembered anything at all. Now that the deed was done, he didn't know how to feel. That was the problem with real life, it was never straightforward.

Dallion looked at the village chief beside him. Without the echoes and his awakening powers, the aura of authority had vanished, making him look like a weak old man. The crowd, the elders, even the Luor family itself seemed relieved, as if they had finally been released from a terrible nightmare and were only now looking at the world with their own eyes.

"So, you really did it?" Veil whispered as he approached. The blond seemed to take the fall of his grandfather rather nonchalantly. Dallion really hoped the Luor wouldn't challenge him to another fight for the sake of his family's honor. "Should have guessed if anyone would manage, it would be you."

"Guess so." Dallion took a deep breath. While he appeared no different than he had a moment ago, the battle against the village chief had left him exhausted. The last thing he wanted to do now was fight. Given a choice, he wanted to go back home and spend the rest of the day sleeping. "Do we have to do it now?"

"Not feeling like it?" There was no smile on Veil's face. "There's no fun taking an easy win. However, you won in public. The entire village knows. If I don't defeat you now, the Luor name will be dragged through the mud."

That was an absurd thing to say. As far as Dallion was concerned, the Luor name had become pretty bad already in the last few generations. Other than Gloria and Veil, to an extent, he couldn't think of a good thing to say about any of them.

"I don't suppose you'd accept a surrender?" Dallion asked. His only advantage was that Veil didn't know about the dartbow. With that, he had a chance, although that would mean Veil would lose his powers.

Veil shook his head.

Damn you, Aspion! Even in defeat, you make a mess of things!

Dallion didn't want to lose against Veil, but he didn't want to win either. If he hadn't been this damned tired, maybe he'd be able to think of a way to think of something.

"Give me a minute to rest a bit?" Dallion took a few steps and leaned against the nearby building.

He always could enter the awakening realm of an item he was carrying and sleep there, though that wasn't going to solve much. Sleeping was only good to rest between awakening battles, not immediately after.

"You don't have a minute." Veil leaned on the wall as well. "This must be settled once and for all."

"I was afraid you might say that. Can I at least—"

Suddenly, a building nearby changed form. Moments ago, it had been a decrepit eyesore about to crumble under its own weight. In the blink of the eye, all the cracks and holes were miraculously fixed. Not only that, the entire structure had become much more solid than before. There was no doubt about it, the building had been improved.

A moment later, the same thing happened again.

"As everyone can see, the task set up by the village chief has been completed," Gloria said in a loud voice. "Two buildings that were in no shape to survive the winter are now ready to become the home of anyone who wants. All thanks to Dallion."

What? Dallion blinked.

He hadn't expected this in the least. Looking closely, he saw Gloria standing suspiciously close to the improved structure. The girl's breathing had become irregular, although only a person with awakened senses would be able to tell.

You improved the building, didn't you? Dallion thought. That was so typical of Gloria, always taking things in her own hands when it suited her. And, of course, she'd only done so after Dallion had done the heavy lifting…or so he liked to believe.

That wasn't all. The building Dallion was leaning on had also undergone a major transformation. He was just about to ask how that had happened when he saw Veil's hand on the wall.

"Her idea," Veil whispered, stepping away from the wall. "I helped."

"Yeah…" Dallion laughed. "What if I had lost?"

"Oh, then we would have ridiculed you," the blond replied without hesitation. "Mercilessly. That was my part of the plan. Just a little something to give you a bit of incentive."

Incentive doesn't work that way, Dallion wanted to say. "Thanks, Veil." *And thanks, Gloria.*

"And this is just the beginning!" Gloria continued. "Today marks a new day for Dherma! For years, Grandpa thought he could protect us from the dangers of the world by keeping us inside and taking the entire burden on himself. As the chainling hunt showed us, there are always dangers lurking about, and it shouldn't be up to a single awakened to face them for us."

That definitely wasn't the way Dallion would have described the situation. When Veil had said that things had to be settled once and for all, this was what he meant. Quite sneaky.

"After hearing what he had been through with the archduke's envoy, my grandfather has agreed that everyone should be helping the village out," Gloria continued. "And to start, my brother and I will help improve more buildings around here. And we won't be the only ones to do so."

Several members of the Luor family turned pale. Decades of comfort and easy life had made them avoid work like the plague. Even with their awakened powers, all they had done was improve a few simple items by a level at most. Getting accustomed to actual work was going to be painful.

Quite a good show. Dallion had to admire the performance. But it wasn't over yet. The final touch remained. Mustering all his strength, he went to the village elder and helped him up. The old man gave him a confused look, still unsure what had happened. In his mind, everything remained a dream, possibly with a little help from the armor echo.

"Thank you for your wisdom, old man!" Dallion said. "For it's thanks to you that I now know what's really important. And so does everyone else! Now it's finally time to put Dherma back on the map!"

NEW DAWN

It was impressive how much things could change after because of one simple action. Not that Dallion would have called defeating the village chief simple. It had taken him a full day of sleep to recover from the battle. Apparently, fighting in someone else's awakening room was more exhausting than two all-nighters in a row. Upon waking, though, Dallion had found himself in an entirely different village. It was as if a mythical entity had come by and cranked up the color saturation of everything to a hundred.

People moved about energetically through the streets, doing chores that had been neglected for years. Crumbling walls were being fixed, doors mended. Dallion even saw his father rearranging the clay tiles on the roof. And all that was done with so much joy and enthusiasm, one would have thought it was a holiday.

"Brother!" Linner rushed from somewhere in typically energetic fashion. He was the only one who appeared the same. Then again, if he had become more cheerful than before, he could well have blinded the sun. "Did you hear? We're going back to our old house!"

"Oh?" Dallion smiled.

"Yeah! Grandpa said there's plenty of room. Also, Veil

improved it, so it's all nice and shiny right now! Just like the pebble you gave me."

Just like the pebble, Dallion thought. He had to admit Veil had taken the whole restoring the Luor name quite seriously. From what Dallion could tell, several more houses had been improved in the last day alone, and several more mended to perfection. That was a good start, although, considering Veil's father, there would still be problems in that household. At least that was not Dallion's problem. Veil and Gloria could take care of themselves. Besides, since the chief had lost his power, they were the highest level awakened in Dherma…after Dallion, of course.

"Let's go there!" Linner grabbed Dallion by the hand and started pulling him toward the village center.

"Hey, wait a bit." Dallion played along, finding his brother's actions amusing. "Do you want to live there?"

"You bet!" Linner grinned.

"What's wrong with our old house?"

The child stopped. This was a question he couldn't answer right away. Dallion could see it written on his face. Linner liked their old home, but he also liked the prospect of living in a new, bigger place as well.

"Can't we have both?" Linner asked, just like someone his age would.

"Why not both, eh?" Dallion crossed his arms.

"Well, it's not like Grandpa has anything against guests. Besides, that house is small, and Dad snores a lot…"

And you want to show off to all your friends, Dallion thought.

"Snores?" Dallion laughed. His brother had no idea how right he was. After Dallion had improved his perception, the noise was worse than a sawmill. "Tell you what. You get all your things ready, and I'll help you carry them to Grandpa's house."

"Yay!"

"Just be sure to get Mom and Dad to agree to it."

"Boo!" Linner crossed his arms. "That's not fair!"

"That's what big brothers are." Dallion winked. "We're very unfair. But who knows? Maybe you'll be able to convince them to let you spend some time there, right?"

That wasn't what the child wanted. He glanced at Dallion, then at their father on the roof. The large man was doing a remarkable job of pretending not to hear a thing. Being a parent involved a lot of that. Thinking back, he had always been there to support everyone in the background. He hadn't meddled in any of Dallion's decisions, hadn't given him any advice concerning awakening issues, and yet there was always food on the table, and the house was kept in fairly good condition. What was more, he made Dallion's mother happy.

"Fine," Linner mumbled. "I'll go talk with Mom and Dad."

"I knew you would. Meanwhile, I'll go have a word with Grandpa. I can't let you have the best room, after all."

"Brother!" Linner pouted. "I wouldn't do that. Not until I kill my first beast outside the village!"

"I know." Cool it there, kiddo. It's a bit too early to set off killing monsters. Enjoy life a little. "See you in a bit, okay?" Dallion waved and set off for Kraisten's house.

The status of the elders was another thing that had changed in the last day. In the past, the council had no real power. The village chief only kept them for appearances. Now, he had turned into the figurehead. Officially, nothing had changed. Everything continued to be done in Aspion's name. The village elders only acted as advisors to the Luor family. Whatever the actual agreement was, it seemed to be in everyone's interest.

A short distance before reaching his grandfather's place, Dallion stopped and looked at the sky to the west of the village. That was where the belltower had been. He had only seen it twice, once on the charts in his awakened library, and once in Aspion's memories of regret.

"The sky's not falling," the familiar voice of his grandfather said. "Although it might rain in a week or two. The weather patterns are usually stable here, but you never know."

"Yeah. One never knows." Dallion nodded.

"I guess congratulations are in order. You're fully awakened now."

"Does it show?"

"Usually not, but I have a nose for those things." The elder moved closer. "Defeating Aspion also gave me a hint."

"And here I thought that getting rid of the echoes would be the thing that gave me away." Dallion smirked.

"Oh, I'm sure you did great. Though...you didn't remove all the echoes."

Dallion felt a chill down his spine. Was there something he had overlooked? His grandfather had told him that as long as he defeated the village chief, everything would return to normal, and it had. Proof could be seen all around. In that case, what echoes were remaining?

"Don't be so glum." Kraisten slammed Dallion on the shoulder like a bear. "You did fine. Not all the problems in the world are your responsibility. All I meant to say is that I won't be of too much help. Aspion wasn't the one who invoked my punishment. There's still a great deal I cannot tell you, but there are a few things that might be of help."

TWO OF A KIND

The elder's house was just as improved on the inside as it had been outside. Every item and piece of furniture within view had been carefully mended, including a large carpet Dallion remembered ripping as a child by accident. The thing had been so old that just walking on it had caused a tear. Now, it appeared brand new.

"You've been busy," Dallion said, impressed.

"A bit." Kraisten went to the living room table—another new addition, made entirely out of stone—and sat. "Others did most of the work. I can't improve much these days."

"Can you still craft?" Dallion joined the elder.

"So, you've heard that?"

"I saw a few things in the chief's awakening room. A suit of armor showed me." He paused a moment. "He told me you were the reason the things around here turned out this way. Is that right?"

"It is," the elder replied with a sigh. "Aspion did a lot of crap, but he's not wrong about this. I made the mistake that set things in motion. All because of a noble."

A noble? Dallion thought the Order of the Seven Moons had punished them both. Well, all three of them—there was the matter of the chief's sister, although by the way everyone referred to her, she was likely dead.

"But that's not what I wanted to talk to you about. Tell me, Grandson, how's Earth these days?"

"Earth?" The only reason Dallion didn't choke was because there wasn't enough saliva in his mouth. Had the old man just said "Earth?"

"You didn't think you were the only one who suddenly awakened here, did you?" Kraisten laughed. "I thought you'd have figured it out by now, especially with the hint I dropped last time we had a talk."

Dallion thought back. The last time was after improving the well. It seemed like ages ago. What hint had his grandfather given him?

"Genetics." Dallion shook his head. "Luck, genetics, or intense training." He recited the phrase. How hadn't he caught on until now? It was so obvious. Of course, there was no way anyone in this realm had heard the term.

The realization felt as if a huge weight had been taken off Dallion's shoulders, a weight he didn't know he had. He was no longer the only Earthling in this realm. Now, he knew for certain his memories weren't a dream. Even better, there was someone with whom he could freely talk to about back home! Or could he? Kraisten had awakened in this world over fifty years ago. Back then, Dallion wasn't even... Heck, there were probably dozens of countries from that time that no longer existed, not to mention the leaps in technology...

"Yep, genetics." Kraisten smiled. "A nice loophole. The echo limitation only lets me talk about things others already know, but it has difficulty catching certain terms so long as I'm subtle. I knew you were from back home from the start, just as I know there are more like us."

"There are?"

"Yeah, though I've only met one other ages ago. Look for people who were confused after their awakening. It usually takes a few days for the mind to clear up. The Order calls it soul confusion. I tried asking them more about it, but they keep to their own. The only way they'd provide information is if you joined them, and that's something I'd advise against."

"Because they'll punish me if they learn that I'm not from here?"

"I can't tell you." The elder frowned. "There are many reasons, but that's a conclusion you'd have to reach on your own."

That was sadly convenient. At least Dallion knew for certain there were others like him. And that meant...

"Is there a way back?" he asked.

"To Earth? If there is, no one has found it. You really want to go back there? Don't know about you, but I wouldn't. Even after everything that's happened, I prefer it here. And by the look of it, so do you." Kraisten rubbed his hands. "You've felt it, right? The power of awakening, the call of adventure, all the possibilities this world offers. Aspion couldn't stomp it out of you with threats and echoes. He tried, but you ended up on top."

Is that what you told him? Dallion thought. All those decades ago, his grandfather had something similar to Aspion. There was no way of knowing what went wrong. Kraisten either couldn't or wouldn't tell him.

"What about you?" Dallion asked. "Will you leave the village? The chief is no longer stopping you."

"He's not the one stopping me, but no." The elder shook his head. "I've no intention of going. I've grown to like Dherma. Now that Aspion's grandkids have taken over, we might even improve it a level or two. You'll leave, though."

"Oh? Why so certain?"

"Because you won't find your answer here."

"What's the question?"

"What lies beyond?" Kraisten smiled. "That's what makes us different. The question that drives us to reach the top just to take a look. My way didn't work, but maybe yours will. Either way, it will be one heck of a ride getting there."

The question that drives people to reach the top just to take a look... Dallion had never considered it this way. All he wanted to do was see what it was like in the city. He had no intention of joining the city guard despite his experience in the hunting party, nor did he want to become a noble. He just wanted to see what it was like outside the village. Maybe that was how it had started for his grandfather as well? The memory he'd seen made it appear that way, but Dallion wasn't his grandfather, even if both of them came from Earth in a manner of speaking.

"So, finish everything you have to, say your goodbyes, and get out of here. Carry only what you must, sleep in the awakened state as much as you can, always be ready to fight, and never trust anything with a dark star on it."

The last sounded particularly specific, but Dallion nodded nonetheless.

"Thanks, Gramps." He stood up. "I think I'll learn a few things about this world. And when I get back, we'll have a proper talk about it."

WISH OF THE WELL

More *people from Earth*, Dallion thought as he made his way to the village square.

It was already an incredible coincidence that his "grandfather" had turned out to be one. Maybe there was something linked to genetics after all?

"What do you think?" a familiar voice asked nearby. It was Veil. Dallion had to admit the blond had improved quite a bit as well since their last fight. Judging by the way he had suddenly appeared, he might have gotten a second skill. "I fixed up the place nice, right?"

"You did?" Dallion smirked. "I thought Gloria was doing most of the work."

"Some of the work," Veil grumbled, although that confirmed Dallion wasn't too far off. "Anyway, what are you still doing here? I thought you'd be out of this place the moment things were over. Weren't you talking about it during the hunt?"

"Can't wait to get rid of me? Should I start calling you chief now?"

"Give it a few years. Also, don't think you'll be ahead for long. Sis told me of your little secret, so don't count on me staying level four for long." He laughed. "Seriously, though. What are you doing here?"

"I came to have a talk with the well," Dallion replied. A while back, he had made a promise to the guardian. And now it was time to deliver.

"Seriously?" Veil arched a brow.

Dallion made his way to the center of the square and placed his hand on the well.

"Seriously," he said.

AREA AWAKENING

The surrounding landscape changed, taking him to the realm of the well. In part, it could have been his imagination, but the place seemed much more cheerful now, and not only because it was mended to a hundred percent. A golden sun shone upon the mountains, making the streams and rivers glisten as its rays bounced off.

You are in the Land of WELL
Defeat the guardian to change the land's destiny.

Just like last time, Dallion thought. Of course, back then, the well was almost crumbling, causing a pack of puma-like creatures to attack Dallion every chance they got. There was none of that this time, though, unfortunately, the climb to the top of the mountain remained. Or did it?

"Hey, Guardian!" Dallion shouted. "I've returned as I promised. Are you ready to duke it out?"

Silence. The guardian wasn't budging from his arena. It would have been too easy if he had. Then again, Dallion was not one to complain. If the battle had taken place last time, there was a large chance he would have been defeated. Instead, the guardian had made him an offer—take the victory but promise to return and level up the well again.

That had been the first time Dallion had actually heard a guardian speak. He had accepted, of course—he would have been a fool not to. Even so, there was a sense of dissatisfaction about it. The victory was a hollow victory, offered only because of their common hatred of the village chief. That was one thing to note, never treat an object or area poorly, for you never know when its guardian might have enough of its owner.

Well, I guess it's back to climbing.

The rest of the day was spent going up the mountain. The increase of his body trait made the experience much easier, although Dallion still wasn't able to reach the peak of the central mountain by nightfall. This time, he could rest calmly, knowing there was nothing to attack him, and even if there was, the dartbow granted him a huge advantage. At the crack of dawn, the climbing continued.

In a matter of hours, Dallion achieved what had taken him nearly a day before. It wasn't even mid-morning by the time he reached the top. What was more, he didn't feel remotely tired, if slightly hungry.

"Hey, Guardian," Dallion said. The air felt remarkably sweet. "I'm here. I'm ready."

On cue, a hole emerged in the center of the stone arena. Moments later, the stone golem appeared as well.

WELL GUARDIAN
Species: GOLEM
Class: STONE & WATER
Health: UNKNOWN
Traits: UNKNOWN
Skills:
- GUARD

- **ATTACK**
- **WATER JET (Species Unique)**
- **ROCK THROW (Species Unique)**
- **UNKNOWN (Species Unique)**

Weakness: TENDONS

Dallion still had no idea how the classification was made, since the creature was as much water as stone. If he were to be pedantic, it should have been stone and water guardian.

"You returned," the guardian said in its echoing voice. For a moment, Dallion swore he could see gratitude and confusion on its face.

"I said I would. Besides, that last fight wasn't a real fight." *Or any fight, for that matter.* The truth was that the guardian had given Dallion the win in exchange for the promise to return when he got stronger.

"Others claimed the same, and they never came."

That sounded ominous. Was it possible the guardian was talking about Dallion's grandfather? More likely it was referring to Aspion, or someone from his family.

"The village chief isn't an awakened anymore. Those who are will be sure not to neglect you."

"I know. I saw you in the greater realm. I would have helped when I heard your call, but you were too far away."

"It happens." At least that meant Dallion's plan had been good. "So, do we start? I know I've been itching to. Just a word of warning," Dallion took out his dartbow, "I have a ranged weapon now."

In response, the guardian shot a stream of water several feet from him. Apparently, Dallion wasn't the only one with an advantage.

Well played, he thought.

Maybe this was a good point to try to make an echo? Dallion hadn't had any practice in that area. In truth, he only had a vague notion of how it was done. The awakening shrine seemed to have planted the concept in his brain but had done little in terms of actual demonstrations. Two Dallions would definitely be able to fight much better than one…

No! Dallion told himself. This was supposed to be a fair fight. He owed the guardian that much. Besides, if he couldn't defeat such a challenge without cheating, he wasn't fit to venture outside of the village.

COMBAT INITIATED

CRITICAL WOUNDS

A week ago, Dallion would have charged directly at the guardian, relying on sheer luck and guard markers. Such an action now would be ludicrous. Both had ranged attacks, not to mention Dallion had gained quite a bit of experience since their last encounter.

There was more in fighting than the actual battle. As he looked at the golem, Dallion saw many of his options—he could shoot a bolt directly at him, he could wait for the guardian to make the first attack, or he could start walking calmly forward. For a split second, images of each action appeared in Dallion's mind, showing him the results. In two of the cases, the resulting counterattack dealt Dallion a minor injury.

Walking it is, then, he thought, making his way around the large hole that separated the two.

For several steps, nothing happened. Then green footprints appeared along with a shield marker in the air. Dallion didn't think, following the guard skill's suggestion without even looking. No sooner had he done so than a stream of water splashed into his buckler.

The force of the attack was significant. Before, it would have knocked Dallion easily to the ground. Now, it only pushed him a step back. Leveling up his body stat was useful after all.

"My turn," Dallion said. Following the guard markers through to complete a full set, he then aimed at the watery area between the guardian's arm and torso.

A weak spot marker appeared. Once the aim was spot on, Dallion squeezed the trigger.

In his experience, slashing and piercing attacks had little effect on water—the third guardian in the awakening shrine had shown him that much. Dallion expected he'd only achieve a minor wound, taking five percent off the golem's health, if that. Instead, the water exploded as if someone had triggered a depth charge.

CRITICAL HIT
Dealt damage is increased by 200%

Lacking its connection, the large boulder that composed the golem's arm dropped off, slamming to the ground.

ARM SEVERED
Enemy will no longer be able to make use of its LEFT ARM

Now, Dallion understood why the dartbows were considered so important. If there was such a thing as a military grade weapon in this world, this was one of them. The bolts had the same effects on water as they did on a solid surface, or even more by the looks of it.

The golem looked at its arm, then back at Dallion. The crack of a smile appeared on its large head.

"Want to give up?" Dallion smiled. "Or do we call it a draw?"

Instead of an answer, water flowed toward the golem's missing limb. Within moments, a new arm was formed. While it lacked any rocks, it very much resembled the one the guardian had lost.

That didn't seem particularly fair. When the rectangle had made its announcement, Dallion had expected it to mean the golem would continue the fight missing an arm. Apparently, all it meant was that the golem couldn't use that specific arm, but there was nothing preventing it from regrowing a new one.

As Dallion aimed at another of the creature's weak points, the golem twisted its body, hurling the fist of its right arm toward him like a giant flail. The green cone marking the impact zone was enormous, larger than Dallion could evade. To make matters worse, there were a half a dozen shield marker positions, each facing a different direction.

Dallion had seen that before with the training guardian, though never with a normal one. Was that the difference between an area guardian and an item one? If so, it was a huge stroke of luck he hadn't tried to fight the village guardian. A being controlling an area that large, even if it was not commanded by Aspion, would definitely have proved too much.

"Attack is the best defense!" Dallion shouted as he launched another bolt at a weak spot in the guardian's left leg. His gamble was that a single hit wouldn't be enough to exhaust the guardian's entire health.

Two of the shield markers disappeared. Apparently, the closer the golem's fist got, the fewer options Dallion had. Dallion could wait slightly more in the hopes that only one option would be left, or he could gamble and choose one now. The difference was that there was no guarantee he had the reaction speed necessary to react later.

When in doubt, go for the right, he told himself and raised his shield to match the right-most marker.

CRITICAL HIT
Dealt damage is increased by 200%

LEG SEVERED

Enemy will no longer be able to make use of its LEFT LEG

MODERATE WOUND
Your health has been reduced by 20%

Dallion's back felt like a pin hit by a bowling ball. The force of the blow brought him to his knees. Simultaneously, the golem's leg dropped off as well, only to be replaced by a second one.

"Crap," Dallion said, gasping for breath. The pain had almost entirely disappeared, although he still felt short of breath. "You're no pushover."

Area guardians really were on an entirely different level. And to think both Veil and Gloria had managed to defeat a few. Granted, they had faced lower-level guardians, but it was still damned impressive.

"There's no way I'm falling behind." Dallion stood up. "Enough warmup. Time for the real deal!"

The distance between Dallion and the guardian was a few hundred feet. Dallion could continue trading long-ranged attacks and hope that his enemy would be out of damage before he was. So far, the odds were in his favor—two critical attacks had reduced the golem's health to sixty percent. Three more hits, and he would be victorious. Of course, the same could be said for the guardian.

"This battle has already cost you an arm and a leg," Dallion shouted as he assessed his options.

Water jet attacks wouldn't be an issue, but while the golem had a functional arm, the rock-hurling option would be a pain. Despite the obvious, the solution was to decrease the distance.

"Darude." Dallion dashed forward, taking aim at the guardian's other leg.

FAMILIAR COMPANION

The instant Dallion squeezed the trigger, the guardian shifted to the side. The creature was fast, not the clunky motion that Dallion had expected. The bolt flew wide by half a foot, but that didn't matter. While it would have been nice if the golem had taken another hit, Dallion's main goal was to get closer.

Three green shield markers appeared. Instinct made Dallion choose to move his buckler to guard his back. This time, he was lucky. The guardian's fist smashed against the small shield, pushing him to the side.

Follow through, Dallion thought.

Forcing his body to remain standing, he followed the set of green steps to completion. A second series of steps appeared. Apparently, the guardian wasn't planning on a single attack either. Dallion saw lines emerge from the golem's body, spreading in all directions like a pincushion. Each of those was a jet of water, and each would take considerable effort to avoid. At this point, it would be much safer to take advantage of the time slow and shoot off the golem's arm. Dallion, though, continued with the next set of green markers.

Just a little more. He spun and stretched as if following an obscure nineties break-dance. Jets of water flew past him like spears, none of them making contact.

Another time slow occurred, bringing with it a new set of green footprints. Two more and Dallion would be able to use his escape attack cheat. It had worked against a level five guardian; certainly, it would against a level three. Dallion, however, had already decided not to use it. Not only wasn't it fair, but it also it wouldn't do more damage in the long term. The village chief had already shown there were ways to negate it. As Dallion's father back on Earth had said: if you have to rely on something, don't.

At the third set completion, Dallion took advantage of the guard skills bonus to leap closer to the guardian, then he fired two bolts at its arm. This time, there was contact.

CRITICAL HIT
Dealt damage is increased by 200%

ARM SEVERED
Enemy will no longer be able to make use of its RIGHT ARM

Yes! Dallion rejoiced. That took care of the strongest attack the golem had. It was all water jets from here on…or maybe not.

Time had barely returned to normal when the guardian rushed at Dallion. The sudden role reversal caught him unprepared. Without its massive, ranged attacks, the golem had no choice but to engage in close combat.

Three instances of his enemy rushed toward him. In each, both watery arms of the golem transformed into blades striking at him. In one instance, they went for his head. In two more, they slashed through his torso.

Three choices, Dallion thought as defense markers appeared once more. Three choices. There was no time to defend against all. His chances of success were one in three—not terrible odds, considering this world. However, there was one option that guaranteed a hundred percent victory. Dallion lowered his buckler arm, raising the dartbow straight in front of him.

"Stop!" he shouted.

The golem did, freezing in place less than two steps from him. Even so, an exchange of blows continued in Dallion's mind. He could see the golem try to attack him in a multitude of ways: direct pierce, evade and strike, point-blank range water jet attack, even a rock attack with its last remaining rock limb. In some cases, wound rectangles emerged, in others not, but, in all, Dallion ended being the winner.

"Draw?" Dallion offered.

There was a long pause. Dallion had no idea of a draw was even possible in the present circumstances but hoped it was. Sadly, the guardian shook its head.

Would have been too easy, Dallion thought. *At least—*

The WELL GUARDIAN has admitted defeat.
Do you accept his surrender?

"I'm fine with a draw," Dallion said. "You could have won the previous battle, after all. Now, we're even." Not to mention Dallion had a new weapon and some new prediction ability. That certainly hadn't been there before. Maybe it had something to do with his full awakening?

The WELL GUARDIAN has admitted defeat.
Do you accept his surrender?

"You're stubborn, aren't you?" Dallion smiled. "You're sure about this?"

The guardian nodded. As during their last meeting, Dallion accepted the offer.

The rectangle burst into dust. Along with it, the golem did the same. There was a bright flash of light, blinding Dallion for a while. When he regained his senses, the guardian was in front of him again, only now it was a new guardian.

WELL level increased
The WELL has been improved to FOUNTAIN WELL

A proper fountain? Beat that, Gloria and Veil.

There was no indication of a skill increase, sadly. Seemed like the level ten cap held even now.

OATH KEEPER
Keeping a promise brings its own reward. Sometimes it might be from your future, sometimes from your past.

That was an unexpected achievement. Dallion had gotten the gist of them, but in the past, all achievements had increased one of his traits. In this case, the description was vaguer than usual, or rather, the promised reward was.

Good thing I came back. To be honest, when Dallion had returned, he hadn't expected a reward. A few seconds later, he saw that wasn't the only thing he didn't expect.

"Mreow?" A black puma cub poofed into existence before him. Slightly larger than a cat, it was the same creature he had petted out of existence when he had mended the well. Of all the well cracks, that had been the only creature that hadn't attacked him.

FAMILIAR COMPANION — CRACKLING CUB

You have gained a Level 1 companion!

While still young, the crackling is loyal and will always follow

you both in the real and in any awakened world. The crackling will guard your awakening room or attack any enemy you command in an awakening realm.

In addition, it can create cracks on objects in the real world. The size of the crack depends on the crackling's level.

"You gotta be kidding." Dallion laughed. "I just got a kitten?"

The creature's appearance was the same as he had remembered it: a black silhouette of a feline with eyes, teeth, and claws. There was no denying it looked cute, though. Recognizing Dallion as its master, the creature leapt up, landing on his shoulder.

"Hey there." While he could feel the crackling's paws, it didn't have any weight, as if a shadow sat on him.

Oh, boy. This will take a bit of getting used to.

PAST WRONGS

cub, of destruction... Of all the things Dallion could have gotten, he expected that the least. It wasn't as good as a new skill but definitely better than a trait increase. According to what the rectangle had stated, it had the power to create cracks on objects, something Dallion was definitely going to try out. To his amusement, the first thought that came to mind was that old YouTube video of a Charles Chaplin movie. With Dallion's awakening skills and the cub, he could earn infinite money by breaking items and repairing them. Then again, he could do that without the cub.

Returning to the real world, Dallion looked at the well. It had improved once more. While the size had remained the same, the stone had turned to marble, and there was a massive statue in the middle acting as a fountain. All was good and well...except the statue was a depiction of Dallion standing in a heroic pose.

You could have warned me this would happen, Golem, Dallion thought. He would have been against it, or at least requested a less embarrassing pose.

"You just couldn't stop yourself," Veil said in jest as he glanced at the statue. At this point, it was difficult to say whether he was impressed or about to burst out laughing. "I think it caught your bad side," he snickered.

Dallion clenched his fist. Last time he was going to improve this fountain!

"Yeah, yeah. Something for you to remember me by," Dallion grumbled. "Also, to remind you that I got to level five first."

The phrase had the desired effect. Within seconds, Veil's smile vanished. Competition was one thing he took seriously. Dallion had no doubt the blond would spend weeks improving every structure in the village, then have a go at reclaiming the village area itself. As petty as that was, it was also a good thing. This way, Dherma might get back to what Dallion had seen it be decades ago.

"Can you say something to Gloria for me?" Dallion asked. "Ask her to see me at the river. I'll pass through there before leaving the village."

"Why don't you tell her yourself?" Veil crossed his arms. "I'm not your messenger boy!"

"I know." *I also know how mad that makes you.* At times, Dallion could be petty too. "She'll understand." When in doubt, it was always good to say something vague to make it sound deep. "Oh, and you better get strong. Next time we meet, I'd expect you to have caught up somewhat."

"Ha! Next time, I'll be twice your level!"

So easy to manipulate. Dallion smiled. But that wasn't the reason he was happy. In the end, he had proven true to his word. He had defeated the village chief and not lost any friends in the process. Not bad for a month's work.

With a wave, Dallion walked away, leaving Veil at the village square behind him. He had kept his promise to the well guardian and now there was one last thing he needed to do before leaving. Well, actually two, but the second thing depended on Gloria. It didn't take a genius to realize she had been avoiding him since the defeat of her grandfather. Dallion knew from experience that, in such cases, it was better to give her some space.

The roof of Dallion's house was still half-complete by the time he got back. Strangely enough, neither his father nor Linner were there.

"Hello," Dallion said as he went inside. They weren't there either. Maybe they had been called to help with something in the village? "Dad? Mom?"

He went to the kitchen. It was empty too, not a trace of food to be seen. At that point, steps approached, followed by a heavy cloth-like object hitting the floor.

Turning around, Dallion saw his mother standing a short distance away in the main room of the house.

"I've packed this for you," the woman said in a weak voice. Anyone could see she had been crying. "For when you leave for the city."

"Mom, I…"

His mother raised her hand, pleading with him to stop talking. This was difficult for her, more difficult than he could imagine. Thanks to his improved perception, though, he had an idea.

"It's okay." She forced a smile, holding her tears back. "After everything you've done, it's normal for you to want to leave. You've been asking for the cities ever since your awakening. And it's not a bad choice, it's just…"

Dallion didn't think. There were many things he could have said, but he chose to say nothing. Instead, he went up to her and hugged her. He had known the woman for less than a month, but he had also known her since he had been born. In this world, she was his mother and had always loved and cared for him despite the pain and sadness she had carried all this time. Dallion's mother back on Earth had also reacted in similar fashion when he had set off for college.

"I'll take care," he whispered. "I promise."

"I know you will. You're an awakened, a full awakened. Just don't rely on your powers too much. Don't overuse them, and be sure to eat and rest well. Awakened need a lot of food, even if they don't feel it immediately."

"I promise."

"I've gathered all your good clothes, as well as some money. It's not much, but…"

"Mom…" *You really shouldn't have. I could ask Veil and Gloria for a pouch or two if I need to.*

"Just a small gift for the start of your journey. You might have awakened, but you're still my little boy."

That was the reason Dallion's father and brother weren't at the house. His mother had asked them not to be. She had known what he would do ever since the day he had awakened in this realm. If that was so, there was one gift that Dallion could give in return.

PERSONAL AWAKENING

THE GIFT

You are in a small, sealed room.
GERTHA SEENE's destiny has been sealed.

There was something ominous and sad about the rectangle. Dallion felt a chill just looking at it. So that was what happened to someone who lost their powers. He had heard the explanation several times, but this was the first time he saw it in person.

"How?" Dallion's mother asked.

It had been decades since she had last entered this place. Looking at her, the memories were painful even now. If Dallion were in her shoes, he would have stopped trying to get back altogether. After a decade, he wasn't sure he'd ever remember how to do it if he tried.

"A guardian told me," Dallion replied. That had been another valuable gift he had received from the guardian of the well, along with the cub.

Apparently, upon defeating Aspion, the village area had lost its owner. However, since Dallion was the last—and only—person to have defeated a structure guardian of major significance, he had been granted certain powers. In the past, Aspion had abused those powers to put echoes in all the villagers. Dallion had no intention of doing anything of the sort, but there was one thing he was definitely going to try—unseal his mother's awakening powers.

"This is your room?" Dallion asked. While still a level one, the place was far more elegant than his own. Clean and tidy, it had no door, just a single object placed on one of the small walls—a golden lyre.

"This *was* my room," the woman sighed. "I haven't been here in so long..." She made her way to the lyre and reached for it. The moment her fingers touched it, the golden surface of the instrument turned to stone.

"You tried to defeat a guardian with that?" Dallion was more than impressed.

"I was young and reckless," Gertha whispered. "Fighting isn't the only way to win a battle. But you are right. The lyre wasn't a good match. I tried and failed, and now my skills will be nothing more than a sculpture."

"Not if I have anything to say about it." Dallion smiled. "Nox, come out."

Several seconds passed. Dallion's mother looked at him with uncertainty and concern. Realizing that, Dallion couldn't help but feel embarrassed, all because the stupid cub didn't respond to its name!

"Come out, Crackling," he sighed.

On cue, the creature appeared on his shoulder like a black silhouette. So much for making a good impression. Now, the only thing he could do was complete the task he had come here for and hope it would be impressive enough for his mother to forget about this minor hiccup.

"Mom, where did the door used to be?"

"You want to unseal my awakening power?" A glimmer of hope resonated in her words, along with fear of disappointment. "I… Thank you, but it's not possible. Your grandfather told me a long time ago."

"It's not possible for him." Dallion smiled. There was no point in telling her the real reason. Thankfully, that was what the crackling was for. "But it is for me."

Before Dallion's mother could speak, the cub leapt off Dallion's shoulder and ran to one of the plank walls. There, it paused for a few moments, sniffed the stone surface and, without effort, walked into it, forming a thin outline of a door.

Useful cub, aren't you? Dallion thought. Now, it was all up to him.

"I want to attack," he whispered. Three red markers appeared on the wall, each on a spot of the outline.

One weak spot for each level? Dallion wondered. From what he could remember, the ring guardian had been level three the first time he had faced it. If the same one had defeated his mother, that meant that each seal was as strong as the being that placed it.

"Here goes." He took aim with his dartbow and squeezed the trigger. One by one, the areas around the markers shattered like shards of glass. When the last one was gone, the entire wall within the outline crumbled to dust.

GERTHA SEENE's destiny has been unsealed.

A blue rectangle appeared in the air. As it did, the lyre regained its previous texture, becoming an object once more.

Wow! I really did it! Dallion beamed. He had hoped he could achieve this. In a way, he knew that he could, but seeing it filled his heart with joy. Everything was back to how it was supposed to be decades ago.

"Mom, you're an awakened agai—" He suddenly stopped. "Mom?"

The woman hadn't budged from her spot. She stood there, still as a statue, her hand gripping the lyre on the wall. Tears trickled down her cheeks.

"Mom? What's wrong?"

"Nothing's wrong. It's just...I never dreamed the day would come again. After all these years, I'm..."

There was little Dallion could add. Seeing his mother cry, even in such circumstances, made him feel uneasy. When he was younger, he'd often run away when it happened. Now, things weren't that different.

"Crackling," he said. The puma cub emerged from the wall and ran back to him. It was time to go. "I'll leave you alone for a bit, Mom. If you can just give me an exit. This —"

"Wait." Gertha took the lyre from the wall and walked to him. "You have no idea what you've given me." She wiped the tears off her face. "After all these years, I'm finally myself again."

I think I get the gist.

"I know it's not much but let me give you something as well." She held the lyre in front of him.

"You're giving me your skill?" Dallion struggled to stifle his gasp. The gamer in him was overjoyed at the prospect at receiving a third skill, a rare one at that. The son, though, refused to accept it. "I can't take this from you. You just became re-awakened..."

"I'm not giving it away. I'm sharing it with you."

Dallion still hesitated.

"If the Seven are against it, your fingers will pass through," the woman encouraged Dallion. "There's no need to worry. Nothing bad will happen to you or me. Consider it a mother's gift."

A mother's gift... Dallion looked at the lyre. It was exactly as he imagined a lyre should look, golden and beautiful as depicted in every cartoon and comic he'd seen. He reached out and grabbed it half-expecting his fingers to go through it as if it were from air. To his astonishment, it felt solid.

MUSIC skills obtained.

You have broken through your sixth barrier.
You are now Level 6
Choose the trait you value the most

THE LAST GOODBYES

You have assisted GERTHA SEENE in her trial
GERTHA SEENE's Level has increased to 2

It seemed that unsealing someone was treated as a trial in its own right. That was a relief. It meant that even if Dallion ever lost a battle, that wasn't the end. There was always a chance of him being unsealed.

In less than a split second, Dallion was back in the real world. The temptation to experiment with his new skills was enormous. After all, it would only take a moment. There were enough items in this room alone for him to increase his skill by five more, at least. However, he resisted. Any excuse Dallion made to stay longer would only make leaving harder. Even now, he wondered whether not to find other people who had had their powers sealed and helped them, then possibly level up the village before he left.

"I have to go, Mom," he whispered, stepping away from her. "I need to find out what's out there."

"I know…you're so much like your grandfather." She took a step back as well. There were still tears in the corners of her eyes, but the air about her had changed. She was no longer the sad, frail woman Dallion had known her to be. There was a new strength emanating from her, the mark of an awakened. "Go and don't worry. I'll take care of things here and keep an eye on your brother. It's only a matter of time before he gets the same idea and rushes out to follow in your footsteps."

That will be the day, Dallion thought. The world was not yet ready for Linner. Thankfully, neither was Linner himself.

"See you, Mom." Dallion took his backpack from the floor and left. It all felt too similar, like the time he had set off for college back on Earth.

Thinking about it, college was an apt comparison. Once he stepped out of the village area, he would also leave its protection. From then on, he'd have to rely on himself to set his path forward, not on area guardians or misguided tyrannical rulers. For all his faults—and there were many—the village chief had kept all the people safe. Outside, there would be no such protection, and while it was unlikely Dallion would face creatures as dangerous as chainlings, there would be considerable threats.

"Did you finish what you had to do?" a female voice asked.

Gloria leaned on a building nearby, looking at Dallion with an amused smile on her face. Now that she no longer feared her grandfather, the girl had improved her clothes to the point it was obvious they were level five at least. Dallion also noticed the building she was propped against had changed since the time he had entered his home.

"Yes, all finished." Dallion walked to her. "And you've been doing your best to impress me."

"Idiot." There was a barely noticeable blush on her face. "I just wanted to remind you that you're not the only one with skills."

"I'm sure. So, will you come along?"

"Excuse me?" Gloria blinked. The question had caught her completely by surprise.

"Will you join me in leaving the village? Any way you look at it, it doesn't have much to offer. Even if you improve it, it will remain a small village at the end of the known world. The cities will be much more suited for your skills. Besides, Veil could handle things fine in Dherma. And he wants to."

"Always thinking about yourself," Gloria sighed. "No, Dal, I won't be joining you. And, no, it's not only the things my grandfather feared. Everyone knows the world is a scary place; you just don't care. Well, I do, and I also care what happens here. It's not about fixing a few houses; it's about making this village mean something, the village I was born in. Sometimes, I feel you take all that for granted."

That was the truth, and more than Gloria could know. Dallion never saw Dherma as his home. Strangely enough, he didn't see Earth as his home either. In his mind, both places had become temporary lodgings that were nice while he remained there, but not the place he wanted to be. It was difficult to explain, so Dallion didn't bother thinking about it much. All he knew was that something was waiting for him out there.

"And when you place it on the map, what then?" There was no spike or bitterness in his words, just unbridled curiosity. "Will you find a husband and become the next village chief?"

"Who knows? Maybe, maybe not. The point is that it will be my decision."

"Everything you've done was always your decision." Dallion chuckled. "Back from the day you got me to help you pass your trial in the awakening shrine."

"Yes." Gloria held firm. "I guess it is."

"I guess this is goodbye, then?"

The girl nodded.

"Take care, Gloria. Maybe we'll see each other again somewhere." He started walking.

"If you ever get tired of the cities, you can always come back," Gloria shouted after him. "We'll be here for you."

I know, Dallion thought but didn't say it out loud. He had made up his mind as well. The Dallion of his memories would likely be furious. He was giving up the chance to lead a calm and quiet life with his crush, but there was no turning back at this point.

Dallion adjusted his backpack and went on. A few moments later, running steps sounded behind him. At first, he hoped Gloria had changed her mind. Soon though, his improved hearing told him it wasn't her. The person running after him was slower, with a heavier build.

"Dallion!" the annoying voice of Vanessa Dull filled the air. "Dallion, wait!"

Some things never changed. Chaos, echoes, and the fall of Aspion had no effect on Dallion's aunt, who rushed toward him a large bag over her shoulder. No doubt she had heard he was leaving the village, just as she heard about everything, and wanted to catch him for some parting gifts. Gifts for her, that was.

"Hello, Aunt Vanessa." Dallion stopped and did his best to smile. After all, this was the last time he was going to see her. Might as well depart on a high note. "How can I help?"

Instead of an answer, the woman dropped the bag at his feet, breathing heavily. She wasn't the type of woman used to running, so this small dash had taken a lot out of her.

"I- I…" She tried to speak, gasping for breath. "I heard you're leaving the village."

"That's right." If there was anyone who hadn't heard by now this scene rectified that. "Don't worry, though. I'll improve everything you've brought before I go."

"This is not for you, it's for me! Some things my last husband left me! Now that things are returning to normal, I can finally put them to some use."

Dallion took a glance in the bag. It was full of statues and decorations. Apparently, the woman wasn't as poor as she had created the impression of being all these years. That was so typical of her. Still, to turn down a free item improvement…that was unexpected.

"Here." Vanessa looked around, then shoved something in Dallion's hand. "Hide it and keep it safe."

Dallion took a glance. The item was small and metallic, very much like a locket or piece of jewelry. The metal, however, was unmistakable—blue metal, the same used for making emblems.

"How did you get this?"

"My late husband gave it to me. What did you expect? He was a traveling merchant." The woman snorted. "You'll need it if you're to walk through the realm."

"You knew about this?" Dallion whispered.

"Of course, I knew." Vanessa crossed her arms. "Just because I ask for a small favor now and again doesn't make me stupid! Why do you think I wanted your parents to send you to the monastery of the Seven? At least there you'd have been free from Aspion's nonsense. Now, get going. The faster you get out of here, the less painful it'll be."

That was it, the last words of advice Dallion received from a friend he never knew he had. All this time, he thought his aunt had only looked out for herself. That was only part of it. She was looking out for many people in ways no one could realize. All the selfish requests, the random pieces of advice, they had all been subtle nudges to get this or that person moving in the direction that would be best suited for them.

She had been a distraction to Dallion's mother, keeping her from thinking about the past, she had done her best to keep her family's spirits up in her own way, and she was the only one to have found a traveler's emblem, which she had now given to Dallion.

"See that, Nox?" Dallion said, more to himself than to his cub.

"The world is filled with hidden gems, so long as you know where to look."

Taking a deep breath, he took one last step, leaving the village behind him. From here on, the future was his to forge.

DALLION SEENE

TRAITS

    AWAKENING: 6

    BODY: 5

    MIND: 9

    REACTION: 8

    PERCEPTION: 6

SKILLS

    GUARD: 10

    ATTACK: 10

    MUSIC: 1

FAMILIARS

    Nox – Crackling puma cub

EMBLEMS

    Traveler's Emblem

ITEMS

    Dartbow – ranged weapon

ACHIEVEMENTS
RECKLESS!
(+2 Reaction)

Decisive reactions, though little thought.

OUT OF THE BOX!
(+2 Mind)

Unorthodox thinking at a moment's notice!

HOTHEAD!
(+2 Reaction)

Charging head on into dangers could be called brave, but it's not always a smart decision.

ALTERNATIVE APPROACH!
(+2 Mind)

Finding an alternative way to a problem always leads to choice, though choice sometimes comes with danger.

COLLECTED
(+2 Mind)

Being calm and dispassionate often helps in difficult situations, although there's such a thing as overthinking.

OATH KEEPER
Keeping a promise brings its own reward. Sometimes it might be from your future, sometimes from your past.

THANK YOU FOR READING LEVELING UP THE WORLD!

We hope you enjoyed it as much as we enjoyed bringing it to you. We just wanted to take a moment to encourage you to review the book. Follow this link: Book 1 to be directed to the book's Amazon product page to leave your review.

Every review helps further the author's reach and, ultimately, helps them continue writing fantastic books for us all to enjoy.

———

ALSO IN SERIES:

Book 1

Book 2

Book 3

Book 4

———

Want to discuss our books with other readers and even the authors like L. Eclaire, Seth Ring, J.F. Brink (TheFirstDefier), Shirtaloon,

Zogarth, Cale Plamann, Noret Flood (Puddles4263) and so many more?

Join our Discord server today and be a part of the Aethon community.

Facebook | Instagram | Twitter | Website

You can also join our non-spam mailing list by visiting www. subscribepage.com/AethonReadersGroup and never miss out on future releases. You'll also receive three full books completely Free as our thanks to you.

———

Looking for more great books?

———

Kullen is the Emperor's assassin. The sharp hand of justice. The Black Talon. Gifted a soul-forged bond with his dragon, Umbris, Kullen is tasked with hunting any and all who oppose the Empire. But when the secretive Crimson Fang murders two noblemen before his very eyes, Kullen must discover the truth of who they are and what they want. What he uncovers is a web of lies and deceit spiraling into the depths of Dimvein. Natisse, a high-ranking member of the rebellion known as the Crimson Fang, has no greater goal than to rid Dimvein of power-hungry nobles. Haunted by her past, fire, flames, and the death of her parents, she sets out to destroy the dragons and those who wield them as unstoppable weapons of destruction. Until she, too, finds herself buried beneath the weight of the revelations her investigations reveal... The Empire is under siege from within, and one man, dressed in black like the night, stands at the epicenter of it all.

Get Black Talon Now!

Ascending should have been the easy part...
But after being thrown into the void, Thorn finds
himself stranded in a strange world filled with
even stranger creatures. Together with his cute
battle pet, the mysterious god beast Hati, and a
sentient AI named Eve, Thorn must forge a place
for himself in this new world. Unfortunately, the
local guilds all have other ideas and soon the
Titan finds himself embroiled in plots that even
his famed strength cannot help him with. Rallying
his strengths and learning how to fix his
weaknesses will be the absolute minimum Thorn
needs to survive, but if he wants to thrive he'll be
forced to take risks that put his life, and the lives
of his friends on the line.

Get Forgemaster Now!

———

Lightning brought her back. Now, it's her best weapon to survive the apocalypse... When the end of the world arrived, Elysia was already dead.Amid widespread destruction, collapsing cities, and dangerous creatures, strange lightning struck her grave. Rejuvenated by the violet lightning, life returns to her broken body. Elysia must find a way to harness the element in her veins or die as she's thrust into a dangerous new world. Better than being dead. She was always a free spirit, and survival is just another challenge. But as she powers up, something constantly nags at her... That maybe, just maybe, her family is still alive somewhere out there.

Get Rebirth Now!

In the West, there are worse things to fear than bandits and outlaws. Demons. Monsters. Witches. James Crowley's sacred duty as a Black Badge is to hunt them down and send them packing, banish them from the mortal realm for good. He didn't choose this life. No. He didn't choose life at all. Shot dead in a gunfight many years ago, now he's stuck in purgatory, serving the whims of the White Throne to avoid falling to hell. Not quite undead, though not alive either, the best he can hope for is to work off his penance and fade away. This time, the White Throne has sent him investigate a strange bank robbery in Lonely Hill. An outlaw with the ability to conjure ice has frozen and shattered open the bank vault and is now on a spree, robbing the region for all it's worth. In his quest to track down the ice-wielder and suss out which demon is behind granting a mortal such power, Crowley finds himself face-to-face with hellish beasts, shapeshifters, and, worse … temptation. But the truth behind the attacks is worse than he ever imagined … **The Witcher meets The Dresden Files in this weird Western series by the Audible number-one bestselling duo behind Dead Acre.**

GET COLD AS HELL NOW AND EXPERIENCE WHAT PUBLISHER'S WEEKLY CALLED PERFECT FOR FANS OF JIM BUTCHER AND MIKE CAREY.

Also available on audio, voiced by Red Dead Redemption 2's Roger Clark (Arthur Morgan)

For all our LitRPG books, visit our website.

BOOK 1 APPENDIX

CHARACTERS

Archduke Lanitol – ruler of the Wetie Province.

Aspion Luor – chief of Dherma Village. Once he was Kraisten's friend and companion, but after getting banished took control over the village, running it like a tyrant. Aspion is also a platinum blond.

Cleric – an albino of the Order of the Seven Moons. Unable to learn spellcraft, he was banished and had his real name erased. Currently serving as Dame Vesuvia's assistant.

Dallion "Darude" Seene – a college boy who mysteriously entered the Awakening World after a wild party just before the first day of college. Also, the main protagonist of the story.

Dame Vesuvia – Noble from the province's capital and

envoy of the Archduke, sent to track and hunt down the chainling that's causing devastation in the lands.

Gertha Seene – Dallion's mother. A former awakened who had her powers sealed by failing Aspion Luor's trial. Her main awakening skill was music.

Gloria Luor – granddaughter of Aspion Luor, and the childhood crush of Dallion's awakened self. She is an awakened and a platinum blonde.

Kierra Luor – Kraisten's companion and Aspion's sister. Never returned to the village.

Kraisten Seene – Dallion's grandfather in the Awakening World. An awakened and also an otherworlder from Earth, he's an elder of Dherma Village. Originally, he was the previous village chief's son, but set out to explore the world and see the cities. Kraisten took part in a war which gained him fame, but was later cursed and banished back to his village along with Aspion Luor.

Linner Seene – Dallion's brother in the Awakening World.

Nox – a crackling puma cub and Dallion's familiar.

Vanessa Dull – a distant relative of Dallion's in the Awakening World who likes to take advantage of people she can.

Veil Luor – Grandson of Aspion Luor. He is an awakened and a platinum blond.

WORLD LORE

Achievements – rewards given to awakened while performing specific feats within the realms. Most achievements boost the awakened's traits or give other rewards.

Awakening – the divine ability granted by the Moons that allows people to enter the realms of items and areas and improve them by defeating the realm guardian. Awakening also grants awakened superior traits and skills.

Awakening Altar – an altar that allows awakened to level up by completing challenges within their realm.

Awakening Gate – a mental trial that occurs when the player reaches a certain level. The trial is conducted by a Moon and poses a simple question or trial. Awakened who pass through the gate gain new awakened abilities, but lose certain protections granted by the Moons. Those that refuse have their progress sealed and cannot advance.

Awakening World – the world where the story takes place, referred to as "the real world."

Chainling – an awakened monster and Star-spawn. It has the ability to shapeshift and corrupt things it touches with void matter.

Crackling – minor Star-spawn monsters within area realms. They are creatures that are the embodiment of cracks in the real world.

Dherma Village – Dallion's home village in the Awakening World. Located in Wetie province of the Tamin Empire.

Echo – a copy of an awakened in the awakened realms. Echoes know all the thoughts of their creators, but have a personality of their own.

Emblem – a talisman blessed by the Moons that protects travelers through the wilderness.

Guardian – the soul of an item or area realm. If defeated, it's reborn stronger, causing the item or area to improve. In the real world, the guardian represents the item or area and can affect people (the reason why items slip or people trip when walking on a level floor).

Limiting Echo – an echo whose sole role is to limit the thought process of the person in whose realm it is in.

Linking – establishing a connection between an awakened's personal realm and another.

Mending Labyrinth – a labyrinth within the realm of an item. If all imperfections in the labyrinth are mended, the item is repaired to perfection in the real world.

Moon – the deity of the world. There are said to be seven, two of which have hidden their face after calamities in the past.

Order of the Seven Moons – the religious order of the Awakened World, dedicated to serving the Moons.

Personal Realm – the awakening realm of a person, containing their skills and traits. It grows as the player levels up.

Platinum Blond – people born with platinum blond hair. They are viewed as extremely exotic, even special.

Realm – also referred to as "awakened realms," the worlds within items and areas that awakened can enter. Depending on their size and nature, realms can have one or more guardians protecting them. The main guardian also acts as the soul and mind of
the realm.

Rectangle – a rectangle containing text and information to the awakened. They include descriptions, combat effects, achievement notifications, creature information, and more. There are believed to be four colors of rectangles: green, blue, red, and white.

Skill Markers – visual indicators that help the awakened make use of their skills. They only appear in the realms.

Skills – skills granted to the awakened by the Moons. There are twelve in total, three of which are unknown to all but the chosen.

Tamin Empire – the greatest empire in the world, composed primarily of humans.

The Star – the great evil and tempter of the world, sometimes referred to as "the Crippled" or "the Crippled Star."

Traits – the traits granted to the awakened by the Moons: Awakening, Body, Mind, Perception, Reaction, and two unknown. The Awakening trait is also considered an awakened's general level.

Wetie Province – the southernmost province of the Wetie empire, ruled by Archduke Lanitol.

Wilderness – the area that lies between settlements. It is extremely hostile and full of monsters. Items and areas in the wilderness have no natural guardians.

Made in the USA
Monee, IL
01 November 2024

69066881R10288